PRAISE FOR
HE NEVER CAME HOME

"A wonderfully compelling and wildly intelligent exploration of moral corruption. The fateful story of John and Regan Peters is a powerful, cautionary thriller, a reminder that the road to hell is, indeed, a slippery slope. And DeYoung does a fine job of mapping the way."
　　　—William Kent Krueger, *New York Times* bestselling author

"Surprising and smart and wonderfully original, this page-turner of a thriller is completely entertaining."
　　　—Hank Phillippi Ryan, *USA Today* bestselling author of *One Wrong Word*

"Brimming with suspense and secrets, this top-notch thriller asks vital questions about identity, marriage, and the stories we tell ourselves. Perfect for mystery-loving book clubs!"
　　　—Mindy Mejia, *USA Today* bestselling author of *To Catch a Storm* and *Everything You Want Me to Be*

"DeYoung writes with a smart, calculated urgency that makes the pages fly by. The perfect summer thriller to keep readers on the edge of their seat."
　　　—Nicole Baart, bestselling author of *Everything We Didn't Say*

"The real deal. Andrew DeYoung sets up his characters with a tactful grit that skillfully mirrors real life even as situations careen out of control."
　　　—Timothy Lane, author of *The Neighbors We Want*

THE DAY HE NEVER CAME HOME

THE DAY HE
NEVER
CAME
HOME

A Novel

ANDREW DEYOUNG

Poisoned Pen
PRESS

Published by Poisoned Pen Press, an imprint of Sourcebooks
P.O. Box 4410, Naperville, Illinois 60567-4410
(630) 961-3900
sourcebooks.com

Library of Congress Cataloging-in-Publication Data

Names: DeYoung, Andrew, author.
Title: The day he never came home : a novel / Andrew DeYoung.
Description: Naperville, Illinois : Poisoned Pen Press, 2024.
Identifiers: LCCN 2023058103 (print) | LCCN 2023058104
(ebook) | (trade paperback) | (epub)
Subjects: LCGFT: Thrillers (Fiction) | Novels.
Classification: LCC PS3604.E9345 D39 2024 (print) | LCC PS3604.E9345
(ebook) | DDC 813/.6--dc23/eng/20240102
LC record available at https://lccn.loc.gov/2023058103
LC ebook record available at https://lccn.loc.gov/2023058104

Printed and bound in the United States of America.
VP 10 9 8 7 6 5 4 3 2 1

For Sarah, Maren, and Rory—
who always bring me home.

PART 1

CHAPTER 1

The day before he went missing, Regan's husband bought her a lake house. A surprise, for her birthday.

She was annoyed at first. Regan had planned the day painstakingly—booked a babysitter months in advance, reserved a table for brunch at her favorite restaurant, a couples' massage at a little spa in the mall after that. Small pleasures, but Regan was looking forward to each of them in turn. She'd been so busy with the kids lately, frenzied even. Etta was four, Philip one and a half, and they both needed her so much, stretching the limits of her ability to give. The two of them had devoured every single moment of her free time, every ounce of her energy. John worked long hours, barely helped with the kids, and Regan hadn't done anything for herself in ages.

So yeah, she was a little irritated when, kid-free for the first time in what seemed like forever, John took a wrong turn, away from the brunch place, and pointed the car toward Lake Minnetonka.

"John," she said as he navigated the car down a twisting road, lakeside mansions rising up on one side of them, a grove of trees huddled thick on the other. "What the fuck?"

"Just a little detour," he said. "You'll like it. I promise."

She crossed her arms, sighing as the car reached the end of the winding lane and the Edina Realty sign came into view. This was something she and John used to do together, in the early days of their marriage—they'd go to an open house in a rich part of town, walk around some huge home pretending like they had a chance in hell of owning it, and dream together about what might be someday. But times had changed. She wasn't interested in reliving their old days. Wasn't interested in dreaming. They were in their thirties now, their *late* thirties. They had little kids. She hadn't had an uninterrupted night's sleep in months. She didn't want to waste time walking through a house they couldn't afford. She wanted French toast, a mimosa. She wanted to close her eyes and lie face down on a table while someone put their hands on her body and made her feel good.

But then, as they walked up to the house, the front door opened and a real estate agent stood inside. She knew John's name, and he knew hers: Diane. And inside there was nothing. No other people. Not even furniture.

"This isn't an open house," Regan said, looking between John and the agent, her annoyance morphing through confusion to a kind of free-falling giddiness. "What's happening?"

John's lips were pressed together. He looked like a little boy, one who had a secret he wanted to share. Bursting with it. Then his face cracked open in a smile, and God, he was beautiful when he smiled. Regan had almost forgotten. They'd both been so busy, him with work, her with the kids, that sometimes they went days, weeks even, without really noticing each other. She couldn't remember the last time she'd looked at his face. Really looked at it, and saw him looking back at her with adoration in his eyes, as he was now.

"It's ours," he said.

Regan felt dizzy. She put a hand to her chest, reached the other behind her to brace against a wall. John went to her, but she waved him away; she was fine. He stepped back, the smile gone, replaced by a look of concern.

"Do you want it?"

Regan let out an airy laugh. "Maybe I should look around a little."

They raced together from room to room, the agent making herself scarce, giving them privacy. The house was huge, three stories, built into a hill sloping down to the lake. A broad deck past the kitchen and dining room on the main floor, and a walkout from the bottom level to the dock and an empty boat lift at the water's edge.

"But how?" Regan asked, once she'd seen it all.

"I started looking a couple months ago," John said. "I wanted it to be a surprise, for your birthday. Wanted to time it just right. I did everything—made the offer, set up the financing, scheduled the appraisal and the inspection. We close in an hour."

"No, not that, I mean—*how?* How could we, I mean… You know, can we really—"

"We can," John said. "It's been a good year, Regan. A great year. I didn't want to say anything at first, in case things went bad, but they haven't—it's been two really good quarters now, and it doesn't look like it's a fluke. I've doubled my client base, doubled my revenue. I've been making some good picks recently, and a lot of people want in. Everything I invest in goes up."

Benevolence flooded Regan's body. All the late nights, the dinnertimes he'd spent on the phone, ignoring her while she struggled with the kids, sleeping obliviously through Philip's midnight wakings, missing playdates, working weekends. At the time these things had enraged her, made her feel abandoned, but it was all forgiven, now—now that she knew what it had been for.

She loved him, at this moment, for working so hard, for being so good at his job. He'd made a future for them.

John looked down, swallowed hard, pulled at the back of his neck. "I just thought, you know, you've been so busy. With the kids. I know you don't think I notice, but I do. I notice. I see everything you do. How hard it all is on you. But you're so good, Regan. You're such a good mom, and a good wife, and you deserve this. It'll be your name on the deed, not mine, because I'm thinking of it as *your* house, *your* place—a place you can go when you need to get away. Leave the kids with me, or your folks, and just…relax."

His voice was full with emotion, and now Regan was crying. She threw her arms around John's neck. He laughed into her hair and clutched her to him—and here was something else she'd forgotten. The feel of his body against hers, his breath blowing hot in the crook of her neck.

At the closing Regan was still too stunned to follow all the details of the documents that passed on the table before her. But still she signed every time the closer asked her to, a flurry of signatures and dates and initials, her handwriting becoming wilder, more shaking and swooping, on every dotted line. And then she was done, the house was hers, and they were driving back, walking through the rooms once more, running their hands over the walls. In a closet they found a left-behind duvet with its cover still on, and like a couple of horny teenagers they brought it to the living room, stripped down to nothing, pulled the duvet over their naked bodies, and made love right there on the carpet.

Afterward, Regan rolled off John and walked out onto the deck, the duvet draped around her shoulders. The cold fall air pricked at her calves, tugged goose bumps to the surface of her skin. She looked out at the lake, listened to the waves lapping lightly at the shore, reflecting on the fact that this, too, was hers now: this view, these sounds. This was something that could be bought. This happiness. This peace of mind. Her stomach rumbled—they'd never gone to brunch—but she didn't care. In every way that mattered, she was full.

John padded up beside her a few seconds later, in his boxer briefs and a T-shirt.

"Think the neighbors can see us?"

Regan looked to the right and the left. They were shielded on each side by trees.

"I don't think so," she said. "We could fuck out here if you wanted to go again."

John laughed. "What's come over you?" he said, then grabbed at her through the duvet, put his hand on her hip, and pulled her close. "I like it."

She leaned into him. "I like my present is all," she said. "Thank you."

He draped an arm around her, and they stood like that for a while. Regan's eyes wandered down to the dock, where the sellers had left something else behind: a little wooden boat lashed to a post, bobbing on the waves. The back-and-forth motion soothed her, and she simply watched it for a while, setting her cheek against her husband's chest. He was a good man, all things considered. Not perfect by any means, and they'd been through their share of storms—the early money troubles, the issues with her family, the strain of caring for the kids. But they'd weathered them all, went on bobbing on the surface through every swell, like that little boat at the dock. Somehow they'd found their way, together, to a safe harbor.

It was a nice thought, a perfect crystalline moment. Then John spoke, and almost ruined it.

"I have to head into the office tonight," he said. "I might be home late. I hope that's not a problem."

Regan struggled for a moment with a surge of annoyance.

He was always doing this, springing things on her, using work as a blanket excuse to leave her with Etta and Philip. John at the office meant that she'd have to feed and put both kids to bed that evening, that she'd have to do it alone, that she'd go to bed stressed and exhausted and be woken up by John hours later, when he crawled into bed sometime after midnight. *I hope that's not a problem*, he'd always say, seeming not to know or perhaps not to care that his sudden absences *were* a problem, every time. She felt herself about to snap at him, felt it rising up inside her like a reflex, until she remembered where she was standing, what had happened today, and her anger sank down as quickly as it had risen, like a pot of boiling water removed from a flame.

"It's fine," she said placidly.

"Is it really? Or does *fine* mean you're angry?"

"It's really fine," she said again, and was surprised to realize that she meant it. John's work took him away from her and the kids too often, left her with far more than her fair share of the parenting—but also, John's work had made *this* possible, had brought in enough money that this house now belonged to them, to *her*. Maybe this was the trade-off, and maybe it was even a payment of sorts, a reward: in exchange for everything she'd done for their family, for giving up her own career to parent two small humans, for all the times she'd agreed to look the other way—a house.

Regan closed her eyes and set her cheek once more on John's solid chest, felt it rise and fall with his breathing. At that moment, she felt no regret, no resentment, as she thought about the choices and compromises that had led her to this.

It had all been worth it.

CHAPTER 2

Regan woke early the next morning to the voices of her children, calling to her from down the hall: *Mama, Mama.* She lifted her head from the pillow and looked to the other side of the bed to find that John was not sleeping next to her. Confused, she reached her hand over and ran it across the duvet, confirming with her hands what her eyes were already telling her: his side was completely smooth, undisturbed, and cool to the touch. She'd fallen asleep before John came home, expecting him to crawl into bed late. But now it appeared that he hadn't come home at all.

She immediately imagined the possibilities, all bad: John, sleep deprived, had crashed his car on the way home; he'd had a heart attack at the office; or he was having an affair, holed up with a girlfriend somewhere. More likely was that he'd worked so late that coming home had become pointless; he'd curled up on the couch in his waiting room last night and was now, this morning, changing into one of the fresh shirts he kept folded in his desk.

Philip's voice came again from down the hall, more insistent now: *Mamaaaaa...* If she didn't get him now, he'd be screaming for her soon. She got out of bed and went down the hall. She changed Philip's diaper in the dim light, then brought him with a sleepy-eyed Etta to the kitchen for some breakfast. As Regan waited for coffee, she grabbed for her phone and sent John a quick text: Where are you, the lack of question mark intended to communicate her annoyance.

Regan brought the food and her coffee to the table, to Philip and Etta waiting in their seats, the older sister making faces at her younger brother, who was babbling and pounding with his fists on his high-chair tray. She put the food in front of the kids: oatmeal for Etta, mushed-up banana and buttered toast cut into tiny squares for Philip.

"Where's Daddy?" Etta asked after the food was almost gone.

Regan glanced at the phone. There was still no reply from John.

"Work," Regan said, scraping banana from Philip's chin with the edge of a plastic spoon.

"Work is boring," Etta said, poking at the congealing gray mass of oatmeal in her bowl. "Daddy is boring."

"*Ba ba ba ba ba,*" Philip babbled, spraying banana across his tray.

"That's right Philip, *boring,*" Etta said, her voice rising to a motherly singsong. "Are you trying to say *boring*? Daddy is boring, isn't he?"

"Daddy's not so bad," Regan said, feeling suddenly guilty to hear her own words, things she'd said about John before, parroted back to her from her daughter. She needed to be more careful about what she said in moments of annoyance—moments which, these days, were plentiful. John was gone a lot, but she still wanted the kids to think highly of their father. "Daddy bought us a house," she added.

That got Etta's attention. Even Philip stopped babbling, looked at her with his mouth half-open, as though he understood.

"You mean this house?" Etta asked.

"No, a different house," Regan said, gathering up the bowls from in front of them, giving up on breakfast. She brought the dishes to the kitchen, dropped them in the sink, then came back with two dampened cloths, for faces and hands. "By a lake."

Etta blinked, her eyes huge. "Can we go to it?"

Regan smeared the damp cloth across Philip's mouth, then wrapped it around his fingers and pulled as he protested.

"Not today," she said. "It doesn't have any furniture. No toys."

Etta began to whine, the sound like an ice pick to Regan's ears. "Please? *Please* can we go to the house Daddy bought us by the lake?"

"Wipe off your face," Regan said, handing the other dampened cloth to Etta. She watched her daughter calm, focus coming to her eyes as she carefully dabbed the cloth to her lips, her chin, her cheeks, her nose. Regan took Philip from the high chair, propped him against her hip, then reached out for the cloth. "Maybe," she said as Etta placed it in her hand, cheeks ruddy with scrubbing. "After naps. If you're good."

———————

But they weren't good, either of them—it turned out to be a day like any other, of screaming and crying and hitting, of stubbed toes and toys on the carpet and spilled milk on the couch cushions. Philip seemed to need her at every waking moment, and Etta compensated for the attention her brother was getting by clinging to Regan's leg, grabbing her constantly, whining for Regan to notice her. They wanted every piece of her, it seemed, until there was nothing left of her for herself, and by midday she'd practically forgotten John's absence last night, the still-unanswered text. (He was probably busy, in meetings with clients, and simply hadn't thought to respond to her.) The madness of the morning even made it difficult for Regan to recall the events of the day before—the house, the lake, her hysterical giggles at closing, sex on the empty living room floor. Impossible to believe it could ever have been real.

But it *was* real, and through lunch she held the house in her mind as a kind of reward, something to pull her through the screams and the messes, Philip throwing his pears and Etta babbling through a mouthful of half-chewed macaroni and cheese. Regan closed her eyes. She was a mother, yes, and some days *mother* seemed like the worst and most difficult thing in the world a person could be—but she was also a woman who owned a house on Lake Minnetonka—the wife of a wealthy man, it seemed—and if they were rich, then couldn't they afford a nanny? Someone to help her with the kids from time to time? Yes, of course they could; it had been a while since Regan had looked at their accounts—John handled all that—but it stood to reason that if they could buy a house that expensive then they could also afford to pay some college girl to look after Etta and Philip for a few measly hours a week. What use was the lake house, after all, if she couldn't get away to actually enjoy it? She'd been slow to put Etta and Philip in childcare but they were getting older now, and maybe it was time. She'd start looking at nannies right away, day cares too, she thought as she put the kids down for a nap—Philip first, then Etta, who protested that she was too big for naps and not even sleepy, but finally agreed to stay in her bedroom with a few toys and the door closed until Regan told her it was time to come out.

Then, finally, the house was silent, and Regan could hear herself think. She came down the hall, down the stairs, surveying the wreckage—the toy-strewn living room, the mess from lunch still slopped across the dining room table. By the time she was done cleaning, the kids would almost be done napping.

"Fuck it," she whispered to herself. She tiptoed through the chaos toward the kitchen, poured herself a glass of wine from a half-empty bottle of Chenin Blanc she'd opened a few nights ago. Then she grabbed her laptop off the counter and stepped through the sliding door to the deck and sat in one of the deck chairs, curling her bare feet beneath her thighs. She spared herself a brief glance to the horizon; the day was clear and bright, but their suburban neighborhood offered her little to look at aside from a smattering of other houses that looked a lot like theirs, roofs angled toward the sun, dotted down a long gentle slope to a frontage road and freeway whose constant, gentle roar of traffic was like the sound of waves lapping against a shore.

Waves, shore—the thought led her back to the computer screen, where she put the lake house's address into her search bar to find the original listing, with staged photos of the interior. Then she brought up other browser tabs: Pinterest, Instagram, a few style blogs. She began trolling through photos of furniture, wall colors, carpets, tiles, kitchens, and bathrooms. The photos soothed her, the stress of the morning beginning to melt away. Looking at wallpaper patterns, she felt her breathing calm.

This had been her thing, once—interior design. As a student she'd gone to the prestigious Minneapolis College of Art and Design, studying graphic design and studio art, but designing spaces had always been Regan's core interest, the thing she wanted to do if her artistic parents hadn't thought it frivolous. Out of school, and before John, she'd done a couple years as a junior art director at one of the city's ad agencies, not enjoying the work very much. It was only after she'd started seeing John, in her midtwenties, that she'd gathered the courage to speak aloud her dream of becoming an interior designer. He'd encouraged her, and after they got married and his business started to take off, she'd actually tried it for a few years, quit the agency job, and got a few clients of her own: rich friends of friends of friends who had so much money, so many houses, that they needed help filling all the different rooms they owned. She'd loved the work, and was even starting to develop a bit of a reputation, a list of clients who used her services and then referred her to other rich friends.

But then the kids came; Etta first and then Philip. She still couldn't quite explain to friends with more conventional careers why the kids had brought an end to her professional ambitions. They didn't understand. Office jobs had maternity-leave policies: six or eight or twelve weeks off followed by a return to work, but when you were your own boss, as Regan had been, there was no such structure. And the business required a certain amount of momentum, the pursuing and signing of clients, one job leading to another leading to another—momentum that dissipated completely after Etta's birth, more than four years ago now. Returning to work after as little as three months at home with a newborn—three months of recovery from childbirth, of sore nipples and midnight feedings, of seemingly endless doctor's visits and weigh-ins—felt so much like starting over that she simply didn't go back, and didn't go back, and didn't go back, until the months had become years and she was suddenly pregnant again, with Philip. And so John's career had taken off while Regan's had stagnated, as if by some unspoken arrangement Regan hadn't actually agreed to: *You make the money, I'll take care of the kids.*

Well, it was time to change the arrangement. John had become someone, built a successful business. Now it was her turn. As Regan flagged photos she liked, beginning to build a mood board, she resolved that this would not just be a new house but a new beginning: a return to the person that she was before the kids, a coming home to her true self. She'd get that nanny, restart the interior design business. Maybe even get John to shell out some seed money for an office space, a design studio, a couple assistants to do her daily bidding. She'd start with a design-focused Instagram account or interior decorating blog, something to build an online following, an audience—starting with photos of her beautiful new home on the lake.

The thought made her realize that she hadn't told anyone yet. Not her family, not her friends. She'd gotten the usual parade of birthday wishes on Facebook, encouragements to *enjoy the day!* and *do something fun!* But nobody knew about the house yet. Nobody but her and John. Her friends would be so happy for her. Happy, and jealous. Envious of her and her perfect life and perfect kids and perfect, rich husband. The thought gave her a jolt of pleasure, and she was just thinking about how to do it—a Facebook post? An Instagram photo of the house?—when the doorbell rang. The chime was clear all the way back to the deck, and it startled her. Made her jump.

She stood, left the computer and the wine on the deck table as she went back into the house. Passed the mess on the dining room table, stepped carefully through the chaos of the living room, and came to the front door. She opened it.

"Mrs. Peters," said the man on the stoop. "Regan Peters?"

He was strikingly handsome, and at first Regan smiled politely, thinking he might be a door-to-door businessman selling siding, or maybe a volunteer, an activist type seeking signatures for something or other. Then she saw the yellow letters on the breast of his dark-blue jacket.

FBI.

"Yes?" she said, clutching at the door.

"I'm Agent Armstrong, with the FBI," he said. "And this is Agent Torres."

He swept his arm to the side, drawing Regan's attention to a woman who stood at the bottom of the front steps. Average height, impassive face, the same blue coat, same yellow letters.

Past her, on the street, were a pair of black SUVs, unmarked, and a smattering of other agents leaning against the fenders or milling about on the grass, eyeing her sharply as they leaned in to mutter to each other. A couple of the agents walked around the side of her house on either side, to the back, and Regan thought absurdly of the laptop and the glass of wine she'd left on the deck—they'd see it; they'd know she'd been drinking in the middle of the day, alone with the kids and the house a mess.

"What are they doing?" Regan asked, panicking, her voice rising. "Can they do that? Are they allowed to—"

"We need to come inside, ma'am," Agent Armstrong said.

"I don't know," Regan said. "It's a real mess in here. I have kids. It's been a tough day."

Agent Torres cleared her throat, and Agent Armstrong winced, as though he was sorry for what he'd say next, and at that moment Regan realized that this—whatever *this* was—was very bad.

"I'm afraid, ma'am," said Agent Armstrong, "that we're not asking. We have a warrant, and our orders are to execute it."

They moved toward the door, Armstrong and Torres, and Regan felt herself stepping back, pulling the door open wide for them, and once they were inside she hated herself. She was always such a pushover—with the kids, with her parents, with John. She gave herself over to people too easily, let herself be swept up in their thoughts and preferences and desires, only thinking to be angry after she'd already given in. Like now. Letting FBI agents into her home without a peep of protest. She was angry *now*, at herself. She should have fought. Closed the door in their faces, made them break it down if they wanted in so badly, though she supposed that would have caused a scene, caused the neighbors to notice, and for what? Okay, then at least she should have asked them to show some identification first, let her look at the warrant before letting them in. She could do it now—all they were doing was standing there, surveying the wreckage of her living room— but she felt foolish, timid. The time to push would've been outside, on the stoop.

"Is your husband home, ma'am?" Agent Armstrong asked.

"He's not," Regan said. "He's at work. He's a financial adviser. I can give you the address for his office if you want it."

Agent Torres turned. There was no warmth in her eyes, no forgiveness, no mercy.

"He's not there," she said. "We just came from his office. We raided it. There was nothing. No people, no documents. It was cleaned out. Completely."

Regan struggled with the words, hearing them and not hearing them at the same time. "*Raided?*" she asked, picturing a SWAT team, cops in full-body gear and assault weapons, taking down the door with a battering ram. Things she'd seen on TV, in movies.

She felt a little bit as though *she* was being raided now. The invasion of her home felt akin to an invasion of her own body, a similar kind of violation. The two agents who'd gone around the side of the house were now coming through the back door and stepping heavily through the kitchen. All around her, footfalls sounded heavy on the floor as more agents poured through the front door, peered down halls and up the stairs.

"What's happening?" Regan asked, her voice not merely alarmed but panicky now. Her heart pounded, but the adrenaline was bringing her a kind of clarity, a sharpness of focus. "What is this? I need to see your badges, I need to see your warrant. I need someone to tell me exactly what the *fuck* is going on."

Some wordless exchange passed between Armstrong and Torres, messages passed back and forth with their eyes. Ultimately Torres shrugged and moved away, and Armstrong was the one to step forward and speak.

"I'm sorry to tell you this, ma'am," he said, "but we have a warrant to search your house and the surrounding premises. And another warrant."

"Another one," Regan repeated. "To do what?"

"To arrest your husband for fraud."

CHAPTER 3

What was surprising, at first, was how unsurprised she was, the words "to arrest your husband for fraud" bringing not an immediate sense of wrongness or inner objection, but clarity, even a sort of acquiescence. It wasn't precisely that Regan had ever expected John to be arrested (though the thought that he might have cut some legal corners in his business had occurred to her once or twice over the years)—more that that word, *fraud*, summoned no feeling of disjunction in her mind when she applied it mentally to her husband. Perhaps he *was* a fraud.

John was, after all, a man of secrets, of long absences and hidden depths. Regan knew very little about his past, had never met nor knew the name of any family member or old friend, hadn't seen a single baby picture or awkward yearbook photo of her husband. John claimed that there was very little worth knowing about him, hinting at a painful past he would rather not talk about, and Regan, in their early days together, had decided not to pry any further. She knew this was strange—everyone had a past, everyone had *people*, and it was impossible to fully understand anyone until you knew what they'd come from, what they'd survived, even what they'd escaped. But every marriage had its

secret price, its unspoken agreements, and this had been theirs—
hers and John's: in exchange for the life he worked long hours to
give her and the kids, she'd do him the favor of never asking him
about his childhood, his family, his friends, his past.

Regan became aware that she'd gone a while without
speaking—only a few seconds, perhaps, but still too long. The FBI
agents were watching her, looking for her reaction. Their faces
had taken on expressions of interested puzzlement, maybe even
suspicion. Seeing their eyes on her, Regan realized how strange
her reaction was. The news of John's being wanted for arrest had
caused her not to lose her composure, not to burst into tears, but
instead to grow calm, to tunnel inside herself. To think.

"He's innocent," she said. "He didn't do it."

The two FBI agents shared a look, and then Torres turned
back to Regan, the side of her mouth turned up. "But we haven't
told you what he did yet."

Shit. Regan realized her mistake at once. All they'd told her
was that they were here to arrest John for fraud. But there were
different kinds of fraud, and by protesting without asking the
details, Regan had implied that she knew the details of his crime—
that he was guilty, and that she might be part of it. An accomplice.

"I just know my husband, and I know that he could never
have done anything wrong," Regan said.

"Well, we have evidence that suggests otherwise," Torres said.

Regan's eyes narrowed. If they had all the evidence they
needed, then why were there agents swarming over her house
right now? She could hear them upstairs, their footsteps creaking
on the floorboards, drawers opening and closing. A door opened,
and Philip started crying.

"Goddammit," Regan said. "He's supposed to be napping.
He's only been going a half hour. He'll be a mess for the rest of the
day. You see what you're doing to my family?"

"I'm sorry, but our guys need to search every room," Armstrong said. "I'm sure no one meant to—"

But Regan was already gone. Up the stairs and into Philip's room to whisk him out of the crib. She fetched Etta too, who wasn't sleeping, only looking at a book on her big-kid bed and babbling some nonsense to herself. Regan grabbed the girl by the hand and yanked her, whimpering, back down the hall and the stairs, glaring at every FBI agent she passed, glad that both kids were crying—they should see the full impact of what they were doing. Should see that they were turning a family upside down. Traumatizing kids. John was the one she should have been mad at, she supposed, not the FBI agents—but he was gone, and these men were here. Men who looked a little like John, some of them, and who were currently ruining her day in real and tangible ways. So they seemed a good place for her anger to rest, for now.

She brought the kids down and got them settled on the floor with toys, popped the pacifier from the floor into Philip's mouth. Etta clambered onto the couch and clung to Regan's side, afraid of the strangers in the house. Regan glared at Armstrong and Torres: *You see?*

Armstrong sat in a chair across from her. "Mrs. Peters. I'm sorry this is happening. But we need you to help us right now. We need you to tell us where your husband is."

"I don't know," Regan said. "If he's not at work, I...I don't know. Maybe he's on a client meeting somewhere. He doesn't give me his schedule."

"Does he have family nearby?" Torres asked, still standing. "Anyone he might go to?"

Regan closed her eyes and shook her head. "No family."

Torres squinted. "What do you mean *no family*?"

"I mean John's got no family. His mother and father are dead. No siblings. I've never met any cousins, aunts, uncles. Nothing.

John has never talked about a single living family member in all the time we've been together. No visits, no phone calls. No Christmas letters. Nothing."

"Doesn't that seem a little strange to you?" Torres asked. "Everyone has family."

Regan put her hands up in a gesture of helplessness. Of course it was strange. But every life, every marriage, had things that looked odd from the perspective of an outsider. This was a strangeness she'd learned to live with, so much so that she no longer knew how to explain it to others.

"Okay," Torres said, regrouping. "How about friends?"

"No friends either," she said. "I mean, he's polite with my friends' husbands, but he'd never call them up for anything, and he'd certainly never hide out from the FBI with any of them. I doubt he even knows where any of them live. He works, that's it. Long hours. He works, and he comes home, and then he goes back to work, and he comes home."

Armstrong and Torres were silent, their looks communicating disbelief. She was aware as she said it of how it must look to them, how ridiculous this must all sound. She must have seemed colossally stupid to the FBI agents to have married John in spite of knowing next to nothing about him, in spite of his having hidden so many pieces of who he was. Armstrong and Torres probably thought she deserved all this—her house being searched and her husband on the run. She wished she could explain herself, say something that would make them understand. Their relationship, hers and John's, wasn't really so different from any other married couple's when you thought about it. What was any relationship but a careful weighing of good and bad, the strengths and flaws of a potential spouse? Who went into their wedding day knowing *everything* about the person they were marrying? A marriage was always a calculated risk, an investment, a long-term bet that the good would outweigh the bad, the known overpower the unknown. She hadn't known everything about John when she'd married him, it was true, but she'd known what she believed, then, to be the most important thing: he loved her, and would do anything—*anything*—to provide a good life for her.

But how could she explain any of this? She couldn't. Not now. Any time before this morning, it might have made sense; the risk she'd taken with John would've looked like it had paid off, with dividends. But not now. Not anymore. Not with FBI agents crawling over her house with a warrant for her husband's arrest. Not with a word like *fraud* hanging in the air. So she stayed silent, seething under Armstrong and Torres's disapproval, her ears turning red as she began to realize what a fool she'd been, all those years ago when she'd said *yes* to John, and every moment since as she'd been building a life with him.

Armstrong leaned forward in his chair, spread out his hands. "Okay, let's get a little more creative here. Does John have any favorite vacation spots or—"

"No," Regan interrupted now, holding up a hand. "I'm sorry, Agent Armstrong. I'm not going to cooperate until you tell me exactly what John has done. What you think he's done. There's a rule, isn't there, a law, or some sort of constitutional thing—you can't make me testify against my own spouse, or something? I'm not saying anything until you tell me what he's done."

Armstrong hesitated. "This is an ongoing case. We can't tell you all the details. But we can give you some broad strokes."

"Okay," Regan said. "So tell me."

Armstrong nodded at Etta, whose face was still half-buried in Regan's side. "You're sure you want your kids to hear this?"

"Oh, for fuck's sake," Regan muttered. Too loud.

"What did you say, Mama?" Etta asked.

There was a tablet and headphones on the glass coffee table. Regan grabbed for it and shoved it in the girl's hands.

"You're going to watch something for a while," she said. "You want to put on *Encanto*?"

Etta slipped on the headphones, her eyes going glassy, as Regan found the movie.

"Go ahead," Regan told the FBI agents after she was done. Armstrong looked at Philip, but Regan waved a dismissal. "He doesn't understand anything. Just tell me."

"Okay," Armstrong said. "Mrs. Peters, do you know what a Ponzi scheme is?"

Regan *did* know what a Ponzi scheme was, the basics if not the specifics. She was a person in the world, after all; she remembered the names of Bernie Madoff and that other guy, the local guy, Tom Petters, who'd gone to jail for a similar crime, his name splashed all over the Minneapolis news networks for weeks. The retort "Of course I do, do you think I'm stupid?" was on the tip of her tongue, until she remembered the FBI agents' knowing looks when she'd unwittingly suggested a familiarity with John's crimes and realized that it might be better—better for *her*—if she feigned some unfamiliarity now. Pretended to be exactly as stupid as they seemed to think she was. She pressed her lips together and shook her head. "Not really," she said slowly. "Maybe you…?"

Torres was the one to explain. "A Ponzi scheme is a fraud where money from one investor is used to pay off other investors—and the person perpetrating the fraud also steals money for themselves. Ponzi schemes fall apart when there's not enough new money coming in, and when that happens, the fraudster will often disappear with the cash. Your husband, John Peters, is a financial adviser. Several of his clients have accused him of refusing to give their money back when they attempted to withdraw from their funds. We've looked at client statements and a large percentage of them appear to be falsified. And looking at you and your husband's joint financial records—"

"You've been looking at our financial records?" Regan cut in.

"Of course," Torres said. "We have reason to believe that your husband stole his clients' money. His crimes are financial. So we've been looking at your shared finances."

"What happens…" Regan began, then swallowed and started again. "What happens to—?"

"The assets you shared with your husband will be subject to possible forfeiture and seizure. That means property and financial assets. Anything that is owned solely by you, you will be able to keep—unless it is determined that you have been an accomplice to your husband's fraud, in which case your assets will be subject to seizure as well, and you will be subject to prosecution, just like your husband."

Regan was dizzy. Yellow spots floated in front of her eyes. She clutched at the couch armrest, trying to moor herself to something. It didn't help—the couch, after all, was something they owned, that they'd bought with money; it was part of the world that was slipping out from under her, disappearing into a cloud of nothingness, leaving her floating in a formless gray void. The furniture. The cars. All the clothes in her closet, the kids' toys, the money in their bank accounts. The house.

The house. Oh God. Thinking of the house suddenly reminded her of the *other* house, the lake house, and her hand darted up to her mouth.

"What is it?" Armstrong asked. "Did you think of something? Have an idea where John might be?"

"No," Regan said, her mind racing for an excuse to cover up her involuntary reaction. "Nothing. It's just a lot, what she was saying." She nodded toward Torres. "You really think I'm part of this? That I had any idea—?"

Armstrong shook his head. "We're not seriously considering that currently. No one thinks that you're part of this, Mrs. Peters. Fraudulent businessmen lie to everyone, including their own families. But we do need your cooperation."

Regan nodded and then was quiet. She wondered at herself—wondered why she'd lied to Armstrong just now when he'd asked if she'd thought of anything. The lake house was something the FBI should know about, something Regan should tell them. A major purchase like that, less than twenty-four hours before John went on the run, was suspicious. It could be evidence. But why didn't the FBI know about it already? Torres said they'd looked at all their financial records; surely they'd have seen evidence of a home purchase. Regan thought back to the closing, all the papers she'd signed, the processes she'd set moving with her signatures. Cashier's checks took time to clear, to pull money from one account and put it into another, and surely the process of transferring a home title and deed from one owner to another wasn't instantaneous. Maybe Torres and Armstrong had pulled their financials days or even weeks ago; maybe they wouldn't notice the lake house for a while.

Regan should say something now, she knew she should, but every second that she kept her silence made it harder to speak up. She didn't *want* to tell them yet, didn't want to make that beautiful home on the lake yet another thing that was slipping out from under her. She'd only gotten a taste of that life, a single afternoon—signing the papers, making love to John on the floor, standing together on the deck and enjoying the view. She wasn't ready to give it up. Not yet. John was gone; he couldn't help her. She was in charge, left behind, like always, to clean up the mess he'd made. She had to be smart. Protect herself. Protect the kids. Hold on for dear life to whatever was left, whatever could be saved. Keep as much of it for herself as she possibly could.

Suddenly another thought hit her, a certainty: John was hiding at the lake house. If he was anywhere, he had to be there. Another reason that she should speak up and say something now—except she wanted to get there first, wanted to find John herself, talk to him, and try to clear this up before the FBI caught up with him and put him in cuffs. Maybe this was all a big misunderstanding, a matter of some paperwork that John had been careless with, some document he'd neglected to file. A miscommunication between him and a few clients. Maybe they could fix it, come up with a plan, make some kind of a deal. All Regan needed was time. Time to find John, to get him to come clean with her about what was happening, then to figure out how to handle it. Come up with a story together—a story that satisfied the FBI but also kept him out of jail, that didn't destroy his business, that let them keep all their money and belongings. First she just needed to figure out how to get away from here, to get out without raising the suspicion of Armstrong and Torres.

Just then, there was a creak at the end of the hall at Regan's back, and across from her Armstrong's eyes angled up.

"Agent Armstrong," came a male voice from behind the couch, "I think I've got something you should see."

Regan looked back. The agent was peering out from John's first-floor study, his home office.

"I'll be with you in just a second," Armstrong said, then looked back to Regan. "Ma'am, you should know that this is probably going to take us some time. Do you have anywhere you can go? Family nearby, or…?"

"My parents live in the city," Regan said.

"You should maybe head over there. We're going to have to go over the whole house; it's upsetting for people, and usually it makes just as much sense to, you know, clear out. Pack a bag, stay the night."

Regan nodded, thinking all the while of the lake house. That was where she'd go.

CHAPTER 4

Regan started packing. Gathering up clothes for the night was unexpectedly difficult, the drawers and closets full of memories. The dress Regan wore to that benefit gala years ago, feeling like a celebrity on John's tuxedoed arm. The smart gray blazer she used to don whenever she'd meet with a prospective new interior design client, the one she put on to make herself feel confident and professional when she'd first walk through someone's home and tell them how she'd transform it if she got the job. The plunging gray top she used to wear, before Etta was born, for barhopping or going to concerts. She hadn't done either of those things in years, but she couldn't bear to get rid of the top, because she still remembered how it turned John on every time she wore it, the hunger that would come to his eyes when he saw her in it, the way he'd peel it away from her skin later when they got home. And the matching outfits she'd bought for all of them—chambray and gray denim—for last fall's family photo shoot in Minneapolis's Loring Park with a paid photographer to capture them at their best and most smiling. A photo from the shoot hung above the mantel downstairs now, making them look every inch the perfect family.

"What's wrong?" asked Torres, who'd trailed after Regan up

the stairs, as though she expected Regan to run away with some key piece of incriminating evidence if she left her alone.

"Nothing," Regan said. She didn't have time to be carried away by these memories or the emotions they brought with them. She began stuffing clothes into an overnight bag, barely looking at what she was packing, not even bothering to fold anything. Then she went into the kids' rooms and did the same with their clothes, packing the diaper bag so full of diapers and wipes she could barely close the zipper. Downstairs, Armstrong intercepted her at the door.

"I'm going to send an agent with you," he said. "He's going to follow you to your parents' house."

"Why?" she asked. "I thought you said I wasn't under investigation. What is it you think I'm going to do?"

"It's not that, Mrs. Peters," Armstrong said. "It's just that John might try to make contact. It happens sometimes when people go on the run; they come back for one last look and get caught. Just until tonight. I'll pull him later."

Regan suddenly wanted to cry, realizing that she couldn't go back to the lake house as she'd planned. It was impossible to deny now that she was hiding the other house from the FBI, preserving it for herself a little while longer. She thought, again, that she should probably say something—it still wasn't too late. She could tell them that she'd simply forgotten about it in the overwhelm of the past hour. But again the moment passed and she said nothing.

Instead she went wordlessly out the door, practically fleeing, the muscles of her arms burning as she lugged Philip and the bags to the minivan, tugging Etta along behind. She wrestled the kids into their seats and then climbed in herself, threw the minivan into reverse, and flew out of the driveway. As she paused in the middle of the street to put the car in drive, she saw the crowd that had gathered outside. Don and Gloria, busybody retirees who lived in the house opposite, were gaping from their lawn. Sydney, the housewife who kept inviting Regan to parties for her multi-level marketing company selling dubious health supplements and drinks for gut health, stood on her front stoop with her fingers flattened over her mouth. And further down the street—*oh God*—was a TV van from a local news station, a cameraman at the curb hefting his camera to his shoulder just in time to catch Regan screeching away, her eyes burning, a hand shielding her face from view. In the rearview, a black sedan slid out from the curb and followed her: the FBI agent Armstrong had assigned to babysit her.

On the freeway, Regan finally let go and cried, squinting through her tears to see the road. She tried her best to cry silently, but Etta called out shrilly from the back seat nonetheless. "Mama, what's wrong?"

"Nothing, sweetie," she said, pulling herself together. "Mama just has something in her eyes."

"Oh," the girl said, sitting back in her car seat. Catching her eyes in the rearview, Regan knew that Etta didn't believe her. Kids always know more than adults gave them credit for. Even Philip was absorbing something from the events of the day. It would all come out sooner or later, in the hours and days ahead; and years later, too, in the expensive therapy sessions that were surely in their future.

"Mama," Etta said, "who were those men at the house?"

Regan's jaw clenched. She wasn't ready for this conversation yet. "They were police, Etta."

"Police?" Etta's voice carried awe and a trace of fear. "Did we do something bad?"

"Not us, honey," Regan said. "Daddy made a mistake. Now the police need to talk to him so that he can fix it."

That seemed to satisfy Etta, or at least to silence her. In the quiet that followed, Regan wondered if she could believe what she'd said herself, if there was any world in which her explanation could possibly be true. How big a mistake had John really made? Was it something he could fix? Something *she* could fix? Some errors couldn't be recovered, and her mind looped ahead to all the possible consequences of the things John was alleged to have done: jail, divorce, public humiliation, bankruptcy, poverty.

Her thoughts turned to the explanation she'd have to give her parents when she arrived at their house in Minneapolis. She hadn't really told them anything, only tapped out a text to her mother that they were on their way for an unexpected visit, that they needed to stay the night. Her mother had come back with a row of question marks, and Regan hadn't responded after that. As she drove, Regan imagined the humiliating conversation she was about to have, ran through the different ways it could go. But she couldn't come up with anything—not as she slid off the freeway into Minneapolis's historic Prospect Park neighborhood, the streets huddled dense with stately Victorian homes; not as she pulled into the gravel driveway off the alley; not even as she walked with the children up the steps into the back entry.

And so, when her mother met them in the hall and demanded to know what was going on, Regan put both hands over her face and said the first thing that came to her mind, the words escaping through clenched fingers.

"John's gone. He's wanted for fraud."

There was a moment of silence, and when Regan peeked out between her fingers, her mother had a small smile on her face.

"Of course he is."

———

"I knew it," her mother said later, in the living room. Philip was down for a nap, and Etta was off playing somewhere with some old toys of Regan's. Regan was relieved to have the kids occupied, but for a flashing moment she wished they were close, filling the room with their play, their noise. The kids being elsewhere deprived her of a distraction, a buffer between her and her parents. More specifically, between her and her mother.

"Mom, Jesus Christ," Regan said. "Could you not, just for today?"

Isabel Cartwright, Regan's mother, put her hands up, the loose sleeves on her flowing linen top sliding to her elbows. "I'm sorry," she said. "I don't want to say I told you so."

Except that saying she didn't want to say it was the same as saying it, wasn't it? Her mother was always going on about what she didn't want to say when actually she meant the opposite—she wanted to, she was *dying* to. And what was it that Isabel was supposed to have told her, anyway? That John was a liar, a criminal, a fraud? Nonsense. There was no way she could have known any of that. All her mother had ever said to Regan—first when she and John started dating, and then again later when they were engaged—was that she just wasn't sure if John was good enough for her. More nonsense. What her mother had meant, Regan was pretty sure, was that John wasn't good enough for *Isabel*. That having him as a son-in-law wouldn't reflect well on *her*. Whether John was good enough for her daughter was beside the point. Isabel had never thought that highly of Regan. Never cared about her. Not really.

Regan thought all this, but didn't say it. This was the way it was with family—the air always thick with the things you couldn't say aloud.

"It just makes sense, doesn't it?" Regan's mother continued. "This is what happens, when all you care about is money."

Regan looked down and tried to breathe slowly. "Not everyone can be like you, Mother."

"What's that supposed to mean?" her mother asked. "Like me how?"

Instead of answering, Regan reached past the arm of the antique sofa she was sitting on and made a show of adjusting a doily on the side table, as if at that moment she couldn't possibly focus on anything else. The two houses, hers and her parents', were opposites in every imaginable way. The house she'd bought with John—the first house, not the lake house—was a suburban McMansion with the kind of open-concept floor plan and minimalist modern design that homeowners were always drooling over on HGTV. But her parents' house was old: a rambling bungalow built in the 1920s, designed in an arts-and-crafts style, with rooms the size of postage stamps. It was a beautiful old house, repaired and added to over the years, and Regan had loved it growing up—but it felt claustrophobic to her now. She wanted to escape. But there was nowhere to escape to.

When she looked back up at her mother, Isabel was giving her a hard look, demanding an answer to her question.

"Not everyone can be like me how, Regan?"

Regan shrugged, waved a hand. "Oh, you know. An artist."

Regan's mother seemed satisfied with that answer, but it wasn't actually what Regan had meant—not entirely. Yes, Regan's mother was an artist, a sculptor of some minor renown, with pieces installed in museums and sculpture gardens and public spaces around the country. But Isabel had also come from money, her father an executive at General Mills who'd retired with a healthy nest egg and then done Isabel, his only child, the favor of dying before he could spend much of it. The money had bankrolled the beginning of Isabel's career, bought the huge three-story in Prospect Park with an expensive one-story addition for an art studio. Isabel had lived a life of complete artistic integrity, it was true; a life unburdened by any concern for money—but the only people who didn't have to worry about money were those who had plenty of it. Integrity was expensive, and Isabel had paid for hers with her inheritance.

An inheritance that was, by Regan's calculation, rapidly dwindling. *Isabel Cartwright* may have been a name known by art critics and sculpture aficionados, but Isabel's meager artistic fame brought in far less money than she spent. The grants and commissions she won often barely paid the cost of materials and fabrication, which she mostly contracted to others after she'd done the concepting and design—and meanwhile the house seemed to constantly need repairs. A new roof one year, a new boiler the next, a sewer line backup the summer after that. Meanwhile, Isabel had hardly been living the life of a bohemian all these years, rarely denying herself the pleasure of designer clothes, expensive restaurants, trips to Paris or London or Madrid with stays at the finest hotels. She seemed determined to die having spent the last penny of her daddy's money, to leave nothing of the luxury she'd known to her own daughter. Isabel's fortune, her reputation, was a little like her house: impressive from the outside, but falling apart on the inside, crumbling at the foundations.

Since she was a girl Regan had known she'd have to make her own way, create her own life. This was, in part, what had led her to John—John who, unlike Isabel, had come from nothing, had to fight for every penny he'd ever earned. Regan felt suddenly protective of him.

"John worked hard," she said, blinking away sudden tears. "He worked hard to make a life for us. For me. The kind of life you have. And maybe he… I don't know. Maybe he cut some corners. But I don't think he did it on purpose. He couldn't have. I'm sure it was just a…a mistake."

Isabel clucked her tongue, cocked her head at Regan with pity. "Oh, honey. You don't actually *believe* that, do you? You poor fool."

Regan's cheeks flared, and she had to turn away from her mother's pity—if she looked at her one second longer she feared she'd burst out sobbing, or screaming.

"Isabel, are you being nice?" asked Peter, Regan's father, as he breezed in from the kitchen with a tray of drinks.

"I'm always nice," Isabel said. A laughable statement—she was, if anything, *rarely* nice.

"I made sidecars," Peter announced in a singsong voice. Regan's father was, by contrast with Isabel, so nice that he could never say a bad word to anyone, even if they deserved it. In rooms where tensions were high, he'd perform complex social contortions to make sure everyone around him was happy all the time, constantly asking if everyone was comfortable, if anyone needed anything, if there was anything he could be doing to help. Generally his remedy was to push alcohol, which he regarded as an emotional cure-all. At the moment he was shakily lowering the tray in front of Regan's face, revealing three frosted coupe glasses with liquid sloshing over the lips and down the stems. "Sweetheart?" he asked. "Want one?"

Regan *did* want one, in fact—it was only three in the afternoon, but she deserved the drink. She'd had a rough day. The worst day.

"Thank you, Daddy," Regan said, grabbing a half-full glass and bringing it to her lips for a desperate pull. The sharp taste of cognac and lemon calmed her as it washed over her tongue and down her throat.

"Dear?" Peter asked, offering a drink to Isabel.

She waved him away. "Oh, just put it on the table."

Peter put another glass on the side table next to Isabel's chair and then took a seat himself, eyeing the last drink with alcoholic anticipation. "So, Regan—how are you holding up?"

Regan paused, wondering how to answer the question. How

was she doing? She wasn't sure herself. She was still thinking when her mother answered for her.

"She's doing terrible, Peter. How do you think she's doing? I mean, look at her. The girl's a wreck."

Regan's jaw tightened and she turned away again, furtively covering her face from her parents' pitying stares.

"The FBI's at her house, her husband is a fraud, and she could lose everything she owns."

"I know the facts, dear," Peter said. "I was just hoping to learn how my daughter felt about them."

Regan's father was an artist too—a writer, if only nominally. He hadn't published a book or article in years, but it didn't matter; his debut novel, a campus satire titled *The Dean's Daughter*, had gotten good reviews and won a minor literary award three decades earlier, and Peter had been coasting on the accolades (and the diminishing royalties) ever since. He allegedly had a follow-up novel he'd been tinkering with for ages, a doorstop of typewriter sheets he described at cocktail parties as "an epic of family and crime and politics and *America*." In reality the pages were moldering in his study, and had been for years. The manuscript would go untouched for months at a time, but once in a great while Peter would march into his study, leaf through the stack of loose sheets, change a comma or strike a few words, and call it a day. The rest of his time he spent teaching literature courses at the University of Minnesota and drinking. Of the two, Regan's mother and father, he'd always been the weaker party. "If your mother says so" was his most commonly uttered phrase. Regan sometimes joked, to friends and therapists, that it should be carved on his headstone when he died. Still, Regan loved her father. If he was ineffectual, he was also kind. Her mother was formidable, impressive, scary. But her father, for all his faults, was a teddy bear.

He was staring at her now, eyes wide and glistening, like he might be about to cry in vicarious sadness at what she was going through. "You're okay, Regan?"

"Really, Daddy," Regan assured him, "I'm fine."

"I called Claire, by the way," he said. "She sends her love. Wishes she could be here, but she has a new show."

Regan bit back a surge of anger. "That's kind of her," she said. She'd wondered how long it would take for one of them to mention Claire, her younger sister. Claire was the favorite daughter and everyone knew it, barely took the trouble to deny it when Regan made joking reference to the fact. Like her parents, Claire had grown up to be an artist—an award-winning playwright, specifically, a fact that in terms of parental pride mostly accrued to Peter, play-writing being closer to his art than to Isabel's. Every time Claire staged a new play, every time the positive reviews came in or the awards started stacking up again, their father was the one who got to puff out his chest as his friends in the literature department mumbled approvingly that the apple didn't fall far from the tree, that the daughter must have inherited her skill at writing from Peter—in spite of the fact that she'd long surpassed him in both accolades and output.

For Regan, the most difficult thing was that Claire's success as a playwright had become another tacit point of resentment between her and her mother. One daughter excelled in writing, following in the father's footsteps; the plan for Regan had been for her to make a name for herself in the visual arts, to be a credit to her renowned sculptor mother. But that wasn't the way things worked out. Regan just wasn't interested in the bohemian life of an artist the way her sister was, opting for the suburbs, a family, and a husband with a stable income instead. All choices that looked foolish now. Regan tried to imagine her sister's reaction to the news. She was probably already thinking about how to use Regan's predicament as a premise for one of her plays, something about a woman who sold her soul for the middle-class dream, then saw it all crumble before her eyes. An American tragedy. The reviews would be rapturous. Christ. Regan felt sick just thinking about it.

Regan's mother ignored the mention of Claire and pulled at a curtain. "I don't see why they have to have someone lurking outside," she said, then eyed Regan. "You're not under investigation too, are you?"

"I'm not," Regan said. "They told me I'm not."

"Are you sure they were telling you the truth?" Isabel asked. "The police don't always tell people when they're suspects, you know. It seems like maybe they don't trust you."

"Maybe I should call Ron," Peter offered, naming a family friend who practiced law. "See what he says about all this."

"Ron's a personal injury attorney, Dad—and besides, the FBI's *not* looking at me as a suspect, okay? If I get a lawyer, it'll only make me look guilty. And I'm *not* guilty. I don't know anything. Whatever John's done, he kept it from me the same as he kept it from his clients."

"But you must've known *something*," Isabel insisted. "Even if he didn't tell you anything, you had to have suspected, right? A wife knows her husband."

Regan shook her head to herself as she drew the coupe glass toward her lips, struggling to keep it steady in her quivering hand. *A mother always knows what to say*—that was the line that was going through her mind. The kind of line that showed up in greeting cards for Mother's Day. And it was true of *her* mother, but in a terrible, backward sort of way: Isabel always seemed to know exactly what to say not to comfort Regan, but to make her even more miserable than she already was. Her mother had a knack for being able to put to words the thing that Regan most feared deep down but didn't want to name aloud.

And yes, *of course* she should have known. She was married to John, shared a life and a house and a bed with him. She was supposed to know him better than anyone else in the world. And there *were* signs, weren't there? Signs that he was, if not a criminal, at least a man comfortable with lying, with hiding things, even with stealing. On some level she *had* known. And even if she hadn't—as she had defensively claimed multiple times now, with the FBI and again with her parents—what did that say about her? What was worse: being complicit or being a fool? Would she rather be a victim or an accomplice?

Could you go to jail for not seeing the thing that was right in front of your eyes all along? For looking the other way?

CHAPTER 5

Regan had first met John at a corporate networking event, the kind of thing where a bunch of hungry young professionals would pack into a hotel conference room, take a plateful of cheese and crackers and a plastic cup of wine, and then simply talk, feeling each other out for opportunities to claw a little higher in the corporate world. Regan generally hated such affairs. She lacked the abilities that others seemed to have: seamlessly getting into and out of conversations with strangers, navigating the exchange of business cards, speaking the corporate language of business models, value-adds, brand promises, key stakeholders. But she was there anyway.

Twenty-eight years old and six years into a professional career as a graphic designer, Regan was looking for a change. Her job at a Minneapolis ad agency was theoretically glamorous, but she'd long since realized that it wasn't going to deliver her the kind of life she wanted. The pay was terrible, for one thing—she hadn't gotten a single promotion or anything more than a paltry cost-of-living raise from her entry-level salary since the day she'd started. And the work wasn't even all that interesting. The fun stuff—major campaign concepting, brand ID redesign—all went to her bosses, male art directors who fancied themselves playboy geniuses, modern-day Don Drapers who plastered their office walls with band posters, wore ripped jeans to work, and left early every afternoon to go to the bar. Regan, meanwhile, was grinding away at a cramped desk in a loud, open-floor-plan office, working late hours on dull, thankless tasks. Social media graphics. Slide decks for client presentations. Email campaigns that went directly to spam.

Regan was a pragmatist at heart; she had looked at her life, studied it as a problem to be solved, and made the necessary calculations years ago. Her parents were comfortable, financially, but they'd inherited their money and spent far more than they made; they'd pass little of what they had on to her when they died. The only life she'd be able to enjoy was one she made for herself. And she'd be damned if *this*—the smallness and loneliness and lack of respect and recognition that was her existence now—was going to be the rest of her life.

So that's how John found her: nervously sipping from a plastic cup of red wine at the edge of a hotel event space, eyeing the crowd, looking for *something*—even if she had no idea what that something might be.

"John Peters," he'd said, walking up and offering his hand like a salesman.

Regan was flustered at the brusqueness of John's approach, and she stammered a bit before introducing herself: "I'm Regan."

"Regan," John had said with wonder in his voice, like he'd never heard such a magical combination of sounds before. "What a beautiful name."

Regan felt herself blush, heat rising fast and unexpected to her cheeks. "Is it?"

"Yes. It's…regal?"

This was pretty corny, but Regan was surprised to find herself laughing—no, *giggling*—as she realized all at once that John was flirting with her and that she actually *liked* it.

"That's me," Regan said. "Regal Regan." She flushed, then added: "I've never liked it so much, actually."

"What? Your name?"

"People sometimes say Reagan. Like the president."

"Regan," John said, pronouncing it correctly. "Ree-gan."

"Right. But even then there's Shakespeare. *King Lear*. One of the evil older daughters. I should be insulted my parents chose it. My dad is even an English professor. He's taught *Lear*."

"That's not very nice. Is there a Goneril? A Cordelia?"

Regan's blush deepened as she realized that she'd unintentionally wandered into personal territory. This was a professional networking event, not group therapy. But there was something about John that put her at ease, something in his manner that coaxed her into dropping her guard. She thought of Claire, her accomplished younger sister.

"My sister's name isn't Cordelia," she blurted. "But she *is* the favorite."

"I'm sorry to hear that."

Regan had the urge to clap her hand over her mouth. What was wrong with her? A kind of drunken feeling had come over her, a carelessness. She brought the plastic cup to her lips and drank the rest of the bad Merlot in a single gulp, hoping the flood of alcohol would wash away her awkwardness. After she'd swallowed it down she made a halting apology for burdening John—this guy she had only met—with her personal problems.

John eventually saved her with a gorgeous, heart-stopping smile, a shrug, and a self-deprecating remark: "I guess we're not very good at this." *This* being, presumably, the professional networking they were ostensibly there to perform. The art of conversation.

He was great at it, actually, effortlessly charming—though he wasn't *smooth,* exactly. No, perhaps the self-mocking remark— John's generosity in pretending that he and not she was the one embarrassing himself—was precisely the nature of his charm; in his presence Regan no longer felt out of place in that hotel conference room but exactly where she belonged, delivered from awkwardness to grace, the bone-deep embarrassment radiating from her body reflected back to her, from John, as unconditional approval. John looked directly at her, seemed interested in what she was saying even when what she was saying was stupid or out of place, didn't dart his eyes to the side like some had the tendency to do at these things, looking for someone better to talk to. Talking to her, John gave the impression of a man who was exactly where he wanted to be—and in that moment Regan found that she was exactly where she wanted to be as well. She'd come to the networking event looking for *something.* Perhaps this was it. She should probably circulate, gather some more contacts, but she didn't want to. She wanted to keep talking to John. Look at his eyes as he listened to her.

And so, when he suggested they get out of there, Regan agreed, with something like relief.

———————

They ended up at a brewery not far from the hotel, taking their frothy pints of beer to the patio, blinking into the sun shining brilliantly in that late-spring afternoon. As John threw his leg over the wooden table bench across from her, Regan found herself wondering what this was. Were they still networking? Or were they on a date?

John was a financial adviser, after all, and the questions he began asking about her might have been the kinds of things an adviser would want to know about a prospective client: her job, her life, her goals. But Regan thought she could sense a more-than-professional interest from John, and she found herself becoming comfortable with him, opening up, sharing more than she might even on a typical first date. Without quite intending to, she ended up telling John *everything*: telling him about her dissatisfaction with her ad agency job, and about her desire to get into interior design, which she'd barely admitted even to herself. At the peak of her confessions, she shocked herself by telling him—this guy she'd only barely met yet somehow already trusted with the most painful facts of her life—that her serious artist parents didn't approve of her ambitions, thought her goals for her life were frivolous, girlish, embarrassingly domestic. Regan looked down, ashamed again at sharing too much, but then she felt the weight of John's hand on hers, and she looked up to find him staring urgently into her eyes.

Oh, this was *definitely* a date.

"Is it your dream?" John asked.

"I guess," Regan admitted after a pause.

"You guess."

Regan sat up taller, drew her shoulders back. "It is."

"Then who cares what anyone else thinks? You should be able to go after what you want."

Regan was moved almost to tears herself by John's concern for her, by his encouragement. It was something she never seemed to get from anyone else in her life—not from her mother, not from her sister, certainly not from herself. It was an amazing feeling, being encouraged, feeling that there was someone in the world who truly saw you and thought that what they saw was *good*. She could get used to it.

But what about John? What did he want? She apologized for talking so much, tried to turn the conversation toward him, but he only deflected.

"The thing about being a financial adviser is that it's about making *other* people's dreams come true," John said. "So I guess that's my goal: to help other people reach their goals. The thing that makes me happy is making other people happy."

Oh, he was good. He may have been young, early in his career as a financial adviser, trying to build his client base—but Regan could tell that John Peters was going to be successful at what he did.

Regan leaned over the table, aware that all traces of coyness, all her reserve, had fallen away. She was openly coming on to John now, and perhaps he'd been coming on to her—*selling* her—all along.

"What about me?" she asked. "How would you make me happy?"

She watched as understanding spread across John's face, a wry smile coming to his lips.

"I'm sure I could think of something."

Regan knew at that moment that this was far from over. That she'd make John fulfill his promise very soon—maybe even that very night.

John *did* make Regan happy, in the weeks and months that followed. In bed he was attentive, generous, even patient—not just getting his dick in her and pounding away, like so many of the other young guys she'd dated over the years, but actually taking the time to find out what *she* liked, exploring her body, making sure she came every time they had sex, using his fingers, his mouth. They went on dates every weekend, and there was rarely a single day that passed where she didn't get some kind of communication—a text or a phone call—from him to let her know that he was thinking about her. They never officially moved in together, but they may as well have, John spending so many nights at her one-bedroom in Uptown rather than his studio in Saint Paul that he basically lived there. Regan thought about complaining, considered wondering aloud at breakfast some morning whether they were moving too fast, spending too much time together, whether John should maybe spend a few days at his place—except that it was so nice to have him around. His things barely took up any space, and he cleaned up after himself—cleaned up after Regan too—wiping down counters, sinks, doing the laundry without being asked. Some days she'd come home late from work at the ad agency and find John in the kitchen making dinner: pasta, a big salad, once a whole roast chicken with garlic roasted potatoes, a salad, and white wine.

The only problem in those early days of their relationship was something that had charmed Regan at their first meeting but which had begun to grate as time wore on: John was keenly interested in Regan, in learning everything he could about her, but rarely—almost never—shared anything about himself.

This was hard to notice at first, in part because the experience of being under John's gaze, being the object of his curiosity, was so intoxicating. When she was with John, Regan felt herself to be interesting and important, worthy of all the attention she was receiving, a celebrity to a fan base of one. Under the glare of John's adoration, it was hard to notice or care that he'd pull away and deflect anytime a question turned to him. He'd dance around and turn the conversation back toward her whenever she ventured to ask about his family, where he'd grown up, if he had any siblings, or what he was like as a kid: loud or quiet, silly or serious.

Not that John didn't have answers to these questions, only that the answers he gave concealed more than they revealed and cut off further inquiry. When Regan asked where he was from:

"Oh, just some shithole town up north. I've worked hard to forget it."

Or when Regan asked about his parents:

"They died. You don't have to be sorry. We weren't close."

As time went on—six months, nine months, a year—Regan became more insistent in her questions. As a kind of challenge to John, she began to expose more of herself, laying out her life in all its detail. She answered every question John had, even told him things he hadn't asked about. And one day in the fall, she brought him home to meet her parents, far earlier than she might have otherwise. It was a disastrous dinner in which Isabel barely concealed her dislike for John and his choice of occupation, but getting her parents to like him hadn't been the point. Regan knew she was daring John, calling a sort of bluff: if she gave him everything, every part of her, he'd have to break down and reveal something about himself to her eventually.

And he did, though not in the way she'd anticipated.

This was when the cons began.

———————

It started on a Saturday morning in spring, almost a year after they'd first met and started dating. They already had patterns by this time, as habit-bound as an elderly couple. Normally they'd sleep in late, let the sun creep into the bedroom. John would wake first and go to make the coffee, then Regan would rise later, with the smell, and find him in her kitchen, frying eggs or making pancakes. Slowly, they'd enter the day, lazing for hours around the apartment before venturing out for a late-afternoon happy hour, dinner, maybe a movie.

On this day, though, John came into the bedroom and shook her from sleep with coffee in a steel tumbler.

"Get up," he said. "I want to go out."

Regan looked at the clock. It was 9:30—a time she'd regard

as impossibly late after the kids were born, but which by the standards of her late twenties was still early on a weekend.

"Now?"

"Yeah," he said. "We're going to open houses."

Open houses? Regan thought she'd heard John wrong, but then after she'd had some breakfast, he packed her in the car and brought her to a succession of homes in the city with real estate signs pounded into the dirt at the curb. Huge, beautiful homes, in some of the Twin Cities' most coveted neighborhoods: Lake of the Isles, Linden Hills, Summit Avenue, the price tags seeming to climb with each home they saw. Regan had a few thousand dollars in a checking account, almost ten thousand in savings, some money in a 401(k) that she never checked. She didn't think she'd ever be able to afford homes like these: $735,000, $859,000, $919,000. Palatial living rooms, gleaming kitchens, master bedrooms as big as her entire apartment, with their own bathrooms and balconies. She didn't know how much money John had squirreled away, but she guessed he couldn't come close to putting a down payment on any of these places either—not by the evidence of his shabby studio apartment in Saint Paul.

The real estate agents at the open houses sensed it as well, seeming to smell John and Regan's lack of money as they came in the door. The agents would turn up their noses as they spoke to them, perfunctorily asking them how long they'd been in the market, what they were looking for—then suggestively mention that they had some other properties they might be interested in looking at. *Smaller* properties. The implication was clear: John and Regan didn't belong here.

"John, what the hell are we doing?" Regan asked after the third house, as John drove them onto the interstate, north toward the suburbs.

"Just having some fun," John said.

"This isn't my definition of fun."

"Don't you like to dream?"

"Dream about what?"

"About what might be someday. About where we could end up."

"John. Come on. We'll never be able to afford a house like the ones we've been looking at."

"You never know," John said. "Anything's possible."

He drove them to North Oaks, a loose suburb of golf courses and lakes, rambling mansions on winding roads set amid evergreen trees. They drove up to one such mansion, a white house with a porch that ran the entire length of the facade and wrapped around to the back, panes of glass vaulting above all the way to the eaves. Inside, they took off their shoes and walked to the kitchen, where Regan picked up a flyer. Something caught in her throat: a gasp, or perhaps a laugh. "Escape to spacious luxury. 5 bedrooms. 5 baths. Deck, pool, lake access, boat house. $1,654,900."

A real estate agent walked up to them and introduced herself to John. So far, everything was following the pattern of the previous houses they'd looked at—but then John gave a fake name.

"Roger," he said. "Roger White."

"I see," the agent said. "Are you preapproved? What kind of financing would you be looking at for a home at this price range?"

"I was thinking about a cash offer, actually," John said.

The agent blinked, her disdain morphing at once into interest. She smiled at John. "And what do you do, Mr. White?"

"Oh, Roger, please," John said. "I'm an investor. Real estate investor."

"Oh really? You're looking at this place as an investment?"

Regan looked to John, wondering what he'd say next. She realized she'd been holding her breath. She let air out of her lungs slowly, trying not to draw any attention.

"No," John said. "To live in. I'm looking at a number of properties in the city and I need a base of operations."

"What kind of properties, Mr. White?"

John frowned at the agent. "Now, what did I just say?"

The agent laughed. "Roger, then." Her cheeks flushed red. Regan looked at her and wondered if that was what she'd looked like back when she'd first met John. He'd made her laugh too.

"That's better," John said. "Luxury apartments, mostly. A few old houses in the city I intend to convert to four-plexes and sell. Maybe a few empty lots, for development."

"Are you looking for partners?" the woman asked.

John smiled, and with a stab of hurt Regan realized that he was flirting with the agent. She'd thought he only used that look with her, but here it was, pointed at another woman, and she found herself wondering how many women John flirted with, how many he turned on the charm for. Was it something he did often, to get clients?

"Oh, always," he said.

The agent seemed too overcome to speak. She turned to Regan. "And you are?"

"Yes, dear," John said. "Introduce yourself."

"I'm…Veronica," Regan stammered.

They walked through the rest of the house, but Regan couldn't see the rooms. She kept thinking about what had happened in the kitchen. Why had John lied?

On the way out, the agent stopped them, gave John her business card. "In case you need to get in touch," she said. Then, at the car, an older man in a gray sport coat stopped them. He'd overheard them talking and he wanted in. He wanted to invest.

"I'm afraid we're not looking for small investors right now," John said. "Anything less than half a million, it's just not worth my time."

"I've got it," the man said, a trace of desperation in his voice. "I can get it. I just need to move some things around."

John sighed. "We were just about to leave." He was projecting impatience, but Regan could tell that he was scared.

Panic came to the man's eyes. He reached into his breast pocket and came out with a checkbook. "How much do you need now to know I'm serious? Five thousand?"

"Ten at least," John said.

The man clicked a pen and opened the checkbook on the roof of their car, somehow not noticing that the Hyundai hatchback John drove was hardly the car of a real estate investor. He started scribbling. Regan looked over his shoulder as he wrote a one. Her panic boiled over as he added the zeros.

"John!" she shouted.

The man's head snapped up. "Wait. John? I thought your name was—"

John shoved Regan into the car, then leapt into the driver's seat and peeled away.

———

More dates followed, more *cons*, outings in which John again made up a character on the spot and forced Regan to play along. After the open house in North Oaks, there was a swank millionaire's wedding they'd bluffed their way into, John pretending to be a distant cousin to the bride and becoming loudly offended when the poor event coordinator with a clipboard at the gate couldn't find their name on the list. She'd finally let them in, and Regan and John spent the rest of the night enjoying the lavish party, gaping at the expensive clothes and decorations, eating catered steaks with the rest of the guests, drinking from the open bar, and walking away at the end of the night with party favors:

a whole gift basket full of expensive hand lotions, bath salts, and face creams that Regan used in the bathroom for weeks to come.

After that came the pinnacle of their cons, a night at a dance club downtown where John targeted some trust-fund kids who were high out of their minds on molly. He concocted some story about a bagful of drug money locked up at the bus station, claiming that they couldn't get at it because the cops were staking out the place and knew their faces—but that the kids could have the key for a thousand bucks, and walk away with fifteen thousand, clean. Regan figured that if John's marks had been sober they wouldn't have gone for it, but they weren't sober, and they did go for it, searched their wallets and went to an ATM and shelled out ten crisp hundreds in exchange for a key that John had found at the bottom of a junk drawer, one he admitted later he didn't even know what it was for—a padlock to a locker at an old gym he used to go to, maybe. He chattered about the con all the way home— *Can you believe it, I didn't think they'd go for it but then they did, they fucking did*—while Regan silently held the money in the palm of her hand, looked at it in the intermittent glow of streetlights. When they got back to Regan's place, she finally spoke up and told him the cons had to stop.

"I don't want to do this anymore. I'm done."

John's mouth closed. He seemed surprised, disappointed, perhaps even hurt. After a second he nodded, accepting what she was saying—but then he also left that night, went back to his apartment for the first time in months, and Regan didn't see him or hear from him for a week after that. It was the longest she'd gone without spending time with John since they met. Maybe he knew that he'd scared her, thought she needed space. And maybe she did need the time to think.

They'd been scary, these dates—these *cons*, John had called them—but exciting too. Regan couldn't deny the thrill of pretending to be someone else, of lying. The steak at the wedding had tasted better than any she'd ever had, and the basket of creams and lotions they'd walked away with (she still had some in her medicine cabinet) felt so good as she spread them onto her skin. There was something exhilarating about fooling those dumb club kids into shelling out a thousand dollars for a useless key. And she still thought about the feeling that had risen up inside her when that businessman in North Oaks had pulled out his checkbook, the heady blend of fear and excitement as she realized that he was willing to give them ten thousand dollars on the spot.

Had it been illegal, what they'd done? Had they broken the law? Stolen the gift basket, the free catered meal and drinks? The club kids had handed over their money willingly, but wasn't it still stealing? What if they'd taken the businessman's check, figured out a way to cash it? Would that have been fraud?

The more unsettling questions had to do with what the cons revealed about John and why he'd thought it would be fun to take her on them. Did he do this often? Did he lie to people—lie to *her*? Was John Peters real, or was she another one of his marks— like the businessman, the wedding guests, the club kids? She'd observed that when John bluffed his way into places, when he got things from other people that didn't belong to him, it was not precisely because of who he pretended to be, but rather because of the way he made others feel about themselves—who he made others believe *they* were. The guy in North Oaks believed he could be a high-rolling real estate investor; the club kids believed they could be the kind of people who made deals with criminals. John had made Regan believe something about herself too: he'd made her believe that she was interesting and beautiful. That she was a person who deserved love.

Perhaps he'd intended the cons as a sort of self-revelation, an answer to the questions Regan had been asking about his family, his background, his past. To these questions, John's reply was that his past didn't matter, didn't define him. He could be anyone, and so could Regan.

John was a financial adviser, Regan reflected. He worked in the world of money. And money, she was coming to realize, had no memory. It wasn't burdened by the past. Money didn't care where you were born, who your parents were, the things you'd done or left undone. In John's world the only thing that seemed to matter was the future. With his clients—his *marks*?—he thought not about what had been, not even about what was, but about what could be. He cast grand visions and dreamed great dreams about what they could become with his help, dreams about what their money—by growing and reproducing and becoming more of itself, more *money*—could change them into.

Regardless of the reason, Regan couldn't deny that the week without him was incredibly lonely. Without John at her apartment, her life suddenly felt emptied out, desolate. She'd become used to having him around, had started taking it for granted. In John's presence, Regan had discovered a state of grace she didn't know was possible. To be loved, truly loved and cared for, was the greatest feeling in the world. Now to be suddenly without that feeling was terrible. She wanted it back. Who cared if it was real or not?

And so, Regan was relieved when she finally got a call from John at the end of that long week asking if they could grab dinner. He'd pick her up. She waited for him in a nauseated state of nervous excitement, then leapt up from the couch to meet him at the door when he arrived. As soon as he stepped into the apartment, he sank to his knees and opened a jewelry box.

"Regan," John said, "I love you. I'll be whoever you want—whoever you need me to be to make you happy. Marry me."

Regan looked at the ring, the gleaming diamond jutting up

from the platinum band like the pistil in the center of a flower, enclosed in the petals of the velvet jewelry box and John's sturdy hands. What he was offering her, she knew, was the opportunity to be someone new with him. To see what people they might become together. He was leading her away from the past, and into the future.

"Yes," she said.

CHAPTER 6

Regan watched the FBI car parked at the curb for the rest of the evening and into the night, waiting for it to leave so she could escape to the lake house. She watched it out the window through an awkward, mostly silent dinner with her parents, watched it as she put the kids down for bed—Philip in the study, Etta in her old bedroom.

"Is Daddy going to say good night to me, Mama?" Etta asked as she laid down her head, arms wrapped around one of Regan's old stuffed bears.

A tightness came to Regan's stomach. John would often sneak in and say good night to the kids when he worked late; Regan didn't know how to explain to Etta that it wouldn't be happening tonight or maybe ever again.

"I don't think so, sweetheart."

"He's working late?"

Regan paused. She'd have to explain eventually, but not now. There'd be too many questions, questions she didn't yet know how to answer. Maybe tears too. She couldn't do it to the girl, not right before she went to sleep.

"Something like that," Regan said. "Really, really late."

Etta's eyes narrowed. "Daddy works too many times. I wish he was here."

"I know, sweetheart. I wish he could be here with us too."

She began to choke on the last words, and wrapped Etta in a sudden hug to hide her tears.

"Good night, my girl," she whispered into Etta's ear, then gave her a kiss on the cheek and left the room.

In the hallway she leaned against the wall and took a breath, trying to calm herself. Her hands balled to fists at her side. Across the hall was a small clock, its short pendulum swinging furiously back and forth, and as she looked at it Regan thought of how nice it would be to grab it off the wall and hurl it to the ground, to break something, like a man might do when he was angry. But she couldn't—not without waking the kids and bringing her parents upstairs to see what was the matter.

She heard their voices murmuring below her right now. They were probably talking about her. Whispering about her. She could imagine what they were saying, her mother especially: *I do feel sorry for her, but she should never have married John in the first place. She made her bed and now she'll have to lie in it.*

She couldn't face them, couldn't go downstairs and join them in the living room. Instead she leaned up against the wall and sank down to the floor of the hallway, settled there with her legs stretched out in front of her and crossed at the ankle. She dug in a pocket and pulled out her phone, thumbed it open, and went to the Facebook page for WCCO-TV, a local news affiliate. She hadn't been able to shake the sight of the news van on her street, the cameraman hoisting a camera to his shoulder as she fled. She'd missed the six o'clock news, could've waited until the ten o'clock, but the only TV in the house was on the main floor, and she'd have to watch with her parents. Regan couldn't imagine the humiliation of a story about John's crimes coming on while Peter and Isabel sat next to her.

She scrolled through the WCCO feed, each post providing a link to a different story, a different segment. State senators arguing about the budget at the capital, layoffs at a local factory, a girl raising money for the homeless with a curbside lemonade stand—and then there it was.

TWIN CITIES FINANCIAL ADVISER ACCUSED OF STEALING CLIENTS' MONEY

Regan heard her own pulse in her ears as the video loaded. She frantically thumbed the volume down low enough that her parents wouldn't be able to hear downstairs.

On the screen, a female anchor looked gravely into the camera. "A quiet neighborhood in the western suburbs was turned upside down today when FBI agents raided the house of a..." The anchorwoman must have gone on talking, perhaps handed things off to a reporter at the scene, but Regan suddenly couldn't hear anything anymore, because there on the screen was her street, there was her house, her blue siding, her white awnings, her red front door and cement stoop, and now—*oh God*—there was her neighbor Gloria, the retired busybody, looking red-faced and upset as she talked into a microphone, and Regan suddenly felt as though she was sinking into the floor, the carpet and the slats of hardwood yawning open to swallow her whole. Regan had to put a hand on the floor to steady herself; the phone fell out of her other hand and clattered down. Regan blinked, gave her head a shake to push away the vertigo, and snatched up the phone again.

"...no idea," Gloria was saying. "They seemed like such nice people, but you never know who someone really is, I guess."

They. Gloria had said *they.* Not *he.* Confirming Regan's fears—John had been the one to commit a crime, but the world would hold both of them responsible.

And now there was John's picture as well, the professional photo he used on the website for his business. The photo looked sinister, his smile put on and fake, his eyes empty. Maybe they'd done something to the colors before running it, sapped the photo of its vibrancy, applied some kind of filter. It was impossible to look at his face and not believe him to be a sociopath.

Then the photo blinked away, and another person's face came on the screen—a woman's, middle aged, with other people dimly visible behind her on the sidewalk in front of Regan's house. Off camera, a reporter asked who she was and what she was doing there.

"My parents were clients of John Peters," the woman said. She had a round face and angry eyes set deep behind sharp cheek-bones. "They invested their life savings with him for their retire-ment. I reported him to the authorities after my parents spent six months—*six months*—trying to get their money from him. We just found out today that he has been charged with fraud, and that the thousands of dollars my parents entrusted him with are gone. I'm here today—with my parents and several of John Peters's other victims—because I want the Peters family to see the people whose lives they have ruined."

The woman looked behind her, extended an arm, and a number of other people stepped around: an elderly couple, an old white man in a trucker hat, a young Latina woman in nurse's scrubs, and others partially cut off by the frame of the screen. Some of them held signs—the angry woman's father, mustached and wearing a Western plaid shirt, held a piece of cardboard with GIVE ME MY MONEY BACK written in black marker. His eyes were distant, as though he didn't know where to focus, and there was a look of pained confusion on his face.

Regan held a hand over her mouth as the picture changed again and she suddenly saw herself, recorded in profile through the window of her car, holding a hand up to the side of her face as she screeched away. She looked guilty. It was impossible to look innocent while running away.

"This is Mr. Peters's spouse, Regan Peters, abruptly leaving the scene earlier today—no word from the FBI yet on whether or not she was involved in this financial scheme with her husband."

Regan pushed herself up and lurched to the bathroom. In the darkness she scrambled on her knees to the toilet and lifted the seat. She waited. She'd thought she might throw up, but now that she was here the feeling had passed, and all she did was breathe slowly into the bowl, smelling the water and the scrubbed porcelain—a smell she associated with shame, with late nights and one too many drinks.

After a while she stood up, flipped on the bathroom light, then slowly washed her hands, staring at her reflection in the mirror. Earlier, on the news segment, she'd barely recognized her husband's image; now she hardly recognized hers. She felt as though she'd aged a decade in the last several hours. There were dark half-moons under her eyes, and her cheeks looked sunken and haggard.

After she was done in the bathroom she went back into the hall, walked to the window at the end, and looked down at the street. The FBI car was gone. Finally.

She checked in on the kids—both were sleeping soundly. She crept down the back steps to the side entrance, then walked softly to her car. She felt bad about leaving the kids, cringing at the scene that would result if they woke up while she was gone— Etta and Philip screaming for her, her parents realizing that she'd snuck away like a teenager. But what difference did it make, now?

What was one more sin on top of everything else that had been uncovered today? The world already thought she was guilty.

Let her be guilty, then.

———————————

Darkness advanced across the sky as she drove, the night pulled tight overhead like a cover. Regan felt like a fugitive. She realized as she pushed through the night that she wasn't quite sure why she was going back to the house—fleeing or finding, running from or running to. Did she really expect to find John there, this late in the day? He was probably in another state by now, maybe even another country. Yet she found herself wanting to get there quickly all the same. So much had been taken away, so much seemed to be slipping away—Regan wanted to make sure that the house was something that still belonged to her. That it was still real.

She made a few wrong turns as she wound through the lake roads, but finally she arrived at the house, its dark mass hulking at the end of a dead-end lane. Her headlights illuminated the brick facade as she came close: definitely real. She hadn't imagined it. At the front door she hesitated, feeling fear, as though John, waiting inside, might jump out of the shadows and stab her when she walked through the door. This was silly, Regan knew, but the thought of John had become so strange over the past twelve hours and she no longer knew what to expect from him, if he was indeed inside.

"John?" she called when the door creaked open. "John, are you in there?" No answer, just the small reverberation of her thin voice bouncing from bare walls, empty rooms. She walked through the house, turning on all the lights, her heart taking a little hop in her throat each time she flipped a switch to illuminate another room—but he wasn't there.

The house was completely empty, in fact—empty but for a single object Regan didn't remember being there before: a garage-door opener. The old owners had given the opener to them at closing, along with the keys, and from there it had gone into John's car. She was certain they hadn't brought it back in with them when they returned to the house to marvel at what they'd just bought and make love on the floor. The garage-door opener had remained on the dashboard in John's car. And yet here it was. Evidence that John *had* been here today, even if he was gone again now.

Regan grabbed the opener, walked out the front door to the driveway. She pushed the button and watched the door rise, revealing John's car inside. Cautious again, she crept to the driver's window, but the car, too, was empty, unlocked, and the keys were in the ignition. This was starting to feel like a scavenger hunt. First the opener, then the car, now the keys. What did John want her to find? She scanned both front seats, then the back seat, and then she went to the trunk.

Inside was a cream-colored leather travel bag with tan straps. It took Regan a moment to recognize it as something of *hers*, a gift from John, for last year's birthday. They called it a *weekender*, something to throw a few changes of clothes into for a short jaunt to someplace beautiful—though John, when she'd opened it, had called it her "getaway bag."

"You could use it for a girls' trip sometime," he'd said, smiling, pleased with his thoughtfulness. "You know. Get away from me and the kids for a bit."

Regan hadn't liked it. Philip was only six months old at the time, still not sleeping through the night, and John was putting in long hours at the office. She couldn't imagine getting away for an afternoon, let alone for a girls' weekend with similarly busy mom friends she hadn't even seen in months. If John had really wanted to give her a gift he'd have actually *planned* a getaway for her, hidden a boarding pass and a vacation rental confirmation in one of the side pockets. Instead, the empty bag had gone in the back of her closet. She hadn't used it once.

It was packed full now, though, bulging and lumpy. Regan reached for the bag and gave it a heave to test its weight; she could barely lift it. Next she eased the zipper open, holding her breath, somehow certain of what would be inside even before she saw it.

Money. Piles of it, stacks of it.

The back of Regan's neck tingled and she closed the garage door behind her, imagining a neighbor, some night owl up late, spying on her from down the street. Then she hefted the bag out and carried it into the house. Inside she took one look at all the windows in the kitchen, dining room, and living room, then turned off the lights and went down the hallway. A bathroom was the first room she found where she couldn't be seen from the outside. She emptied the bag out onto the tile floor, then settled herself down and began counting the money.

The cash was in stacks of bills, bound with rubber bands. Most of the bills were hundreds, some fifties, nothing smaller than a twenty. It took her almost an hour to count it all, unbinding the stacks, counting out the cash onto the floor, then wrapping each pile in the rubber band again and going on to the next. As she reached the end of her counting she thought of the man at the open house from their first con, the one who'd tried to write him a check. All those zeros.

There were more zeros now. A million dollars, and more. $1,010,550, to be exact. More money than she'd ever seen in one place, more money than she imagined she'd ever have—though she knew, dimly, that John had been saving money for them over the years, had it spread over different accounts, mutual funds and bonds and money markets and certificates of deposit and high-yield savings. That was electronic money though, numbers on a screen. Besides. the FBI knew about all those accounts, and had their plans to take them from her—every last cent, to pay for John's crimes. This money was physical. It was real. It was laid out on the floor before her. And it was—for now—*hers.*

As she thought it, she knew it wasn't true. This money surely belonged to John's clients, the ones he'd stolen from. Regular people, people like the ones she'd seen on the news story gathered outside her house to protest, to express their rage: the middle-aged woman with lines spidering out from her eyes, the man in the Western shirt, the young woman wearing nurse's scrubs. She should return it, to *them.*

But then she thought of the bag, the gift from John she hadn't liked at the time. Her getaway bag. John was obviously trying to tell her something by putting dirty money in a bag that had originally been a gift for her, the bag itself hidden in the house that had been his latest and most outlandish gift. He wanted her to keep the money, to use it as an escape.

A getaway.

There were also the kids to think of: their future, their clothes, their food, where they'd live. Summer camps, braces, college funds. John was gone; she was the provider now. It was all on her shoulders. She thought once more of the cons, of what John had been trying to tell her with them. She'd always thought his point had been that he could be anyone he wanted to be and so she should stop asking him about who he *was,* who he'd *been.* But maybe there'd been another message, as well: that she could be anyone too.

She wondered, now, if she could become the kind of person who could keep the money laid out in front of her. Someone like John: unencumbered by the past, unafraid to lie, to steal. Someone with a plan.

Regan stayed in the empty house and thought about it for five minutes, ten, paced the narrow bathroom floor, looking at the money, playing out the scenarios. She could call the FBI right now, tell them where she was, what she was looking at. She should, probably. But then there'd be questions, unpleasant ones—they'd wonder why she didn't tell them about the house in the first place, why she didn't bring them along to discover the money with her. She couldn't face it, not tonight.

Ultimately, Regan decided, it would be easier to hide the money. To give herself more time to figure out what to do with it.

Regan drove back to her parents' house with the bag in the passenger seat next to her. She glanced over at it every so often as the car passed in and out of the orange glow of streetlamps, as if to make sure it was safe, and real.

On her parents' street, she pulled into the alley and rolled quietly to the detached garage. She keyed in the code to open the door, then heaved the bag inside, past her parents' car to a ladder at the back wall. The ladder led to a small wooden platform in the rafters. Her father used the loft for storage—Christmas decorations, some yard tools, a few tarps—but when she was a girl Regan had used the loft as a place to escape, to hide. A place to read a book, to put her thoughts in a diary, to lean her back against the wall and simply close her eyes, imagining herself tucked away from the demands of the world.

She hauled the bag up the ladder, her feet uneasy on the rungs. It was still open, the place she used to sit: a smooth patch of unfinished boards between a box of old photo albums and some folded-up drop cloths. A small spot, but she'd felt safe there, when she was young, the box and cloths pressing against her shoulders, making her feel held. Now she heaved the bag up, placed it on the platform, and shoved it toward the spot. The FBI would never look for it here, and her parents scarcely went up the ladder anymore. Regan had been safe in the loft—the money would be too.

Regan closed the garage door and snuck to the house, coming in the back way. She turned the knob gingerly, careful not to make noise—but her mother was awake, waiting for her in the hallway, eyes wild with anger.

"Where have you been?"

Regan glanced at the clock on the wall. It was just past midnight.

"Did the kids wake up?"

"No," Isabel said. "I'm the only one who noticed you were gone."

"Good," Regan said.

There was a moment of quiet, then Isabel asked: "Well? Did you find him?"

"No. Only his car."

Regan's mother let out a long sigh. "If the police knew you were sneaking around, they'd arrest you. For obstruction. Maybe even as John's accomplice. You know that, right?"

"I know what I'm doing," Regan said, turning away from her mother and running up the stairs before she could answer.

But she *didn't* know what she was doing, and when she finally crawled into bed, careful not to disturb Etta, she lay awake for hours and simply thought about the money. Was there any way for her to actually keep it for herself and the kids? She thought that if she simply hid its existence from the FBI for long enough, they'd eventually move on, lose interest in her. She could sneak back into the garage loft, and then spend the money as if it were her own.

These thoughts were still with her as she drifted off to sleep.

CHAPTER 7

The messages began coming the next day.

The first buzzed on her phone the moment Regan woke up, swinging her legs over the side of the bed and webbing her toes wide to feel at the cool surface of the hardwood floor, the lump of Etta's body still sleeping, still breathing steadily, under the covers beside her. A little vibration came from the bed stand, where she'd left her phone during the night. She angled her head to read the message.

> Regan. Oh my God. I just heard the news. How terrible.
> Are you ok?

Her phone kept buzzing throughout the morning—as she got the children and brought them downstairs, as she made them breakfast and brewed some coffee for herself, as she cleaned up after herself and then took the kids for a little walk around the neighborhood, pushing Philip in the stroller and hectoring Etta to keep up, stay on the sidewalk, don't wander onto people's lawns.

Texts and emails, direct messages on Facebook and Instagram. From neighbors, from former coworkers at the ad agency, from classmates she hadn't seen or heard from in years except to see their wedding photos or birth announcements on social media. Each message a small piece of evidence that the news stories that had aired last night were spreading, shared from one person to the next, growing from a spark to a blaze of rumor and voyeurism. Regan had hoped that it would all blow over somehow, that everyone would just look the other way, mind their own business, and leave her to handle this in peace.

How foolish she'd been. No one could resist another person's drama, another person's misery. Everyone loved to be the one with the juicy story, the inside information, the one to say, *Did you hear, oh my God, you'll never believe it...*

The messages were all some version of the same thing, as though there was only one way to offer condolences: *I just heard, are you okay, if there's anything I can do, please let me know.* Some of them offered the services of lawyers they knew, spouses or family friends who worked in corporate law but might be able to help out with a criminal case—and one woman, someone Regan had known back in high school, even gave her the name of the divorce lawyer she'd used when her own marriage had fallen apart.

"He's great," she said in her email, "a real fighter."

An angry rattle rose up in Regan's throat—who suggests a divorce lawyer to someone they haven't spoken to in years? She shoved the phone back into her pocket, kept on walking down the sidewalk, pushing the stroller a little faster over broken concrete.

"Henrietta Jane!" she snapped at Etta, who'd paused a few steps back to look at a purple flower on someone's front lawn, bending over to stick her nose in its petals. "Keep up."

Etta ran to catch up, her cheeks reddened and her eyes wide at Regan's scolding. Regan immediately regretted yelling; Etta hadn't done anything wrong. Let her stop and smell flowers if she wanted to; let her be carefree as long as she possibly could. It wasn't her fault that people were nosy and meddlesome. And maybe Regan *should* have been thinking about hiring a divorce lawyer. She hadn't thought about it until just then, reading her old classmate's email—but her marriage *was* over, wasn't it? John was gone, and once the FBI caught up with him he'd be in jail. What marriage could survive that? They said you had to work on your marriage, fight for it, but there was nothing left for her to fight for—nothing but the money, her fair share of everything that was left over.

She was thinking about whether she should get a lawyer— maybe a lawyer could work with the FBI to let Regan keep some of John's money, or even talk to the press, make it clear to everyone that John was to blame here, not her—when the phone buzzed in her pocket yet again.

"Oh Jesus Christ," she muttered too loudly. "What the fuck is it now?"

"What did you say, Mama?" Etta asked, her voice high and fearful. "Did I do something bad?"

"No, baby. It's ok, don't worry."

Regan looked at her phone and saw a message from an unknown number. No text, just a picture. Regan squinted at it, unable to make out the fuzzy details in the thumbnail. She tapped on the notification, then entered her security code to look closer.

The photo appeared on the screen and seared itself into her brain.

Regan screamed and dropped the phone to the ground.

"What is it, Mama?" Etta asked, her voice gone high and shrill. In the stroller, Philip began to cry.

"It's nothing," Regan said, willing herself to be calm for the sake of the children, knowing she was scaring them. "I just dropped my phone by accident."

She leaned over and picked it off the concrete, the screen still lit up. Etta clambered over and tried to take a look, but Regan clutched the phone to herself, hiding it from the girl's eyes.

"Can I see?" Etta asked, pulling at Regan's pant leg.

"Stop it!" Regan snapped. "Just be quiet!"

Etta stood back and joined Philip in crying, but Regan blocked out the sound as her attention tunneled into the phone in her hands.

The photo was in black and white, a little grainy, but its details were still clear enough once Regan looked closely. It showed a woman and a man having sex in what could have been a hotel bed. The angle was from above, as though the camera had been mounted on the wall near the ceiling. The woman was on top, her bare back to the camera, dark hair cascading down over her shoulders as she rode atop the man. He lay flat on the mattress, head thrown back, eyes closed, but his face was still clearly visible.

It was John.

Her husband, fucking another woman.

The emotions she felt upon looking at the photo and understanding what she was looking at, the betrayal the image represented, veered wildly across a spectrum from moment to moment. First there was the horror, the reflexive disgust, like a gag reaction, that had made her throw the phone to the ground. Then there was the shame, which she was feeling now, a shame so deep that it was indistinguishable from a desire to die, to disappear, to burrow deep inside herself and never come back out. She'd do anything to prevent anyone from seeing the photo, from knowing that John had cheated on her, not just Etta but every other human being in the world.

The third emotion, which followed quickly after, was anger. Why should *she* be the one to feel bad? She'd done nothing wrong. And yet she was somehow the one who felt guilty, the one who felt she had something to hide, the one making a scene on a city street, snapping at her kids, making them cry.

Then her eyes fell on the woman. Her back was to the camera, her face not visible—but Regan didn't need to see her face. She'd know that shoulder-length hair anywhere. Jet black, gleaming even in the limited light of the gray photograph.

Tamara. John's secretary.

———————

John had had a string of secretaries over the years, assistants to help him with the mountains of paperwork that being a financial adviser entailed. They were almost always young women in their twenties, and attractive, which Regan never liked. Just once he'd hired an older woman, named Linda, semiretired, and Regan had breathed a sigh of relief to think of the two of them in the office together—or rather, *not* to have to think of them. Linda was a grandmother; she'd shared pictures of her grandkids with Regan the first time they met. John could work as late as he wanted and nothing would ever happen with *her*. But before even a year had passed, Linda's semiretirement had become actual retirement, and John had hired Tamara next.

She was twenty-four. Black hair that shimmered in light, smoky gray eyes, a perfect body. She was friendly enough, bubbly even—smiling too widely when Regan would walk into the office with the kids, falling into a singsong voice with Etta, offering Regan coffee while she waited for John to get off the phone. She'd even had them over for dinner once, right after John had hired her. She must have read some article, something about the importance of building a good relationship with your boss. She lived in a two-story townhome along the river in a hip part of the city, a neighborhood with lots of bars and restaurants. John and Regan got a sitter for Etta—there was only her then, though Philip wouldn't be too far behind.

The dinner was awkward. Halting conversation under the light of a dangling pendant lamp. John was Tamara's boss, but she seemed to spend most of the night trying to impress Regan. Constantly refilling her wineglass. Asking her questions about the baby, about her home, about her work. Acting all impressed when Regan told her about the defunct interior design business.

"That's so great!" Tamara had chirped. "You should definitely start that up again."

"I've got no time," Regan said. She was a little buzzed from all the wine. She'd probably had more than half a bottle, while John and Tamara had barely finished a glass between them. "Tell your boss to come home more. *Then* maybe I could get the business up again. Until then I'm too busy being a mom."

Tamara gave John a panicked glance and then darted her eyes back at Regan, her plastered-on smile barely dimming. "There's day care, isn't there?"

Regan felt John tense in the chair next to hers. They'd been arguing about day care recently. John thought it would be easiest to send Etta five days a week, but Regan thought she was still too young, and insisted that so many days—days of her baby in someone else's arms—wouldn't be necessary if John spent a less time in the office. None of this was Tamara's business, though, and Regan acted as if nothing was wrong.

"Maybe when Etta's a little older," she said.

"I hope so," Tamara said, the worry in her eyes easing now that Regan had let her off the hook for her misstep. "It's such a shame when talented women drop out of the workforce. I bet you could do a lot with this space, couldn't you? I bet you could give me a lot of decorating tips."

Regan had smiled wanly, accepting the compliment—even

though Tamara didn't know anything about her work, had never seen photos of a space she'd designed, and had no way of knowing if she was truly good at it or not.

It was only later—after the wine buzz had worn off, after she woke up the next day and took two ibuprofen for the pounding headache she'd been left with—that she realized what felt so off about the evening. The whole thing had seemed staged for her benefit. Tamara's deference toward her had been overeager, practically cloying. It was almost as though she and John had planned it together, to put Regan at ease.

Almost as though they were hiding something from her.

———

Now Regan was screaming outside Tamara's front door, making a spectacle of herself.

"I know you're in there!" Regan yelled as she rang the doorbell over and over, the two-tone ring echoing inside in a furious trill. "I know what you did! Come down here right now!"

A small part of her wondered what she must look like to the people passing by—hipster men with beards walking tiny dogs, women out on jogs, pulling out their earbuds to gawk. She'd become a cliché: the spurned wife, come to yell at her husband's mistress. But she didn't care. Her anger had risen to a boil on the drive over, blotting the edges of her vision. She was angrier about John's cheating than she was about his crimes—this fraud, this infidelity, felt so much more personal, and she was in search of someone to punish for the way it made her feel. Philip cried at Regan's hip; Etta stood at her side gape-eyed, a finger hooked in her lower lip. She was scaring the kids. But now that she was here, she couldn't stop screaming. The fury was only growing inside her, a pressure that mounted even as it was being released.

"Tamara Gray!" Regan shouted, pausing in her doorbell ringing to put a hand under Philip's butt, hoist him higher at her side. "Tamara Gray lives here!" Maybe that would get her to the door—the prospect of being embarrassed in front of her neighbors, called out by name among people she had to live with.

Regan switched from the doorbell to the door, clenching her fingers to pound at it. She hit at the door only once, and then stopped short when the door drifted open on her fist. A puff of cool air escaped, blew against her face. The front hallway was dark.

"Tamara?" Regan called into the house, all her anger suddenly turning to something like fear.

She crept into the house, peeked around a corner. There was a small living room to the right, also dark. Up the stairs, a dim yellow light reached down the hall.

"What are we doing in here, Mama?" Etta asked. "This isn't our house."

Regan crouched, deposited Philip on the floor next to Etta.

"Stay here," she said. "Stay with your brother. I have to check something."

"I want to come with you," Etta said.

Regan shook her head. She didn't know why, but she had the feeling that whatever was at the top of those stairs might be something she didn't want her children to see. Regan had the sudden premonition that she might find John up there, that he'd run away to his mistress, and that she'd now walk in on them in the act, repeating the scene from the photo on her phone. Absurd, since the house was quiet, but Regan had a bad feeling all the same.

"I won't leave you," Regan said. "I'll just be upstairs."

She turned and began to creep up the steps. Etta hovered close behind her, drifting after her mother in spite of everything Regan had just told her, and Regan held back an arm, willing her to be still. At the top of the stairs she looked down the hall, found the light streaming through the doorway to a bedroom. She made her way toward the doorway tentatively, inching along the opposite wall.

"What is it, Mama?" Etta asked from the bottom of the stairs. "What's up there?"

Regan saw the stain on the carpet first. Bright red seeping into the off-white plush, almost reaching to the hallway. She saw the body next, lying face down in the center of the red puddle. A deep gash in the back of the head, a flash of white skull visible beneath strands of black hair. Tamara had taken her shirt off, the black of a bra strap cutting across the pale expanse of her back. She must have been getting dressed to go out when someone hit her from behind; clothes were laid across the bed, still on their hangers. The face wasn't visible, but the body was unmistakably Tamara.

Regan sucked in air and blew it out as hard as she could, like she had back when she was in labor with Philip and with Etta before that. You learned how to breathe through pain when you were a mother. Learned how to bite back a scream, to hide what you were feeling. It was part of the training.

"Mama," Etta demanded, "what is it?"

"Nothing, sweetheart," Regan called down. "It's nothing. Just stay where you are."

CHAPTER 8

"Here's what I'm wondering," Agent Armstrong said. "I'm wondering why you were there in the first place."

Regan was back at her parents' house, staring dully ahead in the living room, gnawing at a cuticle. She scarcely remembered how she'd gotten there, the things she'd done after finding the body. It all seemed like a bad dream, her body sleepwalking through the motions, somehow knowing exactly what to do.

Getting the kids back to the car.

Calling the police.

Waiting.

The cops had barely asked her any questions, just took a basic statement, her name and contact information, then let her go. Maybe they'd taken pity on her. She was with her kids, after all, and Philip had begun to scream, tired and hungry, absolutely at the end of his rope—and Etta, poor Etta, peed her pants and started crying too, drenched in humiliation. Regan had driven them back to her parents' house in a daze, then let her mom instincts take over, changing Etta's clothes and Philip's sopping diaper, brushing off Isabel's frantic questions about where they'd been, what had happened.

Then she'd called the FBI.

"Mrs. Peters?" Armstrong prodded now. "Do you have an explanation?"

"I told you already," Regan said calmly. "I was just checking up on her. Tamara is—was—John's secretary. I just wanted to see how she was doing with all this. Is that against the law? Checking on a friend?"

Armstrong sighed. He turned to Torres, who'd been silent through Armstrong's initial questions, icily calm.

"*Regan*," Torres said now, and Regan noted the difference between the way the two agents were talking to her: Armstrong was using her last name, still calling her Mrs. Peters, but Torres had begun to call her by her first name. Like Torres was a friend, calling Regan out, pleading with her to drop the bullshit.

"We know that's not true," Torres continued. "The police have questioned the victim's neighbors. They say you were pounding on the door, screaming at her to come out. So what was that all about?"

Regan crossed her legs and looked out the window. She still didn't quite know what she was doing, but the past two hours had clarified some things. Tamara's murder meant that the mess with John was worse than she'd thought, more dangerous. People could die because of it. She and the kids might be in danger.

She needed help. She needed protection. She needed the FBI on her side.

But there was also the money. Enough money to get her and the kids through this mess, if she could figure out how to keep it.

She turned back to Armstrong and Torres. She'd made a decision. She'd tell the truth.

Some of it.

"Okay," she said. "You're right. I didn't go to Tamara's place to check on her."

Armstrong let out a breath. "Thank you. Now we're getting somewhere. Why, then?"

Regan's phone was on the coffee table. She reached for it, tapped her way to the photo, then held out the phone toward the FBI agents. They squinted at the screen.

"Holy shit," Armstrong said, his professional composure cracking for the first time since Regan had met him. "That's John?"

Regan nodded as the phone slid from her hand into Armstrong's. "And Tamara."

Torres moved close to Armstrong, looked over his shoulder. "Blackmail?"

Armstrong shook his head. "No. A threat."

"What do you mean?" Regan asked, her voice rising.

"Whoever sent this to you, they wanted you to find Tamara's body," Armstrong said. "They knew you'd see the picture and go to her house and find her there dead. They led you right to her. To let you know what they were capable of. To let you know they could kill."

"Who?" Regan asked. "One of John's clients? Someone he stole money from?"

"No. Someone else." Armstrong turned to Torres. "Let's show her. Maybe she knows something."

Torres nodded, then reached inside a leather briefcase leaning against the foot of her chair and placed a photo on the table. Regan leaned over to look at it.

"Do you recognize this man?"

The photo looked like a mug shot. The man in the photo was white, with unkempt hair. Hard eyes, a salt-and-pepper beard.

"I don't," she said, telling the truth.

"Look closely," Torres prodded. "I want you to be sure."

"I'm telling you, I've never seen him before."

"Does the name Arnold Scovel mean anything to you?" Armstrong asked.

"No," Regan said. "Should it?"

"It's him," Armstrong said, pointing at the photo. "He's one of your husband's associates."

Regan winced. *Associates.* The word sounded so dirty, so grimy. Businessmen had clients, partners, service providers. But associates? Only criminals had associates.

"I don't understand. This guy helped John run the Ponzi scheme?"

"This is a little bigger than that," Armstrong said. "Mrs. Peters, it's time we told you everything. Your husband is wanted for running a Ponzi scheme, yes. But we also believe that he's mixed up with this man, Arnold Scovel. He's a local businessman, officially a construction contractor, who's suspected of being involved in various criminal enterprises. Identity theft scams, illegal loans, armed robbery, drug trafficking—"

"Stop," Regan said, holding out a hand. "What could John have to do with any of this?"

"Well, an illegal enterprise like this—organized crime—it creates a lot of money. Money that has to be accounted for. And we believe that your husband was laundering it for Scovel. Cleaning it so it looked legit and couldn't be tracked to any criminal activity."

"How do you know?"

Torres stepped in. "Because Tamara Gray told us."

Regan's mouth clicked shut, the gears turning in her head. So that's why Tamara had been murdered. Regan had thought it might be a disgruntled client, someone who'd lost money in John's scheme, killing the secretary because he couldn't find the boss. But now she knew: Tamara had been killed because she talked to the FBI. Maybe—the thought made her sick, brought a nauseous heat to the back of her throat—John had even been the one to kill her.

She shook her head, pushing the thought away. She couldn't go there. She couldn't believe John capable of killing. He may have been a liar, may have been a fraud, but he wasn't *that* kind of man. Not a murderer.

"Regan," Agent Torres continued, "we really need to know what you know about Arnold Scovel. This is serious. Someone has died."

"But I told you," Regan said. "I don't know anything." She gestured toward the photo, still on the table. "I've never seen this man's face before. I've never heard his name."

Torres squinted at Regan, seeming to take a moment to decide something for herself. "I don't believe you."

Regan breathed out with exasperation, unsure of what to say. "I don't know what to tell you. I can't win. Nothing I do is right to you."

Armstrong stepped in. "You see, Mrs. Peters, the thing is…" he began, slowly, in a tone that suggested a man who regretted having to say what he was about to say. "The thing is, we've been looking at your financial records. Yours and John's. And we've found some things."

"What?"

"Well, partly what we expected to find in the books of someone running a Ponzi scheme. He gets money from his clients, and then he sort of…moves it around. Uses it to pay himself, to pay other clients making withdrawals. The business records are completely falsified, full of stock and mutual fund transactions that never happened. Then there are some larger cash infusions—we think that's the money from Scovel, which gets recorded as an investment from an LLC. John fabricates some capital gains, and it comes out clean. It's not exactly sophisticated."

"But there's something else?" Regan asked.

"There is," Torres said. "It has to do with your own investments."

"Let me guess," Regan said, bracing herself. "They're fake too. I'm broke."

"Not quite," Torres said. "We're still untangling what is real and fake. But the majority of your personal holdings seem to be legitimate."

"What, then?"

Armstrong was the one to explain. "Mrs. Peters, in the weeks leading up to his disappearance, your husband made some changes to your personal investments. What he seems to have done was, he took out all the assets you shared, the joint accounts, the stocks and bonds, even your house, it would appear—and he took his name off of them. He made you the sole owner of all your wealth."

Regan looked down as it all came together in her mind. What it meant, and what it must look like to Armstrong and Torres.

John must have known that everything was falling apart, that he'd be arrested soon. And so he put everything in Regan's name to make it harder for the feds to seize. To anyone looking at the thing from the outside, it would look like Regan was part of it all. An accomplice from the beginning.

Regan thought of what John had said to her, the day of the lake house—the last day. *It'll be your name on the deed, not mine, because I'm thinking of it as your house, your place...*

What a fool she'd been to think this wouldn't come for her eventually. That the eyes of the world wouldn't eventually turn to her and find her to blame. There always had to be a woman at fault. John had fled, left her with the consequences of his actions. Now she'd be punished in his stead.

"Regan," Torres said solemnly, that *let's-get-real* tone back in her voice, "you need help. You're in over your head. Scovel is a bad man, and he thinks you know something. That's why he sent you this threat. He's already killed one person. What if he comes for you next? What if he comes after the kids? We can help you. We can protect you. We can even arrange for you to be able to keep some of your assets—the house, some of the money. We can do that for you. But you have to tell us what you know. It's not you we're after—even John isn't our primary target. Scovel's the one we want."

Regan was silent, thinking. Armstrong and Torres were offering her a deal, an exchange. If Regan helped them get this Scovel guy, they'd go easy on her. Maybe they'd even let her keep some of her money—the money John had put in her name.

The only problem was that she didn't have anything to offer them. Nothing to cut a deal *with*. Maybe she'd known more than she'd let on—knew that John was not who he said he was. But she hadn't known about the Ponzi scheme, and she certainly didn't know anything about a local gangster named Arnold Scovel. She'd told plenty of lies to the FBI over the past two days, but this much was true: she didn't have anything that could help them in their investigation.

"You say you're going to protect me," Regan said. "Did you protect Tamara?"

Torres and Armstrong visibly winced.

"Tamara was a mistake," Armstrong admitted. "We didn't take Scovel seriously enough. We thought she was safe. We won't make that mistake again."

"Am I under arrest?" Regan asked.

"What?" Armstrong looked confused.

"Do you have a warrant for my arrest?"

Armstrong shook his head. "No. We don't. But—"

"Then leave," Regan said. "I want you to leave. Right now."

The FBI agents sighed, then stood. On their way out of the room, Torres paused and looked back. "You're going to regret this." "Just go," Regan demanded.

Regan discovered her mother lurking in the hall after Armstrong and Torres left. Isabel had made herself scarce while Regan was being questioned, but on some level she knew her mother was listening through the walls, and when she came upon her, Regan knew at once that she'd heard it all, every word. Isabel's eyes were fierce, her lips pulled into a tight, bloodless line.

"Did you enjoy the show, Mother?" Regan asked sarcastically.

"Don't talk to me like that," Isabel snapped. "You're the one who brought this poison into our lives."

The naked disdain in Isabel's voice hurt, but there was something almost comforting in its familiarity. Isabel hated Regan, hated her and was ashamed of her, and Regan was glad for the falling away of any pretense that her mother felt otherwise.

"Go on," Regan said. "Out with it. You've been waiting for this."

"You never should have married him."

"I know. You've told me."

"I knew from the beginning that he was no good. But you tied your life to him anyway, and now look at what's happening."

"I didn't choose any of this, Mother. This isn't my fault."

"But you *did* choose it," Isabel said, taking a step closer and pointing a finger straight at Regan's chest. "You chose *him*."

"At least John loved me," Regan said. "*Loves* me. Which is more than I've ever been able to say of you."

Isabel moved her hand toward her chest, playacting outrage. "Don't you dare turn this around on me. I'm your mother. I did my best. I thought you'd understand that by now. I did my best to love you and take care of you and make choices that were best for you. But sometimes your children make mistakes. Sometimes they disappoint you."

Disappoint. The word made Regan ache inside. Coming from a parent, this was always worse than anger, always more devastating: *I'm not mad, I'm just disappointed.* Something inside her crumpled, but then, like a supernova collapsing and then exploding outward, she felt the feeling in her chest transform into rage, a desire to hurt as much as she was hurting in that moment.

"You want to know the truth, Mother?" Regan said. "I married John *because* of you. Because of who you are—who you've always been. Always so *disappointed* in me. So stingy with your love, with your praise. I knew I was never going to get anything from you. No support, no encouragement. So I went for the first man I could find who was even a little bit kind to me. The first man who treated me like I was special and was happy to see me when I walked into a room. The first man who promised to give me the kind of life I knew I deserved."

Isabel's face had gone pale, and the sharpness slowly drained from her eyes. When she spoke next, her voice was thin, hoarse. "We would've supported you. Always. We're still supporting you."

"Supporting me with what? With Grandpa's money? It's quite a luxury, isn't it? Inheriting money. You think I don't notice? I see you and Daddy wasting it, living like fat cats, spending double what you make. I always knew you'd never pass anything on to me. Some people have to work for a living, you know. People like John. He made some mistakes—God knows he made mistakes. But he did what he had to do to support us."

Isabel's jaw bulged at the hinge, and Regan knew that her mother was regrouping, finding her anger again. "You're just like him," Isabel said. "You're guilty. Just as guilty as he is."

Regan searched for a comeback, but found none. She was exhausted, sick of fighting. She was ready to give in—to give in to the thing she'd been avoiding since the FBI knocked on her door. The truth, at last. *You're guilty.*

"Yes," she said. "Fine. I'm like John. More like him than I am like you. I knew what he was, and I married him anyway. In fact, I *liked* who he was. I still do. He may not have been perfect, but he fought for me. Fought for his family. Everything he did—everything they say he did—was for us. For me and the kids. And now I'm doing the same. I'm fighting to protect us. If you don't like that, then you can get the fuck out of the way."

As Regan spoke, Isabel grew very still. Regan knew there was a storm brewing underneath, just barely held at bay. The effort must have been tremendous.

"Maybe you should go," she said. "Back to your house. If you really feel this way about me—about my help, my advice—it's probably best for you to go back where you belong."

Regan thought of the news, the crowd that had gathered around her house, John's victims come to protest and make a scene. She didn't want to go there. But she quickly realized that subjecting herself to *that* would be better than staying in *this.* That she preferred the blind hatred of strangers to the all-too-familiar contempt of her own mother.

She nodded. "Fine. I'll get packing."

She turned and made to head up the stairs. Her mother's voice stopped her.

"And Regan?"

"Yes, Mother?"

She paused a beat, then spoke. "Maybe you shouldn't come back for a while."

Perhaps this was it, then. The end of her relationship with her mother.

Good riddance.

She'd figure out a way to retrieve the money hidden in the garage later. She couldn't touch it for a while anyway, and her mother and father almost never went in the attic—both of them too old, too shaky on the rungs of the ladder. The money was safe here. Sometime in the future she could come back and sneak it away while they were out of the house.

"Gladly."

———————

Upstairs, in her old bedroom, Regan was shoving her clothes back into a suitcase when a series of texts came in. The phone buzzed once, twice, three times. Regan looked at the screen and saw a series of photos.

First was the sight of Tamara's dead body, laid out on the bedroom floor just as Regan had found it. It was the second time she'd seen Tamara's corpse, but it took her breath away again.

Next was a photo of Regan standing outside Tamara's house, knocking on the door and yelling while Philip cried in her arms and Etta clung to her legs.

Last came a picture of the house she was standing in, a shot through the living room window as she was being questioned by Armstrong and Torres.

She knew the photos were intended to scare her—and they did. But they brought clarity too. She understood now. The messages were from Scovel, or someone working with Scovel. And he was letting her know that he was having her followed. That he knew her every move.

The next message to come in was a text.

You have something that belongs to me

The cash. The leather bag. That had to be what this was all about. Money. John had stolen it from Scovel, left it for Regan— but now Scovel wanted it back.

This was bad, but Regan found herself becoming unexpectedly less scared. That Scovel didn't have the money already was a sign that he didn't know where it was, that he hadn't been following her last night when she'd found it at the lake house and hidden it away in her parents' garage. And if he didn't know where it was, then he needed to keep her alive, at least until she gave it up. She was safe. For now.

Regan texted back.

I want to meet

Three dots appeared. You have what I want?

Regan tapped out her response. Her thumb quivered over the Send button. After a second of hesitation she tapped it.

No. A proposal.

CHAPTER 9

Regan and John got married at the courthouse, with two strangers as witnesses. This was designed to cover up two uncomfortable facts: first, that if they'd had a traditional wedding with a guest list, Regan's side of the ceremony would have been full of family and friends while John's was virtually empty; and second, that Regan's parents didn't like the groom very much. They didn't go so far as to object to the wedding, but neither of them cared for John, and they obviously couldn't hide it.

In spite of all this, Regan was happy on their wedding day. Ecstatic, even. She and John had moved in together for the duration of their yearlong engagement, combined their finances, and just a day before they signed the marriage license and made it official, John told her what she'd already been noticing: the money he was bringing in from his financial adviser business had been increasing by quite a bit, and if she wanted to, she could probably quit her job (which she still hated) and give the interior design idea a try. He also told her that he thought he was pretty close to having saved up enough money for a down payment on a house.

These two facts filled Regan with confidence about the future of their marriage. There had been moments during the engagement when she wondered if she had made the right decision. John hadn't changed; he was as mysterious and reticent to talk about himself as ever. This was simply who he was, and Regan had come to accept it. But his financial successes—his income growing and quickly dwarfing hers—confirmed for her that the trade-off she'd made was the right one. Of what consequence was a mysterious past compared to a bright and comfortable future?

The first few years of their marriage were happy, carefree ones. Regan's interior design business was slow to start, clients difficult to find, but she began to see some success, one small job leading to another, and another after that. The time between, the hours she didn't work, were her own, and there was a luxury to having free time. She shopped, she ate out with friends, she went to yoga classes. During those long hours, she imagined herself a woman of leisure, and she didn't mind it at all.

John's long hours at the office began to increase as his business heated up, but Regan didn't mind being alone, and when John *did* come home, she had his undivided attention, there being no one else in his life except for her. It wasn't so different than when they were dating. They went to restaurants, to concerts, to museums. They went on day trips to nature parks, spent the whole day hiking, packed picnics. They took selfies and Regan put them on social media to collect likes and comments. *So cute! Fun! Beautiful couple!*

Regan loved being married, loved the feeling of being held and cared for by another person. She loved their home together, the house they bought in the suburbs, their furniture, their bed. She loved waiting for John to come home at night, the jostling of the mattress when he crawled into bed, then rolling to him and asking him to stay awake a little longer, to put his hands on her body, to make her feel good. Above all she loved having a husband, the very words—*my husband*—feeling like a sort of passcode to an elite club: the happily married.

What began to destabilize their marriage was having children. Regan always knew that she wanted to be a mother. She wasn't exactly one of those women who ached to have babies, who cooed over newborns and romanticized the state of being pregnant—it was simply that when she closed her eyes and imagined the future, there were always children there: probably two, maybe three. When she told John she wanted to start trying to get pregnant, he reflexively acquiesced the same way he did any time she said she wanted something, blandly expressing his enthusiasm.

"Sounds great," he said, like he always did. "Whatever you want."

She got pregnant quickly, more quickly than she'd anticipated. She took the home test one night when John was working late, and then, when the two pink lines appeared, she waited up for him, sitting with her legs curled next to her on the couch by the front door.

"Oh," he said when he finally came through the front door after ten, the sun having set long ago. "I thought you'd be in bed. Is something wrong?"

In lieu of a response she simply walked up to him and handed him the test, then watched as he looked at it and understood.

"Wow," he said, his voice bland and affectless.

"*Wow?*" Regan repeated. "That's all?"

"I'm adjusting to the information."

"Aren't you happy?" Regan asked.

John blinked. "Of course I am."

But he wasn't happy, and Regan could tell. What he seemed

to be feeling, more than anything else, was *befuddlement*, as if their impending parenthood was something he didn't quite understand and didn't expect, even though they'd *talked* about it. And his air of bemused confusion persisted through the entirety of the pregnancy—through the doctor visits and scans, through the shopping trips for baby supplies, through the preparation of a nursery. As Regan grew larger and larger and the day loomed closer and closer, John went on acting as though all this had nothing to do with him, as if he hadn't had a hand in bringing it to pass.

He was useless during the delivery—perhaps all men are. What do they have to do, after all, but stand there and impotently encourage the person who is doing all the work? Regan remembered little of the process of birth except for a feeling of being all alone in her pain, John and the nurses and the midwife and doula seeming to fall away as she tunneled deeper inside herself, until there was only *her*, Regan, and the thing that was happening to her body, this overwhelming task that she, and only she, could perform. The pressure building, and the pain, and then suddenly there was a sort of break, a sudden release, and it was all over, everyone in the room telling her that she did great, she was beautiful, and there was a baby on her chest, and she was crying from happiness and relief. John appeared at her side, looking a little dazed, and deposited a kiss on her forehead.

"You did it," he said.

"Yes," she answered. "I did."

———

Having a baby completely transformed Regan and John's marriage—or perhaps it only transformed Regan's *experience* of their marriage. John himself didn't change, didn't seem to adapt at all to the fact of being a father. After Etta came home to her nursery, John returned to his usual work schedule, spending long hours at the office and returning home late, in time to help put Etta to bed but little else. Before, John's long absences had been an occasion for Regan to spend time by herself, to enjoy the luxury of having a spouse whose money almost completely financed their lifestyle—but now, with a baby in the house, she merely felt exhausted, and abandoned, and resentful of the man who'd done his part in getting her pregnant but couldn't be bothered, it seemed, to help care for his child. John changed a few diapers when he was home, sometimes gave Etta a bottle, played with her on the floor, but he tired of the work of parenting quickly, and mostly left everything to Regan, even in the rare moments when he was around.

Making things even worse for Regan was Etta's obvious joy whenever she saw John, brightness breaking across her face every time he walked through the door. John was *good* with her when he actually slowed down and took the time; he was sweet and gentle, he rocked her and sang her to sleep at night and was the first one to get a giggle, a real laugh, out of her by making a silly face. And she *loved* him, seeming to know him by instinct, to know that he was a part of her. Seeing these moments filled Regan with grief at what could have been if he'd just taken more time with her. How could he stay away from his daughter for so long? How could he stand to be separated from her? The connection between Etta and John only highlighted, for Regan, an almost sociopathic coldness, a distance, in the man she'd chosen to marry. She stewed, too, on the unfairness of it all, casting herself into the future and hating what she saw: John, who was barely around, would get to be the clown, the fun one, while she, who was always present, would be the administrator, the humorless and hated disciplinarian.

"This isn't fair," Regan said one evening, confronting John after suffering through a particularly difficult day at home. "I'm doing everything."

"That's not true," John said. "You're not doing *everything*. I'm the one making all the money."

"That's not what I mean and you know it," Regan said. "With Etta. I'm doing all the parenting."

"Regan, come on," John said. "You're doing *all* the parenting? I'm home by six most nights, and I put in time with her on the weekends."

Regan's jaw tightened. John always did this whenever she tried to talk to him about something important, especially when it was something he didn't want to hear: he'd poke at the edges of what she was trying to say, argue technicalities, turn her words around until the meaning was gone and even she wasn't sure what she wanted to say anymore. "Don't fucking do that. Listen to what I'm telling you."

John sighed, looked at his lap, and Regan hated this too: the way he'd act like she was the one being unreasonable, like she was the silly woman and he was the rational man. "I'm listening. You're doing more of the work with Etta than I am. I acknowledge that. But there's reasons for it, you know. I'm working. You're not."

"So work less."

"You know I can't do that. What if I lose clients? How would we pay the mortgage? You think I like working long hours? It's for *you*, you know. You and Etta."

The edges of Regan's vision blurred with anger at the absurdity of his logic. He was staying away for them. He ignored them because he loved them.

"Why don't you just put her in day care?" John said. "You could start working again, you know. That would make things more equal."

Regan did put Etta in day care for a time, two days a week, but she didn't start working again, and she wasn't exactly sure why. In part this was because restarting her career simply felt too difficult. Unlike many of her peers, who took leave and then returned to their nine-to-fives, Regan didn't have a stable job to return to. She'd *quit* her job, in fact, left behind a steady paycheck for the risk and reward of running her own business. But the prospect of getting the interior design business going after months away—the frustrating work of generating leads and pitching potential clients before money even began coming in—was simply too daunting to contemplate. Even on the days when Etta was away, she felt so exhausted, so emptied out by the work of being a mother, that all she could seem to do was sit, read a book, watch some TV, maybe clean up a bit around the house before it was suddenly time to pick the girl up again.

Eventually, it got to be humiliating sending Etta to day care twice a week but not managing to do anything productive with the time she was away—at least, nothing John would recognize as productive.

"Why are we spending all this money on day care if you're not bringing anything in?" John asked one day. "I thought the point was for you to start working again."

Regan could've killed him in that moment. He thought it was so easy: send the baby away, get back to your life. He didn't understand what it felt like, carrying another being inside you, being taken over by concern for them and their well-being. Thinking of Etta all the time, even when she was gone—*especially* then. She couldn't explain it to him. John had no trouble forgetting about both of them, Regan and Etta, when he went away.

Regan quietly pulled Etta out of day care. She could've done the opposite, sent Etta to be taken care of five days a week instead of just two, but she didn't want to do that. It felt too much like letting John win, assenting to his logic of loving more by being together less. John seemed to think that the problem was not that he wasn't involved enough, but that Regan was *too* involved, that she cared *too* much. That she could be a better parent by being more neglectful, more like *him*. She couldn't allow this absurd argument to prevail. Regan remembered what it felt like to have a mother who cared more for herself than for her daughter, remembered what it was like to know she'd always come second to her parents' ambitions. That wasn't what she wanted for her daughter—even if, in her more honest moments, she knew that her mother's creative fulfillment was what she wanted for *herself.*

The problem was John. If he was home more, maybe did four-day weeks to give her a bit more time to herself, then she could have it all: motherhood and a career. But he wasn't. And so Regan's unhappiness at home—as Etta grew to be one, and then a very terrible two—was a sort of chess piece in an ongoing battle between her and John—something she held strategically against him, hoping he'd notice and finally change.

They probably should have stopped at one child, all things considered. Regan knew this. They were at an impasse, she and John—he too busy at work to give Regan the support she needed, she never able to find the time to be everything she wanted to be for her daughter and to claw some pieces of herself back. But the impasse was temporary. Everyone said this: the early years were the worst. Things would get better when Etta went to school and Regan had five days to herself.

Having another baby was objectively foolish, Regan knew. It

would only start the clock over again at zero, prolong the amount of time it would take for her to return to her own professional ambitions. Her own life.

But here again, there was her imagination to contend with, the future she'd always pictured for herself. A house, a husband, two kids: that had always been the dream. Maybe it wasn't smart or practical, but she was haunted by regret—not the regret she was feeling now, but the regret she feared feeling in ten or fifteen or twenty years, when she looked back and realized that her family was incomplete, that she should've had that second baby when she had the chance.

And so she did it all again—pressed John, obtained his wan acquiescence, conceived quickly, and went once more through the ordeal of pregnancy and birth. A boy this time, Philip, and he looked so much like John, the resemblance between father and son almost shocking in its uncanniness, that she thought things would be different this time. Surely John would be more involved with a baby boy, nature weaponizing his own selfishness against him by showing him his reflection in the face of his infant son and transforming his self-regard to love, commitment, and care.

It didn't happen. If anything, Philip's birth seemed not just to drive John further away, deeper into his work, but actually to break something in him—though Regan couldn't say what. Holding his son for the first time, in the hospital, John looked neither happy nor indifferent, but *pained*, as though the physical reality of the newborn boy was digging up something inside him that he'd have preferred to keep buried. After a paltry four days at home during which John pretended to be "helping out," he positively fled to the office—leaving behind a Regan still sore, still bleeding, barely mobile after the trauma of birth. Regan experienced this abandonment as a betrayal so fundamental, so raw, that she barely spoke to him for the next few months.

Had she been less stressed herself, less overwhelmed by the demands of motherhood, she might've found her way to wondering what was wrong with John, even to pitying him. She received a hint that John's absence was about more than simple male selfishness and laziness late one night four months after Philip was born, when after a midnight feeding, Regan returned to bed to find John awake and silently crying, his shoulders shaking with sobbing.

Any other time, and Regan would have been shocked—she'd never seen John cry. But she was exhausted, sleep deprived, her left breast in pain from a plugged milk duct that she was pretty sure was turning into mastitis, a miserable infection she'd had twice with Etta and feared getting again. In that state, John's tears didn't shock her, didn't prod her to sympathy. They enraged her. What did *he* have to cry about?

"What is it?" she asked.

"I can't do it," John sniveled. "I can't—I'm not who you think I am. I'm a fraud."

In the darkness, Regan rolled her eyes. She didn't have the time or the patience to deal with this. Philip cried all day, and Etta had become clingy since her younger brother's birth, needing Regan's constant affirmation of the security of her mother's love. She couldn't deal with *three* whining babies.

"Suck it up," Regan said. "Every parent thinks they're a fraud. Get in line. Besides, what are you even doing? I'm the one doing all the work here."

Regan closed her eyes. Gradually, she heard John's tears subside next to her, and she was able to go back to sleep. When she woke again, it was—of course—to the sound of the baby crying.

———————

I'm a fraud. Regan had scarcely noticed the word when John first used it. If she thought about it at all in that moment, she figured he was probably talking about a form of parental impostor syndrome, the feeling most parents have of not being at all equipped to care for the tiny creatures that suddenly come into their lives. Maybe, uncharitably, she assumed in her sleep-addled state that he was offering up an excuse for his lack of engagement, his absences, his incompetence. He didn't think he was a good dad. That was why he didn't try, why he ran away instead of engaging. Perhaps he even hoped that she'd comfort him—solace him for abandoning her.

But as the days wore on, she came back to the word over and over again. *Fraud. Fraud. Fraud.* Was that really what he had said, or had she dreamed it? She'd close her eyes, nursing Philip, bouncing him to sleep next to his bassinet, and try to call up the memory. Each time, the sentences came back to her the same. *I'm not who you think I am. I'm a fraud.* Then she opened her eyes, thinking of everything that had given her pause about John from the beginning: his mysterious past, his refusal to talk about himself, his complete lack of family, of old friends, of photos. His long absences. The money that came in every month, from a source and a business she didn't fully understand. Suddenly, John's late-night tears seemed less to her like the result of impostor syndrome, or even like a play for her sympathy, her forgiveness.

No. John was confessing to her.

So much of a marriage is built on trust, Regan realized. There were whole parts of a spouse, a life partner, that you never got to see. What they did with their days. Who they spoke to, where they went, what they said, and who they were during the hours when they were away. The contents of their mind, of their past. So much that was simply taken on blind faith, never verified, never checked up on. One simply took it for granted that they were who they said they were.

But what if they weren't?

———————

Soon after, Regan visited John's office during the day. She didn't tell him she was coming. Brought the kids, because they were always with her and she didn't want to go through the trouble of getting a sitter. Besides, they provided her with a nice cover story—even to herself. They were simply a family, surprising their father and husband at work. Certainly not spying on him. No, not that—never.

John's office—Greenleaf Financial Consulting—was located in a nondescript office building with reflective windows on a corner of land where two freeways crossed. It sat on a platform of dirt overlooking an on-ramp, with barely any trees nearby to shield it from the beating sun, and as Regan curved up toward it, she felt a welling of sadness at the thought of John spending so much of his time in this plain, ugly place. How pathetic it was that he preferred passing his days and many of his evenings in this shabby building instead of with his family—but she wasn't sure who it reflected more poorly on: her and the kids, or John.

When she arrived inside, he wasn't there. Only Tamara, chirpily greeting them at the front desk.

"Regan!" she said breathily and came around the desk to give her a kiss on the cheek. "What are you doing here?"

"Just thought I'd give the kids an outing. Surprise John at work."

Tamara pressed her lips together and cocked her head in an *isn't-that-sweet* look.

"What a great idea! But I'm afraid he's out on a client meeting."

"I see," Regan said. She felt foolish in front of Tamara, ridiculously encumbered. She was pushing a stroller, one that carried both Etta in front and Philip's baby carrier in back, and a diaper bag was slung over her shoulder. The strap slipped down her shoulder, and she pulled it back up, thinking about why she'd come here. It wasn't *really* to see John.

"I was wondering," Regan said, "if I could see the…the books. For the business."

Tamara's blank smile dimmed into confusion. "The books?"

"Right, the records. John and I talk about the business sometimes. I was just hoping I could check on something." She didn't know what she was expecting—she wasn't sure she'd be able to understand the business's books even if Tamara showed them to her.

"Okay," Tamara said, still sounding hesitant. "Which ones do you want to see? The real ones, or…"

"There's more than one set of books?"

Tamara blinked, seeming to realize what was happening. "Maybe we should wait until John gets back."

"It's fine," Regan said, already turning and trying to maneuver the huge stroller back out the door. "Forget about it."

Or the fake ones. That was what Tamara had been about to say, before she caught herself. It had to be.

John kept fake books at his business. But why? Regan didn't know, couldn't imagine the range of reasons that would lead a financial adviser to cook his books, but she knew it couldn't be good. Couldn't be legal. Evading taxes? Covering up some major loss, or earning?

She went through the rest of the day in a kind of trance, barely noticing what she was doing with the kids, reverting to instinct and habit. Her mind elsewhere, gears turning, thinking about what she'd discovered, what it might mean, and what she should do about it.

It's too late. That was the thought she kept coming back to—calmly, rationally. Whatever trouble John was in, it was too late to fix it. Their lives were entangled now. They had a house, two kids. She'd given her whole life to this man; a man she didn't truly know, when she really sat down and thought about it. What good was knowing now, when knowing could only bring her own life crashing down with his—her life and the kids'? No. She wasn't going to dig, wasn't going to interrogate him or Tamara any further. The only thing left to do now was to make sure that she and her children would be protected if John's mistakes—whatever they were—came calling. To prevent them from being collateral damage.

When she got the kids to bed at the end of the day, she placed herself on the couch near the front door and waited for John.

"Hey," he said when he finally came home. "I talked to Tamara."

"So did I," she said calmly, her breath even. She liked the feeling of clarity that had come over her. She was sitting, John towering above her, but she was the one who had the power in this moment, and she felt it.

"She told me you wanted to look at some things."

"I did," Regan said.

"Why?"

Regan folded one leg over the other, then launched into the speech she'd been practicing in her head for the past hour.

"I need to understand more about our financial situation. You have always handled the money, handled our savings and our investments, and that's been fine—until now. We're parents. We have two little kids. I need to have a grasp of where things stand. Just in case."

"In case what?" John asked.

"In case anything happens to you."

John was silent for a stretch. It was late, the sun gone down, and shadows fell across his face, blurring the edges of his features, obscuring the details.

"Tamara said you wanted to look at the books for the whole business."

Regan shook her head. "She misheard me."

"Is that right?"

"Yeah, it is. I wanted to see our own statements. That's all."

"Okay," John said. "Well, I can do that."

"Good. And another thing?"

"What?"

"I need some of our assets to be in my name, and my name only. In case—like I said. Something happens to you."

She waited for a sign that John understood. After a moment, he nodded.

"Okay."

CHAPTER 10

Regan and the kids returned home that afternoon, as her mother requested. She thought of the money as she drove away, the leather bag hidden in the garage loft, but she couldn't risk moving it. Not yet, with so many eyes on her, so many people watching. Her parents wouldn't go into the loft, she was sure. She'd go back for it when things were safer.

As she drove, her thoughts turned away from the money, from what she was leaving behind, to what she was moving toward. What she'd find at home. The news had shown a group of John's clients, his victims, gathered outside the house to demand their money back. Would they still be there? Regan sucked in a breath as she turned off the freeway, then held it in as she rounded the curve onto her street. When the house came into view she let the air out of her lungs—but not in relief. It felt more like she'd been punched in the stomach.

"No," she said to herself in a low voice.

"What is it, Mama?" Etta asked from the back seat—the poor girl, always so attuned to her mother's moods, her empathy working overtime the last couple days.

"It's nothing, sweetheart," Regan said. "There's just—it's a bit of a crowd at our house."

She'd hoped they would have left by now. But there they still were, a day after the news had broken—two news vans, reporters and cameramen mulling around at the curb, and a small group of about a dozen people in the street. For a moment she considered simply speeding by, but there was nowhere else for her to go. The people outside her house looked bored and aimless right now, Regan saw as the car coasted slower. They were looking at the sky, at the ground, kicking pebbles in the road. She could take them by surprise. Dart up the driveway before anyone noticed.

A cameraman stood at the edge of the lawn, one foot propped up on the curb, and he looked up as the car drew close. Through the windshield, their eyes met.

"She's here!" he shouted, hoisting the camera to his shoulder.

Regan pressed on the gas. The car zoomed forward the last fifty feet and swung wildly into the driveway as people swarmed to it from both sides. The rear wheel caught the edge of the curb, rocking the car, and Regan's heart leapt in her chest. She rocketed up the driveway and into the garage, then pressed the remote button to send the door inching down behind her. When it touched the ground she breathed—really breathed.

"We made it," she said to no one in particular.

Of course, there was still the house to get to—the twenty steps between the garage and the side door where she'd be visible to the news cameras, to the angry people in the street. She got out of the car and got both kids, held Philip against her hip and grabbed Etta's hand.

"Okay," she said, looking down. "You're going to have to run with me, sweetheart."

"Why?" Etta asked. "Are they going to hurt us?"

Regan squeezed the girl's hand. "No, sweetie. It's just—it's sort of a game. We don't want them to see us. All right?"

Etta nodded. "All right." Philip sucked on his fingers.

And then they were out the door, back into the bright light of morning, squinting against it, and everyone was shouting.

"Regan!"

"Regan, look here!"

"Where's your husband, Regan?"

"Regan, where's the money?"

Regan dashed to the side door, fumbled with the key, and then finally they were inside. The air in the house had that stale, musty smell it always got when they were gone for more than a day, and there was a slight stink of rotting garbage coming from the kitchen. Philip clambered down and toddled away, almost immediately finding a plastic truck on the living room floor. Etta stayed close.

"Why were those people yelling?"

"They're angry," Regan said. "Someone took their money."

Etta thought about that for a few seconds. "Did *we* take their money?"

"No, sweetheart," Regan said, the decision coming to her all at once. She'd have to explain sooner or later, and now was as good a time as any. "Daddy did."

"Oh," Etta said, absorbing the information. "Why are they yelling at us if Daddy did it?"

Regan sank to one knee on the kitchen tile and held Etta by the shoulders. "It's not fair," she said. "It's not fair that people are mad at us for something that Daddy did. But they just have to be mad at someone. And Daddy's not here. They're mad at us because we're here for them to be mad at. You understand?"

Etta blinked, her eyes huge, her lashes long and curled like a doll's. "Daddy shouldn't have done that," she said. "He should come back and say he's sorry."

Something in the girl's words pulled at Regan, plucked her to attention. There was clarity in what Etta was saying, in the simple moral judgment of a child. John had done something wrong. He should apologize.

It gave her an idea.

Regan had been planning on the way over, mapping out her moves as she drove the miles back to the house—or perhaps even before that. Regan wondered how long. Since finding Tamara's body? Since the FBI first came to her door? Earlier, even? When she'd gotten married, perhaps. When she first knew John wasn't who he said he was.

Either way, her first move was clear. She had to deal with the crowd outside. With the public. She had to make herself innocent in their eyes, get them on her side.

As if summoned by her thinking of them, there came a sharp knock on the door.

"Who is that, Mama?" Etta asked, her voice rising. "Is it the angry people? Do they want to come in and yell at us some more?"

Philip went on playing obliviously on the floor, banging the plastic truck on the carpet, drool running down his chin. At the door, the pounding went on. The shouting. A woman's voice.

"I know you're in there! Come out and answer for what you've done!"

A resolve began to form in Regan's mind. She thought of Etta's words: *Daddy shouldn't have done that. He should come back and say he's sorry.* Clarity. And here too, in the rage of the woman on the other side of the door, was clarity. She was right: they *did* deserve an explanation. They all did. Regan too. They were all victims.

Regan stepped forward, and before she quite knew what she was doing, she grabbed the knob and whipped the door open. Air from outside whooshed into the house. The woman on the other side looked stunned, her fist still raised in the air, ready to pound a door that was no longer there in front of her.

"Yes," Regan said, "here I am. I'm ready to hear what you have to say to me. I want to hear it."

The woman let her fist drop to her side; she licked her lips. She looked as though she hadn't been quite prepared for Regan to actually answer the door, didn't know how to start now that it was open. Behind her, on the sidewalk, stood the reporters and the cameramen—they'd come up the walk when Regan had opened the door and now huddled close on the lawn, microphones out, ready to capture whatever would happen next. Further back, on the sidewalk and the street, were the others—John's other victims, some old, some young, some angry and suspicious with their arms crossed, others looking sad and bereft, confused, as though they didn't know how they'd gotten here.

Regan looked once more to the woman. She looked young—late twenties, maybe early thirties. Her hair was brown, swooping across her forehead and cropped at the ears; she wore a white T-shirt and an unbuttoned blue denim jacket. Her eyes were sharp on Regan's face, but cautious too, as though she sensed a trap. She'd fallen back a few feet, stepped down off the stoop, and was looking up at Regan from a lower level.

"Go ahead," Regan said. "I'm listening."

"My name is Anna Herrera," the woman said. "My parents are David and Marta. They're regular people, not rich. They worked hard for everything they had. My father worked as a car mechanic; my mother cleaned houses and worked as a part-time bookkeeper. They put me through school. Through college. All they wanted was a good life for me, and a little left over for themselves so they could retire and not be a burden."

The words sound rehearsed to Regan's ears. Anna Herrera had been practicing, working on her statement for the cameras.

"My parents gave money to your husband, because he told them he could turn their little bit of money into a lot of money.

Over five years, they gave him seventy-five thousand dollars. Their whole life savings. Your husband told them that he turned this money into more than five hundred thousand dollars. He sent them statements in the mail that told them this, with charts and graphs showing how their money had grown. But it was all a lie. Not only is there no half-million for my parents' retirement— your husband has refused to even give them the seventy-five thousand they gave him at the beginning. Now, my father..."

The woman, Anna, looked down, her voice cracking. Regan stepped outside and went down the stoop to her, held her by the forearms, and propped her up. Anna's eyes lifted. There were tears there.

"Go on," Regan said, conscious of the camera lenses pointed at them, the hush that had come to the air. Everyone was listening.

"My father is so ashamed," Anna said, a sob in her voice barely held at bay. "Your husband has made him a fool. And last night he...he tried to end his own life. My mother doesn't sleep well; she takes pills at night. He swallowed a whole bottle of her pills, and—that's why my parents aren't here today. They're at the hospital. My father is so angry with himself that he wants to...to..."

Anna stopped, unable to go on, and Regan pulled at her arms, pulled her close, and the other woman didn't resist. They fell into each other. Regan put her arms around Anna's shoulders, felt the rough denim of the woman's jacket against her hands. Anna didn't return the embrace, only sobbed against Regan's chest, her body quaking.

"Shhh," Regan whispered. "It's going to be okay." This was something she knew how to do: to listen, to comfort. To be a mother.

After a few seconds Regan withdrew from the embrace and softly turned Anna around, faced her toward the cameras so that they were standing side by side. Regan marveled at herself as she slipped an arm around Anna's shoulder, wondering how she knew to do this—wondering at the sudden calm that came over her as she opened her mouth and began to speak, projecting her voice for the microphones.

"My husband has hurt people," she said. "He's hurt his clients. He's hurt this woman right here, hurt her parents. He's hurt me too. Hurt his whole family. His children."

Just then she felt something brush the back of her legs; she looked down and behind her to find that Philip and Etta had crept out of the house to see what was happening and were now crowding close at her legs.

This was good. She grabbed Philip and hefted him to the usual place at her hip, then moved Etta so she was standing in front of her, visible to the cameras.

"I stand with John's victims. I stand with the victims because I am a victim too. My children are victims. John lied to you—and he lied to us. John stole from you—he stole from us. My own life savings is gone. The police will take it from us, as punishment for John's crimes. All our possessions, including the house we stand in front of, could be gone in a heartbeat. My children could be homeless, because of my husband's irresponsible actions."

She picked a cameraman, one standing straight down the front walk, and looked directly into his lens. Behind it, in the street, she saw the small crowd of John's clients. Onto their blurry faces she inscribed the visages of her mother and father, of Armstrong and Torres—everyone she wanted to prove herself to, to insist that none of this was her fault, that it was John they should be hounding, that they should just leave her alone. Last of all she pictured John. Her husband.

"John, if you're out there, if you're listening to this—come home. Don't be a coward. Face your victims. *All* your victims, everyone you've stolen from. Make this right. Don't force us all to suffer for your mistakes."

CHAPTER 11

The press left soon after—they'd gotten their footage, their sound bite for the evening's news—and after a while, so did all of John's angry clients, even Anna. Regan wasn't sure if what she'd said would work, if it would convince the world that she wasn't to blame for everything that John had done. There'd probably still be people who blamed her, who called her a rich, whiny bitch. There always were. People who had no trouble blaming a woman for a man's misdeeds. But her impromptu statement had at least taken the edge off of the mob's anger, made them realize, maybe, that the person they were mad at wasn't here—he was gone. Long gone. And so, for the moment, were they.

Step one: get John's clients and the media off her back. Done.

———

Step two of Regan's plan came the next day: the day she'd set to meet with Scovel. She'd lined up a babysitter for midday, a college girl named Audrey she'd used for some extra help around the house with Etta when Philip had been an infant. The girl knew about everything that had happened; Regan had heard it in her voice over the phone, the way it turned up too high when she realized who was calling, but Regan didn't care. She was desperate. She'd already subjected her children to stumbling on a murder scene. She couldn't bring them along to a meeting with a criminal too.

Regan left shortly after Audrey came. A strange feeling came over her as she gathered up her keys and purse, as she gave kisses to Etta and Philip's foreheads. Before all this, the only time she ever got a sitter was when she was going out, either alone or on a date with John, taking a break from parenting to be a real person for a few minutes. And now, again, as she left the house and climbed into her car without having to strap anyone into a car seat, the feeling that came over her was one of freedom, as though she was fleeing her responsibilities for a drink with a friend or a midday movie.

The strange, carefree feeling persisted as she made her way south toward the place she'd picked for their meeting: Minnehaha Park, a green space in Minneapolis with trails, a playground, lots of picnic space, and a waterfall. There were almost always people there, enough that she'd feel safe with this man who'd threatened her—but not so many that they'd be conspicuous, and the roar of the falls would make it impossible for others to eavesdrop on their conversation.

Regan pulled up in a lot at the edge of the park, paid the modest fee, then jogged down toward the falls. She walked past a pavilion and made her way toward a footbridge crossing the creek just above the falls. Her gut plunged just a little when she saw Scovel waiting there, hunched over, his forearms against the rails. Then she took a deep breath and blew it out. She'd called this meeting. She was in control. She could do this.

Scovel looked up when she came close, and she felt another chill when she saw the face she remembered from the photo Armstrong and Torres had shown her: gray stubbly facial hair, hard slate eyes, a greasy forehead. There were a few other people on the bridge: a couple posing cheek to cheek for a selfie, a young family on a walk with little kids. But there was also the roar of the falls just below. Nobody could hear them.

"You have what I want?" Scovel asked, his voice low.

Regan stood away from him, half afraid that he'd do something to her if she was within arm's reach.

"I don't," she said. "Not here. I know where it is, though. That's what I wanted to talk to you about."

The man looked at her for a long moment. He was still leaning on the rail, looking at her sideways like her existence meant nothing to him, like she was only a minor obstacle to getting the thing he wanted, like he held all the cards. Except he didn't, Regan reminded herself. She had his money. She straightened her spine, raised herself a half inch higher. Standing that way, the man hunched, Regan erect, she was taller than him. He was vulnerable, even, standing like that. Leaning over the edge. She could attack him, throw herself at him, maybe even heave him into the water, before he knew what hit him. She wouldn't. But she could. It made her feel powerful, thinking like this—like a criminal, someone desperate enough to do anything.

Scovel sighed and looked ahead, returned his eyes to the place where the creek disappeared over the falls.

"Fine," he said. "Let's hear it. And you can come closer. I'm not going to hurt you."

Regan inched closer, moved to the rail.

"I'll get you your money," Regan said. "But I've got some questions first."

Scovel looked back at her, an eyebrow raised. "You wearing a wire?"

"You want to frisk me? You want me to take my shirt off, here in the park?"

The man glanced around at the other people close by—the crowd at the restaurant patio, the couples and families milling around at the top of the falls, taking in the view.

"Just go ahead and ask your questions," he said, his voice gruff. "You want to know my name, is that it?"

"Scovel," Regan said. "Arnold Scovel."

He gave her a sharp look. "John told you about me?"

Regan shook her head. "No. The FBI. They know all about you."

The man chuckled. "You think that scares me? They don't have shit on me. Nothing they can prove."

"Just thought you might like to know."

"Well, thanks. Anything else?"

Regan's mind reeled with all the things she wanted to know. She should have written her questions down, read them off a notepad. "Did you kill Tamara?"

"I'm not answering that," Scovel said.

That was as good as an admission, Regan thought. If the answer was no, he would've said it, whether she was wearing a wire or not.

"You were following me, though," Regan said. "You had pictures of me. At Tamara's house. And then pictures of me being questioned by the FBI."

"What makes you think it was me?" Scovel asked. "I'm an important man. I've got employees, the same as other businessmen."

"That's what I want to know about," Regan said. "I want to know about John. I want to know what he was doing for you."

"Look," Scovel said, "this is going to be a frustrating conversation for you."

Regan sighed, squinted out over the falls. The brilliant midday sunshine combined with the mist to make rainbows at the edge of her field of vision.

"How about this," she said. "I'll just tell you what I think."

"You can talk all you want," Scovel said. "I don't know what you're trying to accomplish."

"Just listen," Regan said. "John was laundering money for you, right? I know he was. He was already running a fraudulent investment scheme, moving imaginary amounts of money through his clients' accounts. It wouldn't have been hard for him to add you to his client rolls. You make money from—I don't know, whatever illegal thing it is you do. You hand it over to John. He logs an investment in his books, manufactures a false gain or dividend, then you walk away with the money clean, as a capital gain. Am I close?"

Scovel spread his hands on the rail, made a show of examining his fingernails. "Just keep yapping," he said. "You're so intent on it."

"Okay," Regan said, taking the non-denial as confirmation that what she was saying was true. "So the million dollars. I figure that was a new pile of money you gave to John. But I think he hadn't laundered it yet before he disappeared. And you figured he ran off with it, had some scheme to keep it all for himself. Which is why you came after me. And maybe Tamara? Because you thought that she was in on it somehow?"

Scovel turned around, switched from leaning forward on the rail to leaning backward. He regarded her with something like respect.

"Look," he said. "You've got guts, I'll give you that. Coming here, without any of my money. Trying to ask all these questions. You're smart. I can see why John liked you."

Regan bristled. She didn't want to hear John's name. Not now, and not from this man.

"But what's this all building to?" Scovel asked. "What's the point of this?"

"I told you I had a proposal, didn't I? Do you want to hear it or not?"

He sniffed out a sarcastic laugh. "I have a feeling I'm going to, whether I want to or not. Say what you have to say. I have things to do today."

Regan licked her lips. "Okay. Well, if I'm right about any of this, you have a problem, don't you? You've got more than a million dollars of dirty money."

Scovel pointed at Regan without lifting his elbow from the rail, a bend of the wrist. "*You've* got it, actually. That's the first problem I'm trying to fix."

"Okay, yeah, *I* have it. But once I get it to you, you still have to clean it before you can do anything with it, right? And John, the guy who was doing your money-laundering, he's long gone. In the wind. Disappeared. His business is finished. The FBI has his books. So how are you going to clean your money now?"

Scovel sucked at his teeth, glanced away. "We'll find someone."

"Yeah, you will," Regan said, her pulse quickening as she walked up to her pitch. "You're looking at her."

Scovel's eyes snapped back to her. "The fuck you say?"

Regan suddenly felt jittery. Her heart was going wild in her chest. An uncontrollable energy vibrated through her limbs. Her fingers fluttered. She had to move.

"Let's walk," Regan said. She turned around and walked away without waiting for Scovel to push himself off the rail. She meandered off the bridge and around the stone wall overlooking the falls, waiting for the sound of Scovel's footfalls. They came seconds later—heavy, pounding against the pavement. He was running to keep up with her.

"Where the fuck do you think you're going?"

"Just listen to me," Regan said. "Before I had the kids, I had a business of my own. Interior design. Fixing up people's houses, making them look nice. It wasn't a huge business, but I did pretty well for myself. Had some decent clients, some pretty major jobs. I stopped doing it when the kids came along, quit to let John focus on his work. But now that John's career is over, I'll need to start it up again."

"Interior design," Scovel said. "You've got to be fucking kidding me. That's not going to—"

"Just shut up for a second," Regan said. "Jesus Christ, do men ever just let women talk? You know how much money gets thrown around on an interior design job? Tons. There's my design fee, for starters, but that only scratches the surface. Once the client has a design they like, there's all the subcontracting to think about, if you can get in on the build side. The construction contractor, for one, if there's a renovation involved. You're in construction, aren't you? I mean, that's your cover? That's what the FBI said. So you should know how complicated these jobs can be. Electric, plumbing. Permits, the inspections. The materials, the tile and the paneling and the rugs and furniture and finishes. Deliveries, installation. Dozens of financial transactions. Dozens of opportunities to tweak the invoices, pass dirty cash into the job and have it come out clean."

They went on walking. Scovel didn't say anything for a few steps. That alone told Regan that she'd given him something to think about. She'd shut him up, for a second.

"How much money?"

"Depending on the job?" Regan said. "For a rich client, a big reno, maybe a hundred thousand, maybe more. And if we go in together on an actual space—a design studio where I can sell furniture, drum up clients? Even more. It would be a lot safer for you too. Harder for the feds to find anything going on. John's business—that was a dirty business even without your money passing through it. He was running a Ponzi scheme. It was bound to come down on your head eventually. With me, you'd never get found out, because aside from the money-laundering, it would be legit. One hundred percent clean."

Another long silence. Into the void rushed the sounds of a bright Minneapolis Saturday: children shouting, people laughing. Bike bells, birds chirping. And all around, the rush of water. The roar, still, of the falls. The mist cool on Regan's face.

"Let's say I find this…this *proposal*—let's say I find it interesting," Scovel said. "Why should I trust you?"

"Why did you trust John?"

"Because he was already dirty," Scovel said. "And because I had something on him."

Regan's stomach clenched. The photo. Of course. Scovel had shown it to her as a threat, to lead her to Tamara and show her what he was capable of—but before that, the photo was blackmail, Scovel's leverage over John. *If you don't cooperate, I can ruin your marriage.*

"Maybe you can trust me because John screwed me over too," Regan said. "He left you with a pile of money you can't do anything with. And he left me without a livelihood. Without a future. The FBI's going to take most of my money—I know they are. The rest of it, whatever they keep, I figure that's probably gone too, to lawsuits and legal fees. John's victims, they're going to sue me for everything I'm worth. We need each other, you see? You need me to clean your money. And I need you to help me relaunch my business, get it off the ground, so I can keep my house and feed my kids even after this—this thing that John's done—burns my whole life to the ground."

Scovel didn't say anything for a while. He did that, Regan had noticed—let silences draw out. Made her wonder what he was thinking as she waited for what he'd say next.

Finally, he laughed. A real laugh—slightly cruel, perhaps, but with real amusement in it.

"Goddamn, lady," he said, and Regan felt a whir of anger: *Don't call me lady, asshole.* But she kept her tongue.

"I have to admit," Scovel continued, "I'm impressed. John was a scheming son of a bitch, but you put him to shame. Maybe we should've been working with you from the beginning."

"I'll take it as a compliment," Regan said.

"Now let me tell you something," Scovel said. He drew up to a stone wall overlooking the falls, a jagged gorge, and the thread of the creek below as it continued on from the plunge of the falls to feed into the Mississippi River. He pointed to the bridge they had been standing on. "You see that guy there? The one in the red cap?"

Regan saw him, a young guy whose face was not quite visible under the shade of his hat brim.

"He's one of mine. I had him come along with me to keep an eye on things. Make sure you didn't bring any cops with you. And back there," Scovel continued, pointing in the other direction, toward the pavilion. "By the trees. Dark hair, sunglasses, black polo shirt. See him?"

She did. Heavyset, threatening, leaning cross-armed against a tree.

"He's with me too," Scovel said.

"Why are you telling me this?" Regan said.

"You want to enter into a business partnership with me? Well, then we need to put all our cards on the table. You need to know: you try to fuck with me, I can fuck with you too."

"I know," Regan said. "You've made that abundantly clear."

"Well, consider this a reminder then," Scovel said. "John forgot. And look at him now."

"I'll remember."

"Okay then," Scovel said. "So how do we do this? How quickly can you start?"

"I've got past clients," Regan said. "I could use them for referrals. Maybe get a job in...two weeks? And I can start moving the money after that."

She wasn't actually sure that she could pull this off—she'd been out of the business for a while, and she wasn't sure if she'd be able to get a big client this quickly—let alone several of them, enough to move Scovel's million dollars. Besides which, she wasn't sure if the FBI would even let her move the money around—the legitimate money—to start the business again in the first place. She'd have to get a lawyer to argue on her behalf that she should be allowed to start earning money for herself, make an income, since John was gone. But all those details could wait. For now, all that mattered was convincing Scovel. Closing this deal. And then getting back home to Etta and Philip, safe.

"And I'll need to see results," Scovel said, "to know you're serious about this."

"What kind of results?"

Scovel thought for a second. "Half. In a month."

"Five hundred thousand," Regan said. For a moment she felt dizzy. She'd made big promises only moments before, but now that Scovel was going for it, she wasn't sure if she could pull it off. She wouldn't just have to land one client, then. She'd have to land a few, and big ones. "Okay. I'll make it happen."

"And don't forget," Scovel said. He made two fingers into a claw, pointed them at his open eyes, then at her. "We'll be watching."

CHAPTER 12

In the car, Regan pounded the wheel with the heel of her hand, a sudden giddiness coming over her. She felt the way she used to feel back when she was working, when she'd sold a big client on her services, closed a big job. Effervescent, a little lightheaded, and momentarily invincible.

Her phone rang, and she punched the button, took the call on speaker as she drove.

"Is this Regan Peters?" A man's voice.

"Yes, this is she. Who is this?"

"I'm your neighbor," the man said. "Your new neighbor."

"Oh. Did you just move in?"

"What? No, I didn't just move in. You did."

"Huh?"

"I'm your neighbor—at the lake."

The lake house. Of course.

"I'm sorry," said the man on the other end of the line. "Maybe I have the wrong number. Is this the Regan Peters who just recently bought a home at—"

"Yes," Regan cut in. "That's me. I'm sorry. It's been a hectic few days. My brain doesn't work so well sometimes."

"I know the feeling."

"You were saying?"

"Well, I suppose I should introduce myself. I'm Steve Larsen, my wife and I have a house across the lake from you, and—well, this is about your boat."

"My boat?" Regan asked. "I didn't know we had a—"

"Just a little rowboat. You inherited it, I suppose, from the previous owners. Jim and Tammy. Nice couple."

"Yes," Regan said, recalling the little wooden boat bobbing at the dock, looking down on it from the deck with the chill of the air against her bare calves, the duvet draped around her shoulders. "Yes, okay, what about it?"

"It got loose is what's happening," said Steve Larsen, "and it drifted over to our side of the lake somehow. And I figure you probably want it back on your side of the lake."

"Okay," Regan said, glancing at the clock, thinking of the babysitter and getting back to the kids. "Okay. I'll come. But the thing is—I've got kids, you see? Little kids. And I really need to get back to them."

"Oh heavens," Steve Larsen said. "I've been there. I have kids of my own, you know. Grown now."

"That's nice," Regan said, her impatience growing. She wanted to get off the phone, start turning her attention to the million things she had to do. Get back to the kids. Pay the sitter. Then relaunch her defunct interior design business and start laundering a million dollars in dirty cash.

She didn't have time for this. For some dumb problem with a shitty little rowboat.

"Thing is…" Steve Larsen began.

"What?" Regan asked, her annoyance beginning to come through in her voice. "What is it?"

"Well, the boat's been over here, bumping up against my

rocks, for going on three days now," he said. "Ever since your husband was over here fussing with it."

Things seemed to slow. Regan pulled the car to the side of the road, stopped, cars honking as they whooshed past her.

"Wait, what did you say?" Regan asked. "My husband?"

"Shoot," said Steve Larsen. "I'm sorry, I'm so old. I forget that people don't always do things the way we did back when I met my Gloria. Your partner—"

"It's not that," Regan interrupted. "I'm married, I am, it's just—you saw him? You saw my husband?"

"Well, I guess I assumed it was him. It was after dark. I was getting ready to go to bed, and then I glanced out the window across the lake and I saw a man at the end of the dock, fussing with that rowboat. I figured, well, that must be the new neighbor. I should go over and say hello tomorrow. Then I went off to bed and didn't think anything more about it. I don't know what he was doing with the boat, seemed like a weird time to be taking it out, but he must have left it loose by accident, because the next morning it was bobbing on our side of the lake without anyone in it."

"Three nights ago, you said?"

"That's right," he said. "It took me that long to get ahold of you. I had to track down the listing agent first, and then explain the issue, and then get your number, and…"

Regan did the calculations as the man babbled on. Three nights ago. That was after John had bought her the lake house, said he had to go to the office, then never came home. The night before the FBI came looking to arrest him.

"I'll be there in half an hour," she said.

———————

A sleek frame house built into a slope, glass windows reaching all the way to the peak of the roof. A stand of trees below that, a pile of rocks leading to the shore. And then the boat, so absurdly buoyant that it seemed to bob on the waves without even touching the water. Every so often there was the sound of the hull bumping against a rock; she'd have thought the planed boards would have cracked apart by now, started letting in water, but the boat stayed strong.

"What do we do?" Regan asked.

"This," Steve Larsen said, handing her some kind of tool she'd never seen before: a pole with a hook at the end of it. "Sorry, I'd do it myself, but I'm not as steady on those rocks as I used to be."

He wasn't what Regan had expected. In boat shoes, straight-legged shorts cropped above the knee, a Carleton College windbreaker, and chunky clear-framed glasses, Steve Larsen cast a hipper vibe than Regan had anticipated, even in what Regan guessed were his late seventies. He looked a bit like the old ad men Regan used to work for in her agency days—a copywriter or designer turned CEO, or a retired architect, maybe.

"Just hook it and push it toward the dock," Steve said. "I'll catch it and lash it to a post."

Regan studied the tool in her hand, then looked back at Steve. "Okay."

The kids were still home with the babysitter. She felt bad about foisting them on the poor girl, but there was no other choice. She'd called on the way over, let Audrey know that she'd be a little longer than she planned, that she'd pay extra—double, even. The sitter insisted it was okay, but still Regan wanted to get this done with as quickly as possible, see what John had left in the boat, if anything, and then get out of there.

Steve walked toward the dock, and Regan inched down toward the water. She wobbled on the rocks, put down a hand to keep herself from falling.

"Careful," Steve said.

"Thanks a lot," she muttered under her breath, too soft for him to hear. "Be careful. Hadn't thought of that."

Near the edge of the water, Regan could see into the boat. It didn't look like anything was inside. But John could've stowed something under the bench.

"Just hook it," Steve called. "Around the edge, then push it this way."

Regan threw the hook out, nearly losing her balance again. The hook splashed in the water.

"Almost," Steve said. "Just reach a little farther."

"You do it," Regan muttered, "if you know so much."

"Huh?" Steve asked, his voice nasal.

"Nothing," Regan said. "Just waiting for it to come back in."

Some low waves were coming in; they carried the boat back toward the shore. Regan waited until it was close, waited for the sound of the hull knocking against the rocks again—then she threw the hook out once more, flung her arm out as far as it could reach without losing the rod.

"There you go!" Steve shouted. "Now bring it this way."

Keeping the hook looped around the edge of the boat, Regan walked carefully along the rocks toward the dock, then gave the hook a shove. The vessel wobbled on the waves, riding the light momentum Regan had given it toward the dock.

Steve crouched. The dock creaked under his knees. He reached out.

"Almost, almost—got it!"

Regan climbed back up the bank as Steve worked with a length of rope, looping it around the cleats at the boat's side and one of the posts of the dock.

"Is there anything in there?" Regan asked as she stepped onto the dock.

"I don't see anything," Steve said. "Just the oars."

"Under the benches?"

"Nope," Steve said. "Were you expecting something?"

Regan didn't know what to say. What had John been doing with the boat, then, if not hiding something there?

"Hang on," Regan said. "What's that?"

She pointed. There was a smear of something brownish-red on the wale. Dried liquid, and a bit of matter, something globby and knotted.

Steve hissed in a breath. "Looks like—"

He didn't finish, but he didn't need to.

Blood. It looked like blood.

———

An hour later Regan was across the lake, in the empty house, waiting while the police dragged the lake. Regan stood at the sliding glass door, watching divers fall backward off a police boat, while two more officers watched from the shore, muttering to each other and leaning against the hood of a cruiser parked on the grass.

Regan glanced down at her phone, thumbed the screen bright, and looked at the time. She thought again of the kids, of the babysitter, still at the house more than an hour after Regan had said she'd be home. She should really get back, but the cops had told her to wait until someone could come and take her statement. She was expecting Armstrong and Torres any minute now, with their questions, their suspicions. She needed to find someone else to sit with the kids, but she only had one option, and she was dreading the phone call.

She stabbed at the phone, hit the name on the screen like she was attacking it, then held her breath as it rang.

"Regan," came the voice on the other end—cold, withdrawn. Her mother. "What is it?"

"I'm sorry," Regan began, immediately hating herself for apologizing when it was Isabel who should have been saying sorry to *her*. "I wouldn't be calling if it wasn't important."

"Yes?"

"I need someone to go to the house and sit with the kids," Regan said. "They're with a sitter, but I need to let her go and I'm stuck somewhere, I'm—it's John, they think they may have found him. Found his, well, his…"

Silence on the other end of the line. Isabel was going to make her say it.

"His body."

Finally her mother's voice came back—hushed, softened.

"Regan. Oh my God."

"Yeah," Regan said, her voice catching. She cleared her throat. "So if you could just head over to the house and let the sitter go. I'm not sure when I'll be back, and I know this is so inconvenient, but—"

"It's fine," her mother cut in. "Don't worry about it. I'll be with them. As long as you need."

Regan breathed out, a tightness in her unwinding. She felt tears rising to her eyes, blinked them back. Isabel would never apologize to her, Regan knew, never own up to all the ways her coldness, her subtle disapproval and withholding of love, had unmade Regan psychologically, damaged her since childhood. Regan knew not to expect that from her. But a mother was still there for you when you needed her most—the same way she'd be there for her own children until the day she died.

When the call ended, she looked up, back to the lake. A diver came back to the surface, made some hand signal to the men on the boat, and then he went down again. Continued his search of those dark waters.

Regan turned away from the window and wandered around the house, running her hands along the walls. Here was the kitchen, with the huge center island where she'd imagined making elaborate meals; here was the dining room, where they could've hosted friends for dinner parties; here was the living room, where she'd have liked to sit reading a book while a fire crackled in the hearth. The house full not of memories, but of possibilities—a future that would never be. All except that corner in the den, where the old left-behind duvet still sat in a lump: the spot on the floor where she and John had fucked like horny kids after the closing.

Their last time—ever, now. They'd never make love again. And Regan would never be as happy, as hopeful about the future, as she'd been in that moment.

The doorbell rang, and she walked to answer it. It was Agent Torres.

"It's you," Regan said. She stepped away from the door and walked back inside. "Come in, I guess."

"Sorry to be bothering you," Torres said. Somehow all the usual sharpness had gone out of her voice.

"I suppose you want to ask me some questions," Regan said, coming back to the sliding glass door. Outside, she saw that Armstrong had walked around the house to join the two cops by the shore watching the divers.

"The usual, I suppose," Torres said. "I didn't realize you had a lake house."

"I didn't keep it from you on purpose," Regan lied. "I honestly forgot about it. We closed three days ago. John hadn't even told me about it until that day, and when all this mess happened it was like it just got knocked out of my head. I hadn't had a chance to get used to it yet. I'm honestly surprised you didn't already know about it. Haven't you been looking at all our assets?"

"Looks like John paid cash, so there was no mortgage application. And since you hadn't closed yet…" Torres said.

"Ah."

"It's in your name, isn't it?" Torres asked. "Like the rest of your assets?"

Regan sighed. "It was a gift. For my birthday. John said—" Regan cut herself short, sensing some commotion outside.

Torres stepped to the sliding glass door next to Regan. At first Regan looked to her, but then she saw that Torres was staring intently through the glass. Regan followed her gaze.

"What is it?"

Regan's heart sped up. Through the trees, the head of one of the divers bobbed to the surface, like a black ball floating on the waves. The diver lifted his hand above the water. Regan had to squint hard through the trees to see what he was doing.

Pointing down. To the murky bottom.

On the boat, a man standing with his foot propped against the wale lifted something to his face. A radio. Regan's gaze snapped to the shore, where one of the police officers pushed himself off the hood of the cruiser and lifted his own radio to his mouth. The two men talked for a few seconds, then he turned to Armstrong, and Armstrong turned toward the house.

"What's happening?" Regan asked, panic washing over her. "I want to know what's happening."

Torres rapped her knuckles on the glass of the sliding doors, and Armstrong's eyes came up to find them. He nodded at Torres, then made a little cutting motion with the flat of his hand close to his throat.

Regan turned to Torres, who was already looking at her, waiting.

"Mrs. Peters," she said, "I'm so sorry."

Torres went on talking, but Regan could no longer hear her.

She saw the FBI agent's mouth moving, but it seemed that no sounds were coming out. It was as if Torres was speaking to her from a long distance. As if they were underwater.

———————————

"It doesn't look like him," Regan said.

The young medical examiner's assistant holding the sheet flinched, looked confused. He looked down at the body on the metal slab and blinked. They stood opposite each other in a harshly lit room, fluorescents buzzing overhead from a drop ceiling, stone floors, a wall of square steel doors. The assistant scanned the doors now, perhaps wondering if he'd opened the wrong slot, pulled the wrong corpse.

"It's him," Regan rushed to clarify. "I know it's him. It's just—"

How to explain? The body before her had to be John's, there was no doubt about that. And yet it wasn't John. Her husband was still gone, still missing in some crucial way. She'd never see him again. All that was left of him was this…this *thing*, this lump of meat. The face puffier than that of the man she remembered, more swollen, and half-gone besides, covered with weeping red sores of some kind.

"It's the water," the assistant explained. "Bodies puff up after a couple days in the water."

"And the…" Regan trailed off and waved her hand in front of her face.

"Oh, that," the assistant said, seemingly embarrassed. "The fish got at him. I'm sorry, I know it's disturbing. But the police wanted to get the ID out of the way. For the file."

"It's fine," Regan said. "I understand."

The assistant put the sheet back over John's face.

"What are they saying?" Regan asked.

"We'll have to do an autopsy," he said, then leaned in and lowered his voice. "But it looks like suicide. He'd tied his ankle to a cinder block. Put it over the edge."

"Oh," Regan said. "What about the blood?"

"Blood?"

"On the boat. There was some blood on the edge of it."

"He's got a knock on his head," the assistant replied. "The ME thought maybe he hit it on the way down, as the cinder block pulled him out of the boat. It's possible he went in the water unconscious. The autopsy will tell us that. There will be a full report soon."

"I see," Regan said, wondering if there was something she was supposed to be doing, some way she was supposed to be acting. In the movies, people wept after they identified their loved ones' bodies on metal slabs, put their heads in their hands. Maybe that's what this young man was expecting from her. But she couldn't manage it. Her eyes were completely dry. She searched inside herself, dug down all the way to the core of her, searching for some emotion she could drag to the surface, but she couldn't find anything. The only feeling she could muster was exhaustion.

"Is that all?" Regan said.

"That's it," the young man said. "You're free to go."

CHAPTER 13

By the time Regan arrived back home, it was late afternoon. She opened the door to find Philip and Etta playing on the carpet with their toys, her mother on the couch above them with her legs folded up next to her.

Isabel rose at once when she saw Regan.

"Is it," she began, then cut herself off and began again. "Is he...?"

Regan nodded, and Isabel crossed the room to her.

"Regan," she said. "I'm so sorry."

Regan received her mother's hug but didn't return it. Isabel held her stiffly for a moment, then withdrew.

"Do you want to talk?" Isabel asked.

"Not really," Regan said. "Not right now." She declined to speak the sentence her mind added: *Not with you.* Regan was grateful for her mother's help, and maybe she even *needed* Isabel's support now that John was officially gone for good and she was a single mother. But she was determined not to let her mother back into her life so easily—not without boundaries, not without being able to set her own terms. She was done putting everyone else first. It was time to think about herself for a change.

"I guess I'll go then," Isabel said.

Silence descended. Regan glanced toward the children, who'd paused in their play and were looking up at their mother and grandmother, seeming to sense something in the air.

"Did you tell them anything?" Regan asked in a low voice.

"No," Isabel said. "I didn't know what to say."

Regan sighed. "I'll talk to them."

Isabel left, and the children went on staring at Regan. Regan sat in a chair in the living room and stared out the front window. She thought about what she had to say to the children, thought about how to tell it to them. Her mind wandered to John, imagining his final night—the FBI closing in, his life about to fall to pieces. She imagined him rowing out to the middle of the lake in the darkness, throwing the cinder block over the edge. Wondered at his final thoughts, as the weight pulled him over the edge. Pulled him under. Had he thought of her? Of the children? Had there been a fleeting moment of regret as the water rushed into his lungs, a split second when he wanted to take it all back and return to them?

How could she explain any of this to the children when she couldn't understand it herself?

"What's wrong, Mama?" Etta asked.

Regan blinked, and suddenly she realized she was crying.

Peter toddled up and grabbed Regan by the legs, put his chin on her knees, and looked up at her. "Mama okay?"

Regan sank to her knees and wrapped both children in her arms. "I'm going to be okay," she said. "Mama's just…thinking about something."

Etta blinked, her eyes cartoonishly huge with vulnerability. "Thinking about what?"

"About Daddy," Regan said.

"Thinking that you're mad at him?"

"No," Regan said, surprised to realize that, for once, it was the truth. She wasn't mad at John. Not in this moment. "Thinking about how nice he could be sometimes. How he tried his best to make a nice life for all of us. He wasn't perfect, but he tried. He tried to make us happy, didn't he?"

Regan's voice faltered, and suddenly she was actually weeping, and the children threw themselves at her, completely terrified.

"Is he coming back soon?" Etta asked.

"No," Regan said. "He's not."

"Because he doesn't like us anymore?"

"No," Regan said, her heart seeming to pull apart in her chest. "Sweetie, no. That's not it."

"Why, then?"

Regan gathered a breath, held it, then spoke. Said the thing she had to say. "He died, sweetie. Your dad can't come home because he's not alive anymore."

Etta's face crumpled. She started bawling, and Philip followed, and again Regan gathered them in her arms, cried with them on the floor. They stayed like that for a long time.

She passed the rest of the day in a stupor—but once she'd finally gotten the kids to bed in the evening, a feeling of urgency came over her. She still had things to do, a plan to execute. She went to the kitchen, found Agent Armstrong's card in a drawer, then called him.

"Hello?"

"It's me," she said. "It's Regan Peters."

"Mrs. Peters," Armstrong said. She heard rustling, the click of a lamp, and she knew she'd caught him after hours, perhaps at his hotel room. Unwinding at the end of a long day.

"I need to talk."

"Now?"

"Yes," Regan said. "Please come as quickly as you can. Alone. No Torres."

There was a silence on the other end of the line. Regan could almost feel him wanting to ask her why. But then he didn't. "Okay," he said, then hung up.

After the phone went dead, Regan busied herself like a woman preparing for a dinner date. She tidied up the living and dining rooms. Wiped down the table and counters, swept the floors, picked up the toys. Upstairs, she put on slippers and comfortable pants, stripped down to her camisole, and slipped a shawl sweater over her shoulders. She fluffed up her hair in the mirror, patted her cheeks, put on sheer lip gloss. She was pouring herself a glass of Cabernet Sauvignon when Armstrong came to the front door.

"Agent Armstrong," she said with a slight note of surprise, as though she hadn't been the one to call him. "I was just pouring myself a drink. Do you want anything?"

Armstrong stepped into the house. Regan was pleased to notice that he'd showered and shaved before coming over—his cheeks clean of stubble, a slight scent of lavender clinging to his skin.

"I don't think so," Armstrong said. "We're not really supposed to accept gifts."

"It's not a gift," Regan said. "It's a drink. You'd be doing me a personal favor. My husband was found dead today."

Armstrong winced. "I know. And I'm sorry."

Regan walked to the hutch in the hallway, opened the door, and grabbed at the stem of an empty glass. "You'll have some, then?"

Armstrong shrugged, sighed. "Fine. A small glass. It's late."

"You've said." Regan put the glass on the coffee table, gave a generous pour. Armstrong would never know—the glasses were huge globes, obscuring how much liquid they held, and a person never really knew how much they were drinking when they were drinking it. She handed him the glass by the stem, their fingers brushing as he moved to cradle the goblet.

Armstrong put his lips to the wine, took the tiniest of sips, then let the glass fall against his chest.

"I was sorry not to be there with you, you know," he said.

"Be where?"

"At the coroner's," Armstrong said. "Identifying the body. You were all alone, I heard—I didn't want that. It's just this case. It's sprawling. Keeps us busy. The whole team. Scattered."

"Hither and yon," Regan said, returning to her seat by the window, crossing one leg over the other. She held the wineglass between her two hands, but didn't drink. Armstrong probably wouldn't notice if she didn't drink. "That's what my dad always used to say. *Hither and yon.* He's a writer, so he's given to floral language."

Armstrong was in the midst of another sip, a larger one this time; he lowered his glass, clicking his tongue on the back of his teeth as he swallowed the wine down. "Florid, you mean?"

Regan smiled placidly. A man couldn't resist correcting a woman. It didn't matter who the man was.

"I'm sure you're right," Regan said. "So what was it that scattered you hither and yon? That's making the case sprawl?"

"Oh, I don't know if I could—"

"It's about Scovel, isn't it? You don't care about John anymore—now that he's dead. You want his associates now. Whoever he was mixed up with."

Armstrong took yet another drink of wine, then held it in his mouth, grimacing. He seemed to like it a lot for a guy who'd protested at first, which was good, because it had cost Regan more than fifty dollars at Haskell's, and she wanted to get her money's worth.

"It's really nothing you have any reason to know about," Armstrong said. "But yes, actually. Now that you mention it. Your husband was tied up in a large criminal network. And we're trying to untangle it."

"Any arrests?"

Armstrong gave her a patronizing smile, the kind of smile that said she'd already pushed things far enough and wasn't going to get anything more out of him. Regan put a hand to her chest—put it between the folds of the shawl sweater, on the swath of bare skin that stretched pale above the low-cut camisole. An exaggerated gesture of offense, to match his exaggerated expression of scolding.

"Don't I have a right to know?" Regan asked. "That man threatened me. He killed Tamara. He may have even killed John."

Armstrong's brows hooded over his eyes. "We don't know for sure that he killed Tamara. And John was a—"

"A suicide, I know," Regan said. "As I understand it, though, that's not official yet. And you don't think this man can fake a suicide? There was blood on that boat; the kid at the medical examiner's office told me that they're thinking he hit it on his way down. But what if that's not right? What if someone hit him over the head to knock him out, took him out to the middle of the lake, then dropped him in?"

Armstrong thought about that for a few seconds, trailing his fingers around the lip of the wineglass.

"That's possible," he said. He looked down, practically put his chin on his chest, and sighed. "Okay. You've got a point. So no. No arrests yet."

"That's what I wanted to talk to you about," Regan said.

"What? The fact that we haven't arrested anybody yet?"

"No," Regan said. "The fact that I can *help* you arrest somebody."

"How would you do that? Last time we talked, you told us you didn't know anything."

Regan explained her plan. It was identical in every way to the plan she'd proposed to Scovel, with one key difference: she'd wear a wire and try to get Scovel on tape admitting to his crimes.

Armstrong listened. "What's in it for you?" he asked when she was done.

"You let me keep half of everything," Regan said. "All the assets I shared with John. I get what I would've gotten in a divorce settlement. I keep the house. And the business—the interior design business I start up as a front for the laundering scheme. It stays mine after you arrest Scovel and his people."

"That's going to be hard to negotiate," Armstrong said. "I don't have the power to make that kind of deal."

"Who does?"

Armstrong shrugged. "My bosses. Guys at Justice. Federal prosecutors."

"Talk to them, then," Regan said. "Tell them I want to make a deal. They can negotiate the details with my lawyer."

"You got a lawyer?"

Regan shook her head. "Haven't gotten around to it yet. But I will."

Armstrong looked at her for a long moment. Then he burst out laughing. "You're something else, Regan Peters. Your husband was not a smart man to step out on you like he did. He should have kept you close. I would have."

Regan narrowed her eyes. "I'm not sure what you're saying. Is that a compliment?"

"It is."

"Well then that's how I'll take it."

Armstrong set the glass of wine on the coffee table, then leaned back on the couch and laced his fingers behind his head.

"Let me ask you this," he said. "Why did you want only me to come here tonight? Why not Torres?"

Regan felt her lips pulling into an expression of distaste, and she lifted the wineglass to her lips to cover it.

"She's not on my side," Regan said.

"Neither am I, technically," Armstrong said. "I'm on the side of justice. Of figuring out what's really happening here. Whether that's good for you or not."

Regan bristled, wondering if Armstrong had fallen to insulting her on purpose. She decided to ignore it. "It really means something to you, doesn't it?" she asked.

"What?"

"Justice."

Armstrong looked away and made a pained face, as though he was embarrassed to be caught believing in something.

"It does," he admitted.

"And can you often find it?" Regan asked. "In the FBI?"

"Not always," Armstrong said. "Sometimes law enforcement is the last place you'd look for justice. You know that, if you pay any attention."

"I do," Regan said. She may have been a suburban housewife, but she watched the news. Cared about things in the world, the same as anyone else.

"It can be good, though, if you're in the right unit," Armstrong said, looking down, a distant look coming to his eyes, like he was getting lost in his thoughts. "I like Financial Crimes. I requested it specifically. Some people think it's boring, all those numbers, going through files, analyzing lines of data, but it's where the real action is. The real crimes—real theft, the real corruption. The criminals are rich, mostly. Powerful. And the money that they're stealing—it's outlandish. More than most people could dream of in their whole lives. Stealing it from regular people. From poor people."

He blinked, looked up at her. "The truth of it is… I got into this job to bust men like your husband. I know you just found out he's dead, and I'm sorry about that—but it's true. In this world, it's men like him who are the real criminals. Rich men. Men who know their way around money, and who manipulate it to hurt other people. Whether it was your fault or not, Regan, you lived with that kind of crime, you lived *in* it." He lifted up a hand to encompass everything they were sitting in: the house, the furniture. Then he let the hand drop back to his lap. "So no. I'm not on your side, Regan."

Regan blinked, her eyes suddenly feeling hot. "You are, though," Regan said.

Armstrong let out a sigh through his nose. Halfway through, it turned into a disbelieving laugh. He shook his head.

"You say you're not on my side with your words," Regan pressed on. "But then I see the way you look at me, the way you treat me."

"My mother taught me to be polite."

Regan shook her head. "No. It's more than that. You're *kind*, Agent Armstrong. And you don't hate me, as much as you might claim otherwise. We're on the same side—you can see that. John was a criminal, yes. The exact kind of criminal you joined the bureau to catch. Okay. *And I'm one of his victims.* I am. He lied to me, he drew me in, made me love him; he built our lives around his lies and made me a part of them. He conned me, made me a mark. That's the kind of victim I am. And now I'm trying, you see? I'm trying to make it right. To…to—to get my *soul* back. You see that, don't you?"

Armstrong's eyes grew wide as Regan spoke, and she realized she'd begun to cry again. These felt different than the tears she'd shed for John, the tears she'd cried with Etta and Philip. She found herself wondering how she looked, if the tears would appear real or fake to Armstrong. She bent over at the waist, covered her face, and went on crying.

After a while she heard footsteps, the rustle of shoes on carpet. And then she felt the warmth of Armstrong's hand on her shoulder. His hands—Regan pictured them. His beautiful hands.

"It's okay," Armstrong said. "It's going to be okay. I believe you."

Regan sniffed and looked up at him. "And you'll help me?"

He seemed to hesitate for a moment, but then he nodded.

"Okay. I'll help."

CHAPTER 14

The next days passed in a blur. Out of guilt or pity—Regan didn't care which—her mother went on taking the kids for stretches of time. But even without Etta and Philip around, Regan still felt frenzied, beleaguered, beset by responsibilities and troubles. She'd made promises—promises to Scovel, promises to Armstrong. Now she also had to deliver. She had a month to launch a business, get a few high-paying clients, and start moving huge amounts of cash.

She built a simple website, paid a fee, used a template. Made a list of every client she'd ever had before the kids were born, every connection she could exploit, and then called them one by one for references. ("I don't know anyone who's looking to have anything done *that* quickly," most of them said. "But Regan, didn't I hear something about your husband? Something about some financial problems?")

John's death was on the news. The police ruled it a suicide, as the medical examiner's assistant had predicted. Some said—in man-on-the-street interviews and the comments sections of *Star Tribune* and *Pioneer Press* articles—that John had taken the coward's way out, ending his life rather than facing his victims.

The ruling of suicide also caused problems for Regan, a fact she discovered when she called their insurance agent to make a claim on the term life policy she and John had taken out years before. Half a million dollars.

"It's a little complicated, Regan," the insurance agent said on the phone. His name was Chris, a soft-spoken guy who'd talked in their first meeting years ago of the importance of *protecting your future* and *going with someone you can trust*. Now he was going to fuck Regan over. She knew it by his voice.

"Complicated," Regan said. "How?"

"Well, here's the thing," Chris said. "You're insured for five hundred thousand on John's death. That's true. But—and I really hate to be telling you this in the middle of your bereavement and all that—but there are some stipulations on cause of death. The policy doesn't pay out for suicide. And according to the death certificate I'm looking at here—"

Regan closed her eyes. "Why is that a rule? I don't understand. We bought the insurance, paid all the premiums on time. And now he's dead. I have bills to pay. A funeral, a burial. Not to mention the kids. They no longer have a father to provide for them. The lost income alone—this is why we bought the life insurance. You *sold* it to us."

Chris clicked his tongue. "I understand that, Regan, I really do. But you have to understand it from the company's standpoint. They don't want to be in the position of *encouraging* people to kill themselves, you see. I mean, you can imagine—a person gets in financial trouble, they worry about their ability to provide for their family, maybe they get depressed. And they've got this life insurance. It could seem tempting to just end it all, right? It's really a sort of…of *fraud*, if you think about it."

Fraud. That word again. She wondered how long it would be before she'd never have to hear it again.

"You're not going to pay."

"I'm sorry. It's out of my hands."

Regan only wanted the money to offset everything that the feds would take from her in the prosecution—there wouldn't actually be a funeral. Regan couldn't bear it, cringed to even imagine it. At first she figured that nobody would show up even if she did have a funeral. John didn't really have any friends, and he had no family to speak of. But then she realized the truth: *everyone* would show up. Everyone she'd ever known, from close friends to slight acquaintances. Forgotten classmates from high school, elementary school, maybe even preschool. Her childhood pediatrician, the Lutheran pastor who'd baptized her as a baby, her kindergarten teacher. They'd show up because of the news stories, because of the spectacle. They'd come to gawk. To look at the wreckage of her life, like rubberneckers inching past the site of a car crash.

No, there wouldn't be a funeral. Not even a burial. She'd burn John's body, put the ashes in the cheapest urn they had, the whole thing costing her less than five hundred dollars.

She didn't tell anyone about the death, didn't put any announcement on Facebook or Instagram—but the messages came anyway. The condolences. Texts, direct messages, cards, flowers. It had been on the news, after all, the whole sordid story. Sorry for your loss, the messages said. Thinking of you in this time of sadness.

But Regan didn't know if she was sad, didn't even know if she was supposed to be. She and John had been together seven years, married for five. They'd had children together, bought a house, built a life. But he was also—it turned out—a bad man. A liar. A con artist. A *fraud*. Did you grieve a man like that? Did you cry for his death? Or did you only mourn what he'd done to you, the sad joke he'd made of your existence, and celebrate the fact that he was gone? Regan probably should've gone to therapy to talk about it, and one day she even did some research, looked at some local grief counselors online. But then she shook her head, closed the laptop, put it away. A therapist would only tell her something like, *There's no right way to grieve.* Or: *Feel your feelings.* Why pay for something like that? She didn't want to feel her feelings. She wanted to be done with them as quickly as possible. Wanted to rush through this horrible chapter of her life and get on to the next thing.

———

She got a lawyer, to help her cut a deal with the feds and figure out the money side of things. Nobody special, just a business card she'd picked up somewhere, a middle-aged guy named Bill with a receding hairline and a paunch that had a tendency to bulge out between the unbuttoned halves of a navy sport coat. He began by working with the FBI to get his hands on all the financial records they'd subpoenaed for their investigation. After he'd finished this task, Regan was shocked to find that she was, on paper, a rich woman: almost a million in savings and investments, and she owned both homes—the house and the lake house—outright with no debt. That made sense, she supposed; John was alleged to have stolen more than ten million from his clients and had reported thirty million in false capital gains. That money had to have gone somewhere.

Not all of it was liquid, though. She couldn't spend it. Much of the savings was in retirement accounts, so she couldn't get her hands on it until she was almost sixty, even if the FBI let her keep any of it. The savings accounts amounted to a couple hundred thousand. She could also sell the houses, or take out a mortgage on the equity, to pay off legal bills if she had to.

"You're never going to get half," Bill warned her. "Even with what you're offering them. We'll ask for half, as a negotiating position. But you won't get it."

"How much, then?" Regan asked. "How much, if not half?"

"Maybe half of the savings if we're lucky. One of the houses. You'll get to keep your car. That's probably it."

Half, plus one of the houses, and the car. She hoped it would be enough. A group of John's clients had recently notified her of their intent to sue, and she was certain that much of the cash left over would have to go to a settlement. More lawsuits might be coming. She was afraid she'd be broke when all was said and done—broke or even in debt, working for decades to come to pay off the price of John's crimes.

Armstrong came back to her with a deal two days after their meeting. It was exactly as Bill had predicted: she'd get to keep half, plus the house—not the lake house. The rest would be seized and given to John's victims as restitution, though there wasn't nearly enough to cover what he'd stolen, and there'd still, most likely, be lawsuits.

There was still the cash in the garage, the million dollars in the cream leather travel bag. She hadn't gone near it since putting it in her parents' garage attic, afraid that either her parents, Scovel, or the FBI would catch her with the money and rob her of her one remaining bargaining chip. She was more determined than ever to find a way to keep the money for herself, a pile of cash that no one—not the FBI, not the courts, not John's victims—could get their hands on. Something for her and the kids. She just couldn't quite see it. How she'd pull it off.

Not yet.

Isabel had taken the kids the morning Regan finalized her deal with the FBI. A meeting with a pair of nondescript men in suits whose names she forgot as soon as she heard them, her lawyer and Armstrong looking on as she signed the papers they gave her. Afterward Regan drove home alone, thinking about the deal she'd just made, what she'd signed her name to. The stereo was on in the car, tuned to public radio. A local news segment came on; the top story was about John's suicide and speculation about where the case might go next. Regan stabbed her finger at the power button almost desperately, flipping the sound off.

Silence. God, she loved silence. It had been years since she'd really been able to enjoy any for herself—four and a half years, to be precise. The four and a half years since Etta had been born. Children were noise. They came into the world with noise— with screaming and pain. And then, once they were out, they took over the screaming for you. Crying, colicky, through the night as newborns. Then, when they learned to walk, they kept on crying every time they fell. Soon came the whining, the fits, the temper tantrums. The incessant questions, the *why why why*. The begging for things in the store—for toys, for treats. Even when they were happy they were noisy, unable to have a good time without screeching. She'd gone through it first with Etta, then again with Philip. Four and a half years of unceasing racket, so much that sometimes she felt as though her own thoughts were being screamed right out of her head, the noise going into her ears and lodging in her brain, crowding out everything that was *her*.

Regan pulled into her driveway. She scarcely noticed the car parked at the curb, the driver's door that opened when she pulled in, or the woman who stepped out and crossed the grass to come close to her—not until the woman was almost on top of her and she turned to see her standing there.

Regan shrieked, and the woman jumped, startled.

"Holy shit," Regan said, a hand to her chest. "You scared the hell out of me."

"I'm sorry," the woman said softly.

"It's okay," Regan said. She looked at the woman, took her in. She was in her sixties, plump, with blond hair that came to her shoulders and cheap-looking glasses. Her lips were thin, the corners of her mouth bracketed by deep parenthesis-shaped wrinkles, and though she wasn't frowning, Regan had the overpowering sense that she was sad, and not just at that moment, but that sadness was a condition of her life, a baseline reality. "Can I help you?"

"Your name is Regan?" the woman asked. "Regan Peters?"

"Yes?" Regan said, growing cautious.

"I saw you on the news."

"You're here to yell at me? Call me a greedy whore? Tell me my husband deserved what he got?"

The woman blinked as though she couldn't understand a word Regan was saying.

"I'm your husband's mother," the woman said.

Regan stood silent for a second, thinking she must have misheard. Then she laughed.

"What did you say?"

"I'm John's mother," the woman said again. "Though he was never John to me. That's not the name I gave him."

Regan shook her head, sputtering. "That's impossible," she said. "You're supposed to be dead."

As though she didn't know by now. As though everything John had told her about himself hadn't already turned out to be a lie.

But something about what Regan had said pleased the woman. She smiled, the parenthesis wrinkles growing deeper, like a smiley face a child might draw. She nodded.

"Don't I know it, honey."

CHAPTER 15

Regan invited John's mother inside.

"Make yourself comfortable," Regan said. She glanced at the clock. It was still early—ten in the morning. "Can I get you something to drink? Coffee? Tea?"

"Tea would be nice, honey," the woman said. "I can't really do coffee. The caffeine makes me jittery."

Regan began to move into the kitchen. Then she stopped. "What should I call you?" she asked, half-worried the woman would say *Mom*.

"My name is Darlene," she said. "You can call me that."

Regan nodded, relieved. She went into the kitchen and got the pot started on the stove. She looked for mugs and teabags, picked an English breakfast for herself, chamomile for Darlene. She went back into the living room a couple minutes later with two steaming mugs.

Darlene was on the couch, gazing at the family pictures on the wall.

"There are kids here, aren't there?" she asked when Regan handed her the mug. "You have kids?"

"They're not here right now," Regan said. "They're with

their grandma." She bit her lip when she realized what she'd said; Darlene was their grandma too.

"I'd love to meet them."

"Maybe," Regan said. "We should probably talk a little first."

Darlene nodded. She blew on her tea, her eyes still wandering the space, taking it in. Then her face brightened. "I brought pictures. Do you want to see them?"

"Sure," Regan said.

Darlene reached into her purse and came out with a pile of postcard-sized photographs held together by a rubber band. She pulled off the rubber band then began shuffling the photos.

"These are of…John?" Regan asked. She felt off-balance, not sure what to call her husband in Darlene's presence.

"Well, I know him as Casey," Darlene said.

Casey. Regan gave her head a tiny shake. It didn't seem right. The name didn't seem to match her husband. Didn't fit the man she'd known.

"Here's one of him as a baby," Darlene said, slapping a photo face down on the coffee table and sliding it toward Regan. "And one of him when he was…oh, maybe three or four. Some time in elementary school. And high school." She sent more photos across the table. Regan picked them up one by one and flipped through them.

The baby picture was taken in the hospital, with John no more than a few hours old, sleeping, swaddled tightly in a blanket. The picture could've been of anyone, the newborn features still unformed, squishy and shapeless, and yet there was something— something in the mouth—that reminded Regan of her husband. The next photograph, of John as a toddler, showed him in the snow, knee deep, wearing a burgundy-red bodysuit with attached mittens and a matching stocking cap. His cheeks were rosy, his eyes squinting against the sun reflecting off the brilliant white, and he was not smiling.

The next photos—of John in elementary school and high school—showed a boy taking shape into a man, the man she knew. He could've been anywhere from seven to nine years old in the first: ratty blue jeans, a navy-blue T-shirt with horizontal stripes, a bit of baby fat. In the second, the boy had become a brooding pre-teen sitting on a rusted lawn chair, slouching low, legs stretched out and crossed at the ankle, floppy hair parted down the middle and falling into his eyes. Again he smiled in neither picture, and Regan found herself wondering if he'd ever smiled throughout his childhood—if the sadness she'd sensed in Darlene had made itself a part of his life too, and if that—that melancholy—was what he'd run away from.

"Where were these taken?" Regan asked. "Where are you from?"

"You ever been to Grand Marais?" Darlene asked. "Up on the Superior Shore?"

"Once or twice," Regan said. Lake Superior's North Shore was a bit of a vacation destination for people in southern Minnesota, and she'd vacationed there a couple times with her family, before John—who never seemed interested in going there when she suggested a trip up north. "You're from there?"

"Not quite," Darlene said. "A little bit further north from there, almost to Canada. A couple of houses, an old resort on the shore, and a general store. Some maps don't even have it." She added the last bit as a sort of wry aside, almost as though it was a point of pride.

"That's where John grew up?" Regan said. Try as she might, she could not bring herself to say the name *Casey*; he'd always be John to her.

"That's right," Darlene said. "Edge of nowhere. Pretty rough place. Abandoned. I ran the general store, inherited it from my daddy, but it wasn't much of a business. Not many people stop there. Not since the resort closed down. Nobody but the hardcore outdoor types—half of them are hippies, the other half are antigovernment crazies. And truckers. We lived pretty much on the edge of poverty."

Regan looked at the photos again, new details popping out at her. The snow suit John was wearing in the preschool-aged picture, for instance: it was old, tearing at the seams, white batting oozing out at the shoulders, the knees. In the elementary school picture, she suddenly saw the dirt smudged on John's young face, the baby-fat gut hanging below the too-short T-shirt, the patches on the knees of his jeans. And in the high school picture, John was sitting on the lawn next to a house with peeling white siding, a crazily angled back stoop.

And suddenly it was all rushing out of her—everything she'd been trying to hold back the past few days, since John had turned up dead. All the sadness. All the grief. It didn't have to be like this. He could've talked to her. He could've told her the truth about what he'd come from, about who he was. She wouldn't have judged him for it, wouldn't have stopped loving him. If anything, it would've made her love him *more*, knowing what he'd fought to escape, how far he'd come to be what he was today. Regan thought about what it must have been like for him to lie for all those years, to lie and lie and lie, and then, when the lies began unraveling, to think that there was no way out but to end it all. To leave behind a wife and children—to leave them with a bag of money, and then to row out into the lake in the dead of night, tie a cinder block to his ankle, and then drop it in the water.

"Oh, honey," Darlene said. "You're crying."

"I'm okay," Regan said, drawing the back of her wrist across her eyes. "I am."

"Do you need a tissue?" Darlene dug through her purse once more, but Regan waved away the offer.

"Who's *we?*" she asked.

Darlene blinked, putting down her purse. "Sorry?"

"You said, 'We lived on the edge of poverty.' Who's *we?*"

"Oh. Me and Casey, and his brother Randy."

"And John's father?" Regan asked.

Darlene made a pained expression. "Casey didn't really know his daddy. He wasn't around much. One of those truckers. He'd stop through sometimes on a haul, stay a night. Give us some money, bounce the boys on his knee. We'd see him twice, three times a year. He stopped coming when Casey was about two. I'm ashamed to say we weren't married, their daddy and me. My boys were born out of wedlock, which could be a point of gossip up there, where we were from. But they have the same daddy, Randy and Casey do. I can say that at least. And I've found the Lord since those bad days. I've asked forgiveness for my sins. Praise God for that. You and Casey, are you believers? Are my grandbabies baptized?"

Regan ignored the question, not so much because she didn't want to answer (Etta and Philip had been baptized Lutheran, though they went to church only twice a year, at Christmas and Easter), but because she was growing dizzy, disoriented with all the information Darlene was giving her. What she now knew of John's life felt like little more than points on a blank piece of paper. She knew that he had been a boy named Casey, growing up impoverished in the middle of nowhere; that he'd later shown up in her life as a struggling young financial adviser named John Peters. But she couldn't gather these bits of data into a coherent story, couldn't draw an arc between these dots that led to the man she'd known.

"When did he leave?" Regan asked.

"He didn't exactly *leave*," Darlene said. "Well, he did, but it wasn't a send-off with a big tearful goodbye or anything. He just sort of disappeared. It's a bit of a story, actually."

"I'm listening," Regan said.

Darlene was quiet before she began, settling herself where she sat. She set down her purse by her feet, then reached for the steaming mug on the coffee table. She grabbed at the paper tab of the tea bag, lifted the bag in and out of the water a couple times, then set it on the saucer Regan had brought out with the mugs. Darlene brought the tea to her chest and settled back against the cushions, sank deep into them.

"The thing you have to understand about my boys," she began, "is that they were as different as night and day. They had the same daddy, and they looked a lot alike—they looked like brothers—but in terms of how they acted, who they were deep down, they couldn't have been more different. Casey was a pleaser. The kind of kid who always liked to be on good terms with everybody. Who'd get real upset if he thought that anyone was angry with him. He followed all the rules, made sure that whatever he did, it was just right. Just what people wanted him to be doing. Whether that was me or his teachers at school. He almost never misbehaved. But oh, if he ever did something wrong, it would suddenly be, *I'm sorry I'm sorry I'm sorry, don't be mad at me*, crying and crying until you were the one apologizing to him just to get the poor kid to stop beating himself up. I never had to punish Casey. Never had to whup him, never had to send him to his room. Because he always punished himself."

"And your other son?" Regan asked. "Randy?"

"Randy was my wild one," Darlene said. "Always pushing the limits. Anything I said, he did the opposite. Little things at first. Kid things. Not eating his supper, not doing his chores. Getting into things he wasn't supposed to be in. Breaking things. But then when he was about eight or nine years old, it started to be more serious with Randy. I barely saw him anymore. He'd disappear from the house for days. I wouldn't even know where he was sleeping. And then someone would drag him into the store by the scruff of the neck, tell me they caught him doing something or other. Stealing, usually. A trucker, a tourist, a hiker, or a camper. Going through their stuff, looking for money, for valuables. Things he could sell. A lot of the time he got caught, and without much law enforcement up there, the people he was trying to steal from would just take care of things themselves. Bring him in to me sometimes. Or rough him up a little themselves. Try to teach him a lesson."

"They'd beat up a child?" Regan asked.

"It's a lot of rough folks who end up there, like I said. People with old-fashioned ways of handling things. Besides, a lot of what I'm talking about, he was getting to be not so much of a child anymore. It was hard for me to keep track of Randy, like I said, but I'd hear rumors—gas stations or liquor stores a ways down south getting robbed, houses broken into. And I'd wonder— maybe that's Randy. He'd come back sometimes, every couple weeks or so, every month, and he'd sometimes bring stuff with him. Money. Or things: lamps, watches, pieces of jewelry. He'd tell me to sell them secondhand, or pawn them the next time I got down as far as Duluth. I'm a little ashamed to say I took them. I needed the help—needed the money to keep from going hungry. To keep feeding Casey. To keep the heat on. It gets plenty cold up there, you know. I had my reasons, but I'm still not proud of it. It's another thing I've had to ask forgiveness for. From the Lord. Supporting Randy's sins like that. Letting him stray. God help me, I've made some mistakes." She lifted a hand, raised her eyes to the ceiling.

"And John's disappearance?" Regan asked, prodding Darlene on.

"Yes," Darlene said, her gaze dropping again. "I don't know everything about that night. Nobody does, really. But Casey left the house one day. Looking for his brother."

Darlene paused to take a sip of tea. Regan felt her hand quiver, her heartbeat pulse in her wrists. Her breaths were shallow, almost as though she was afraid to make any sound.

"Casey looked up to Randy, you see. He was the older brother—only by a year, but still. Casey was a homebody, a goody-goody, a kid who played it safe. But Randy was the risk-taker. The macho one. And I suppose Casey might have wished that he was a little more like Randy. That he was brave like his big brother was."

"What happened?" Regan asked, her voice barely above a whisper.

"It seems that Randy got it in his head to stick up a store," Darlene said. "A little place along the highway catering to tourists—gifts and camping supplies and, oh, smoked fish and whatnot. You know, the kind of everything-but-the-kitchen-sink store you get in a tourist area. But they only took cash, and Randy must've known they'd be flush with it around closing time, and he took his little brother along with him as a kind of test. To toughen him up, you know? The way boys do. Randy was eighteen. Casey was seventeen. Boys, still."

Darlene shook her head, heaved the kind of sigh that Regan recognized—a sigh of motherly disappointment, of a woman who just can't *believe* what her children have done, that they could be so stupid.

"Randy had a gun," Darlene said. "And I guess it went off. Nobody knows how. The shop owner, he had a gun, a sawed-off he kept under the front register, but he didn't go for it—it was still strapped to the underside of the counter when the cops showed up."

"He died?" Regan asked in a hush.

Darlene closed her eyes. "Yes. An old man. Just a harmless old man who'd owned that business for years. A family man. Bled out before the police even came. Before they could get an ambulance to him."

"And then what?" Regan asked. "How did Casey disappear?"

"There was an accident," Darlene said. "A car accident. They found Randy in the driver's seat fifteen miles away. He'd gone too fast, lost control, flipped the car. But Casey wasn't there. When Randy got pulled up for it, went to court for the crime, what the prosecutors tried to say was that he'd killed Casey, actually; tried to make it into a double murder. Their theory was that Casey threatened to tell what Randy had done and then Randy shot him, dumped his body in the woods, maybe even buried it, then flipped the car in the getaway. But they couldn't make it stick. They couldn't find a body. So Randy went up for killing the old man, and that was it."

"Did they list Casey as a missing person?" Regan asked.

"I suppose maybe they did," Darlene said. "But nobody seemed to look for him too hard. I think everyone thought he was dead somewhere. Besides, who cares about some poor kid from out of nowhere? And I didn't have any money to hire a private investigator. Some people suggested it, some of my friends, but I couldn't afford it. I could barely afford to keep myself alive, what with Randy and Casey no longer bringing in any money."

"Casey earned money too?" Regan asked. She noted with a bit of surprise that she'd fallen into calling him by his real name, *Casey*, instead of *John*.

"He worked part-time at a resort about a half hour down the shore," Darlene said. "Odd jobs, cleaning up, doing little repairs. It wasn't much money. Not as much as Randy brought in. Crime pays better than honest work, it turns out."

Regan sniffed. Maybe it did. If so, it was a lesson John had learned a little too well.

"Randy got out recently, actually," Darlene said. "About a year ago. On parole."

She set down her tea and began riffling through photos again.

"I wish I'd brought a picture of him. These are all of Casey. I figured those were the ones you'd want to see. And the kids, those grandbabies; I thought they'd want to see their daddy as a boy. I still wouldn't mind meeting them, you know, if—oh, wait. Here's one. A picture of Randy."

Darlene flipped it down onto the table, pushed it across with her index finger.

"It's of both of them, actually: Randy and Casey. From a time when we all got down to Duluth. I brought them to J.C. Penney's, did one of those photo shoots. I saved for months, for the shots and for the boys' outfits. I think they turned out nice."

Regan reached for the photograph. It was larger than the others, portrait sized. She guessed the boys were around eight or nine. John—*Casey*, Regan corrected herself—sat on a block covered by a velvety throw blanket. He wore a sweater that looked like it might have been hand knit. A white button-down poking above the neckline, a ring of grime around the collar.

Next to him, standing, was the older brother, leaning against Casey with his elbow on the younger boy's shoulder. He wore a similar outfit, but what struck Regan—what sucked all the breath from her lungs and caused her to drop the photo to the ground—was the boy's face. His face and the mental image of the man he might've grown into.

Regan had seen him before.

CHAPTER 16

Regan hit the road just an hour later, before noon. She didn't pack anything—no change of clothes, no food, not even a bottle of water to drink in the car. Her mind was too full, too addled, to think of anything she might need over the next few hours. Anything she'd forgotten, she could buy along the way.

She climbed in the car, set the address on her phone, then started the route. She backed down the driveway too quickly, rocking back and forth onto the street, the bottom of her car scraping at the curb. Then she threw it into drive, jerked forward with a staccato squeal. She got on 494, then exited to Interstate 35, going north. It was a simple route from here: I-35 to Duluth, then onto State Highway 61, skirting Lake Superior's northern shore across rugged terrain until she reached an unnamed clutch of houses and a couple stores just a few miles from Canada. The tiny, unmapped outpost where John—where *Casey*—had grown up.

She called her mother from the car.

"Can you take the kids overnight?"

"What's that, dear?"

"I need you to keep the kids. Overnight."

"Well, I suppose. Though I'm not sure we have—"

"Thanks," Regan said, stabbing the call silent with her finger and then turning off the phone.

She didn't notice the white repair van a few car lengths behind her. Didn't notice that it had been parked a few houses down from hers, that it had been following her since she'd left, that it was keeping pace with her now.

She was too busy thinking.

Thinking about what she'd do when she got where she was going. What she'd say.

Thinking about everything Darlene had told her.

———————

"What's wrong?" the older woman, Regan's mother-in-law, had asked after Regan dropped the photo to the floor.

"You said Randy got out of jail," Regan said. "A year ago? Where did he go after that? Did he come here? To the city?"

"No, he's living on some land my daddy owned. It's mine now, I guess, has been for years, but I always think of it as my daddy's land. I'd sell it, but I don't think anyone would want it. It's not really worth anything. Randy's there, in a little cabin—almost a shack, really. I wanted him to live with me, but he's gone a little reclusive since he got out."

"Does he go anywhere?" Regan said. "Is it possible he came here without you knowing?"

"I passed the cabin maybe two weeks ago," Darlene said. "Randy's truck was gone. He might've gone somewhere. But it was back again yesterday when I went to tell him that I might've found Casey, that I saw someone who looked just like him on a news story from down in the cities. He wouldn't answer the door, though. Like I said, he's a bit of a—"

"What's the address?" Regan cut in.

Darlene squinted at Regan, but told her how to find the cabin anyway, wrote some directions on a pad Regan slid across the coffee table.

"Do you have somewhere to stay?" Regan asked when she had what she wanted.

"I got a hotel," Darlene said.

"I've got some things to do," Regan said. "I hate to hurry you out the door, but…"

It felt urgent to get the woman out of her house. Regan could hardly wait for her to leave. She burst to her feet, unable to sit still any longer. It was suddenly clear what she had to do, where she had to go. This was it, the confrontation she'd been destined for ever since the FBI showed up on her doorstep to tell her the truth about her husband. It had all been leading to this. The answers she'd been seeking—who John was, what he'd done, what had really happened on the lake and on a dark abandoned road two decades ago—these answers weren't here, in the city. They were out there. In the woods. In the wilderness.

"I was hoping I'd get to meet those grandbabies of mine," Darlene said, annoyed. "I didn't even know I had grandbabies until a couple days ago."

Regan went to the front door, opened it, waited for Darlene to stand.

"You will," Regan said. "I'll set something up. I'll call you."

Darlene sighed, gathered up her photographs, and heaved herself to her feet.

Now Regan was driving, alternating between too fast and too slow, both wanting to get there as quickly as possible and afraid of getting pulled over. The buildings thinned as she drove north, shopping malls and big-box stores replaced by sprawling car dealerships, trucking lots, warehouses. And then she was free of the city completely, in the midst of trees that clustered so thickly around the two-lane road she was on that she couldn't see the interstate lanes heading the other way. The names of the towns attested to the growing ruggedness of the landscape: Pine City, Askov and Finlayson, Moose Lake, Otter Creek. And then the interstate veered, slid through a long flat expanse, and the trees opened and the ground dropped out to reveal the long slope of Duluth in front of her—houses clustered up on the hill, the docks and shipyards and piled mountains of ore and coal down below.

Regan stayed on the interstate through the city, took it all the way to its unceremonious end, where the sleek four lanes terminated in a stoplight. She skirted the big lake, the rocks and water visible between mansions of different eras: Victorian, Craftsman, contemporary. Soon she was on the next road, State Highway 61, which hugged the lake's shore all the way to Canada. Regan pictured a map, remembered how Superior always looked like a wolf's head to her. She was on the nose right now; she'd drive up between the wolf's eyes to the middle of its forehead. She had two hours yet to go.

The landscape grew still more sparse, more rugged. Forests, rock formations. Here and there along the highway there were resorts: cabins, lodges. Gift shops selling snow globes, agates, smoked fish. The road twisted, tunneled here and there through salmon-colored rock. The views were breathtaking. She went through Two Harbors, passed Gooseberry Falls, Split Rock, Temperance River. In Grand Marais she stopped for gas, a bottle of water, a protein bar, and a banana. Then she kept on going.

She was maybe fifteen minutes away from the turnoff in the directions Doreen had given her when she rounded a curve and an object leapt out in the lower-right corner of her vision. A large rock, maybe about the size of a person's head, at the side of the road. Regan swerved, but it was too late: her right front wheel caught the rock, bringing a thundering crack. The impact shook the whole vehicle. The car continued rolling down the road, but it was juddering dangerously.

Regan's stomach sank. She slowed to forty, then thirty, then twenty, but still the car shimmied, parts clanking and scraping around somewhere beneath her feet.

She pulled off into a scenic overlook. They were everywhere on this road—overlooks, historical markers, lake access points. The car rolled into a gravel parking lot with spaces marked off by boulders. Past the parking area was a shelter, a square brown kiosk with placards warped by rain, and a little stone path through the pine trees to a rocky shore.

Regan got out and came around to look at the tire. Flat, as she'd feared. The rim had gone concave on one side where it had hit the rock; she'd need to pay for a new one. There could be something wrong with the axle, too; the terrible scraping sound had to have come from more than just a shredded tire.

Regan looked at the sky. It was still light out, but it wouldn't be for too much longer—an hour, maybe two. She couldn't drive the car, but she was too far from any town to walk. It would get cold soon. She pulled her thin jacket close, feeling the frigid wind off the lake cutting right through the fleece.

She checked her phone: no bars.

"Shit," she said.

Then there came the low groan of an engine, of wheels crunching gravel, and Regan looked up. A black sedan rolled toward her.

"Oh thank *Jesus*," she muttered to herself and began walking slowly to the car, waving with both hands.

The driver's door opened and Agent Armstrong climbed out.

Regan froze.

He came toward her, leaving his door hanging open behind him.

"What's going on, Regan?" he asked. "Why are we all the way out here?"

"I can explain."

"You can explain," Armstrong said. He drew in a breath, looked off toward the lake, where the horizon disappeared in a gray haze. He dropped his head and gave it a shake. "You always have an explanation, don't you?"

"I came here to find something," Regan said.

"You mean the Canadian border?" Armstrong said. "We're about thirty minutes from it, aren't we? Looks to me like you're making a run for it."

"Without my kids? Come on. You know I wouldn't do that."

"I don't think I know you very well at all. You lied to me, Regan. You made me stick my neck out for you. And now you're making me look like an idiot."

"Just listen. Could you listen? John grew up around here. Really. The truth about him—it's here."

Armstrong put up a hand. "Enough. I'm done listening to you. Giving me wine, pouring out your sob story. You manipulated me."

"I didn't manipulate you. I'm telling you the truth. I've always told you the truth."

"Save it," Armstrong spat. "I'm bringing you in. Whatever you came here to find, it'll have to wait."

Armstrong dug his cell phone from his pocket and turned it on.

"What are you doing?" Regan asked.

"I just have to check in with my superiors. Let them know where we are, when we'll be back in the city." He dialed, put the phone to his ear, then pulled it away and looked at the screen again, squinting.

"There's no coverage here," Regan said. "I was going to call Triple-A, but—"

Armstrong put up a finger to silence her and walked away, lifting up his phone to find a signal. "Wait here," he called back, wandering off the gravel and into the grass, toward the lake.

Regan stood where she was, watched Armstrong walk ten, twenty, then more than thirty feet away. She heard him muttering, cursing the bad reception. Eventually, her eyes wandered to his car. Why was it that these FBI guys always drove black cars—black SUVs, black sedans? The door was still hanging open, she noted. Her eyes sharpened. Armstrong had come out of the car fast, rushing to catch up with her. The car was still running.

Her mind drifted up the road, to the remote cabin Doreen had told her about. She was so close. Armstrong would be furious at her when he caught up with her—but he was furious at her now. No matter what she did, she was in trouble. She'd have to talk herself out of something either way. And she'd come this far. She might as well try to make it the last few miles, see what revelations lay waiting for her.

She at least had to try.

She gave one more glance at Armstrong—his back was turned, the phone to his ear—then she bolted. The gravel slid under the soles of her shoes and she almost went to her knees, but she managed to keep her feet. Halfway to the door she heard Armstrong shout, heard his footsteps begin to pound on the grass, but she kept going. She was almost there.

She threw herself into the driver's seat and pulled the door closed. A fraction of a second later Armstrong was there, his palms slamming on the glass. She scrambled for the lock as he went for the door handle; the locks thudded on just a moment before he got his hand under the latch and pulled up.

"Fuck!" he yelled, pounding the glass.

Regan glanced around her, then saw the car's key fob in the cup holder next to her. He'd left it behind, just as she'd hoped.

"Regan," Armstrong said, his voice muffled, "don't do this. Be smart, Regan. Don't make it worse for yourself."

She backed the car into the lot, gravel crunching under the tires. Armstrong advanced, keeping himself in front of the front bumper, waving his arms, preventing her from moving forward and getting out of the parking lot. Instead she gunned it even further in reverse, to the back entrance of the parking lot, then threw the car into drive and turned sharply to the left, exiting the lot through the entrance before Armstrong could run to reach her.

She saw him in the rearview as she pulled onto the highway, running toward the road then slowing as she gained speed. He stood and watched her go. Then the road curved, brought the car around the other side of a rock face, and the next time she looked in the mirror, Armstrong was gone.

She was alone again.

———————

She'd left her phone in her car, which meant no more GPS—but she remembered the directions that Darlene had given her. She passed slowly through the outpost John had grown up in. Darlene had been right; it wasn't much to look at. A couple warehouses and squat commercial buildings; a half dozen ramshackle houses, each either neglected or abandoned. One house had a square little shop attached in a single-story wing, a gas pump outside. That must have been the general store. John's house. Or Casey's—he'd never lived there as John. John had been the man he'd created to get out of this place.

A mile out of town she made a turn onto an unmarked gravel road. She drove for a while, trees so close on either side that there were times she feared the road would simply disappear and she'd be driving in the forest, unable to find her way out. But then the trees opened up into a little open space, and she saw it. The cabin.

It was a shack, really. A brown rectangle slapped together and elevated off the ground on cinder blocks. Angles not quite right, sagging in the middle. Three crooked steps leading up to a scratched white door.

Outside the shack was a truck so rusted Regan couldn't say with any certainty what its original color had been. She pulled Armstrong's black sedan up next to the truck, then got out of the car, taking the keys with her. She paused for a second, considering whether this was a good idea—whether she should just get back in the car and drive away. Face the consequences with Armstrong. Never know the truth.

Then she walked up the steps and knocked three times on the door.

"Hello? Is anyone home?"

No answer. Not even movement.

She knocked again.

"It's me. Regan. I'm—oh, just answer the door. Just talk to me. I know you're in there."

She waited. Listened.

After a couple seconds' silence, she heard something. A rustle. Creaking footsteps. A hand on the doorknob.

The door opened, and there he was. Alive.

"Hello, John," she said.

PART 2

CHAPTER 17

People always said they looked like twins. Travelers would come off the road—tourists looking for gifts for the folks back home, truckers looking for coffee or caffeine pills to keep them awake on a long midnight haul, campers or hikers looking for replacement supplies, a lantern or a compass or a pocket knife. They'd scan the general store's shelves, looking disappointed by the paltry selection, and then, sometimes, their eyes would fall on the boys. Randy and Casey. Half-feral, greasy hair mussed up, dirt around their ears, holes in their shirts and blue jeans. They'd frown.

"They look so alike," they'd say, then turn to Darlene. "Are they twins?"

"Yes," Darlene would say. "The Irish kind." And then she'd laugh.

Casey hated the joke, cringed every time she made it. The joke reminded him of sex, of the fact that his mother was having it, which no boy wanted to think about. It made him think about the strange men off the road who sometimes came to his mother's room, of the creaking and moaning sounds that came through the thin walls at night, of the groceries that filled the fridge and the cupboards the next day. (*Fucking*, Randy told him on one of those creaking, moaning nights. *That's what it's called.*) Casey was only ten months younger than his big brother, and he knew exactly how that had happened: their dad, a trucker who hauled timber from Canada to paper mills in Wisconsin, paid extra to... to *fuck* Darlene without a condom. Then, not even a month after Randy was born, he came through on another haul and paid to fuck her again.

That was his story—the story of how he came into the world. He hated it.

Casey also hated the fact that people could confuse him and Randy, that people could think them anything alike. Casey was quiet, thoughtful, even (he thought, and his teachers said) *special*. He liked to read, to draw—to ponder, imagine, and dream. Randy was the opposite: brash where Casey was shy, rough where Casey was soft. He spent most of his time outside: fishing, hunting, breaking windows, playing with matches. Slicing open roadkill and poking at the entrails, scattering roofing nails on the highway and hiding in the ditch to watch the blowouts, tying toads to M90 firecrackers and lighting the fuse. Randy's word for Casey was "pussy"; he used it more than he used Casey's name. Randy got into even rougher activities as he grew; fighting and stealing and getting blackout drunk—even as Casey threw himself into school, into books, hitching rides to the community library, where he'd spend hours at a time just sitting, reading, surfing the internet. Anything to keep from going home.

But because he and Randy looked so much alike, it was as though Casey had a shadow self roaming around in the wilderness outside, a doppelgänger sowing chaos while wearing a face that looked almost identical to his own. Casey felt, at times, as though he was in two places at once. And when, years later, Randy got out of prison and tracked him down in the city, seeing his face felt like looking through a portal to an alternate reality:

the person Casey might have been if he hadn't gotten away, hadn't climbed out of that truck and disappeared into the night. Casey had spent most of his life trying to get away from Randy, adopting names and identities to put as much distance between them as he could. But now here he was again, and on some level, John (sometimes he forgot his own name, he'd had so many) knew it would always come down to this—a confrontation with the true, secret, and shameful self he'd managed to outrun, for a time, but could never truly escape.

But now he was getting ahead of himself.

CHAPTER 18

As a boy Casey stocked shelves in the general store, worked the front register, swept the floors. But as soon as he was old enough he took a job that took him out of the house, down the road a couple miles to a small resort with boxy little cabins tucked into the rocks along the shore. In the summers Casey would walk to work each day, his shoes crunching in the gravel of the highway shoulder, trucks whipping by just five feet away. At the resort he'd cut the grass. He'd chop firewood and tie bundles together with orange twine for guests to buy. He'd cut brush, clean cabins, scrub the bottoms of the rental canoes and kayaks.

The owner paid him in cash; less than minimum wage, but since they paid him under the table they weren't withholding any taxes either, so he came out ahead. This is what they told him. He didn't spend any of the money. Instead he stashed it, wrapped it with a rubber band and tucked it in a rust-pocked coffee can he kept under his bed. He'd count it sometimes at night, taking pleasure in the feel of the edges of the bills against his fingertips, the numbers counting up above five hundred. It was his getting-away money; someday he'd use it to leave this place, start a new life somewhere else.

Casey observed the guests, watched them as they drove in with their gleaming, unrusted cars and parked on the asphalt pads next to their cabins. The license plates mostly said Minnesota, but sometimes he saw other states too. Casey wondered at their lives, made up stories for them. The men were gruff and confident, the women tanned, the children—if they had them—loud and scrubbed so clean they were almost pink. They weren't rich, probably, but they had money, more money than Casey or anyone he'd ever known. They'd have thought his coffee-can stash paltry. After a few days, a week, or a long holiday weekend, they'd leave, drive away to the lives that were waiting for them back home. While Casey stayed. Worked. And kept saving.

Once, a guest noticed him. A girl. It happened while he was washing the dock, scrubbing it slippery with a bowl of soapy water and a hard-bristled push broom. He was just finishing up, preparing to start up the power washer to rinse the suds off the slats, when he sensed a presence behind him. He turned, and saw her.

She was his age—sixteen, maybe seventeen. Dirty blond hair pulled back, blue-gray eyes, thin lips that were just a little bit shiny. Casey had seen this before and always wondered how girls did it, made their lips gleam, made them sparkle. She wore a baggy hooded sweatshirt that hung around her waist, shorts so short Casey thought at first she wasn't wearing any pants. Long tanned legs that he allowed himself to glance at, then darted his eyes away.

"Hi," he said. "Can I help you?"

"No," the girl said, "I'm just bored. Wandering around."

"Oh," Casey said. He examined the handle of his push broom, not quite knowing what to say. "Are you here with your family?"

"My mom and dad," the girl said. "They don't want to do anything. Just sit and watch the lake."

Casey looked out at the water, let his eyes move all the way from the waves crashing against the rocks to the place on the far horizon where the sky met the lake in a muddled blur of gray haze.

"It's pretty, isn't it though?" Casey asked. "Guests like it, watching the lake. Listening to the sound of the water. They find it relaxing."

"I guess," the girl said. "They're just sitting there and reading."

"Don't you like to read?" Casey asked.

The girl frowned. "I read enough in school."

"Like what?"

"Oh, I don't know. *To Kill a Mockingbird. The Great Gatsby.*"

"I read those," Casey said. He'd been enchanted by *The Great Gatsby*, sympathizing with Gatsby's plight, with the gleaming, untouchable life he'd wanted to build for himself in that house at the edge of the water. He'd even cried a little at his ultimate fate, and at the last line, "*boats against the current, borne back ceaselessly into the past.*" His teacher had challenged him, asked if Gatsby was really a character worth looking up to, and in the end she'd told him about another book that he later looked up in the community library, *The Talented Mr. Ripley*, about a man who lied and stole and killed his way into a life of unimaginable luxury. Casey understood. Jay Gatsby wasn't necessarily a tragic hero; looked at a different way, he was a villain, like Tom Ripley. That was his teacher's point, the reason she'd recommended the book. It could be dangerous, running away from who you were, because there was no telling what you'd become in the process. Still, Casey couldn't help but admire these men, Gatsby and even Ripley, who'd escaped poverty and humiliation for a better life of money, and parties, and traveling the world.

"I'm Tricia, by the way," the girl said.

"Casey." He set down the push broom and began rinsing off the dock, using the low setting on the power washer so they could still hear each other. So they could still talk.

"Is there anything to *do* around here?" Tricia asked, speaking just a little bit louder over the sound of the washer.

Casey flicked his wrist back and forth, rinsing the bubbles off the dock and into the water, thinking. Based on her attitude toward reading, Casey didn't think she'd be very impressed to hear that the only thing he really did—when he wasn't working or at school—was go to the library, find a book in the stacks, and pore through it until closing time. He didn't like being home, didn't like talking to his mother or hearing her questions, so he never checked the books out, never even bothered getting a library card, only read while he was there, put the book back on the shelf, and remembered the page number he'd left off at for when he came back.

"Grand Marais isn't too far," he said. "There's stuff to do there."

"Like what?"

"Restaurants and stuff. Shops. Art galleries. You could go on a hike around here; there are lots of trails. Or I could rent you a kayak, show you how to use it. Water isn't too rough today."

He glanced at Tricia to see how she was taking these suggestions. She wrinkled up her nose with distaste and he forced himself to laugh, like he knew everything he was suggesting was lame and he was just testing her to see if she was cool or not. Like he hadn't even gotten to the real stuff yet. The good stuff.

Tricia saw his face and asked, "What?"

Casey shut off the washer and began telling her stories.

Stories about Randy.

He told the stories as if they were his own. Told about how he sometimes fought other boys for money in an older guy's backyard a few miles up the road; fought in front of a hooting crowd until one of them either gave up or got knocked out; fought guys ten years older and twice his size and won, every time.

He told Tricia about how to get booze, how to get a fake ID, where the best parties were, who sold the best pot.

He told her how to get high off a pressurized duster can from the gas station, fill a balloon up with the chemicals and suck them into your lungs; told her how to juice up cough syrup or cold medicine and end up with something pretty close to meth.

He told her that he sometimes broke into houses—half the homes around here were vacation homes anyway, empty half the year, and full of amazing stuff. Told her how you can just live in them for weeks at a time, sleep on their thousand-thread-count sheets, drink their fancy booze, then bug out with all their TVs and pawnable jewelry.

"Don't tell," Casey said. "I'll kill you if you tell." And then he laughed, like it was just a joke, and Tricia laughed too, light and airy, and he could tell he was scaring her a little bit—scaring her and impressing her, which was what he wanted.

They didn't do any of the things he suggested that day—didn't go walk on a bridge railing blindfolded, didn't hot-wire a car and take it joyriding, flipping the headlights on and off as they hurtled through the darkness—but over the next few days Tricia kept coming back, kept appearing over his shoulder as he worked around the resort, and each time she did, he gave her another of Randy's stories, presented it as though it was something that had happened to him.

Sometimes he'd ask Tricia about what it was like back home. She was from Minneapolis ("Edina, actually," she corrected herself), and she insisted that it was all pretty dull—that mostly she and her friends would go to the mall, go to each other's houses, watch movies, try to get their hands on booze, mess around. Sometimes they'd go to a concert or a show, one of their parents playing chaperone. It sounded amazing to him, but Tricia insisted it was boring.

"Cool," Casey said, as if he understood—things were boring pretty much everywhere. When the whole world was yours for the taking, you had the luxury of thinking it was boring. "Cool."

———————

New guests checked in the next day, in a sleek Lexus SUV. Two adults, a teenage boy. Casey scarcely noticed them, rushed through his work for the day—cleaning two cabins that had just been cleared by customers checking out, cutting the grass on the north lawn, rewinding the line on the weed trimmer, replacing empty propane tanks on the gas grills the guests used when they had a steak or fish fillet they wanted to cook. Then he went looking for Tricia.

He encountered her dad instead, sitting on the deck outside their cabin with a laptop and a clear glass, a finger of brown liquid sloshing around in the bottom.

"Can I help you?" he grunted, looking up. He was a gruff man, intimidating—some sort of banker, Tricia had said. Dark hair, broad shoulders, a big gut that he didn't seem the least ashamed of, carried it like it was a sort of birthright. His wife was thin, athletic, always out on hikes. She was kind of hot, actually; Casey saw where Tricia had gotten her looks from, and he was awed by this man's ability to keep his wife while evidently letting himself go: a plump monarch in a kingdom of beautiful women.

"I was looking for Tricia," Casey said. He and Tricia's father hadn't spoken before; Casey had only overheard the man speaking to the owner, his boss, demanding this and that amenity for their cabin.

"What do you want with Tricia?" the man asked, narrowing his eyes.

"She asked me a question," Casey said. "About some…trails. I found a map for her."

The man sat back in his chair. "You just missed her. She went off with that boy who just checked in. Paul, I think his name was." He turned back to his computer. He was probably answering work emails, Casey thought. An important man. He lifted a finger without looking up from his screen and gestured vaguely toward the woods. "That way."

Casey walked. Skirted the rocks leading down to the shore, then made for the trees. He didn't have to go very far; they'd only barely walked out of sight of the cabins.

Tricia was on her back, the boy on top of her, kissing her, his hand slid up the inside of those long tanned legs, right to the top of her inner thigh. At first Casey thought she was in trouble, that she didn't want what was happening, and his blood surged in his veins, but then he saw that Tricia's hands were up around the boy's neck, pulling his mouth against hers.

He stopped. A twig broke underneath his feet. The boy's head snapped back toward him.

"The fuck, bro?" the boy asked, his eyes sharp with the quick fury of an adolescent male interrupted while hormones raged through his body.

Tricia's shoulders came off the ground; she propped herself up on her elbows. Her ponytail was undone, the hair mussed, leaves and twigs tangled in the strands. Her cheeks were red.

"Casey," she said, breathy with surprise. "I—this is Paul. We were just—"

"Get the fuck out of here," Paul demanded.

"I'm sorry," Casey said, backing away.

As he walked away, he heard light laughter coming from the trees. Murmuring. Rustling. Then silence.

Casey walked home, cursing his stupidity. It was a four-mile walk, forty-five minutes on foot most days, but it seemed to go faster today. He kept picturing it, the sight of Tricia on her back with Paul on top of her. The hand curled up on the inside of her thigh, so casual, like he'd done it dozens of times before. Tricia's surprise in seeing Casey, the speed with which they'd gotten rid of him.

And then he looked up and there was the town, there was the general store, the attached house. He walked around to the back, not wanting to see his mother behind the register inside, and went to his bedroom. He lay on the bed, laced his hands behind his head.

What hurt the most in retrospect was how quickly it had happened. Paul and his family had checked in…what? Two hours earlier? Three? And yet it had taken him and Tricia no time at all to find each other, to go to a spot in the woods, to start making out. Maybe they'd even had sex by now, if Paul had convinced Tricia to do it outside, and if they didn't, they would soon; they'd find a room, a bed, a stretch of time when his family or hers wasn't in their cabin. Whereas Casey had spent days talking to Tricia, telling her stories—God, those fucking stories. He cringed thinking of them now, wanted to die so he'd never have to remember the things he'd said. He couldn't believe how foolish he had been, thinking that the stories would impress her, that he'd ever be anything more than a curiosity to her.

With a kind of involuntary movement, he lurched to the side of the bed, reached underneath, and grabbed for the coffee can. Payday wasn't until next week. The money would be the same as it was the last time he counted it—seven hundred and eighty-three dollars. He wanted to count it anyway. It calmed him to have the bills in his hand, to feel the pile growing, the day of his escape coming nearer and nearer.

He knew something was wrong the moment he laid his hand on the coffee can. The weight of it was different. He snatched it up to the top of the bed, ripped the plastic lid off, and looked inside.

It was empty.

His mind raced: Randy was the first person he thought of, but that couldn't be right; Randy hadn't been home in days, weeks even. Which only left one other person.

"Mom!" he shouted as he stomped into the general store from the side door, the one that connected from the house.

Darlene startled at the front register; she'd been reading a *People* magazine, elbows propped on the counter. There were no customers.

"Where the fuck is my money?"

"Keep your voice down," Darlene said, glancing to the side as though someone was listening—as though they weren't completely alone.

"Seven hundred and eighty-three dollars," Casey demanded, practically crying. "I want it back. That's *my* money, Mom. I earned it. I worked hard for it. It's not yours, it's *mine*."

Darlene slumped, sighed with what sounded like real regret, real guilt—which only made Casey angrier.

"I needed it, Case," she said. "I needed it to stock up the store, and to pay the electric. I'll pay you back. I swear I will. As soon as business picks up."

"As soon as business picks up, Mom?" Casey yelled, his rage growing until it felt bigger than his body. He raised up his hands and looked around at the empty store, at the sparse shelves—she couldn't even afford to stock the business properly. "It's the height of tourist season. When is business going to pick up? When winter comes and we fucking freeze?"

Darlene reached for him across the counter. "I'll think of something."

Casey snatched his arm away. "You'll spread your legs, is what you'll do. Right? That's what you do when you need money, isn't it?"

Darlene's mouth went thin as she pressed her lips together. She looked down. "I don't know why you're saying these things to me."

"Except they're not coming anymore, are they?" Casey said. "Nobody wants you anymore. Now that you're old."

Darlene lifted a hand, shielded her face from Casey. "Are you trying to hurt me? Are you trying to hurt your mother?"

Casey couldn't see her eyes, but from the way she talked he knew she was crying.

Good.

He went out the front, let the door slam behind him. In the parking lot he paused, deciding what to do next. Then he crossed the highway and walked into the woods.

He was looking for Randy. His big brother. For the first time in his life, Casey actually wanted to find him.

Randy would know what to do.

CHAPTER 19

Casey threaded his way through the forest, stepped high to keep his ankles from tangling in the undergrowth, glanced down every once in a while to look for poison ivy. *Leaves of three*, the rhyme danced through his head, *let them be*. He hiked for about an hour, four miles inland, then the cabin emerged between the trees, rose up as if out of the ground.

It had been his granddaddy's cabin, but they'd let it go to seed since he'd died. The rocky patch of land it sat on was basically worthless, and the cabin wasn't much more than four clapboard walls slapped together. Randy was hard to find most days, went weeks at a time without coming home, but if he was anywhere, Casey knew, he was here.

Casey pounded on the door. "It's me!" he yelled, then walked in without waiting for an answer.

The smell was the first thing to hit him. Must and shit and damp. He blinked, his eyes adjusting slowly to the dim, and then he took in the wreckage. It was a single room, the concrete floor scattered with trash. There were only two pieces of furniture: a card table with a hot plate on it, and a brown padded recliner, the upholstery torn and the guts spilling out. It took Casey a moment to realize that Randy was there, asleep on the recliner, his head lolled to the side and a trail of drool running down from the corner of his mouth. A half-full handle of Evan Williams and a twelve-pack's worth of Busch Light empties lay scattered around the recliner, and a pile of porno magazines slumped against the side of the chair with the pull bar. Behind the recliner, on the wall, Randy had drawn a target in black marker; the wood was pocked with straight gashes, and right now a couple knives and a hatchet were embedded hilt deep, nowhere close to the bull's-eye.

Casey cleared his throat. "Randy," he said quietly, then more loudly when his brother didn't so much as move: "Randy!"

The older boy startled awake, and suddenly Casey found himself with a gun in his face.

"Who is it?" Randy demanded of the darkness. "Who the fuck is it?"

Casey's arms shot up and he squinched his eyes shut, certain that he was about to be shot through the forehead. His legs shook and his bladder felt loose; good thing he'd taken a piss in the woods just before coming upon the cabin.

"It's me!" Casey screamed. "It's Casey! Don't shoot!"

There was silence. No gunshot. Casey was still alive. He cautiously opened his eyes, saw his brother blinking, rubbing the sleep from his eyes with the heel of the hand that held the pistol.

"Casey," Randy said. "Goddamn, you scared the everloving shit out of me."

"I'm sorry," Casey said.

"You can't sneak up on people like that," Randy said. "You could get yourself shot."

"You sleep with a gun?" Casey asked. "Aren't you afraid of shooting yourself?"

Randy grunted and rocked himself out of the chair. He set the gun on the table and then walked over to the corner of the room and pulled the elastic waist of his shorts down, leaned a hand against the wall, and began to piss into a white plastic bucket. Casey turned away and put the back of his wrist over his nose and mouth, gagging at the smell that Randy's cascading urine was bringing up from the bottom of the bucket. Randy hocked up something from the back of his throat and spit it into the bucket as he shook himself off, finished up.

"What are you doing here?" he asked, turning around.

"Mom stole my money," Casey said.

"Shit. The money you make at that little resort place? How much?"

"More than seven hundred."

Randy was quiet. His muscles twitched. The way the light was falling, his face wasn't visible but his chest and arms were—a walking torso, an embodied threat of violence.

"That bitch," he said at last.

"And…" Casey added, then trailed off.

"What?" Randy asked.

Casey told him about what had happened at the resort. Tricia and the rich boy.

Randy walked over to the table and grabbed for the gun he'd been sleeping with. He grabbed something else with his other hand, tossed it toward Casey.

"Heads up," he said.

Casey barely caught it, something hard and smooth and cold. Another handgun.

"What's this for?" Casey asked.

"We're going shooting."

———

Casey was afraid Randy actually wanted to go out and kill

someone—their mother, maybe, or the rich kid, Paul—but he only meant target practice. He led Casey outside, walked around to the back of the cabin by an old fallen tree trunk. They set up the empty beer cans on top of it and tried to shoot them from a hundred feet away.

"So your first mistake," Randy said between clips, "was in going for a girl like that."

"I know," Casey said.

"A rich girl, a city girl," Randy continued. "She's never going to go for a shit-ass country kid. Not even one who's a brainy little pussy boy, like you are."

He slammed another clip in his handgun, a Glock 9mm. "You gonna shoot?" Randy asked.

Casey shook his head. "No, you go."

Randy lifted his hand, cigarette hanging from his lips, and fired off at least a dozen rounds. Four empty beer cans disappeared from the limb, flew into the air, and dropped somewhere in the woods.

Randy loosed the clip to the ground, then he turned back to Casey, took a long drag on his cigarette, then flicked it in the dirt as he exhaled the smoke through his nose. "See, the problem is, fancy girls like that, they like to be with their own kind. And they know you're not one of them. They can smell it on you. What you need, if you ever want a girl like that, is you gotta become one of them. A rich, fancy city kid. Until you do that, they're always going to smell it on you. Country poor. That shit's hard to shake. You know?"

"I know," Casey said. "That's what the money was for."

"What," Randy said, "the seven hundred Mom stole?"

"Seven hundred and eighty-three, actually."

"Whatever," Randy said. "It doesn't matter. That's nothing. Shit money. You really want to get out of here, make it so girls like

Tricia will drop their panties for you? You need to stop being a bitch, doing bitch work, getting bitch money."

"What did you have in mind?"

Randy sucked at his teeth, looked off into the distance.

"There's a store up the shore a ways," Randy said. "A tourist trap kind of place. They sell smoked fish—no joke, it's just a shitty little smokehouse—but don't laugh. They clean up during peak season. And they don't take credit cards, see? Cash only. I've been keeping an eye on the place a few weeks, and I swear they've gotta clear seven hundred, a thousand in a single day. Bring the money to the bank once a week, so the rest of the time it's just sitting there, piling up in the safe. And here's the thing— they make the bank run tonight. Tomorrow they start over again at zero. Tonight's the night when they've got the most cash in the building."

"How much?" Casey asked.

"I don't know exactly. Five thousand? Maybe more?"

Five thousand. Twenty-five hundred for each of them.

"So how come you haven't done it already?" Casey asked. "You've hit plenty of places before."

Randy grimaced. "It's a little busy around there is the problem. Lots of cars, people passing by even at closing time. If we hit it, it needs to be fast. You see?"

Casey blinked, shook his head. "I'm not really—"

"I need a driver," Randy said.

"A driver," Casey repeated.

"Yeah. Someone who's ready to hit the pedal as soon as I jump in."

Casey was quiet for a long moment, marveling at how quickly it had come to this, how quickly his mind had adapted. He felt like a different person than who he'd been that morning. What's more, it didn't even scare him. What he was contemplating, what

Randy was laying out for him, didn't seem outlandish. On the contrary—it seemed necessary. Logical. Even right.

"Okay," Casey said. "I can do that."

He cocked his gun, stretched out his arm, and fired toward the tree trunk. One of the beer cans disappeared, rocketed into the woods. Casey didn't see where it landed.

———

They took Randy's pickup, an old Chevy beater he'd once bought off someone in Two Harbors for less than five hundred dollars. Dark fell as they hurtled down Highway 61, and as the sky changed, so did Casey's mood. Suddenly he was regretting everything, and the truck's cab felt like a prison. As Randy slowed down to make a turn onto a winding smaller road, Casey eyed the door latch and wondered what would happen if he jumped out right now.

He stayed in the car, too afraid to move, to run. They reached the store a few minutes later: a single-story wood building with a roof that sloped in one direction, neon beer signs in the window, ice freezer out front, a gravel parking lot stretching all the way to the road.

A car was pulling out as they pulled in.

"They're closing," Randy said. He glanced at the time on the truck radio. "Right on time. Now the guy will take a few minutes to clean up, he'll empty the safe, put all the cash and change in a bag, then lock up and leave for the bank drop. That's when you need to go in. After he's opened the safe. That's when you'll be able to get in and out the fastest."

Unease dropped into Casey's stomach like a sugar pill and spread through his body. "What did you say?"

"You're going in." Randy reached across him, went for the glove box, and dug out a ski mask. "Put that on."

Casey's arms and legs went cold. "You said you needed a driver."

"It's time, brother. Time to pop your cherry."

Casey shook his head. "That wasn't the deal."

Randy nodded toward the store. "There he is, see him? Just a pathetic old man."

Casey looked, saw the man through the windowed front of the store. An old man, like Randy had said, maybe in his seventies, wiping down the counter.

"You want to be a pussy your whole life?" Randy asked. "You want girls to step out on you like you're nothing? You want your mommy to keep stealing your money because she knows she can—because you won't do a damn thing about it? Or do *you* want to be the one who takes? The one who takes what he wants and doesn't fucking apologize for it?"

Casey's body felt distant. It was as though his senses had dropped out—all but his hearing and his sight. He blinked and saw his vision go blurry. He was practically crying.

"I don't want to," he said, feeling like a little boy. A pathetic little boy. Randy had always forced him to do things he didn't want to do, for as long as he could remember: sat on his chest and punched his shoulder until he said something embarrassing like "I eat farts"; forced him to touch the carcasses of squirrels and raccoons and deer on the side of the highway; pressed a shoplifted bag of potato chips or a bottle of soda into his hands and made him carry it out of the Dollar General in his hoodie pouch. No matter what it was, Casey had always ended up doing it, so upset he'd practically hyperventilate right there, blinking back hot tears that stung his eyes.

"You're fucking doing this," Randy said now, and Casey looked at him to see that he was holding his gun at his side, his finger on the trigger. "You're doing it now."

Casey looked at his lap, at his own handgun and the ski mask. He took a breath, pulled the ski mask over his head.

"You go in shouting, okay?" Randy said. "The moment you open the door, you scream like a fucking monster. Scare the piss out of him. He won't dare to try anything. You'll be out in thirty seconds."

Casey stepped out of the car, the gun a dull weight in one hand. He walked toward the store, the movement feeling odd, sitting wrong in his body. He had to think about everything: step, step, step. Reach for the door handle. Pull.

A bell rang. Maybe he shouted, like Randy had told him to, or maybe he didn't. Maybe he was completely silent. Either way, the man behind the counter looked up, registered his presence with an almost eerie calm, like Casey was just another customer and not a kid in a ski mask with a gun.

The gun. Casey lifted it, pointed it at the man. Said something. A single word.

"Money."

The old man was still for a second. He wore a cap, a dusty collared shirt, overalls. Then he moved—so quickly. Went for something under the counter.

Casey didn't intend to fire the gun. But when he saw the man's hands go down under the counter, his whole body clenched at once, including the hand that held the gun, and it went off, almost as though it had become an extension of him, an animal thing that had lashed out in instinct. The sound of it roared in the close air of the shop, and the man staggered, grabbed on to the counter, a spot of red blooming through the dusty shirt. Then his grip on the edges of the counter slackened and he went to the ground.

Casey turned and ran.

"What did you do?" Randy asked when he got back to the truck. "I heard a shot."

"Get out of here," Casey said.

"Where's the money?"

Across the road, a woman had come out onto her lawn; a teenage clerk at the gas station next to the shop peered out the glass door to look for the source of the noise. One of them would call the cops, then it would all be over.

"Just go!" Casey shouted.

Randy threw the truck into gear. Gravel clattered in the wheel wells like a hailstorm, then the tires let out a screech as they hit the highway. The truck fishtailed, then straightened, and they were hurtling into the night.

Fleeing.

The needle on the truck's dashboard surged above sixty, seventy, eighty, then held.

"What the fuck did you do?" Randy demanded.

He wasn't watching the road. The truck drifted to the white line at the shoulder. A rattling hum shook the truck as the wheels went over the rumble strips. Randy pulled the wheel hard, brought the truck back to the center line. Casey's stomach lurched, his knuckles white on his knees.

"Watch the road," Casey said.

"I asked you a question," Randy said.

"He was going for a gun," Casey said. "He was going under the counter."

"Or maybe he was grabbing the fucking money," Randy said.

"You told me to go in there," Casey said. "You made me."

"I didn't think you'd lose your goddamn head."

The road unfurled ahead of them like a scroll. Past the headlights, all was dark. Further up, something flashed blue and red.

"Slow down," Casey said.

"The fuck you say?"

"Slow down!" Casey said louder and nodded forward. Randy looked, then Casey felt the truck slow as he pushed the brake, brought them down to fifty-five.

The police car, a state trooper, passed them doing at least eighty in the direction of the store. As soon as he was past, Randy sped up again.

"Where did you shoot him?" Randy demanded.

"*Where?*" Casey repeated, not understanding.

"On his body," Randy said. "Where did you get him?"

Casey closed his eyes, brought back the sight of the blood blooming beneath the dusty blue shirt. "His chest," Casey said.

"Goddammit, Case," Randy breathed. "You could've killed him. You probably did. You know what that means? It means *murder*. If you hadn't shot him maybe we could've got out of there without anyone seeing us, but after the gunshot, people came out to look, and they probably saw the truck. They'll have a description even if no one got the license plate."

Casey felt calm. He understood everything Randy was saying, understood what it meant. But at the same time, he felt as though it couldn't possibly be happening—not to him. He wasn't a murderer. He wouldn't end up in jail. He couldn't. That was not how his story ended.

"I'm telling you one thing, I'm not going down for this," Randy said, practically talking to himself now. "I've done a lot of wild shit but I've never killed anyone. The cops catch up with me, I'm giving you up in a goddamn second. You hear me? What happened in there—that's all you. You can go down for it."

What happened next happened, somehow, without Casey's wanting it to, without his thinking about it or willing it in any way. He didn't even look at what he was doing. His eyes stayed forward as his left hand shot out and grabbed the wheel, yanked it hard to the right. The truck swerved in a scream of tire rubber. They went sideways. The road disappeared. The headlights hit the trees. The truck pitched left, and there came a giddy, free-falling moment when no part of the vehicle seemed to be touching the ground.

Then the truck slammed back down onto its side—the left side, the side Randy was sitting on—and a sudden chaos of noise and pain blotted out Casey's consciousness.

He woke up in agony. His spine lit up white hot, and there was a bone-deep ache in his shoulder. It took him a minute to realize that he was upside down, that the pain in his collar bone was from the seatbelt holding him in place. He wiggled his fingers, moved his arms, testing each bone and muscle separately. Then he unlatched the seatbelt.

He tumbled out of his seat onto the roof, screaming in pain when he hit it, his body crumpling where it landed. The pain passed over him in a wave, blotting everything else out, then receded, and he found that he could move. He curled straight, reached his arms through the shattered side window, and pulled himself out by his fingertips. Then he stood, finding that both his legs worked. A couple of his ribs were probably broken, and his left collarbone was screaming at him, but everything he needed to move was intact.

The truck had flipped right off the road. It was leaning against a couple of trees, headlights still on and cutting a shaft of light through the long grass at the road's edge. The way it was leaning, the driver's side of the car was obscured by the trunks and the underbrush. Casey couldn't see Randy. And he didn't want to, either. Maybe he was alive, maybe he was dead; Casey didn't want to know any more than he wanted to know what had happened to the old man in the shop.

Casey's head snapped left, back to the road. Sirens. Growing louder. He walked out to the blacktop, looked down the long dotted yellow line to the horizon, where blue and red lights flashed. Maybe they'd gotten to the store; maybe one of the people who'd called the cops had described the truck; maybe the trooper they'd passed had made the connection. Either way, they were headed his way. The lights disappeared, then crested a near hill.

Casey walked away from the road and slipped into the woods. He kept walking until the darkness devoured him. Until he became a part of it.

CHAPTER 20

Casey hitchhiked through the night and into the morning, catching rides from truckers on midnight hauls. They looked at him funny the first time he climbed into the cab, seeing the cuts and bruises on his face, but they didn't ask questions. Casey slept as well as he could, awakened through the night by the lights of towns he'd heard of but never been to: Brainerd, St. Cloud, Mankato. The last time he awoke it was to the glow of the sunrise.

"End of the line," said the trucker, a man who'd picked up Casey on a blacktop road somewhere south of the Twin Cities. "This is where I stop."

Casey blinked, sat up. The inside of his mouth was fuzzy and foul tasting, and his stomach ached with hunger.

"Where are we?" he asked, sniffing. There was a smell of sulfur in the cabin from a chemical plant at the edge of town; as they rumbled in on a four-lane road, they passed a chain-linked lot lined with propane tanks, a scrapyard, general stores and hardware stores, and bars in low-slung plywood buildings. The road curved and the trucker pulled into the driveway of a big machine plant.

"This is Windom," the trucker said. Casey'd never gotten his name.

"Minnesota?"

"Yep. Iowa's about a half hour farther that way."

"Where are you going after you unload?"

"Home," the trucker said. "In St. James. It's up the road."

Casey blinked, thinking about what to do next. Through the windshield, the morning sun was coming down gray and harsh. The darkness had been kind, made Casey believe that he could actually escape somewhere, let himself be swallowed by all that blackness, but the light showed this to be a foolish delusion. Outside, a man had come out of the plant and was waving the truck in. Past the machine plant lot, across the border of a chain-link fence, small houses lay spaced far apart. The land was flat here; it was farm country. Nowhere to hide.

"Could I maybe come with—" Casey began, but the trucker cut him off.

"Sorry," he said. "This is as far as we come together. I picked you up because you obviously needed to get away from something. Someone beat you up pretty bad, I can see."

Casey looked away, pointed his face in the other direction. The man didn't need to know that these marks were from a car crash, not a fight—and from a car crash he'd caused. That he'd shot a man, maybe killed his own brother. No one ever needed to know.

"I got you away from whoever did that to you," the man continued, "but that's all I can do. I've got a wife, kids of my own. Our house is small. No, I can't take you in. Here on out, you're on your own. Okay?"

Casey nodded, still not meeting the man's eyes. He opened the door and climbed down.

"Town's that way," the man said, pointing. "There's a grocery store, McDonald's, gas stations. More highway too, if you want to keep hitching."

"Thank you," Casey said, and began walking.

The grocery store wasn't open. The McDonald's was, people just past the windows unwrapping breakfast sandwiches and taking the plastic tops off cups of coffee to let them cool. He caught a whiff of hash browns, of potatoes and hot fryer oil, but he kept walking. He didn't have any money. Not twenty-four hours ago he'd had more than seven hundred dollars to his name; he'd even briefly had a line on thousands from the smokehouse— but now he had nothing. The clothes on his back. A body that ached. That was all.

He crossed the street to a gas station. There was no one by the pumps, just a dark-blue truck parked at a careless angle just outside the front doors. He walked inside.

Just past the doors, a man stood speaking to a young woman behind the counter. The man must have been telling a joke as Casey opened the door, because the young woman had her head thrown back, laughing, brown curls dangling down. They went quiet when the bell rang. They looked at him. Casey saw in their faces how bad he looked. The man nodded at him gravely, but the young woman made no greeting, only lifted her fingers to her mouth, pressed them flat against her lips. Casey turned away and went to the back, looked for a bathroom.

He used the toilet, washed his hands, checked himself in the mirror. His cheeks and forehead were covered in little cuts from all the broken glass; both his eyes were puffy and encircled in blackened half-moons. He hadn't hit his face, he thought, but perhaps the accident had rattled his body hard enough to burst blood vessels. There'd be more marks under his clothes, he knew—more bruises.

He wiped the water off his hands, dropped the paper towel into the trash, then walked back out. The man and the young woman were still at the front, talking in low voices. Casey walked the aisles, keeping away from their eyes, looking at the food on the shelves. Doritos and Slim Jims and Funyuns. Little sleeves of salted nuts, butter crackers with cheese, snack cakes. All of it so cheap, ninety-nine cents, a couple bucks at most, but he couldn't afford any of it. He wandered to the front to smell the hot food: breakfast sandwiches under heat lamps.

He felt eyes on him.

"Do you need help, kid?" the man asked. "You don't look so hot."

Casey half turned to get the man in his field of vision, but kept facing away, toward the food.

"I was…I was thinking," Casey said, shame and desperation washing over him in equal measure, "I was thinking I might like to buy some…some breakfast. Except I can't really—"

"What do you want?" the man asked. "One of those breakfast sandwiches? A donut?"

"Yeah," Casey said softly, hoping he'd end up with both.

The man and the young woman exchanged glances, nods, and she moved toward the food cases.

"One of those biscuit ones," the man said. "With egg and sausage and cheese."

The young woman took it from under the heat lamp with tongs, put it in a paper bag. Saliva rushed into Casey's mouth; his stomach groaned with anticipation.

"Donuts too, Leah," the man said in a low voice. "Make it a few."

She added donuts to the bag: glazed, chocolate, vanilla with sprinkles. She rang up the food, then looked from Casey to the man.

"I got it, Leah," the man said, putting some money down. He took the bag off the counter and handed it to Casey. To take it, Casey turned toward him and really looked at him for the first time. He had paint-splattered hands, dark facial hair, a dusty cap on his head. He winked. "There you go, kid."

"Thank you," Casey said, his voice a thin croak. Tears came to his eyes, made the man and the young woman blurry. He willed himself not to cry.

"You going to eat it?" the man asked.

Casey opened the paper bag, took out a donut.

"Nah," the man said, "you gotta eat the sandwich first. It'll get cold."

Casey put the donut back, unwrapped the sandwich, began eating it. It was nothing much—just a shitty gas-station breakfast sandwich—but Casey thought he'd never eaten anything so delicious in all his life.

The man and the young woman—Leah—watched him eat.

"You in trouble, kid?"

Casey swallowed down the last bite of the breakfast sandwich. It made a painful lump in his chest. He wished he had some orange juice.

"I don't really know how to explain it," he said.

"Running from the person who did that to you?" The man squinted at his face.

"Something like that," Casey said.

"You got a place to stay? Any money at all?"

Casey studied the man's face. He sensed that this was the time to tell the truth.

"No," he said.

The man sucked a hissing breath through his teeth. Took off his cap, held it by the bill, and scratched at the top of his head with the edge of his thumb before putting it back.

"Okay," the man said. "Come with me."

———

The dark-blue truck belonged to the man, and he drove Casey

a couple blocks to a house—small, one story, but nice. Freshly painted blue to match the truck, with white gutters and the heads of flowers poking above window boxes. The man pulled into the driveway, got out, and began to walk around the house. He looked back.

"You coming?"

There were ways for this story to end badly, Casey supposed. The man could be a sex pervert, a serial killer. But Casey didn't have much to lose. A basement dungeon would at least be a roof over his head. He got out of the truck and followed the man.

They went down a narrow walkway around the side of the house. In the back was a square of scraggly lawn, a stone patio with a table and chairs, and cement steps leading down into the ground toward a basement door. The man went down the steps, fussed with a ring of keys, then opened the door. Casey went down after him and found a small apartment: a stove and sink and mini-fridge, a small sitting area with a shabby coffee table, couch, and chairs, and through a small doorway, a narrow twin bed.

"It's vacant," the man said. "There's linens and blankets in the dresser. Shower and toilet behind that curtain back there."

"I can't pay you," Casey said. "I don't have any—"

The man waved him silent. "Save it. I've got jobs today." With that he disappeared, went back up the stairs to the lawn, and Casey was alone.

The shower was little more than a spigot jutting from the wall and a drain in the floor, but Casey washed off anyway, relishing the feel of the hot water against his skin, the warmth that curled its way into his aching muscles. As he'd expected, his body was covered with bruises. He toweled off gingerly, put his clothes back on, then made the bed and crawled in, asleep almost before his face hit the pillow.

He awoke hours later to a banging on the back door. He rolled out of bed, trudged to the door, and opened it. There was the man again, looking the same but for a fine layer of white dust on his hands, his shoulders, his beard, his face. The sky was dark. Casey had slept through the whole day.

"What is it?" Casey asked.

"Dinner," the man said, and lifted his arms. He held two plastic bags, a smell of meat and fryer grease coming off of them. "Come upstairs."

Casey sat at the man's kitchen table as he unpacked the food: a dozen hard-shell tacos from Taco John's. With a flick of his hand he scattered packets of hot sauce across the tabletop. "Eat up," he said.

They ate without talking, using napkins and the papers wrapping the tacos as plates. Casey devoured six tacos and the man pushed him one more. The man drank a beer; he offered Casey an orange Shasta from the fridge, but he opted for tap water instead. When they were done, the man swept the trash into a waste bin he took from under the kitchen sink.

"I don't suppose you're very tired after passing out all day," the man said. "But if you can, you should get some more sleep tonight. We're up early tomorrow."

"Up early?" Casey repeated.

"That's right."

"Doing what?"

"You'll see."

Casey stood and went to the front door, getting ready to go back around to his basement apartment. But the man stopped him.

"Hey, kid," he called. "What's your name, anyway?"

He thought about it for a second before answering. People would be looking for him—the cops, his mother, and his brother, if he'd survived the crash. His name might be in the news already. His face. *Missing*—or, maybe, *Wanted*.

"Paul," he said, thinking of the boy—the rich kid who'd stolen Tricia out from under him without even trying, as though it was nothing. "My name is Paul."

He smiled for the first time in what felt like forever. *Paul.* It felt good. Maybe it was as easy as this, becoming someone new. Maybe all you had to do was pick a new name. He felt as though his old self—his pathetic self, his loser self—was disappearing, receding as though into water, swallowed by crashing waves. Maybe he *had* died in the car crash by the shore after all. Died and been born again.

He was Paul, from now on.

"It's nice to meet you, Paul," the man said. "My name is Darryl."

CHAPTER 21

Darryl woke him the next day before the sun was up. Pounding on the back door like he was trying to rattle down the house.

Casey—no, *Paul*, goddammit. *Paul.* His name was Paul now, he reminded himself as he padded out of bed; he'd have to practice, since the other one, the boy with the other name, was dead and gone forever—Paul answered the door, bleary eyed.

"What?"

"Time to get up," Darryl said. The moon was at his back, still the brightest thing in the sky. He threw Paul some clothes. Paul caught them, held them against his chest. "Got some clothes for you. They're mine, old stuff, but they still oughta be good. Good enough for working."

"Working?"

"Still got that job from yesterday. Going to need a hand to finish it up."

"What kind of job?" Paul asked.

"Get dressed," Darryl said. "I'll see you upstairs in ten minutes."

———

They had breakfast, coffee and hard-boiled eggs and toast, and then they piled into Darryl's truck and left just as the sun rose over the cornfields. They drove from the edge of town to the center, where Darryl pulled into a gravel warehouse lot and opened a garage door to reveal a mess of tools and building supplies. They loaded up the truck and then went off to the worksite, a new-looking house at the edge of town.

Darryl led Paul into the basement and put him to work, teaching as he went. They were finishing a basement, screwing drywall to the studs, taping, mudding, sanding. It looked like mindless work to Paul, but as he got more into it he realized that it had an art to it as well, and by the end of the day he was finding pleasure in hanging a slab of drywall just right, in driving a screw perfectly flush so there'd be no hole to fill later, in placing a piece of tape with no bubbles, in smoothing the mud over the joints and imagining what the wall would look like when their work was done.

Once, the owner came down to check on them. He was an older man, gruff like Darryl was, but he had a smile in his eyes.

"Who's this, then?" the man asked.

"This is Paul," Darryl said. "He's helping me a few days."

"You'll finish faster?"

"That's the hope," Darryl said. "Couple more days. You can't rush the final steps."

The man nodded. "Well, get to it, then."

They finished for the day, had another dozen tacos and two pounds of fried potatoes that evening, then came back the next three days. Mud and sand, mud and sand; then came the painting, a couple coats, and then they were done. The owner inspected the work, nodded, handed Darryl a check. They drove to the bank. Darryl deposited the money, but kept some cash back. He counted it out and handed it across to Paul. Paul counted the money.

Three hundred dollars.

"That's your share," Darryl said. "Minus rent and what you owe me for all the food I've been feeding you."

"Rent?" Paul asked. "You mean—"

"I've got another job starting tomorrow. Baseboards and door moldings."

"I'll be there," Paul said. "We leave early?"

Darryl nodded. "You know it, kid."

———

Paul bought his own dinner that night. Walked to the grocery store in the middle of town, got milk, bread, bananas, peanut butter and jelly, and some boxed mac and cheese. He made the mac and cheese on the little basement stove, the kind with black coils that heat to red. He was settling down on the couch with his food, eating with a fork straight from the pan, when there came a knock at the door—soft, almost dainty. Darryl didn't knock like that.

He opened the door and saw the girl—the girl from the gas station. Leah.

"Darryl told me you're living with him," she said. "I thought you might want a little company." She bent her elbow and lifted her arm to show him what she'd brought: a six pack of beer, Grain Belt Premium.

"I'm not twenty-one," Paul said.

"Neither am I," Leah said, walking in. "I'm only twenty. But I know the guy at the liquor store, and he doesn't card me. Plus there's jack shit to do in this town." She sat in a chair near the couch, took out a bottle, pulled the sleeve of her hoodie over her hand to twist off the metal cap. "How old are you?"

"Twenty," Paul said—a pointless lie; in reality he was turning eighteen in a couple months. He wasn't even sure why he'd lied, since Leah didn't seem to care how old he was, but it was out now, and there was no going back. He'd changed his name, why not his age too?

"You want one, then?" Leah asked. "We're almost legal. No cops in the basement, anyway."

She handed him a sweat-beaded bottle; he took it by the neck and sat back down.

"Eat," she said. "Don't let me stop you."

They sat for a little while in silence while Paul finished the rest of the macaroni and cheese, began drinking the beer. He'd never had any before. Drinking beer had been Randy's thing, and as Paul tasted the stuff now, he thought he might know why his older brother liked it so much. It tasted odd, but refreshing, and halfway through the second bottle his fingers and his lips went tingly. He set the empty pot on the coffee table and leaned back, feeling pleasantly dizzy, slouching low enough on the couch that his knees were almost parallel with his body.

"So what's your story?" Leah asked. She propped her legs up on Paul's knees, crossed them at the ankle, and he didn't protest.

"Not much of a story," he said.

"Your face says otherwise," Leah said. "Your black eyes are looking better, though. How'd that happen?"

"I got in a fight," Paul said, the lie sliding out easy. He was getting better at this.

"With who?" Leah asked.

Paul sensed that she'd keep asking and asking if he didn't come up with a story right now, that she'd always be curious. He and Darryl didn't have to talk; men could leave things unspoken. But a woman would want to know about him as a prerequisite to any relationship. If he told her to fuck off, she'd probably leave and wouldn't come back, and he didn't want that. He liked her here, liked drinking beers with her, liked feeling the weight of her legs, the warmth of her calves on top of his knees.

"My dad," he said. "I got in a fight with my dad."

"Oh my God," Leah said. She looked at him like he was an injured puppy dog, eyes big and wet, and he didn't mind that either. No one ever felt sorry for him. No one ever tried to take care of him. "Was he…I mean—did he do that a lot?"

Paul looked away and played with the label on his beer. The condensation on the bottle had made it start to peel off. "He's a bastard," Paul said, the blanket condemnation meant to close off further discussion. The truth was that he didn't know his father; there was one picture of him and his dad together, from when he was maybe two years old, but after that the man (he didn't even know his name) had gotten a different job, a different trucking route in a different part of the country, and from then on they didn't see him again.

"How about your mom?" Leah asked. "What's she like?"

Paul thought about Darlene—the pathetic, failing store, the money stolen from the coffee can, the moaning sounds that came through the bedroom walls sometimes at night. He was in a better place now in this tiny town, in this small basement apartment. When you came from *that*, anything was an improvement.

"My mother is dead," Paul said.

Six months passed more or less like that: Paul helped Darryl with jobs at houses in town and in the surrounding countryside. He saved his money from the jobs—minus rent to Darryl—this time in a plastic gallon freezer bag. Darryl told him he should probably put it somewhere safer, like a bank, but Paul didn't know how to start a savings account—not without a driver's license or a social security number or any of the things you needed to be a person in this world.

Sometimes he'd walk to the library in town, sign up for an hour at one of the computers, and search for anything related to his old name, his old self. Every time, there was nothing. Somehow he'd disappeared without a trace, made it through eighteen years of life without making a single mark on the world.

It was when he searched under his brother's name that things started to appear. News stories out of Duluth about the robbery, the shooting. The old man behind the counter had died; they were trying to pin the murder on Randy. Paul wondered sometimes why his old name didn't come up in these stories, why no one was looking for him. Maybe no one had seen that there were two people, not one, in the getaway truck; maybe Randy was trying to tell the cops that his brother was the one who'd done it but they all thought it was bullshit; maybe even his mother thought he'd simply run away to start his own life. She was probably too busy just trying to survive to look for him. He was almost eighteen, after all, an adult in the eyes of the law. Maybe she was even glad that he was gone. One less mouth to feed.

Leah kept visiting at night, after her shifts at the Speedway ended, and they started having sex pretty quickly, the third or fourth time she came by. It was Paul's first time, but he lied and said he'd been with other girls before—if he was supposed to be twenty years old, which Leah still believed, it was too embarrassing to be a virgin. Soon they were a couple, of sorts, though they never went out, never went to restaurants or to movies or did any of the other things that couples did. They only sat in the basement of Darryl's house, talking languidly over beers or day-old donuts Leah brought from the gas station, then went to the bed when they ran out of conversation. That usually happened fast—not much happened to them; they didn't have much to talk about.

It wasn't much of a life, Paul realized, this thing he'd run away to. But it was better than what he'd left behind. And it was enough. For now.

CHAPTER 22

The events that eventually drove Paul away from Windom and into another life—a third life—as a husband, father, and crooked financial adviser in the Twin Cities began when Darryl landed a job in the spring a couple miles outside of town. It was a huge house, being built from the ground up, at the top of what passed in that flat part of the state for a hill, with a view of gently swelling crop fields stretching for miles.

The owner was a man in his fifties with dark hair and nice clothes who stalked around the grounds with the imperious ease that came from having more money than he could spend. He had an army of workers piecing together the house: landscapers smoothing and grading, planting shrubs, and rolling out sod; electricians installing wires and outlets; plumbers putting in pipes and sinks and toilets; heating and cooling guys putting in the vents and pushing thick, downy slabs of insulation between the studs. Last came Darryl and Paul and a few other guys they'd pulled together for the job, rushing in to finish each room with drywall and paint and baseboards after the guts had been laid in the walls. There were (Paul counted) six bedrooms, three full bathrooms, an office, a game room, and a basement den with a massive flat-screen laid into the wall behind a pocket door that slid back like a curtain at a vaudeville show or an old-timey movie theater.

They worked on the house for two weeks, the last crew to leave. The owner would pop his head in every now and then to check on their progress, ask them how it was going. Darryl would always do the talking—he was in charge of the relationship with the client, while Paul's job was to keep his head down and do the work with the rest of the grunts. But Paul couldn't help staring at the man every time he showed himself, look at his tanned, lightly weathered face, observe the ease with which he took command of every space he entered, and wonder at what he'd done to get all this for himself. He'd seen mansions before, of course—there were rich people on the North Shore, folks who took the money they'd made from other places and took it to the edge of the water to build their castles. But he'd never been inside one before. He'd never seen one up close. He understood now why Randy had sometimes broken into the rich people's vacation homes, squatted in them. Just being close to that kind of luxury made you feel a certain way. Like anything was possible. Like you could be good too, if you had all this. If you could only find a way to get some of it—even a slice of it—for yourself.

Paul stayed quiet throughout the job, let Darryl do all the talking—until the last day. Paul waited by the truck as he watched the owner pay up, cut Darryl the last check. Then the man walked with Darryl to the truck, shook his hand. Paul stayed outside as Darryl climbed in. He stepped close to the man and offered his hand too.

The man blinked with surprise, but grabbed Paul's hand and pumped it.

"Son," he said, "thanks for the work."

"It's a beautiful house," Paul said.

"Yes it is," the man said, turning to look at it. "I've worked hard for it. I believe I've earned it."

"What do you do, anyway?" Paul asked.

The man turned back to him. There was a crooked smile on his face. He reached into a back pocket, came out with a sleek metal case. He opened it and slid out a business card, put it into Paul's hand.

DONALD BELL
FOUNDER
BELL FINANCIAL PARTNERS

"What does that mean?" Paul asked.

"I take people's money," the man, Donald Bell, told him, "and I turn it into more money."

Paul found the office on Main Street. It was a small storefront with a red awning and the name of the business etched on the front window. He'd passed it dozens of times before without noticing it, paying more attention to the other businesses: the Ben Franklin general store, the hardware store, the bakery. But now he saw other small, nondescript offices just like it. A State Farm insurance agency; another for Farmer's Insurance. *Robert Odin, Accounting Services*; *Johnson Mortgage*; *Burch and Holloway, Attorneys at Law*. Paul wandered past the doorways and wondered if a rich man sat inside each of them, a man with enough money in the bank to build a mansion from the ground up, a man whose life was warm and spacious and easy.

Paul walked through the door marked *Bell Financial Partners*. A bell dinged above his head, just like at the hardware store, and when he looked back down there he was: Donald Bell. He stood at a doorway with a cup of coffee in one hand. The walls of the office were done up in shabby wood paneling, but the desk was broad and dark; oak finished with stain and lacquer and polished to a shine. Bell crossed to it and sat down, setting his coffee on a brass coaster.

"You're the kid from the house," Bell said. "You were part of the drywall crew."

"I have money," Paul said. He walked forward, took the envelope from his coat pocket, and put it on the top of the desk. "That's twenty-five hundred dollars. Everything I've saved."

"What do you want me to do with it?"

"You told me that you turn people's money into more money," Paul said. "What can you do with that?"

Bell shrugged. "Double it, maybe," he said, grinning. "Then double that. Five thousand, then ten thousand. You give me enough time, add some more dollars to it, I could make you a millionaire."

"How?"

"The miracle of compounding interest, son," Bell said. "You invest in assets, they increase in value, you have more money than you did when you started."

"Okay," Paul said. "I want that. Do that."

Bell was still for a moment, his mouth held in something like a sneer. He turned, went for a drawer, came out with a sheaf of papers that he handed across the desktop.

"Fill those out," Bell said.

Paul picked them up, glanced through them. There was a questionnaire about something called *Investment Risk Tolerance*, about *Short-Term Financial Goals*, about *Preferred Portfolio Asset Mix*. More forms below that asking for legal name, date of birth, mailing address, social security number. Account numbers, routing numbers. Things Paul didn't have.

"Take them home with you," Bell suggested. "Bring them back when you're done. I'll also need a voided check."

Back in the apartment, Paul threw the forms in the trash, took his envelope of money back out of his pocket, and hurled it on the coffee table. It slid and fell onto the floor. Paul plopped onto the couch, put his hands on his eyes, threw his head back. He didn't want to see the money right now. It had been a comfort to him before—counting it, watching it grow with each job he and Darryl completed—but now all he could see was the paltriness of his stash, the long distance that lay between him and real riches. What he'd dreamed of was a life without limitation, a life of abundance and plenty, but somehow it felt further away than ever. The doors that mattered were still closed to him. He'd run, somehow, from one prison to another.

His phone buzzed in his pocket. Leah had bought it for him at the gas station, a burner flip phone with limited minutes. It didn't matter, since he didn't call anyone, didn't talk to anyone. It was only so that Leah could contact him, see if he was home, if he wanted to do anything.

It was her. It was always her.

"Hey," Paul said. "What is it? You off work? Want to come over?" Paul didn't really want to see her right now, but maybe she could distract him, make him forget this feeling. That was what sex was good for, Paul had come to believe—it made you feel a different way, for a little while. Made you forget who you were, until it was over, and then you remembered again.

"I don't have a shift today," Leah said. "Maybe you could come over here, actually."

"I don't know," Paul said. Leah lived with her parents, and

Paul had worked hard not to know them, to be such a marginal presence in their lives, a shadow at the edge of their peripheral vision, that they wouldn't want to be introduced to him or know anything about him.

"My parents are gone," Leah said. "Just come over. I want to talk to you."

The ceiling creaked under the weight of Darryl's footsteps. He could hear the dull murmur of the upstairs television. The walls were like cardboard; Darryl could probably hear them when they talked, even when they fucked. Maybe Leah's place wouldn't be so bad, this once.

"Okay," he said. "I'll be there in the next ten minutes."

Leah and her parents lived in a white house a few blocks over from Darryl. A stone birdbath lay askew on the grass out front, with wilting hydrangeas clustering around the front stoop. Paul knocked on the front door and heard Leah's voice shouting from within. The front door was open.

He found her in the living room, sitting on the couch with her feet in socks curled up around her. She wore a Vikings sweatshirt, purple and gold, and a blanket was spread on her knees. On the opposite wall, the TV was on, turned to the news, a weatherman waving at a map. Rain was coming.

"Hey," Paul said, plopping down next to her. She barely seemed to notice him, eyes ahead, but she wasn't really watching the TV either—more like looking through it. She chewed at the edges of her fingernails, lost in some thought.

Paul's eyes wandered back to the screen. The weatherman was gone, and the picture had gone back to the anchorman and anchorwoman at the desk setting up a new story. The picture flipped again, showed a landscape Paul recognized. Trees, rocks, water. The North Shore. And now there was a street Paul recognized, in Grand Marais; there was the county courthouse. Paul's body tensed, his senses sharpening to a point. The TV was old, not even a flat-screen, and the volume was low, but the picture seemed crisp and hyper-real to Paul, and he could hear every word spoken.

"*A robbery gone wrong, a murder—and now, a possible case of mistaken identity,*" a reporter's voice said over the establishing shots. "*That's only scratching the surface of this case that has shocked a community here on Minnesota's North Shore, and stumped authorities here in Cook County.*"

The picture switched again, and Paul's stomach dropped out. On the screen was a picture of Randy—a mug shot. His face was battered, cut up from the crash. But he'd survived.

"*It all began with the arrest of Randy Whitacre six months ago. Whitacre was accused of shooting and killing a store clerk in a failed robbery. He was picked up by police after fleeing the scene and losing control of his vehicle. Whitacre was known to authorities, and they were certain they had their man. But now that the case has come to trial, Whitacre and his court-appointed defense attorney say that it wasn't Randy who killed the clerk, but his brother Casey.*"

Now a photo of Casey came up on the screen—a school photo in which he was smiling against a matte glamour-shot background. Paul glanced at Leah, but somehow she wasn't noticing what was on the screen, still looking through it with glazed eyes, her mind on something else.

"*Locals say that the brothers have a strong family resemblance, and Casey's whereabouts have been unknown since the time of the robbery and shooting. However, no missing persons report was ever filed, and so far the defense has provided no additional witnesses to the younger brother's involvement in the crime. The Cook County prosecutor, meanwhile, speculates that Randy Whitacre might be responsible for his brother's disappearance, killing Casey and hiding the body due to his knowledge of Randy's crimes. But Randy Whitacre and his defense attorney insist that Casey Whitacre is still alive, and they ask anyone in the public with information relevant to his whereabouts to come forward."*

"*Sounds like a regular murder mystery up there,*" the anchor said.

"*That's right, Tom…*"

Paul began to breathe a little easier as the news broadcast moved on to other stories. Leah still hadn't said anything, hadn't seemed to notice. But others in town would've seen the story. Maybe they'd recognize him.

"Paul," Leah said, "I have something I need to tell you."

"What is it?" Paul said, only half listening—he was thinking about getting out of there, going back to the apartment, throwing some things in a bag, and leaving. He was wondering if he could get his hands on a car, if the used dealership on the south end of town would take cash and let him drive something off the lot without a title transfer, when Leah's voice broke through again.

"I'm pregnant."

Paul was back at his apartment, throwing his few possessions into a pair of pillowcases, when Darryl appeared at the door. Paul froze.

"You're leaving," Darryl said.

Paul breathed out. This was one of the things he liked most about Darryl—he never asked questions. Never made Paul explain anything. The most important things Darryl just seemed to know, was content to leave unsaid.

"I wanna thank you," Paul said, squaring up to Darryl. "For putting me up. For the work, the cheap rent."

He put out his hand, and Darryl accepted it.

"Where are you going to go?" Darryl asked.

"I don't know," Paul said. "Anywhere. Anywhere but here."

"You need a plan," Darryl said.

"That's the plan."

Darryl half sighed, half laughed. "That's not a plan."

"It's the best one I got."

Darryl was silent a moment, pulling at the back of his neck with a hand. Then he let the hand drop, pulled up straight, and spoke.

"Paul," he said.

"What?"

"You think I don't notice things," Darryl said. "But I do. I'm not stupid."

"I don't know what you're talking about." Paul turned back to the bed, went on stuffing things into the pillowcases. Toothbrush, toothpaste, deodorant, shaving cream, and a disposable razor. Underwear, socks. The burner phone he'd leave behind; he wanted no link with this place. No link with Leah. He should've never started anything with her.

"I notice things plenty. Like, I've never seen you show a driver's license. Never seen you carry a wallet."

Paul paused and listened.

"I notice," Darryl went on, "how you don't open a savings account at the bank even though it would be a hell of a lot safer than putting your money in a damn freezer bag."

Paul gathered the folds of the pillowcases in his two hands, tested the weight. It wasn't much. Everything he owned, and it weighed less than a couple sacks of potatoes.

"Paul isn't even your real name, is it?"

Paul closed his eyes, a quiver in his breath as he drew air in and out of his lungs slowly, deliberately. Darryl had been watching

TV when Paul left for Leah's; he must have seen the story, made the connection.

"Are you going to turn me in?"

"No."

Paul turned back to him. "What, then?"

"Son," Darryl said, and it almost took the breath out of Paul to hear him say it—*Son*, like he might actually mean something to the older man, like he'd finally found someone who cared about him, who gave a shit about whether he lived or died. "If you want to *be* someone," he said, "then you're going to have to be *someone*. You understand what I'm telling you?"

Paul paused, then nodded. "I think so. What do you suggest?"

"I know a guy," Darryl said.

"A guy."

"Yeah. From when I did time."

"You were in prison?"

"It was a long time ago," Darryl said. "I did some dumb things when I was a kid. I wouldn't recommend it. Anything you can do to stay out of jail, you do it, you hear?"

Paul drew himself up straight, nodded. "And this guy...he...?"

"He gives people new identities. Papers. Birth certificate, social security, driver's license. He can give you a whole new life."

"But my past. The thing I'm running from. What do I—"

"You'll lay low for a while," Darryl said. "You'll keep your head down until it blows over. You'll forget it ever happened."

Forgetting. Paul didn't know if it was possible to forget everything that had happened to him. But if his life could forget *him*—if the people he'd known before this moment simply failed to recall his existence, never came looking for him—that might be enough. The only one he'd be sad to leave behind was standing in front of him.

"Will I ever see you again?"

"No," Darryl said without flinching, and at first it hurt Paul's feelings a little bit—maybe he didn't mean as much to Darryl as Darryl meant to him. But then he understood. Darryl would never see Paul again not because he didn't care, but because he did. Because Paul's life turning into anything good depended on his leaving all this behind and never looking back.

"Okay," he said. "What do I do next?"

"I guess the first thing to do," Darryl said, "is you should pick a new name."

CHAPTER 23

"John Peters," he said, offering his hand.

There was a quaver in his voice as he said it—but not because of the lie. He was used to that by now, almost ten years after he'd taken the name. He'd lived so long as John Peters that he could go days or even weeks without thinking of the people he'd been before this, their names like shadowy talismans from a dimly remembered dream. Most days it didn't even feel like a lie anymore, didn't feel like something he had to pretend was true. He was John. It was his name. As simple as that.

He'd even started to feel safe in his assumed identity, had stopped fearing that his past would somehow catch up with him: the familiar face in the crowd, the police officer tapping on his apartment door. Safe enough, secure enough, that he'd returned to Minnesota after years of staying away: shit jobs and sleeping in a car in Wisconsin, slightly less shit jobs and an efficiency apartment in Michigan, night school and financial-adviser-certification classes in Illinois. He wondered sometimes why he didn't run farther: New York, California, even Mexico. But locations had a sort of gravitational pull to them; maybe you could only orbit the place that had made you, never really leave it. Now he was back in an even closer orbit: Minneapolis, six hours by car away from the place where he'd grown up. So far he hadn't seen anybody he'd known, nobody had recognized him—he'd changed so much—and he felt safe enough to assume that they never would.

So no, if there was a shake in his voice, it wasn't because he was lying about the name he was giving—it was because the woman he was introducing himself to was stunningly beautiful and he'd spent the last five minutes watching her from the other side of a hotel conference room, trying to gather the courage to speak to her.

She looked at his hand a split second before accepting it in hers, grasping it with her fingers. Her other hand held a wide-mouthed plastic cup of red wine, a square napkin folded at the base.

"I'm Regan," she said, then withdrew her hand.

Her tone was cool, but John was enchanted. "Regan. What a beautiful name."

She blinked. "Is it?"

"Yes!" John blurted. "It's...regal?" He flushed hearing the rhyme—only one letter's difference—but then she laughed, a delighted laugh, not a cruel one, and John relaxed.

"That's me," she said. "Regal Regan."

She seemed to be trying to play off his awkward compliment, but John thought she *did* have a queen-like air about her: something in the cast of her spine, the way she held her shoulders, the red-brown hair cascading perfectly over her temples and curving underneath her chin, slate-blue eyes whose color reminded him of the sky after a rain, red lips full and just a little bit pouted. It looked to John like a face that should appear in oil paintings in museums, or on the faces of coins and paper currency.

"I've never liked it so much, actually," Regan said.

"What?" John asked. "Your name?" He couldn't imagine that she could dislike anything about herself. He found it offensive.

"People sometimes say Reagan. Like the president."

"Regan," John pronounced. Then slower: "Ree-gan."

"Right," she said. "But even then there's Shakespeare. King Lear. One of the evil older daughters. I should be insulted my parents chose it. My dad is even an English professor. He's taught Lear."

"That's not very nice," John admitted. "Is there a Goneril? A Cordelia?"

Regan gave him a sharp glance, and John drew in a breath, wondering if he'd overstepped. "You know the play?"

John let his silence be the answer to that. He'd read it, years ago, in the library. A previous name. A previous life.

"My sister's name isn't Cordelia," Regan said. "But she *is* the favorite."

"I'm sorry to hear that," John said.

Regan gave a shrug and bolted the wine from her cup. "Oh, don't be. Every family has their stuff."

"That's the truth," John said, using a somber tone he'd developed over the years that usually cut off any questions about his own family, his own past.

"Listen to me," Regan said. "Treating you like a therapist when we're supposed to be here making contacts."

It was a networking event for young professionals, an under-thirties thing, which John still was at twenty-eight. He'd come looking for clients, not dates, but he was finding it difficult: circulating, passing out business cards, breaking off conversation with one person and transitioning effortlessly to another. That terrible moment when you were waiting outside a new circle of people who seemed to know each other, hoping to be let in.

"I guess we're not very good at this," John said.

"No," Regan said. "Shall we start again?"

She put out her hand for another handshake. John accepted it with a chuckle, noting that her grasp was stronger this time, less hesitant—her fingers touching his palm, their thumbs interlocked all the way to the base. John found himself wanting to hold on, to pull her close, to find other places where their bodies could touch, overlap, interlock.

"Regan Cartwright," she said as their hands parted. "I'm a graphic designer at an ad agency."

"Do you have a business card? I could maybe use some marketing help."

"What's your business?" she asked as she looked in her purse.

"I'm a financial adviser."

She took out a metal sleeve, popped it open, and handed John a card. "That's my personal card, actually."

John looked at it. It was colorful, splashy, Regan's name done in hand lettering with geometrical shapes flying off the tips of the letters like sparks.

"I'm here more for myself, I guess," she explained. "I'm trying to get out of the ad business. Too stressful. Anyway, if it's marketing help you want, our firm might not be right for you. We do larger clients, big campaigns. You probably want direct mail, fliers, referral campaigns. Maybe a bus stop bench. We don't really do that."

"Well," John said, sliding the card into his back pocket, "at least I know how to reach you. Either way."

Regan blushed. It was amazing—a real blush, like a cartoon character, red circles coming to her cheeks. John allowed himself to hope.

"Do you have one?" Regan asked.

"What?"

"A card."

"Oh!" John blurted, embarrassed, realizing he'd been staring, saying nothing—maybe he was blushing now too. He fumbled with his card carrier, flipped out a card, and handed it to her. It wasn't as interesting as hers, just one of the standard designs at Office Max with his details laid in. "I might need some help with my branding. Maybe you could do that for me. A nice logo, a website?"

"Maybe," Regan said. "Yeah, that could be fun. Freelance."

And then it came: the moment when they'd part, break off this conversation and go elsewhere in search of a new one. But they didn't. Everyone else in the room seemed to be embedded in conversations already. Or maybe—John again allowed himself to hope—Regan wanted to stay close to him. Didn't want to leave.

"This is going to sound a little forward," John said. "But—"

"*Yes*," Regan said, leaning hard on the word, relief palpable in her voice. "Please. Let's go somewhere else."

"I think there's a brewery in this neighborhood," John said.

Twenty minutes later they were sitting at a long wooden table just outside a metal garage door that had been pulled all the way up. Inside was a curving bar with bearded men pulling at tap handles, can lights hanging from the ceiling, exposed brick. On the gravel outside, John sat in front of a pint of IPA with a foamy head that stuck to the sides of the glass as he drank it slowly down to the bottom. Regan had gone for the blond (John had paid, over her objections), and now she sat hunched over the glass, elbows on the table. She'd pulled her shoulders up and curved them inward in that delicate way that women sometimes did.

"You cold?" John asked. "I have a jacket in the car."

"No," Regan said, looking up over the tops of the warehouse roofs to squint into the sky. "It's beautiful out."

It was late April, an unreliable month in Minnesota, but that year it had tilted into an early spring, sun and unseasonably warm temperatures blasting away the snow and plucking a shocking green up from the dirt. Everywhere people seemed to be emerging into the light, pale and squinting, delighted but a little terrified, like animals surprised to be woken from winter sleep.

John barely noticed the weather, though. He was too busy looking at Regan—her hair, her lips, those dainty shoulders angled inward, and especially, right now, her neck, long and thin and smooth. He searched for something to say; if he didn't talk, then all he'd be able to do was stare, and he'd freak Regan out.

"I'm glad we came here," he said. "I hate those networking things."

"Didn't you say you were a financial adviser?" Regan asked. "I thought guys like you were good at talking to people."

John looked down at his beer, gave the glass a little swirl, bringing back a little foam. "Yeah. I'm supposed to be. I'm still pretty new at it. Trying to build my client base."

"Maybe you should go back. I'm not much of a prospect. I don't have much money to invest."

"No?"

"My parents do. But not me."

John cocked his head. He always thought that having rich parents meant that you were rich—apparently not. He recalled the hint of sadness when Regan had mentioned her family, the passing comment about her sister being the favorite, and knew not to pursue it any further.

"Well, it's not about having a lot of money. Just a little bit every month can add up over time. Right now is exactly when you should be investing."

"Oh, so you *are* trying to sell me?" Regan asked. "And here I thought you enjoyed my company."

"I—no, that's not…I *do*."

Regan reached out and touched John's hand. His eyes snapped up, surprised by the sudden warmth of it.

"John," she said. "Relax. I'm just teasing you."

He breathed out and smiled. Regan took back her hand, but he could still feel the place where she'd touched him.

"What about you?" John asked.

"I don't know. What *about* me?"

"Well, back there you told me that you're trying to get out of the ad business. Tell me about that. What are you looking for?"

"Oh, I don't know," she said, angling into herself further, a hand rising up and across her body to curl around the side of her neck—her beautiful neck.

"You sure about that?" John asked.

"It's silly."

He shook his head. "I bet it's not. Come on, tell me."

"Well, so I do graphic design, right? Web, print, branding. But what I'd really like to do is…*interior* design."

John didn't understand all the buildup, didn't understand what could possibly be embarrassing about that—but on the other side of the table Regan clapped her hand over her eyes, then peeked at John for his reaction.

"Is that stupid? You think it's stupid."

John shook his head, honestly bewildered. "No. Why would I think it's stupid?"

"My parents think it's stupid."

"They do?"

"They're serious artists, both of them. Well, my mom more than my dad."

"I thought you said he was an English prof."

"He wrote a novel a bunch of years ago. An important one."

"I see," John said. "And they think interior design is…?"

"Frivolous," Regan said. "They're not exactly huge fans of the ad work, selling my talents for corporations or whatever, but interior design is too… I don't know what they think exactly." She looked off, thinking. "Girly? Domestic?"

Now John was the one to reach across the table and touch her—just a couple fingertips, brushing against her elbow. Her gaze snapped back to him, surprise in her eyes, but he left his hand where it was.

"Stop," he said. "Don't do that to yourself."

"You don't think it's true?"

John withdrew his hand. "Is it your dream?"

Regan pressed her lips together, tilted her head back and forth, sighed through her nose. "I guess."

"You guess."

"It is."

"Then who cares what anyone else thinks? You should be able to go after what you want."

She took a dainty sip of beer, the tiniest pull—at this rate he'd have two before she'd even drunk half of hers—then set the glass off to the side and leaned forward, suddenly animated, talking with her hands.

"It's really a very serious craft, when you think about it," Regan said. "A lot of people think of it as just *decorating*, but it's so much more than that. It's form and it's function and it's *experience*, you know? You're designing an experience for someone— the experience of their home. It's really an intimate thing."

"I bet you'd be really good at it."

"You think?" Regan smiled. She laughed and gave him another touch on the arm—a joking slap, but soft enough to feel almost like a caress. They kept finding excuses to touch each other, he noted. "You're sweet. You don't know enough about my design style to know if I'd be good or not. But you're sweet."

John didn't know what to say to that. The only things that came to mind were *You're beautiful* or *You're amazing* or *I think I might love you*, but he was afraid to say any of that, so instead he took his glass off the tabletop and drank the rest of the beer down to the dregs.

"God, I can't believe how much I've been talking about myself," Regan said. "You must be so annoyed with me."

"Not in the slightest," John said. "You're interesting. I like hearing you talk."

Regan blushed and looked down at her beer—God, that blush again; it killed him every time.

"Okay, but what about you? I've told you about my goals. Do you have any? Being a financial adviser, is that your dream in life?"

John grimaced. "Sort of?"

"Not very compelling, John."

He thought for a second. What *did* he want? Then he came across it, sitting like a kind of hidden treasure in his mind: the perfect way to explain. The perfect pitch.

"Well, the thing about being a financial adviser is that it's about making *other* people's dreams come true. So I guess that's my goal: to help other people reach their goals. The thing that makes me happy is making other people happy."

Was that true? John wasn't sure. But he thought it sounded good. Across the table, the pitch had brought Regan up short, sent her into quiet consideration.

"Huh," Regan said. "That's good. I like that."

"Well, I'm glad," John said. "I guess I'll use it the next time I'm talking to a prospective client."

Regan laughed, then tilted her head to the side and regarded him coyly, her hand dangling over her beer glass, fingers lightly touching the rim.

"And what about me?" she asked. "How would you make me happy?"

John smiled, understanding that they were not talking about financial investments.

"I'm sure I could think of something."

CHAPTER 24

There'd been girls before—awkward dates, fumbling one-night stands—but what John had with Regan was his first real relationship. His first since… Well, he didn't like to think of her name, didn't like to remember what he'd done to her. And maybe that's what this thing with Regan was. Penance.

He treated Regan well, worked hard to be good to her. He bought flowers, devised elaborate dates, went broke paying for everything. Met her friends, surprised her at work with lunch dates, cleaned up his apartment, and cooked her fancy meals over candlelight.

And he listened. Such a simple thing, and yet it was the thing most guys simply failed to do. Listening, John discovered, was an aphrodisiac, it was foreplay; it turned Regan on and made her love him more and more each day. And so John became a detective, an interviewer, a scientist specializing in the study of her. Call it Reganology. All through their dates he'd simply ask questions, let silences stretch out waiting for her answers and elaborations, drawing her further and further outside of herself. He'd turn his head to the side as she talked, look intently at her face, make little murmurs, little sounds of reaction to show he was paying attention. When she turned the questions back at him he'd mumble and stutter, he'd deflect, he'd insist that there was nothing interesting about him, nothing interesting about his family, nothing interesting about his past—and then he'd carefully tilt the conversation back toward Regan, make her the center.

His most surprising discovery came when he met Regan's family and found that they did not, in fact, adore her. John was stunned. To him, Regan was a celebrity, someone in whose company it was a privilege to be. He felt grateful for every moment she gave him, honored beyond words that someone like her would choose to spend time with someone like him—and when she let him kiss her, let him put his hands on her body, took off her clothes, and climbed into bed with him, he'd been stunned almost to tears, the gift of her plucking at some deep and wounded thing in the depths of him.

But Regan's family—her mother and father—somehow seemed to think that she was utterly ordinary, even shabby. An evening at their house for dinner felt like navigating an obstacle course of broken china: delicate but sharp. Their manner with each other was both polite and cutting; their kindness masked cruelty.

"So you're the *financial adviser*," Isabel said when she met him, pronouncing his profession as if he spent his days torturing small animals. "It seems my daughter is quite taken with you."

"I don't know about that," John said. "I like her a lot, though."

"I'm sure you do," Isabel replied, then breezed into the kitchen to check on the roast, leaving John standing in the living room, wondering what had just happened. He felt vaguely insulted in a way he couldn't quite name; more than that, felt that Regan, the girl he was falling for, had been insulted too, and by her own mother.

Nursing his drink (something brown and ridiculously strong Peter had mixed for him), John began to realize what it was: Isabel had somehow implied that Regan and John were each the best the other could do, that they were together because neither of them could expect any better. She thought he was ridiculous, Regan too, and she looked on them both with pity and scarcely concealed derision. The realization deepened throughout the dinner that followed. Isabel made perfunctory and condescending inquiries into Regan's work at the ad agency and "how you're coming along with that little decorating idea." Peter drank and got quiet. John, after Isabel's initial inquiry, was mostly ignored. The conversation became most lively, the brightest and most effortlessly joyful, when it turned to Claire, the absent sister, who was young—barely out of college and a couple terms into an MFA program in New York—but already an up-and-coming playwright with plays in production and commissions coming in.

"You don't like them," Regan said afterward in the car.

"I don't know about that," John said, ever careful, always holding back some portion of himself and what he really thought. "Do you?"

Regan looked away. "Oh, I don't know. I've never really thought about it. They're my family. It doesn't really matter if I like them."

"It doesn't? It seemed to me like they were a little shitty to you."

"Oh, they were," Regan said. "They can be like that. It's true."

"And they clearly don't like me very much."

"You're too straight for them," she said. "Too square."

"Square?"

"The financial adviser thing."

"Is that a problem for you?"

"Oh, John," Regan said. "You're hurt."

"I'm not," he said, though he was—hurt and scared that she felt the way her family did, deep down. Afraid that the dinner had pulled away some kind of mask for her, worried that she saw through him now, saw that he was not good enough for her or her family.

"Look, my family—all they understand is art commissions and foundation grants and cocktail parties and being important and admired by the right people. My mother inherited all her money from my grandfather, and my father married into it, so they don't know what it's like to have to work for something, to strive like you're doing with your financial adviser business."

John gritted his teeth. "You make it sound like a bad thing. Was it that obvious? That I'm the poor boy trying to sit at the table with rich bohemians?"

"Is that who you are?" Regan said. "A poor boy? I didn't know that."

John gritted his teeth in the darkness—he'd revealed more than he'd intended to, talked about who he used to be. Not that there was any specific danger in the detail that he used to be poor. It didn't have to lead anywhere. But Regan had a tendency to seize on any detail about his past as a pretext to ask for more, and John still hadn't figured out what to tell her, hadn't concocted a story that satisfied her.

"I don't know who you are," Regan continued. "My family isn't perfect, but they're part of me. They made me who I am."

"I don't believe that," John said. "You're not limited by who your family is. You don't have to be what they say you are. You can be whoever you want to be."

"You're not listening to me," Regan said. "I'm not saying that you don't get a say in who you are, that you can't change if you want to. But where you came from—that's a part of you, John. My family is a part of me. You know something new about me now that you've met them. What do I know about you? What have you told me? Anything?"

John was silent, not sure how to answer, and Regan didn't press any further. The silence lasted for the rest of the car ride—the rest of the night, in fact, as they brushed their teeth in silence. In bed, Regan flipped off the light and turned onto her side, showing John her back. They slept side by side without touching.

––––––––––––

John thought about it for days—thought about the terrible dinner with Regan's parents, the fight he and Regan had afterward. He knew somehow that this was a thing that could break them, pull them away from each other, this fundamental disagreement. Not just his refusal to tell her anything about his past (though that was part of it), but something even deeper: their beliefs about the world, about life. Regan thought a person was determined in part by what they had come from, but John thought—no, he *knew*—that people could become whoever they wanted. This was what he'd discovered, escaping Casey and then Paul to become John Peters: that the word *person* referred to little more than a collection of behaviors, a set of habits, that such theoretically immutable and stable things as *personality* and *identity* were much more changeable than people believed. All you had to do to become someone else was to change your name, dress differently, spend a few months acting a new way, doing the things the person you were trying to become would probably do, and then, somehow, you became that person. Even someone you'd known in your old life, your past life, could have a face-to-face conversation with you and they'd scarcely recognize you; John hadn't tried this, but he thought it was probably true.

He wished he could show Regan. She didn't have to occupy

the shabby role her mother had relegated her to. She could leave her family behind and become whoever she wanted to be.

Perhaps this was where the cons came from. He hadn't taken her out that first day intending to lie with her, to adopt false identities. It just sort of happened. Initially, he'd only brought her to a series of real estate open houses on an autumn Saturday to dream with her about what might be some day, to draw her into the future with him by leading her to imagine living together in a huge home, maybe even to impress her by the size of his ambition. But things didn't go the way he'd planned. Walking into these expensive houses only made John feel small, the large price tags on the fliers so much more than he could ever imagine affording, the real estate agents seeming to see immediately that he wasn't a real prospect, only a pretender. Rather than impressing Regan, he felt certain that he was diminishing himself in her eyes, that she could see right through him to the poor boy underneath—through the transparent shell of John, all the way down to Casey.

At the last home they saw, a true mansion on the water in North Oaks, he felt like the help wandering into the clubhouse. The real estate agent stationed by the huge kitchen island wore pumps and pearls, and several of the older men touring the property with their tanned, fit wives had on sport coats with cuff links. Seconds after they walked in the door, John almost grabbed Regan by the hand and whispered to her that he wanted to leave, but the real estate agent intercepted them before they could flee.

"Welcome," she said. "And you are…?" John saw the unfriendly look in her eyes, heard her suspicious tone, and suddenly felt himself becoming angry.

He thrust out his hand. "Roger," he said, feeling Regan's body pull taut next to him at hearing the fake name. "Roger White."

"I see," the agent said. "Are you preapproved? What kind of financing would you be looking at for a home at this price range?"

"I was thinking about a cash offer, actually." The lie was so absurd that he figured she'd call him on it right then and there, perhaps kick them out of the house. Who could believe that he was the kind of person who had millions of dollars lying around? But to his surprise he saw the agent's entire attitude toward him change, the visible transformation from derision to admiration spreading through her face, the way she held her shoulders, her entire body as she inclined subtly toward him.

"And what do you do, Mr. White?"

John improvised, spun a story about being a real estate investor—he didn't know anything about it, but he'd seen some online videos of people who recommended it as a way to get rich, buying one property and then another and another after that, renting them out until you were wealthy enough to retire early. Making everything up as he went along, he said something about needing a base of operations while he acquired some properties in the city, luxury apartments and empty lots for new construction, and to his shock the real estate agent seemed to buy all of it, seemed even, at the end, to be flirting with him a little bit.

"Are you looking for investors?" she asked, curling a finger underneath her chin.

"Oh, always," John said, playing along.

Then the agent turned to Regan. "And you are?"

John turned toward her, wondering if this would be where the lie would end—wondering if he'd be disappointed or relieved when Regan refused to play along and dragged them back to their car.

But to his surprise she smiled and, with supreme confidence, extended her hand and gave her own fake name. "I'm Veronica."

The agent took them through the house then, mostly talking to Regan—to *Veronica*—explaining the different features, drawing their attention to different design elements of different rooms. Regan leaned into the part of the wife or girlfriend of the rich man, asking questions, wondering aloud about this repair, that renovation, moving this wall over here, upgrading the kitchen with new appliances. The agent enthusiastically agreed with everything Regan suggested, probably smelling a sale, and John marveled at how natural she was at this, at the life wealth made possible. She was born to be the kind of woman people catered to, the woman in the room whose needs everyone else served.

While Regan talked to the real estate agent, the other men at the open house—the sport coat wearers in their forties and fifties—asked John questions about his business. They'd been listening while he'd been spinning his lie in the kitchen, and now they were interested.

"What neighborhoods are you looking at?" one man asked, stopping John in the dining room.

John rattled off a list of what he thought of as Minneapolis's cool neighborhoods, the places he wished he could afford to live. "Uptown, North Loop, Warehouse District."

"Existing properties or new build?" another man asked, cutting in from the edge of the room.

John turned, mystified to have somehow drawn so much attention. Had he been talking that loud?

"Mostly existing. But there's a few sites we're looking at, distressed properties, that'll probably be tear down and build."

"You got the permits you need?" the first man asked. "It's hard, building in the city. Lot of legal hoops to jump through."

Somehow these men had each detached from their wives, and John himself had lost sight of Regan. She was off somewhere, talking curtains or bathroom fixtures with the listing agent.

"I've got a guy in the city planner's office," John said impatiently. "I'll be fine. If you'll excuse me."

He strode out of the room, then went upstairs and found Regan, who, as he expected, was with the real estate agent, her arms out and hands framing the air in front of her as she sketched out some sort of major reconfiguration of the owner's suite.

"Let's get out of here," John said. He suddenly wanted to be gone from there, wanted to be away from these people and their questions. Regan came with him reluctantly, and the agent pressed a business card in his hand as they went out the door.

At the car, one of the men from the dining room was waiting for him.

"I want in," he said. "I want to invest."

John sighed. Couldn't these people leave him alone? The sight of John's car—a rusting Hyundai hatchback with almost two hundred thousand miles on it—should've tipped off the man that John's story wasn't true. Why couldn't he just let him go in peace?

"We're not looking for small investors right now," John said. "Anything less than half a million, it's just not worth my time."

The man's eyes narrowed, seeming to focus on a point in the air between him and John, and John realized why the man couldn't see the signs of his lie—because he couldn't see *anything*, nothing except the possibility of getting in on something that could make him more money. Somehow John had awakened his greed with his story, whipped the man into a frenzy where logic and reason no longer applied.

"I've got it," he said. "I can get it. I just need to move some things around."

"We were just about to leave."

"How much do you need right now to know I'm serious? Five thousand?"

"Ten at least," John said, hoping to make him balk.

But the man clicked a pen and opened a checkbook on the roof of their car. John stayed back, stunned at what was happening, but Regan moved close, watching over the man's shoulder as he wrote, and when he came to the numbers she turned to John with a strange, fierce look in her eye.

"John!" she gasped with some mixture of shock and delight.

The man's eyes came up. "Wait, John? I thought your name was—"

John brushed past him, pushed him away from the car, shoved Regan in the passenger's side, and then scrambled into the driver's side. When he drove away, the man was still standing at the curb, his mouth agape, pen in one hand, open checkbook in the other.

When they were on the freeway, Regan laughed, her voice high and airy.

"Oh my God, I couldn't believe that. He was actually writing you a check."

"I know," John said.

"I mean, I saw him writing out the zeros. Ten thousand. He was going to give you ten thousand fucking dollars. He didn't even know you."

"No," John said. "He didn't."

"Could we have cashed it, you think?"

"I don't know. Maybe. We probably could've figured something out."

Regan turned toward him in her seat, reached across the gear shift. Keeping his eyes on the road, John felt her hand slide up his thigh.

"Would that have been, like, a crime?" she asked, her voice suddenly low and smoky, her breath hot in his ear. "If we cashed it?"

"Probably," John said. "Does that excite you?"

"A little," Regan admitted. She slid her hand a little higher on his thigh, and he felt himself growing hard to meet her fingers where they brushed against him.

John drew in a sharp breath, swerved on the highway, corrected himself. "Careful. I'm driving."

"I thought that was really hot," Regan said. "The way you took charge back there. I like to see that side of you."

His foot sank on the accelerator and he sped back to her place. As soon as they were inside she was on him, grabbing at his clothes, pushing him toward the bedroom. She seemed ravenous for him in a way she never had before, taking him so deep into her throat that she gagged, tears leaping to her eyes. After he climaxed she climbed on top, used her hand to get him hard again, then put him inside her and moaned as she bucked against him.

"I love you," she said as she came—the first time either of them had said it—and then, as she climbed off of him and slumped onto her pillow, he said it back: "I love you too."

She sighed and closed her eyes, blew a breath out through pursed lips, strands of hair plastered to her sweaty forehead. John simply watched her, realizing the magnitude of everything he still didn't know about her, the things that were still and would always be a mystery.

———————

More cons followed. Crashing a rich couple's wedding by the river in downtown Minneapolis—they went as Roger and Veronica again—got them a free steak dinner and access to an open bar, but Regan seemed nervous the whole night, and when they went home that night they didn't have sex, just went to bed. Thinking back and realizing that it was perhaps the money that had so turned Regan on the last time, the check with all the zeros, John speculated that the problem with the wedding was that it was too safe, too boring—not enough like a real con.

And so, for the next con, he brought them to a club and concocted a whole story for a pair of high-as-hell club kids: he and Regan were high-end drug dealers who'd just made a big score, but the money was stuck at a storage locker at the bus depot (he didn't even know if they had storage lockers) and the police were casing the place, knew their faces. Fifteen grand, just sitting there, but if someone the cops didn't know would go in and pick up the money, they could get it out without anyone knowing. The catch was that they just couldn't trust a stranger to retrieve the money—what if they ran off with it? So, in exchange for the locker key (just some random padlock key John had found lying around), they'd need some money, just as insurance: a bit of incentive for the retriever of the money to come back and split it, or a consolation in case they still bolted.

Of course, there was no money, no locker—but the kids bought it, went to the ATM for a thousand dollars, and shelled it out, a wad of bills, as John put the key on the table. As he and Regan left the club, John realized that he hadn't even given them a locker number.

In the car, he couldn't hide his excitement. "Can you believe it? I didn't think they'd go for it—the girl seemed suspicious for, like, a second—but then they fucking did, both of them. God, my heart was going so fast when he was giving me the money."

Regan was silent in the passenger's seat next to him, holding the money in her hand. Just looking at it.

"What is it?" John asked. "Are you all right?"

"I'm fine," Regan said. "It's just…"

"What?"

"When they realize what really happened. What then?"

241

"Did you see how high they were? They won't even remember what we look like. We're never seeing them again. It's ours."

Regan smiled at him, and John felt something stirring in his chest. He'd made her happy.

Back at Regan's apartment, John was the one to make the first move, the one to reach for her. She accepted his touch, opened herself to him, drew him toward her on the bed.

"You didn't give a name this time," she whispered in his ear.

"What?"

"You didn't give them a fake name."

"Casey," John said without thinking, as he slid his hand up her leg, past the folds of her skirt to the soft flesh of her thigh. "My name is Casey."

Regan blinked and her breath caught in her throat, the name seeming to pass through her head without catching anywhere. She clutched at his arm, her fingernails clawing into his skin, bringing pain.

"I'm a poor boy," John said, exploring with his fingers, pushing past lace to the wetness beneath. "Trying to be good enough for you."

"Yes," Regan said, gasping. "Yes."

"I did something terrible," John went on. "Years ago. I committed a crime. And now I'm running from it. You're the only one who can save me—the only one who can save me from these things I've…"

"Stop," Regan said. Her eyes wide open and alarmed, her body suddenly gone stiff beneath John's hands. She pushed him away, nudging his forearm until his fingers came out of her. She scooted up on the bed, crept away from him, drew her knees toward her chest.

"I'm sorry. Did I say something wrong?"

"I didn't like that," Regan said. "I'm nobody's savior, John."

"It was just a joke," John said. "Just a story. You know, a poor boy trying to make it with a rich girl. I thought it could be like, I don't know, role-playing."

"I know what you were trying to do. I just…" She slid away, to the other side of the bed, and sat with her back to him. "I don't want to do this anymore. I'm done."

John gulped, felt the hurt spread through him as he realized belatedly what had just happened. The way she'd recoiled after he told her the truth about himself.

"Maybe…" he began.

Regan looked back at him. "Maybe what?"

"Maybe I should go."

Regan nodded, accepting it.

John left her in the bedroom and found his keys on the kitchen counter. That night, he went back to his apartment and slept there, alone, for the first time in months.

CHAPTER 25

You're the only one who can save me.

The phrase came back to John many times in the long, lonely days that followed. An echo. Each time he heard it, played it back in his mind, he closed his eyes and groaned, humiliated that he'd said such a thing out loud to Regan.

The fact that it was true made it worse. Worse because the truth about him was what had made Regan pull away from him—and also because this same truth was what bound him to Regan, what made it impossible for him to leave her. It pushed him toward her even as speaking it aloud seemed to push her away. She *was* the only one who could save him. John couldn't say quite why this was true, but it was. Ever since he'd first laid eyes on her, he'd sensed it. This beautiful woman emerging from the dull scrum of a corporate networking event, an angel in a hotel conference room. Something in his soul had fixated on her in that moment, had oriented itself toward her as the one thing he lacked, the one thing that was keeping him from wholeness. Though in his mind he knew there were other women in the world, other relationships that might make him happy, John couldn't reason his heart out of its obsession, its primal want.

He'd applied himself to the study of Regan so diligently that he no longer knew how to be interested in anyone else. Only by being with her, he felt, could he finally shake loose the shame that hounded him wherever he went—the grime of sin and poverty and *Casey*, poor pathetic loser *Casey*—that clung to him everywhere he went.

Only by convincing Regan that he was good enough for her could he finally be *good*. If John could make her love him, make her happy, then, he felt, he'd know that he himself was someone worthy of love and happiness.

But maybe she couldn't love the real him—couldn't love Casey. She'd made that clear by the way she'd pulled away from his absurd role-playing confession, the story he'd half-jokingly whispered in her ear when his fingers were inside her. Fine. If that was the price of Regan's love, it was a price he was willing to pay. He'd be whoever she wanted.

But who did she want him to be—and how could he turn himself into that thing?

He thought, reflecting back on the open house in North Oaks, that who Regan wanted him to be might be who he'd been, temporarily, in that lakeside mansion: the man who was in control, who convinced others to give him things, even if it came at the cost of lying.

And she'd been excited, too, by the older man's willingness to write John a check for thousands of dollars—excited, John thought at the time, by how close they'd both come to committing a crime. But there was crime and then there was *crime*: crime that felt like crime, and crime that didn't. There were thieves and con men in the world, but there were also respectable businessmen who fleeced their marks in socially acceptable ways, who got rich and also got *off*, scot-free.

Regan, John thought, wanted him to be *that* kind of man, the kind of man whose crimes—ethical lapses, momentary compromises with morality—were indistinguishable from the legitimate work of the world: finance, sales, and politics. Maybe what had turned her on was her momentary vision of him as a man who could get her everything she wanted: money, freedom from her parents, and a gleaming, spotless life at the water's edge. If it took some corner-cutting to get there… Well, maybe she didn't want to know about that.

This thinking led John back to his business—the financial consulting business, which could, theoretically, make him a rich man and Regan a rich wife, if he succeeded at it. But he wasn't succeeding at it. His client list was building too slowly. Some of the people he reached out to didn't get back to him; others agreed to meet with him but then he'd never hear from them again; and even those who agreed to become his clients generally didn't have that much to invest—a couple hundred a month, most of them, put right into a mix of mutual funds with modest returns. Even after taking his fees, John was barely making enough to pay for his little one-bedroom apartment, for food and electricity and health insurance and all the dates with Regan. Somehow, each month he ended up behind, overdrawing his checking account, putting expenses on a rotation of credit cards, his debt a little worse every day. About six months into dating Regan he thought about getting a side job, but quickly rejected the idea. A job would give him even less time than he already had to build his client base, and if Regan ever found out that he was delivering pizzas or driving an Uber on the side, she'd know that he was not a successful financial manager. That he was failing.

This was his greatest fear, greater even than the fear of

his past coming to light: the fear of being seen as a failure. As someone who couldn't make money. John wanted Regan back, even wanted to marry her someday—but how could he marry her, how could he give her a family, if he couldn't provide for her? From the day they'd met, he'd made promises to her: promises that he could somehow make her dreams come true. But he couldn't, not yet, and every time he was reminded of that fact—a credit card denied, a text message from his bank telling him in angry capital letters that he had insufficient funds—an icy terror knifed its way all the way to his bones and he became, once more, the poor backwoods boy who walked in on a pair of rich kids making out in the trees, who had his whole pitiful life savings wiped away in a single day. The boy who could never be anything more than nothing, no matter how many new selves he created.

He was thinking about all this, still, on a bright and sultry August afternoon. John was at a golf course in Bloomington, on the driving range, taking his frustrations out on a bucketful of golf balls. John didn't like golf—the clubs and the fees were yet more things he didn't have money for, things he'd used his credit cards to pay for—but he'd attended a client-development workshop a couple weeks prior, and the guy teaching it advised them all to learn how to play golf. Rich businessmen liked golf. John's clients at this point were mostly young professionals working entry-level corporate jobs, spending more money than they saved, pulling or halting their monthly investments when their job situation changed, and John needed to find a different class of investor. More money, more reliability. What he needed, if he was going to get Regan back, was a whale—and a golf course was a place to find them.

He'd gone through a bucket of balls and was resting from

the heat in the clubhouse, seltzer and lime in his glass, when his whale found him. Walked up to the bar a few stools over and ordered a Scotch, neat.

"Blended?" asked the bartender. "Or single malt?"

"Lagavulin if you have it," the man said. "The sixteen year."

The man glanced at John as he waited for his drink, caught John glancing back. The man smiled, then returned his eyes to the mirror behind the bar and sat down. He had dark hair, glasses, khaki shorts, a black polo, and a large gut that he carried with comfort, like he was entitled to a bit of extra weight.

"I saw you at the driving range," the man said. "I was a couple slots behind you."

John grimaced. "I'm terrible," he said, which was true. His shots always seemed to veer off in strange directions, never taking the predictable, beautiful arc he expected. Watching the white orb curve left or right after it left the head of his club, John would get the sinking feeling he felt every time he looked at the growth chart on a mutual fund he'd picked for one of his clients and failed to see the steady up, and up, and up he'd promised.

"You just need to fix your grip," the man said. "And your follow-through. Beginners swing at the ball. The pros swing through it."

"As simple as that?"

The man smiled. "There might be a little more to it." He offered his hand and John took it. "Tim Hansen."

In lieu of offering his name John gave Tim Hansen a business card, sliding it across the bar top with his index finger.

"Financial adviser," Tim said, then looked back up at John out of the corner of his eye. "And you're learning to golf. Can I ask why?"

"Thought I needed a hobby," John said.

"No you didn't," Tim said. "You hate it. You're learning to play because you need clients. That it?"

John hissed air through his teeth and gulped down the rest of his club soda. The ice cubes clinked at the bottom of the glass with a wedge of lime, brown at the edges. "My swing must be even worse than I thought. And here I thought I was getting better."

Tim Hansen laughed. "I think it's smart. You're thinking about your future. You'll get better. But don't get too good. You'll get more clients if you let your prospects win."

John smiled. "I'll remember that."

Hansen climbed off his stool and came closer, sat right next to John. "What're you drinking?" he asked. "You need another one of those?"

"This? It's just club soda and lime."

Hansen slapped his hand on the bar top, and the bartender came within seconds. "Brandon, could you get this kid one of what I'm having?"

The bartender nodded. "Right away, Mr. Hansen."

"I don't know," John said. "It's, what, three in the afternoon? I probably shouldn't—"

"Take the free drink, son," Hansen said. "This is the good stuff. If you're going to get into golf, you should get into Scotch too. You're in the business of making people money, aren't you? Well, then you gotta think rich. Project it to your prospects. It's gotta ooze out of your pores."

The glass appeared in front of John, two fingers of brown liquid at the bottom of a tumbler.

"Drink up," Hansen insisted. "Go slow."

John grabbed the tumbler and lifted it to his lips. He took a careful sip. What followed was a complicated flavor of caramel and smoke and some other element he couldn't quite place. It was his first time drinking Scotch, and the most he could say was that he didn't hate it.

"How about that?" Hansen asked.

"I'll need to think about it." He felt dumb immediately after saying this, but apparently Hansen liked it, because he nodded.

"Well said. A good Scotch deserves to be pondered."

A long silence stretched out as the older man took a long pull of his drink and held it in his mouth, breathing slowly through his nose as he swallowed it down.

"So tell me," he said, leaning close, breath sour with an alcohol funk, "what's your investment theory?"

John had no answer for this. He didn't realize that an *investment theory* was something he needed to have. But the man was waiting, looking at him expectantly, and so John opened his mouth and said the first thing that came to his mind.

"I take people's money," he said, "and I turn it into more money."

It was what the financial adviser in Windom, the one with the huge new house, had told him years before, and as soon as he said it John feared he had blown it with Hansen—blown whatever *this* was, whatever was happening right now. The older man blinked a couple times, not responding. Then he arched back on his stool, threw back his head, and laughed. It boomed throughout the half-empty bar, people at the round tables looking up from their salads and club sandwiches to see who could be making that noise, but Tim didn't seem to care. He might as well have owned the place. He reached out and slapped the bar with his hand as he came back toward John, came in too close, and spoke directly to his face.

"That's a good one! I like that. So when you're picking investments for your clients, what do you focus on? You go big? Or you do little pussy shit?"

John didn't know for sure what Tim Hansen was talking about, but he had an idea. This was the part of the conversation when most financial advisers would talk about the importance of understanding risk tolerances, of diversification, of having a balanced portfolio—but John knew that wasn't what this man wanted to hear.

"I go big," John said. "If my clients are into it, I go big."

"Glad to hear it, son. So what are we talking about? Stocks mostly?"

"Stocks," John said. "Bonds. Money markets, currency arbitrage. Precious metals. Cryptocurrency. Whatever my clients have the stomach for, I'll do it to make them money."

This was patently false—at that point, one hundred percent of John's client base was in relatively conservative mutual funds, at his urging—but he could tell that Tim Hansen wanted someone with a bit of swagger. He sensed a whale, and he didn't want the conversation to end.

"Okay," Hansen said. "Okay. Now let me tell you a little bit about me."

Tim Hansen was a rich man—he referred to himself this way completely unselfconsciously. He'd made most of his money in car sales, winning salesman of the month for years on end early in his career, ultimately making enough money that he bought out his boss and then set up new dealerships in his name all over the Twin Cities. But he was semiretired now, sold three-fourths of his stake in the business to younger business partners, spent most of his time on the golf course. He still had a sizable income from the car dealerships, though, money that came in each month without his having to do anything to earn it. He was getting bored, John sensed.

"I've got financial advisers already," Hansen said. "But they don't seem to work too hard for me. They take my money, move it around, and I suppose I should be happy with them—they're not losing money, though they take plenty in fees. It's just that they're happy getting four, five percent returns each year, and they tell me I should be too. They say that at my age I should have a low-risk investment portfolio."

"Pussy shit," John offered.

Hansen snapped his fingers. "Exactly right."

"So what do you want?" John asked. "What's your goal? Cars, houses? A trust for your kids or grandkids?"

"I've got all that," Hansen said. "I've got everything I want."

"What, then?" John asked. "What's wrong with modest returns if you've got enough money already?"

Hansen bared his teeth, angrily aspirating a long pull of the Scotch—his third pour—on his palate. He swallowed it down with a wince. "I should probably be content," he said. "But it goes against the way I'm wired. I came up working my ass off for more, more, more. More sales, more commissions. More revenue, more market share. Now I'm out of the business and everybody's telling me to take it easy, enjoy the spoils. But I can't. I don't know what to do if I'm not pushing."

"You like to watch the numbers go up," John said, thinking of years ago, how it felt to count out the money he was saving, the meager stack of bills growing in that rusted-out old coffee can. "You like to watch a pile of money grow larger."

Hansen surprised John by actually slapping him on the back, grabbing him by the scruff of his neck, and pulling him close, shaking him with excitement.

"That's it," Hansen said, releasing him. "That's fucking *it*."

John rubbed the spot on his neck where the older man had grabbed him. "I get it," he said. And he did. He hadn't felt that feeling himself in a long time—these days, the numbers in his bank account were a little larger than they were when he was a teenager, but they were going in the wrong direction. He hungered for it just as much as Hansen did. More, maybe.

"Look," Hansen said, "this may be stupid, but I'm having fun talking to you, and I *see* something in you, kid."

"Yeah?" The whiskey had dulled John a little bit—he wasn't used to it—but he felt himself perking up. Hansen was definitely a whale. Maybe he was even a whale John could harpoon. The rarest of prospects: one who *wanted* to be reeled in.

"I think you're a kindred spirit, maybe," Hansen said. "You could be successful in your chosen business, like I was—if you do what I did."

"Which was?"

"Never be content. Always push those numbers up, and up, and up, and when you think they can't go any higher, push them a little further still."

"I'm trying," John said.

"You don't try," Hansen said. "You fucking do it."

"I will," John said. And then, sensing that the older man was egging him on, that he was a salesman expecting to get sold, was in fact begging for it, he added: "Maybe I can start with some of your money."

CHAPTER 26

They talked through the details right there at the bar: Hansen would give John fifty grand, then see what he could do with it in a week.

John almost fell off his chair when he heard the number—Hansen's investment alone would double John's income for that month. A week wasn't much, though. The conventional wisdom among financial advisers was that investment was a long game: you put money in the market and then didn't touch it for years, riding out the big swings up and down to end with a modest year-over-year gain. The fee on Hansen's money would help John make all his payments that month, pay down his credit cards, maybe even put some money away in his own emergency savings account, but to keep the rich man coming back for more with only a week's worth of performance, he'd have to pick a couple stocks that would just happen to move big in the next few days, then sell fast before there was a market correction.

He spent the rest of the weekend researching hot stocks, obsessively reading the *Motley Fool, Morningstar, Bloomberg*, kept CNBC on in the background. He looked at growth charts, visited the websites of startup companies that had just gone public. If a stock was going to break big, it would usually be one from a newer company, not an established one. In the end he picked a pharmaceutical company that was alleged to be on the verge of some breakthrough for rheumatoid arthritis; the buzz said that they were going to bust out big in the coming week. He might have picked a few other stocks, maybe some fund shares, to even out the risk on Hansen's investment, but that would reduce his gains, too, and Hansen seemed to be expecting a lot. He put in an order for the full amount. His whole future as a financial adviser, it seemed, riding on the fluctuations of a single drug manufacturer.

That Monday the market opened big and the stock spiked up 10 percent. Then it quickly dropped five, then fifteen, below the level of John's initial investment—then back up twenty. All within fifteen minutes of opening. John was breathless with nerves.

He had some meetings later that day, new prospective clients, so he turned off his market tracker and drove to them. He didn't have an office yet, so he was relegated to meeting people in coffee shops, buying his prospective clients whatever they wanted while he stuck with cheap cups of brewed coffee.

"I just don't understand why I need you," said his ten-thirty appointment, a woman in her twenties who he'd met at another of those young professionals' networking things. They had proven to be a decent source of clients, the networking events; he could usually walk away from them with at least a dozen business cards, the young corporate climbers who attended them usually had money to spend and a low cost of living, but if they agreed to invest with him, the amounts they committed each month were often small.

"Tell me more about that," John said.

"Well, I've got my 401(k)," she said. "Money goes into it from every single one of my paychecks."

John suppressed a sigh. A part of him wanted to end this

meeting right now, check on the stock—but Hansen had told him to sell himself, to always push the numbers higher. If it were him sitting across the table from this young woman sipping a caramel macchiato and picking at a scone he'd bought for her, he'd go for the close. Hansen would be relentless. That's how he'd become a rich man.

"That's good," John said. "A 401(k) is good. But tell me this—do you actually know what you're investing in?"

"Not really," the young woman said. "There was a whole list of things, different funds, and I just picked some."

"That's right," John said. "That's what most people do. Because there's no one to help you, right? There's no one to tell you where you should be putting your money. What the right mix of assets is. You could be under-leveraged—you could be making less money on your investment than you're able to. Or you could be exposing yourself to too much risk by putting too much money in just one sector of the economy. You're probably not doing yearly rebalancing. And you might not even be investing enough. What percentage of your paycheck are you putting in the 401(k)?"

"I don't know. Five?"

"That's not *nearly* enough. You're, what, twenty-six? These are the years when you should be investing the most. Because it could grow so much in the years ahead. If you get aggressive with your investment strategy *now*, by the time you're in your forties, fifties, sixties, you could be *so* rich. So comfortable. But you have to start soon, stop wasting your time. You have to get serious. And getting serious means partnering with someone like me—someone who can tell you where to put that money, someone who can keep an eye on it for you." He paused, licked his lips, and used his usual line—the line that had captured him, years ago. "Someone who can take your money and turn it into more money."

The young woman pursed her lips. Then she nodded. "Okay.

Yes, you're right. I have to get serious. This feels like something—like something my dad would want me to do, if he were here."

John forced a laugh. "That's a good thing?"

The young woman shrugged. "He's a smart guy."

They rushed through the paperwork, filling it out right at their table—then the young woman left and John dove for his phone. He thumbed to his stock app, checked the pharma company.

John's stomach plunged when he saw the chart, as though the jagged line of the stock's fluctuation were a roller coaster he was riding.

It had declined more than 50 percent.

He had lost half of Tim Hansen's money.

John watched the stock for the rest of the week, praying for a spike that never came. Online, the chatter was still that the stock was poised for a big gain, but around Thursday the buzz on it began to turn sour—rumors of mismanagement, high turnover, a rejected patent, looming legal troubles, and the stock sank still lower. John pulled out Hansen's money and socked it in some low-yield bonds, a full retreat, but it was too late to matter much: he'd turned Hansen's fifty thousand into just a little over ten thousand.

The call came on Friday, just as John had expected it would.

"John," Hansen said, "where are we with that fifty grand? Tell me something good."

"Yes," John said. "It's good to hear from you. How was your week?"

"Cut the small talk," Hansen said, his voice gravelly. "What are you, stalling? You're making me nervous. I put a lot of faith in you, son. Don't tell me it was misplaced."

"No," John said, "it wasn't." Even though it was.

"Okay," the older man said, "then get to the good stuff. How are we doing?"

"We're doing—we're doing great," John found himself saying. Somehow his mouth simply couldn't form the words to tell the truth.

"Yeah? How great? Where'd you put my money?"

John was in his apartment, sitting on the couch with his laptop on his lap. He quickly glanced at the screen, tapped a couple times to bring up a list of that week's best performing stocks, the big movers. He picked one that showed a nice gain since Monday; big, but not too outlandish.

"Altravex," John said, vaguely aware that he was probably breaking the law.

"Huh," Hansen said. "Never heard of it."

"Me neither before this week," John said. "It doesn't matter. It's up more than thirty."

"Thirty *percent?* Damn. My money still in there, or did you get out?"

"We're still in," John said, thinking maybe the stock would go down before the end of trading and he'd somehow find the courage to tell Hansen about the loss sometime over the weekend. Either that or he'd have to come up with forty thousand.

"Get out," Hansen said.

John's heartbeat pulsed in his temples. He felt lightheaded. "You're cashing out? You don't mind paying the capital gains?"

"Not cashing out, I just don't want to lose if this is one of those pump-and-dump things," Hansen said. "Sell the stock, put it somewhere safe for a while, then do it again. Okay?"

John breathed out. Hansen didn't want his money back. John had time to make up the loss, work his way to some real gains so Hansen would never know that he'd lied.

"And John?" Hansen said.

"Yeah?"

"I'm sending you some more money, okay? You're my guy from here on out."

"How much are we talking about?"

"Millions, John. But I can't send it to you all at once. Have to move some things around. You know how it is."

"Of course," John said, as though he knew anything about what it was to be so rich that you didn't even know where all your money was, what it was doing.

"I'll start you with a hundred grand," Hansen said. "Let's make the transfer before close of business if we can."

"Sure thing," John said. "I appreciate your faith in me."

"Yeah, yeah," Hansen said. "It's not faith. If you hadn't made me money this week, I would have dropped you like a handful of dog shit."

"Of course," John said. "I won't let you down."

"I hope not."

"Mr. Hansen?" John said timidly.

"What is it, son?"

"I appreciate referrals."

There was silence on the line, then a laugh. "I bet you do. I'll call some people."

"Thank you."

"I'm gonna make you rich, son."

———

John knew he should probably forgo the fee on the incoming one hundred thousand—he had a loss to make up, after all—but he couldn't bring himself to turn down the money. Hansen would be unforgiving if he knew what had really happened, but at the same time the man seemed so uncaring about what actually happened with his money, seemed unable to keep track of it. Perhaps, when all was said and done, he'd barely notice the loss of forty thousand dollars. Given enough time, there were things he could do to cover the losses—maybe he could divert some money from one of his existing clients, or a new one if Hansen's referrals came through. Jittery with adrenaline, John suddenly saw that money coming in the door could cover a multitude of sins, if there was enough of it. He just had to be careful, claw his way back to even, then do everything above board from then on out.

He called Regan that evening.

"Hey," he said. "I'd like to see you. I want to talk."

Regan breathed out on the other end of the line, and John realized that she was as relieved to hear his voice as he was relieved that she'd picked up.

"Talk?" she asked. "Uh oh."

"No, it's nothing bad, it's just—I feel like we fell out of touch this week."

"Work was nuts," Regan said, and John perked up again. Maybe she wasn't giving him the cold shoulder. She seemed normal, seemed as though she was willing to act like the club, the money, the cons—all of it—had never happened.

"You gotta get out of there," John said. "Start your interior design business."

"I'm trying," Regan said. "I need some startup money."

"You'll get there," John said. "We'll get there."

"We? What's this we?"

"I don't know. I'm part of your life, aren't I?"

"All right," Regan said. "*We*, then."

"So can I see you?"

"I was planning on some drinks with friends. I could blow it off."

"Do it."

"You want me to come over? Is this a booty call?" John could hear the smile in her voice.

"No," he said. "Dinner. I'll pick you up. Wear something nice."

John expected another joke—*Oooh, something nice, huh?*— but something in the way he was talking had put a hush into Regan. "Okay," she said.

He hung up the phone, then went online and made a reservation at the most expensive restaurant he could find.

Then he drove to the mall, went to a jeweler's, and bought an engagement ring.

CHAPTER 27

One evening, some years later, John came home from work late—a frequent occurrence. The business was bigger now, enough to warrant an office. No more working from home, no more client meetings at coffee shops. He and Regan had been married a year, and they had a house in the suburbs. Everything had changed. It was about to change even more.

Regan was waiting for him in the living room, sitting on the couch facing the door. She stood and walked to him, put something in his hand. He looked at it. The plastic object was something he'd never held before, but he'd seen enough commercials to recognize it, after a beat, as a pregnancy test. The indicator window showed two pink lines. He didn't know what that meant, but the way Regan had presented it to him gave him a pretty good hint.

"Wow," he said. In the moment, it was all he could muster. The day had been long, and on the way home he'd been soothing himself with the thought of a beer, something from the fridge, maybe a bit of TV. Not this ambush as soon as he walked through the door.

"*Wow?* That's all?"

"I'm adjusting to the information."

"Aren't you happy?"

John saw that Regan was hurt. He stopped himself, actively tried to reorient himself to the situation. Regan had probably been sitting with this information all day, bursting with it, dying to share it with him.

Maybe this was how it happened, John thought. One minute you were going along with your life, head down, then you looked up and everything had changed. A house, a wife, a baby on the way.

Regan was waiting for his response.

"Of course I'm happy," he said. He smiled, barked out a laugh. Then he closed the distance between them, wrapped her up in a hug. It seemed like the thing to do. In movies, people were always tearfully celebrating when they found out that they were having a baby, the news drawing joy from some place deep within them, but John merely felt self-conscious, like his reaction was being watched not just by Regan, but by someone else, some hidden camera outside the house, piercing the walls with its gaze. The people in movies were actors, and that's what he was doing too: he was acting.

"This is great, Regan," he said into her hair. Her body was stiff in his arms. She pulled away from him.

"Is it?" she asked. Her eyes sparkled with tears. "I wasn't sure what you'd think."

"I'm happy," John said, but even he could hear the dullness in his voice. "I really am. Just a little surprised is all. I didn't even know you were taking a test. Why didn't you tell me?"

"Because I didn't know," she said. "I didn't want to do the thing from the commercials, waiting together—if it wasn't positive I don't know what I would've done. I couldn't… Not in front of you. I needed to do it alone. I'm sorry."

She burst into tears. John laughed and grabbed her by the shoulders, ran his hands up and down her arms. "Regan, don't apologize. It's okay. This is a good thing, okay?" This was something he was used to—comforting his wife, being what she needed. Safe ground; a place where his routine, his act, was more practiced. "It's what we wanted, isn't it?"

"It is," Regan admitted. "It's just so fast."

This was true. They'd been talking about having a baby for months—well, Regan had done most of the talking while John had mostly listened. But they'd agreed in the end that they were open to it, and had recently decided to stop taking precautions. If John was honest, it *had* happened a little fast. Too fast.

"Some people it takes a really long time," Regan said.

"I know," John said softly, still fully committed to the role of supportive, wonderful husband. Maybe he could do this. "But it's a good thing, right? That we didn't have trouble? That's a painful thing for a lot of couples."

"It still isn't a definite," Regan said. "I could have a miscarriage."

That took John by surprise, and he didn't know what to say at first. It was amazing the things women held in their heads, all the things they had to think about that never crossed men's minds.

"Maybe," he said after a moment's consideration. "But maybe not. If that happens, we'll deal with it. We'll try again. And anyway, shouldn't we let ourselves be happy about this right now?"

Regan nodded, blinking hard, and John hugged her again. This time she melted into him and put her cheek against his chest, breathed slowly in and out.

"Everything's going to change, John," Regan said. "Everything."

"I know," he said, letting his face go slack now that Regan could no longer see his expression. He was feeling something now, finally.

Fear.

How did I get here?

John asked himself the question all the time. He'd chosen everything, technically—his wife, his house, his job, even his name, which most people had given to them when they were babies. And yet, when he paused and looked around, he couldn't precisely remember how it had happened, how he'd ended up with *this* life and not a different one. He couldn't remember choosing *this*, couldn't remember a moment when he'd decided that *this* was how he wanted to live, who he wanted to be. He hadn't chosen the anxiety, the fear that seemed to live inside his chest every minute of every day—the fear of losing it all. Of being found out, exposed as a fraud and a failure.

The house was big and beautiful, the kind of home upper-middle-class people moved to the suburbs to be able to afford. A three-car garage, a curving brick path to the front door. An open-concept floor plan, the living room flowing into the dining room and the kitchen. A basement with a huge TV and gym equipment, a deck overlooking the backyard, spacious bedrooms and a study upstairs. In some ways it was a lot like the house he'd hung drywall for years ago, the one built up from the dirt out in the country for the financial adviser who'd fed John his best sales line: *I take money and turn it into more money.* The house was a dream, the thing John had always wanted—and he also hated it.

The mortgage payments were huge, and they had a home equity payment on top of that. They made the payments each month, paid their bills with some to spare, but the mortgage was simply a reminder of how much they owed, the anchor tugging constantly at their lives, the level of income John would have to maintain to keep them afloat. They couldn't lose the house; that would be too humiliating. The only thing to do was to work like hell to keep it.

A big house also needed furniture and decorations to fill it, repairs and improvements, and this was largely Regan's domain. The home equity loan had gone toward knocking out some walls, setting up that open concept on the main floor. Kitchen tile, an island with stone countertops, a gleaming backsplash, and a breakfast nook overlooking the backyard. Regan chose all the furniture, and her tastes ran expensive; her parents were rich, so she was used to nice things. "They last longer," she said. "IKEA stuff falls apart. I want the house to look nice." Aside from the decorating, there was also the stuff in a house that fell apart and needed fixing. The privacy fence was wobbly in the northeast corner, the plumbing was a little weird, the furnace was old, and they needed a new roof.

Now, on top of it all, there was a baby on the way. They'd have to turn a room into a nursery: there'd be painting, a crib, a dresser, a rocker, a changing table. Clothes, diapers, food. Everything was money; everything led back to the business.

And the business was not going well.

From the outside, Greenleaf Financial Consulting was a huge success. John had a large list of clients, with money coming in every month, and a steady stream of new prospects. He'd rented an office in a gleaming glass building with a dentist, a chiropractor, a couple lawyers, and a center for diagnostic imaging and lab tests. The office granted him legitimacy, made people more likely to sign with him and give him their money. As did the website and the string of secretaries he stationed in the reception area to welcome his appointments and offer them coffee while they waited. He could never keep a secretary for long—it was an entry-level job, and the young women he hired generally moved on fast—but it didn't matter. There was always a new girl waiting to take the place of the one that had left, and she didn't need any particular experience; she only needed to be young and polite and pretty, needed to charm the men—it was mostly men, the ones who had money and were dumb enough to hand it over without asking too many questions—upon whom his livelihood depended.

Because, on the inside, the business was crumbling, forever on the verge of collapse. A fragile house built of paper, of spreadsheets and charts and numbers, insubstantial as gossamer. John needed that constant influx of new clients, of new money, because without it, everything would fall apart.

The Hansen investment—choosing poorly, losing most of the money, then lying about it—had been the original sin, the error from which the whole fraudulent scheme sprang. Hansen's money kept flowing in, as did his referrals, men who'd made modest fortunes in home renovating, in carpet cleaning, in appliance sales, or in local restaurant franchising. But John was never able to cover the original loss, never able to put together a string of investment wins to bring the value of the portfolio up to the false gains he'd reported to Hansen. He took to diverting money from other clients to cover the losses in Hansen's account, but that only created deficits in their accounts, which had to be covered by money from yet other clients, and so on, the lie ballooning until it touched every part of his business. By the time Regan dropped a positive pregnancy test on the arm of the couch, John had no client whose reported investments were not at least partly fraudulent—put not into the market, in stocks or in bonds, but into the business, into another client's partial payout, or into John and Regan's own bank account.

For the first couple years of the fraud, John never took more than the fee to which he was legally entitled as a part of every investment. This was his last redoubt for a time, the one ethical principle he took refuge in, even as he flouted every other: he would not take more than he was owed. The rest of the money he took from people, he said to himself, would go toward trying to recoup the hidden losses. In this way he fooled himself for years, told himself the delusional lie that the deficit was still recoverable long after it had ballooned well past his ability to manage it, that he could turn things around and return the business to legitimacy.

But during Regan's pregnancy he dropped the delusion. He began skimming larger amounts for himself, starting small at first—a few hundred extra here or there for a crib, a dresser, a stroller, a car seat. John felt extraneous to Regan's pregnancy; he'd supplied half the genetic material to make the baby, but after that, everything about it was something that was happening to Regan, not to him. He looked on with fascination as her body bloomed, as her breasts grew larger and her belly bulged, listened to her complaints of nausea and back pain, put his hand on her when she asked if he wanted to feel the baby kick. But try as he might, he couldn't understand or empathize with what she was going through. It was too alien to him.

No: if he had any contribution to make, he thought, it was to support Regan and the baby financially—to keep bringing in the money to keep the roof over their heads, to put food in the refrigerator, and to have a few hundred dollars extra when Regan needed it for a fancy bassinet that rocked and played lullaby music, for a couples' birthing class, for a doula who'd stand by the bed and cheer her on when it came time to push the baby into the world.

John was extraneous at the labor and delivery too. Regan did everything—Regan and the army of nurses and midwives she'd gathered around her. John was lost, a man in a world of women.

The doula they'd paid to be there mostly brushed him aside, rushed into the space next to the bed where he should've been standing, sent him on errands for Styrofoam cups full of ice chips. When it came time to push, he went to the other side of the bed and held Regan's hand, but when the pain got really bad, she let go of it, braced herself against the mattress, but went on gripping the doula's hand on the other side of the bed.

He was useless here. Good for nothing—except perhaps to pay the hospital bill once it was all done.

Even after the baby came out, after Regan fell back against the pillow sweaty and exhausted, John had little part in the proceedings. The nurse put the squalling baby on Regan's chest, and she cuddled up under her mother's chin and stopped crying.

"Do you have a name?" the nurse asked.

"Henrietta," Regan said, saying the name they'd agreed upon. "Etta for short."

"Beautiful," the nurse said.

Regan looked to John. She seemed to be expecting him to say something.

"You did it," he said.

"Yes. I did." She looked down at the baby on her chest, then back to John. "Do you want to meet her?"

John smiled, something in him cracking. "I do," he said. "But the two of you look so peaceful. She's sleeping."

"Just give her a kiss," Regan suggested.

John moved close and leaned over the bed. Whorls of dark hair were matted to the baby's head, and there seemed to be a fine white down all over her skin. John gave her a little kiss right behind her ear. She squirmed and cooed.

Regan let out her own little sound of surprise and delight. "Oh, John! She likes you."

"She likes *you*," John said. Thinking of his own mother, of

Darlene. Had she ever held him like this? Had he ever, in some dim prehistory he couldn't remember, snuggled up to her like she was the absolute center of the universe, the sun and moon and stars in his sky? "Kids always love their mothers. You'll be her whole world."

"We *both* will," Regan insisted. "John, we have a baby. A little girl. We'll love her more than anything, won't we? We'll give her a good life and make sure she's safe?"

John nodded. "We will," he said. "We'll do whatever we have to."

Parenthood sat uneasily on John. He wasn't a natural. Baby Etta tended to cry when she was in his arms, quieting down only when she was returned to her mother. This was a point of stress between John and Regan in the early days, as it meant that John was basically useless in getting Etta to sleep. He'd try to rock her, to give her a bottle, but it was no use; the girl just didn't want him. After five or ten minutes of trying to get her back down in the middle of the night, Regan would appear in the doorway, frazzled and exasperated, telling him to go to bed—she'd take care of it. Soon she didn't expect him to help with the baby at all, and John went back to the office after two weeks thinking that was it, his daughter just didn't like him. Maybe he was cursed when it came to fatherhood. He'd never known his own dad; now he was missing some crucial gene.

Something changed, though, when Etta was six months old. A light came on in her eyes when he walked into a room; she'd smile and gasp with joy when he came home from work. When he was doing something else around the house—looking at his phone, watching TV—she'd crawl to him, grab at his pant legs, demand that he drop to the floor and pay attention to her, making faces or playing peekaboo until she giggled. He felt himself becoming a father then, studying his daughter's face, putting his nose on the top of her head and breathing in her smell, squeezing her chubby arms, feeling her hands and her tiny fingers, hugging her gently against his chest when she reached for him.

"I don't think there's ever been a person so happy to see me," John said.

"I know," Regan said. "Isn't it great?"

It *was* great—and a little unnerving. Sometimes John would look at Etta's glassy little eyes looking back up at him and wonder what he might be to her. Some sort of deity? A god walking the earth? It scared him; he couldn't live up to it. There'd come a time when she'd begin to see him for what he was. Children always realized their parents weren't perfect eventually. And what *he* was was a fraud, a liar, a cheat. He'd begun to realize he couldn't keep lying to his clients forever; he'd read about Ponzi schemes, knew how they ended. What would it do to his daughter to see her father brought low before her eyes, to see her idealized image of him so violently fractured? He looked at Etta's eyes and imagined those same eyes watching him get marched away in handcuffs, escorted into a black car by men in suits. It broke his heart.

There was a push-pull to fatherhood, he learned; Etta's adoration, the extent to which she loved him and wanted him and needed him, drew him in and drove him away at the same time. John had helped to make Etta, helped to bring her into the world; she hadn't asked to exist, hadn't asked for the thousand little hurts and miseries and indignities of being alive. The least he could do was provide for her, make sure she'd have a comfortable life, no matter what happened to him.

Regan, meanwhile, delayed and delayed her own return to work. She'd quit the ad agency long ago, had started a little decorating business at John's urging, and it had been going well before the baby came, bringing in a nice stream of extra cash. But now she didn't want to go back to it.

"I think I just want to be a mom for a while," she said.

"You sure?" John asked. "You were so excited about starting your own business."

"I was," Regan said. "I still am. But I can start that up again anytime—and Etta's here now. She'll only be a baby once. I don't want to miss it."

John paused. He didn't think jumping back into the business someday would be as easy as Regan thought, and he was nervous about his income being their family's only revenue stream in the meantime. But what could he do? Making her happy was the thing he'd always promised to do, the premise of their entire relationship, and right now, she was claiming that the thing that would make her happy was being a stay-at-home mom.

"Of course," he said. "If that's what you want, we can make it happen."

"We'll be fine, financially?" Regan asked. "You're making enough with your clients?"

"We'll be great," John said. "I promise."

CHAPTER 28

John began taking more risks at work, began stealing more money for himself, Regan, and Etta. Fearing that he'd one day be arrested or have to go on the run, his new goal was leaving Regan with a pile of money she and Etta could live on for a time—maybe even the rest of their lives. He'd devised a way to siphon off more money for himself and make it look legal, laundering bad money through a series of small, legitimate, low-risk financial transactions: bonds, precious metals, money markets. Each transaction represented a fee he could legally take and put into accounts with his and Regan's names on them. He wasn't sure if that would make the money impossible to seize, but if he got arrested, at least the authorities would have some trouble getting at it.

Things changed for him yet again when he hired Tamara Gray as his latest in a long string of secretaries.

"I really want this job," she said in her interview. "And I think I'd be good at it. Your clients will like me. And, you know, I really want to be an investor myself someday, so this will be a great learning opportunity for me. Maybe I can even add some value."

"Yeah," John said, not really listening. "I bet you can."

It was an easy job. Welcome appointments, offer coffee and

water. Do some paperwork, mail the quarterly statements (fake statements, designed by John to show the lines always going up, up, up). John's business was mostly one of perception—to get a constant stream of new investors, new money, he needed to create the image of a high-rolling investor making fortunes behind a gleaming oak desk. Having a pretty girl stationed out front was part of that perception, and Tamara was that.

He offered her the job before the interview was over.

But Tamara *did* turn out to be different. The others had all seemed to be waiting for something else, working each day like any moment they expected something better to come along. Tamara was more interested, more engaged. She wanted to know John, asked him questions about himself, about his family, about Regan and Etta and what they were like. She even invited them over for dinner once.

She had questions about the business too, questions about his investment strategy, about marketing, about how to bring in clients and keep them happy, keep them from taking their money elsewhere. It made him nervous, but he tried to answer her questions anyway, almost as a test for himself: How well could his lie stand up under scrutiny? He even showed her some of the financial paperwork—the fake paperwork, stuff he'd roughed up after the fact to show investments in assets that happened to perform well, even when he'd actually put money in assets that ended up losing money. The real books were elsewhere; he'd never show them to anyone.

John stood over her desk and watched her as she looked through the papers, waiting for any crack, any show of suspicion.

"Amazing," she said, blinking up at him with her huge doe eyes, her long black lashes.

"What's amazing?" he asked.

"You're obviously doing something right," Tamara said. "Everything you invest in…it always goes up."

Something changed in the air between them in the days and weeks that followed. Tamara was no longer merely politely interested in him, giving him the attention any employee might give her boss. She seemed, John thought, to be *attracted* to him as well. She'd linger at his desk when she brought something to him to sign, lean over and put her elbows on the desktop when she had a question, giving him a clear view down her shirt; she'd touch his arm, play coyly with her hair when they talked, let out airy laughs at things he hadn't even meant to be funny.

Her questions for him also changed, subtly but noticeably. She'd always been interested in his family, in Regan and Etta, would often ask on a Friday what they had planned for that weekend, remember Regan and Etta's birthdays, ask after Etta's health when she was recovering from a cough or a runny nose. But now she began to ask more probing questions, about John and Regan's marriage specifically.

"People always say marriage is so hard," Tamara said once, during a lunch break, both of them eating salads out of plastic bowls that she'd picked up from a takeout health food place at the strip mall across the street.

"I suppose they do," John said, poking at his salad, wondering why he hadn't asked for a sandwich—he was always still hungry after a salad.

"Is it true?"

John glanced up at Tamara but didn't say anything right away. He wasn't offended, wasn't annoyed, just unsure of what she was driving at. This was a delicate dance they were engaged in, and John didn't want to be caught misreading Tamara's intentions.

"I'm sorry," Tamara said. "I don't mean to pry."

"No," John said. "I don't care about that. Just trying to figure out how to answer. What do you want? Relationship advice? Got a boyfriend, wondering if he's marriage material?"

Tamara laughed. "I'm single as a nun," she said.

"No boyfriends? No dates?"

She shook her head. "Nope."

"I find that difficult to believe," John said, leaving the crucial part of that communication unsaid: *You're beautiful. I find you extremely attractive. I'd want you, if I were a single man.*

Tamara blushed, seeming to read his mind. "Well, it's true."

"So you're not looking for relationship advice."

"No, I guess I'm just curious. We spend so much time together in this office, after a while small talk gets boring. And I—you're going to think this is silly, but I feel like I'm a part of your family a little. Sometimes it's Regan on the phone when I answer, you know, and sometimes you're in a meeting and I can't just pass her through to you. If I knew a little more about the two of you, maybe I'd be able to help you with that more."

John thought about this for a moment. "Okay," he said. "So your question was: Is marriage hard? And the answer is: it can be. Even a good marriage has problem spots. Times when it seems like all you do is fight, and you have to work on it to get to the other side of it." John paused, realizing that these were all meaningless platitudes. He hadn't yet offered anything real. "Regan and me, for instance. Our big tension is how much I work."

"You're still here when I leave most days," Tamara said.

"Yeah, and meanwhile Regan's at home with Etta," John said. "Parenting a one-year-old is hard work. It's… How do I describe it to someone without kids? It's really consuming, it takes all your attention, but it's also really boring at the same time, a lot of the time. That's Regan's day-to-day: consuming and boring. While I'm here, she's doing almost all of the parenting. And that causes problems."

Tamara looked down at her salad, chewing daintily, thinking. "My older sister had a baby with her husband," Tamara said. Her voice was even, slow—cautious. "She told me once…"

"What?" John asked. "What did she tell you?"

"She told me that for the first two years afterward, they basically didn't have sex at all."

John froze. This seemed to him to be a pretty clear declaration of something. Tamara was asking about his sex life. Wondering if he was satisfied.

And he had no clue how to respond.

It was true that John and Regan were having far less sex than they used to before Etta came along. In the early days there were the changes to Regan's body to think about, the damage that childbirth had done. Sex hurt for her for a long time afterward, and she just simply didn't want to do it—understandably so.

But even after she'd fully recovered, after there was no more pain, they kept not having sex—and not having it, and not having it, and not having it. In fact, it seemed to John that they'd often go days, weeks even, without so much as touching each other. He'd try sometimes, reach for her after crawling into bed at the end of a long day. But almost always, these overtures ended before they even started.

"John, I'm so tired," Regan would say. "Etta's in a really clingy phase. She's all over me, all day. I just—I need to not be touched for a little while. You understand?"

"I do," John would say, though he didn't—he hadn't been with Etta all day. No one had been touching him. Regan was drowning in affection, in human touch, but John lived in a desert of it. He could be aroused by as little as a hug; a peck on the lips turned him on. A glimpse of skin—a flash of thigh, of cleavage—could turn him incandescent with lust. He was full of sexual energy that had no place to go. Burning with it. Angry with it.

277

"Yes," John said, finally, to Tamara. "Yes, for some people that can be a real problem."

Things came to a head between them a few days later. Tamara poked her head in John's office around five thirty.

"Need anything before I go?" she asked.

"No," John said. "I think I'll be okay."

He was preparing himself for a late night. He needed to create his clients' quarterly statements, an easy job for most financial advisers, who simply output the totals from the same software they used to make and track their investments. But John wasn't most financial advisers. He had to build fake financial statements, weighing the real financial situation of the company against how much gain he had to promise his investors to stay in their good graces and how much false gain he'd told them they'd made last quarter. It was exhausting, holding these two competing realities in his mind—the real one and the false one—and he hated the job, the four-times-yearly reminder of the distance between what he was and what he claimed to be. Perhaps that was part of the reason for what happened next: he was feeling sad and small, and Tamara's attentions made him feel wanted and important and good again.

Tamara came into the office even though he'd told her he didn't need anything, and as she came out from behind the half-closed door, John noticed that she wasn't wearing her coat, even though she claimed to be heading out the door.

"You work so hard," Tamara said.

"It's a big job," John said, "taking care of people's money."

"I wish you'd let me help you," Tamara said. "I can take on more, you know."

John's hands clenched on his keyboard. So Tamara had

started to realize that not everything was normal about her job; most financial advisers would've given the job of preparing the quarterly statements to an assistant. But John couldn't, because to do it for his firm required a knowledge of his fraud and just how deep it went. Any task more complicated than answering the phone, than scheduling appointments, than making coffee and arranging the flowers in the sitting area required an accomplice— and so far John had acted alone.

"I like to do the statements," John said. "Keeps me close to the portfolios."

This was a reliable deflection, one John had used before: *You don't need to pay attention, because I'm so dedicated. I pay attention for you.*

"At least let me get you a drink," Tamara offered. She moved across the room toward a sideboard with glasses and a crystal decanter of blended Scotch.

He let his silence be his assent. If he had to do this miserable job, he might as well be drunk while he did it. The tink of glass on glass, the burble of liquid falling and pooling at the base of the tumblers, came from the side of the room. Tamara turned and walked to the desk with two glasses.

"Hope you don't mind," she said. "I thought we could share a nightcap. I've got no plans tonight."

"No hot dates?" John asked.

"You know I don't," Tamara said, pushing his glass across the desktop. There were two fingers of whiskey in his, barely half a finger in hers. "Cheers," she said, then leaned a little forward to touch her glass against his over the desk, her breasts bulging out of the top of her blouse.

John drank carefully, watching her over the top of the glass. She bolted the whiskey in one gulp. Then she laughed when she saw the way he looked at her.

"What?" John asked.

"You're so serious," she said. "You need me to rub your shoulders or something?"

"You don't have to," John said, but she was already coming around the desk. John hurriedly minimized the window on his computer screen that showed the fake statement template, the numbers and charts and graphs he manipulated every three months for his clients. The screen went blank, and then her hands were on him, warm and soft.

"Is that good?" Tamara asked.

"Yes," John said woodenly. "Very nice. Thank you."

"It's my pleasure," Tamara said. "I'm your secretary. It's my job to make your job easier. To make you…happy."

Her hands began creeping down past his shoulders to his chest, then lower. John sucked in a breath.

"Tamara," he said, swiveling his chair around.

And then, suddenly, she was straddling him on the chair, her thighs squeezing hard against his hip bones, her skirt hiking up so far toward her waist that he could see her panties: black, silky, just a little bit shiny. Her mouth was on his, open wide, and he found that his was open too, that his tongue was moving against hers, tasting her. God, it had been so long since he'd touched a woman, really touched one, and without quite deciding to, he reached a hand up and set it on her breast, reached into her blouse and moved aside her bra to feel her nipple. She moaned against him; he felt the vibration of it in his teeth.

"I don't do this," he said, pulling his head back, breaking the touch of their lips. "This isn't something I do."

Tamara studied him, brushed a finger from the line of his chin up to his temple. "You sure about that?"

"I am," John insisted, though even as he said it he knew that he didn't mean it, that he was only putting up this last bit of resistance for the pleasure of knocking it down, blowing past it, giving in completely.

"Just once, then," Tamara said. "Just once—then it won't be something you *do*. It'll be something you *did*. A fun little memory to have as your own."

CHAPTER 29

But it wasn't fun. John's blood came down as they drove to the new Holiday Inn Express down the highway, and while he waited in the car for Tamara to get them a room the whole thing started to feel seedy, not sexy. Once they got in the room, things went too quickly; John hadn't had sex in so long that he couldn't last, couldn't keep it going. Tamara climbed on top of him, guided him into her, rocked against him a couple times—and then it was over. Pathetic.

He'd imagined that it would feel amazing to fuck Tamara, that the newness of it would make it exciting. But instead he found himself wishing for the familiarity of what he had with Regan. With his wife, climaxing brought with it a feeling not just of physical pleasure, but of deep emotional satisfaction. But now, with Tamara, the physical sensation felt shallow, passing too quickly— and all that was left was a feeling of deep shame. He cried as she climbed off him, as he slid out of her, covering his mouth so she wouldn't hear.

"I have to go," he said. "I can't be here."

She was quiet as he dressed, as he walked out of the room. He ran to the car and drove home, took a shower in the extra bathroom downstairs before crawling into bed beside his wife. Her body was still, a shadow in darkness—then the sheets began to rustle and she rolled toward him.

"It's late," Regan said. "You work too much."

"I know," John said.

"You had a drink," Regan said. "I can smell it on you."

"I'm sorry," John said. "I showered. Brushed my teeth."

"It's okay," Regan said. "You don't have to apologize."

For a few moments she was silent, and John thought maybe she had drifted off to sleep.

"You have to work the weekend?"

"No," John said, even though he probably did. He still hadn't gotten to the quarterly statements, because of the thing with Tamara. Thinking of it again made him want to die. In the dark, he drew a fist up to his mouth and bit hard on the knuckle of his index finger, clamped down until he tasted iron and salt.

"Good," Regan said, patting his arm. "We've barely seen you all week. We need you."

———

He arrived at the office early on Monday, before eight—but Tamara was already there.

"Mr. Peters," she said when he walked in. "In your office there's—"

"We need to talk," John said. He'd made some decisions over the weekend. He'd thrown himself into the duties of fatherhood on Saturday and Sunday, spent long hours playing with Etta on the floor, took her for walks, changed all the diapers. During her naps he cleaned the house, told Regan to get out and do something for herself—get a cup of coffee and read a book, go shopping, watch a movie. On Sunday evening they'd made love, and then afterward, as they lay together naked, with Regan's cheek resting against his chest, he made his plans: Tamara would have to go. He couldn't fire her, that wouldn't be fair, but he could tell her to look for a new job. And the business... He'd have to fix that too. Maybe he could start putting up losses with his clients, drive the fake quarterly statements toward the real ones, stop trying to make up the gap with a string of investment successes that would never come. Turn the business legitimate without anyone knowing there'd ever been anything wrong.

He'd be a new man. And he'd never tell Regan what had happened with Tamara—never tell her his rock bottom, the thing that had driven him to finally change.

"Look," he said now, standing in front of her desk with his briefcase in his hand and a coat draped over his forearm, "what happened on Friday was a mistake. We shouldn't have done it. And now I'm thinking it's probably best if we—"

"John," Tamara cut in, "you have to listen to me. You have an appointment. He's in your office."

"An appointment? It's not even eight. I don't remember anything on my calendar."

"It's sort of an impromptu thing. I couldn't say no."

"Who is it?"

Tamara winced; the question seemed to cause her some internal pain. "Just go in and see him, would you?"

John walked into the office and saw a man sitting in his chair. He was heavyset, wearing jogging pants and a windbreaker; the hair atop his head was stringy and thinning, and there was stubble on his chin and cheeks. The man had lifted a picture frame off John's desk and was looking at it, a family shot of him and Regan and Etta that had been taken on a cobblestone street by the river in Minneapolis.

"Nice photo," the man said. "You've got a beautiful family. Lovely wife, lovely daughter. You're a lucky man."

"That's my desk," John said.

"Sure it is," the man said, and he moved around to the chair on the other side while John took his seat.

"What can I do for you?" John asked.

"You're in investing," the man said.

"That's right."

"Tamara tells me that, everything you buy, it always goes up. Is that true?"

"I've had some good luck."

"See," the man said, "but that doesn't sound right. The way I understand it, the market is volatile. Up one day, down the next."

"Well, yes," John said. "Day to day, there's a lot of volatility. What you want to look at is the overall trend."

"Right," the man said. "And your trend is up."

"It is," John said.

"Bullshit."

The word hung between them for a second. John's blood felt cold in his veins. He realized that he was afraid of the man who sat across from him. "Who are you?" he asked.

"My name is Arnold Scovel," the man said. "I'm a bit like you."

"How so?" John asked.

"I make money doing things that aren't quite legal."

"Now hold on a minute," John said. "I don't like what you're insinuating."

"Oh, knock it off with that," Arnold Scovel said. "You can drop the act. I know you're cooking your books, but I don't care about that, so you can save your breath denying it. What I'm here to talk to you about is a partnership."

"A partnership."

"Yeah. I make my money doing things the cops wouldn't exactly like, if they could prove it. A lot of money. More money than I'm able to explain. You understand what I'm driving at."

John thought for a second. "Money-laundering."

Scovel nodded. "I figure you make money appear out of nothing for your clients. Maybe you can do it for me."

"No," John said, remembering all his plans—becoming a new man, being there for his family, his wife and his daughter. "No way."

Scovel grimaced, sucked air through his teeth. "See, here's the thing," he said. "I'm not fucking asking."

He reached into his pocket, and John's hands clamped white on the arms of his chair, thinking Scovel might be about to pull out a gun. But it was only a phone. He put it on the table and slid it toward John.

What was on the screen made John's body seize up again.

It was a grainy black-and-white photo, showing him and Tamara having sex in the hotel room.

"Like I was saying," Scovel said, "you've got a lovely family. A beautiful wife. There's no reason for her to see something like this. You made a mistake—but it doesn't have to ruin your life."

John stared at the photo—stared at the black-and-white image of himself, his head thrown back and his eyes closed as Tamara rode him. He looked pathetic, weak. In that moment, he'd have done anything to prevent anyone from seeing the photo, anything to destroy it, to expunge it from his memory even as it imprinted indelibly in his mind.

"If I agree," John said, "you'll delete that?"

"Oh, I don't know," Scovel said, putting the phone back in the pocket of his windbreaker. "I think I might hold on to it, actually. I need to trust the people I do business with. Having this helps me trust you."

He stood and began walking toward the door.

"I'll be back in a couple days to work out the details," Scovel said. "You think about it in the meantime. Get used to the idea."

And then he was gone.

A few minutes later, Tamara crept into the room.

"Mr. Peters?" she called from the door.

"Go away."

But she didn't go away. She came inside, went to the sideboard, poured a glass of Scotch, and brought it to him. It was so much like how things had started between them on Friday night that he felt his stomach turn, felt himself overcome by the sudden urge to stand up and shove her away from him, send her sprawling across the floor. He kept still, though. Stayed in his chair, unmoving.

"It's early," John said. "I haven't even had breakfast yet."

"Just drink it," Tamara said, and he did, threw it down in one gulp.

Tamara sat across from him, in the chair where Scovel had been minutes before. "I'm sorry," she said. "I really am. I owed him money. A…a drug thing. I party, sometimes, buy stuff for the weekends, and I got a little ahead of myself, and my paychecks from you aren't quite enough to—anyway, I owed him, and he said I could pay it off another way."

"Just stop," John said, putting a hand to his forehead, bridging his thumb and forefinger across his temples. "Stop talking, please."

The thing that hurt the most right now was not the betrayal, not the shame—it was the embarrassment, the humiliation, of realizing that Tamara had never wanted him. He'd enjoyed being the one pursued, for once, but it had been a lie all along. She hadn't been attracted to him. She'd only been setting him up.

"Look, I know you probably don't want to talk about this right now," Tamara said, "but I was hoping that maybe…you could *not* fire me? I really need this job."

"Fine," John said in a kind of exasperated surrender, almost laughing at the ridiculousness of it. This would be his life now, he realized: doing what others told him to. The moment he kissed

Tamara, he'd given up the right to be the master of his own fate. This was what he deserved, now. "Fine. Fuck. Whatever."

"I can help you, okay?" Tamara said. "I can make it up to you. You're going to need help moving that much money. And I've been thinking. I've got some ideas for how we can make it work."

CHAPTER 30

Laundering money for Scovel actually wasn't so bad at first. The task came, for John, with a sense of resignation and even relief— the relief of taking orders rather than being in charge, of no longer being responsible for what he did, because he had no other choice. Before, John had been alone with his mistakes, the only person to bear the weight, the unbelievable anxiety, of the things he'd done: the money moved from one account to another, the fraudulent reporting of gains, the desperate desire to claw his way back to even. He'd been the only one accountable, the only one to know the truth; if his crimes were made public one day, he'd be the only one who'd deserve punishment, since he'd kept everyone else in the dark and had no accomplices.

Not anymore. Now he was following orders, taking direction. It was still technically John's business, his name on the paperwork and on the nameplate down in the lobby, but he was no longer in charge. He'd gone from boss to employee, and there was something about that that was nice, something that relieved him of a portion of his anxiety about being found out. Now, if he was ever discovered, he'd have an excuse, someone else to point the finger at. *It wasn't me. It was him. I didn't have a choice.*

Scovel called the shots. Tamara too; she all but ran the financial advising business now, created the money-laundering scheme from the ground up. At first, John had figured that he'd just do for Scovel what he'd been doing for his clients—reporting false investments on stocks that happened to have made big gains in order to justify the sudden appearance of previously unreported sums of money. But Tamara pointed out that this method was too vulnerable to detection if anyone came looking, and in partnership with Scovel, the chance of someone coming looking increased exponentially.

What she devised instead was a system in which a collection of shell companies—LLCs listed in the filing paperwork as consulting firms or logistics companies—invested excess cash in each other's businesses, an engine into which money entered dirty and exited clean, scrubbed shiny by a cloud of false valuations and dividend payments, hundreds of thousands of dollars appearing as if from nowhere. John couldn't keep track of it himself. Tamara ran the show; she turned out to be an accounting whiz, halfway to an MBA in finance from Carlson School of Management, an institution far better and more distinguished than the shitty night school from which John had obtained his license to practice financial management.

Another thing that was not just tolerable but actually good about laundering money for Arnold Scovel was the sudden influx of cash—dirty money that came every week in stacks of fat yellow envelopes. John's Ponzi scheme (he'd started to use the term in his own mind, to admit to himself that that was what he'd been running) had required a constant flow of cash, new clients, and investors to cover his losses and fraudulently reported gains. The thing that usually brought Ponzi schemes down was investors deciding to cash out, trying to withdraw money that wasn't actually there. But Scovel's dirty money gave John a nice cushion. If any of his clients decided that they wanted their money back, he'd now probably have the cash to cover the difference between what was actually in their accounts and what they expected to be there. Scovel might even float John the money to keep his clients from going to the cops if it came to that—surely the gangster (that was what he was, wasn't he?) would want the man cleaning his money to stay out of jail. John's usefulness to Scovel was protection, a shield from ever being found out for what he truly was.

For a time, John was even home more, being attentive with Etta and Regan, leaving the office and the business and the money-laundering almost completely to Tamara, who was an accomplice now, as complicit in it all as he was. She could carry part of the burden now—maintain the shadow books, create and send the fraudulent quarterly reports—while John tried again to be a father and a husband.

"What's this about, all of a sudden?" Regan asked one day, surprised to see him once more returning from the office early, at only three in the afternoon, when normally he came up the drive at six or seven o' clock. "Did you lose some clients?"

"It's fine," John said. "The new girl I got at the office—Tamara, you met her. She's great. She's helping, more than I even thought she could."

"So this is a regular thing? You're going to be home more all the time?"

John shrugged. "We'll see. I hope so."

Regan made a noncommittal noise, like she'd believe it when she saw it, but when John next got a glimpse of her face she was smiling. He sank to the ground, not even removing his suit jacket or taking off his wingtips, and began playing with Etta, who was then about two and a half years old.

In the weeks that followed, they entered one of the best eras of their marriage, as carefree and happy in its way as their newly-wed days had been, before Etta. John went to work a little late each day, arrived home a little early, and used that extra time to help around the house, to take Etta to the park and on walks, to make Regan's life as a mom just a little bit easier, a little less stress-ful and more enjoyable.

John was surprised to find that the small amount of extra work he did around the house and with Etta made a world of difference to his wife's mood, the time they spent together as a family no longer characterized by seething resentment, by passive aggressive comments and barely concealed sighs, but by laugh-ter and happiness. As he was making dinner or cleaning up the toys from the living room floor, Regan would surprise him with a hand running up his stomach to his chest, a kiss that was more than a peck, her mouth opening, her tongue darting past his lips.

"What was that for?" he'd ask, something stirring deep in his belly.

She'd simply smile and shrug coquettishly as she turned away and left him to his work.

At night, they started having sex again—not every night, still not as much as they had when they were dating or engaged or newly married (they were still parents of a young child, and went to bed most nights exhausted), but more often than they had during the long drought years following Etta's birth. Maybe once or twice a week. And in its own way, the sex was good, even great, better in some ways than it had been when everything between them was so new and full of discovery. Now the surprise was how good sex could be when it was familiar and safe, when there was no element of fear or of performance or self-consciousness about their bodies. Afterward, when they'd roll away from each other, John would drift off to sleep completely satisfied, as contented as a baby, thinking to himself that *this* was always where real life had been: *here*, lying next to his wife, with a toddler sleeping in the next room over. How foolish he'd been, to have forgotten, to have strayed. But he was back now, and he'd never leave again.

He'd think about the business sometimes during those lovely months of reprieve, his mind turning back to the Ponzi scheme and the money-laundering, Tamara and Scovel, as he watched Etta come down a slide at the playground or measured out a glass of milk for her at dinnertime. He'd think about it—his ongoing crime—and worry. But not too much. Criminals like Scovel went years without being caught, even lifetimes. Maybe John could have the same luck. With Scovel, he was safe—safe to build the good life he'd wanted from the beginning: life with a beautiful family, and a house, and enough money to be comfortable.

————————

John did wonder, sometimes, where all the money was coming from. What Scovel's business really was. He asked Tamara once, at the office, but she only gave him a pained look, as if he'd made some social faux pas, said something that would've better gone unsaid.

"Do you really want to know?"

"I don't know," John said. "I think so."

"What good would that do? Would it make you feel better about it, you think?"

Implied in Tamara's questions, John realized, was that knowing would actually make him feel worse, that whatever Scovel was involved in was so bad that the best defense was simply not to know about it. Which only wanted to make him know more.

"What is it? Drugs? I know it's drugs—that's how he got you. But what else? Does he steal stuff? Run fraud schemes? Does he kill people? I need to know where it's coming from, Tamara."

"*John*," she said, using the voice of someone who needed the other person to just stop already, "you're running a Ponzi scheme."

John bristled. Tamara had been doing this with him lately, ever since they'd had sex. Something about that night had flipped the power dynamic between them, put her on top. She thought less of him than she used to—or perhaps she'd never thought much of him and only now felt free to show it. Either way, she was the boss now, he the underling. She seemed to be implying that he was no better than Scovel, that he was dirty too and had been for a long time, so who was he to complain? What grounds did he have to be offended at anything Scovel did to earn money? He'd been compartmentalizing his own crimes for years now—keeping them from his clients, from Regan, keeping them even, for long stretches of each day, from himself. He needed to, in order to survive, to go on being a person who could function. What right did he have to demand the truth from Scovel when he could barely tell the truth to himself? His only job was to keep his head down and count the money.

Still, he stayed curious, and one day, when John was getting ready to leave the office—late again—he locked up and turned around to find Scovel waiting for him in the hallway. John jumped when he saw him standing under the red light of an exit sign, scenes from *Goodfellas* and *The Sopranos* playing through his head: surprise whackings, parking garage executions, the sound of a gunshot and the spatter of blood.

"Jesus Christ," he said, putting his hand to his chest. "You scared the shit out of me."

"Come with me," Scovel said. "We're going for a ride."

"Where?" John said, his eyes darting down the hall, toward the elevators. The thought of running occurred to him.

"I just want to show you some things," Scovel said. "Come on."

He pushed through a doorway toward the stairwell. John followed him.

In the parking lot, they got into Scovel's car, a black SUV, and drove into the night.

"Tamara tells me you've been asking things."

John felt his heartbeat in his neck, his wrist, his thumb. "Not really. I mean, I wouldn't say I've been *asking* exactly, maybe just wondering some things aloud, but I didn't think Tamara would—"

"John," Scovel cut in, "relax. I get it, okay?"

"You do?"

"Of course. A man has a business. Maybe it's not the best business—I mean, your business, when I came to you, I don't have to tell you—but it was yours. Now it's not anymore, it's mine, and a man wants to know. What he's a part of."

John began to relax in his seat. There was no one else in the car but them, no one hiding in the back seat with a gun to the headrest, and Scovel couldn't pull anything while he was driving. He was safe.

"Yeah," he said. "I suppose."

Scovel pulled the car off the highway onto a dimly lit road next to an industrial park. They turned again down a gravel road, the car rocking on its shocks, and drove through some dark curves before they came out on a low promontory overlooking an abandoned parking lot where trucks and backhoes sat, asleep for the night.

John glanced at Scovel. His eyes were on the parking lot, sparkling with the reflection of the amber light below.

"What are we—"

"Just wait," Scovel said.

They sat in silence for five minutes, ten, fifteen. Nerves rumbled in John's stomach. Just when he thought this was all a ruse, that he was about to be dragged from the car and beaten to death, there was movement below. An unmarked delivery van pulled into the lot, followed by a pickup truck, the loaded bed covered with a blue tarp.

"Here we go," Scovel said.

Men poured out of the two vehicles and then simply stood around with their hands slung low in their coat pockets, glancing to each other and mumbling. They seemed to be waiting for something.

Minutes later, more movement: a large delivery truck rumbled into the lot. Another couple of guys came out, walked over to the guys from the delivery van and the pickup truck, and began talking.

"This is you?" John asked. "They're with you?"

"The guys in the delivery truck," Scovel said. "The others—they're not with me. But we do business with them. We do today, anyway."

The guys from the truck looked inside the van, peeked underneath the blue tarp in the pickup truck, and nodded. A brown package changed hands—money, probably—and then the men went to work, flung the tarp to the ground, opened the doors of the delivery van wide. They began transferring boxes from the van and pickup truck to the larger delivery truck, while Scovel's two guys looked on. The boxes came in various sizes, and it was impossible to tell from that distance what might be inside, though some of them were shaped like flat-screen TVs.

"This is what I do," Scovel said. "It's mostly just things changing hands. Sales."

"Sales," John said, nodding, as though Scovel had said something profound. So much of the world of work came down to this. Sales. Distribution. Imports, exports. Items moving out of one hand and into another.

"Say someone finds themselves in possession of something and they don't know what to do with it," Scovel said. "Doesn't matter what it is. Electronics, car parts, high-end clothes, credit card numbers. Prescription drugs. Doesn't matter how they got it either. Could be stolen, could be obtained legally; I don't care. What I care about is: I know what to do with it. I know how to get it sold. You see? I'm a businessman, just like you."

After the boxes had gone into the delivery truck, the guys piled into the van and the pickup truck and left. The two guys with the delivery truck waited.

"What happens now?" John asked.

"There's another thing," Scovel said. "Just wait."

About ten minutes later, another car passed into the light of the parking lot. It was another SUV, like the one Scovel drove. Two more guys got out of the front, then opened the truck and pulled out a man who'd been stripped to his underwear, a gag tied around his mouth, his arms zip-tied behind his back. John drew in a sharp breath. The man's face glistened under the lights with blood and tears, and one side of his face had swelled up purple. The man looked to be middle aged, his body soft and wrinkled, every vulnerability exposed in the cold air of night.

Next to John, Scovel started the car.

"What are we doing?"

"You'll see," Scovel said.

He backed the car, turned it around, and then drove down toward the parking lot. The man's eyes snapped toward them, panicked, when the car came onto the lot.

"Come on," Scovel said. "Get out with me."

John looked at him and shook his head. "I don't want to be part of this."

"You wanted to know," Scovel said. "This is what you asked for."

"I never asked for this."

"Get out of the fucking car, John," Scovel said, pulling his coat up to reveal a gun and putting his hand on it.

John opened the car door and came around. He felt the man's eyes on him, but he couldn't meet his gaze. If he looked at the man and saw the pleading look in his eyes, then he'd feel a need to help him—and he didn't want to help him, didn't want to put himself in danger. All he wanted was to survive whatever happened in the next few minutes.

"Put him on his knees," came Scovel's voice.

One of Scovel's men kicked the man in the back, and he fell down with a groan, all the way to his face. Then Scovel's guy picked him up by the neck, faced him toward Scovel.

"Take the gag out. What do you have to say for yourself?"

The gag was removed from the man's mouth, and he immediately started blubbering.

"Arnold, please, don't do this. I made a mistake, okay—I know I did a stupid thing, but I know better now and I won't do it again."

"You stole from me," Scovel said. "I don't take very kindly to people who steal from me."

"I know," the man said. "I know, and I promise you it'll never happen again. It was my kids, Arnold—my oldest is going to college, and my daughter needs braces, and—"

"That sounds to me like an excuse," Scovel said. His eyes turned up. "You believe this? Guy's half naked in a fucking parking lot, beat to shit, he's trying to make excuses with me."

Scovel's goons laughed, but the man sniveled harder, began to cry. "I'm not, Arnold. I'm not making excuses, I'm just trying to make you understand—it was a moment of weakness, okay? Just a moment of weakness. I'll pay you back."

Scovel itched the back of his neck, winced. "Thing about trust is: once it's gone, it's gone. I can't trust you anymore. So there's only one thing that can happen here."

He reached to his side and came out with the gun. The man cried out, hung his head in despair. John closed his eyes, afraid of what would come next. But the next thing he heard was not a gunshot, but his own name.

"John."

It was Scovel. He opened his eyes. Scovel held the gun out to him.

"You want to do the honors?"

John was silent, staring at the gun. He hadn't held one in years—not since that day. The day he shot the old man. The day he became a murderer.

Scovel laughed and let the gun drop to his side. "I'm just kidding with you."

John sighed with relief, and so did the man on the ground.

"Thank you, Arnold," he said. "Thank you. You're not going to regret this. I'm going to make this up to you. You'll see, I'll—"

Scovel pointed the gun at the man's head and fired before he had a chance to finish his sentence. He moved so quickly that the recognition of what was about to happen had barely come upon the man's face before he fell back dead, the gravel behind him spattered with blood.

———

Back in the car, John didn't talk. Scovel did all the talking for him.

"So you might be wondering why I showed you this today," Scovel said. "And the truth is, John, even if you hadn't asked—even if you hadn't been getting so fucking *curious*—this was something that needed to happen. Some guys like me, they keep their people on a *need-to-know* basis, and that's a fine approach. But I look at things a little different. Way I see it, one of the things I need anybody working with me to know is what happens. What happens if you fuck with me. You see?"

John didn't answer. Didn't seem like he was expected to.

"The thing about this job you've got is it's sort of a lifetime thing, you know? The only way it ends is you die. Best case scenario, you die in your bed an old man, rich as fuck, never got caught, never squealed. Some guys, they die in jail—but only because they made a mistake. You're not going to make a mistake, are you? No, I don't think you are. You're too smart for that. Other bad way to die is… Well, you just saw it, I suppose. Is that all clear to you?"

A silence drew out, and now John knew that he was expected to say something.

"Yes," he said. "Crystal."

"Good," Scovel said. He was pulling into the parking lot outside John's office now. John's own car was the only one that was left. Everyone else had gone home for the day.

"Now let's get you back to your family."

John drove home in a stupor, thinking about what had just happened. Add it to the list of things he'd seen, the things he'd done. Sometimes it all felt like too much to live with, but it was easy, really: all you had to do was push it to the back of your mind, keep on existing moment to moment, and eventually it receded to nothing.

At home, Etta was asleep, but Regan was waiting up for him. Drinking tea. She sat him down at the dinner table, put a tumbler with a finger of whiskey in front of him, then told him that she was pregnant again.

"Whoa," John said, feeling himself begin to separate from his body, to watch himself and his reactions as if from the outside. "How—I mean, when did—"

"A month ago, I think. You remember. That time when you were home so much and it was like we found our way back to each other again. Like we rediscovered each other."

John nodded. He remembered. The time after Tamara, and Scovel, when John thought he could rededicate himself to his family, be a good husband and father, even if he was also a criminal. Now Regan was having another baby, and he should have been happy, but it was a terrible thing instead. He was bringing another child into *this*—this horrible world, this horrible life, this edifice of sand that was going to crumble at any minute.

"Are you happy?" Regan asked.

"Of course," John said. "Why wouldn't I be happy?"

Regan put her hand on his, slid it up his arm to his bicep.

"I hope it's a boy," she said. "I want you to have a son."

CHAPTER 31

What he found impossible to describe, even now, was what it was like to be him in the interminable months that followed, the daily, hourly, moment-to-moment reality of life in the prison of himself, the unrecognizable-to-himself man he'd become. The best he could do was to outline a state of blended resignation and despair. This was his life, there was no escaping it. And he hated it. Hated himself. Sometimes, late at night, he found himself wishing fervently that he could simply cease to be—a wish that was different than a desire to die. He didn't think about killing himself, didn't make plans, never contemplated methods. More accurate to say that he simply wished he'd never been born, like George Bailey in *It's a Wonderful Life*, with the difference that if an angel ever came to show him what the world would be like without him, everything about it would be better. The old man would be alive. Randy, his brother, wouldn't be in jail. And Regan would be married to someone else. Someone better.

The kids didn't help—Etta, and then Philip, who was born in the natural way of things some months after Regan had told John she was pregnant. The kids made things worse, actually: Etta with her adoration of John, her joy whenever he came home from work, her footsteps as they pounded up to him, her little arms that curled around his calves and squeezed him tight. She loved him so much, but he didn't deserve it. Philip made things even worse for John, more painful, by looking so much like the boy he'd once been (*Casey, his name had been Casey*) that John could barely stand to look at him, so overcome and confused was he by the emotions that flooded over him when his son looked in his eyes. There was, at once, a deep sadness for the lonely child he'd been, grief and shame at the utter wreck he'd made of his life, a desire to make things better for the boy sitting in front of him, and a fear that he couldn't. The things he'd done would catch up with him—with all of them—eventually.

Philip reminded him of one specific thing he'd done: he'd walked out on Leah, his girlfriend for a time, when she told him she was pregnant. He'd become an absent father, just like his own dad had been. He'd kept tabs on Leah—it was easy these days, with Facebook and Instagram. Easy to lurk, to spy, to look up photos and torment himself with what he'd done, with what might have been. He'd seen pictures of his son online; his name was Matthew, he was a teenager now, and he also looked like John. Leah wasn't married, Matthew didn't have a stepfather, and John compensated for this fact by sometimes sending them money, cash in an envelope, mailed to Leah's parents' house in Windom, from a mailbox an hour outside the Twin Cities, so they'd never be able to track the postmark.

Plagued by all this guilt, all these memories, John ultimately came close to a real breakdown in the wake of Philip's birth. It happened late one night, another sleepless night with the baby. He slept terribly, Philip did, and as a result they slept terribly too, Regan and John splitting the nighttime feedings. On this particular night, Philip had woken up every hour, and when he woke up yet again, like clockwork, at one in the morning, it was John's turn, since Regan had breastfed Philip then rocked him to sleep at midnight. John pulled himself out of bed, trudged practically sleepwalking to the kitchen to warm up a bottle of milk Regan had pumped from her breasts, then brought it in to the baby. This was how he remembered it.

He settled in the wingback chair they'd bought for the nursery, then began feeding his son. Philip quieted immediately when he got his lips on the nipple of the bottle, latched, and then began pulling at it with his gums, made the clicking sound that was the sign that he was eating. John gazed at his face; it was like looking in a mirror. They said newborn babies look like their fathers to create a bond with their male caretakers, but John found Philip's similarity to him more off-putting than anything. Holding his son, John found himself remembering—or reflecting, since he couldn't actually remember—that he'd been a baby once as well, unmarked by life, full of possibility. How he'd squandered it. There was no possibility in his life now. He was who he was. He'd become something he hadn't anticipated, and there was no undoing any of it.

John finished feeding Philip, then put him into his crib asleep, milk-drunk, and slunk back to the bedroom. When he reached his side of the bed, he was surprised to realize that he was crying. He put his fingers to his eyes and they came away wet. His shoulders quaked. He was astonished at himself, unsure where this was coming from. He put a hand on his chest, felt his shaky breath, and then realized that what he was feeling was envy. He was jealous of his own son. In that moment he wanted nothing more than to go back to the beginning, to do it all over again. He turned around and put his hand on Regan's shoulder, lightly shook her sleeping form. She came awake and then said, with some annoyance, "What?"

John didn't know how to answer. Why had he woken her up?

"I can't do it," John said, sniffing tears. "I can't—I'm not who you think I am. I'm a fraud."

Was it a confession? A cry for help? Even John didn't know what he was trying to communicate. But he knew what he wanted. He wanted Regan to comfort him, to hold him and rock with him, the way they did with their children. Surrounding them with love, with safety. That's what he wanted for himself—the thing he'd never gotten.

She told him to shut up and let her sleep.

No, Regan and the kids weren't a solace, weren't a refuge—they were a complex trap, like one of those gift-shop contraptions that squeezed tighter on your fingers as you tried to pull out of them. Being with them made him feel guilty, reminded him of the ruin that was waiting for them if he failed, which drove him deeper into the Ponzi scheme, the money-laundering, the need to take as much for his family as he could, to make a soft place for them to land in the event that he was arrested or killed. Sometimes he even found himself hating them, because it was the pressure to provide for them, to make a good life for them—houses and cars and food and toys and college funds—that had driven him to these lengths in the first place. What they needed from him most of all was not his time, not his presence, not his love. It was money. So much money.

Ultimately, the mix of emotions—loving Regan and the kids, but hating them and himself at the same time—was too confusing to process, so he just stayed away as much as he could.

He haunted the office, stayed late even when there was nothing he had to do, made excuses to Regan. Often, he drank late into the night, emptied the crystal decanter of Scotch. Watched the orange lights come on in the parking lot as the sky above darkened.

Sometimes, he realized that he was waiting for something. But he wasn't sure what it could be.

It was on one such night that John looked out the window and noticed a man in the parking lot waiting by his car. John waited and watched for about an hour, nursing the Dewar's rolling around in the bottom of his glass. As the parking lot emptied, he became more certain—yes, the man was definitely waiting by his car. Leaning against it, in fact; sitting against the bumper with his eyes to the building.

John couldn't see the man's face, but clearly he was waiting for John to come outside. And then do what? John couldn't imagine. He thought about calling the police, but then decided not to. He had become uncomfortable around cops, his jaw tightening when he saw one on the highway. He thought that they must know on some level that he was breaking the law, that they could smell it on him. An absurd fear—*but still*, he thought, *no cops*. He could sleep in the office; he'd done that plenty before, on nights when he just couldn't bear to drag himself back home. But he'd been spending long hours at the office for the last week or more, and if he didn't get home at a reasonable hour tonight, or some night soon, there'd be a fight with Regan.

Finally, as the lights of the parking lot blinked on against the darkening sky above, John had an idea. He dug his keys out of his pocket, fumbled them onto the floor (he was a little drunk by then), then grabbed them again and hit the panic button on the fob. Out in the middle of the parking lot, an island in a sea of empty lines, the car came to life. The headlights and taillights flashed; the horn honked, then went silent, then honked again.

The man seemed unperturbed. He stood slowly, then raised

his hand in a wave. John realized that the man must be able to see him now that dark had fallen. His was the only light on in the whole building.

The man began walking toward the office building, and John tapped the fob again to turn off the alarm. He stood and put his head almost right against the glass as the man came close, trying to see his face (was it one of Scovel's men?), but the man disappeared into shadow just as he passed under the window. Now John couldn't see him; he was at the entrance, which was locked this time of evening. A few seconds later, John heard the entrance door rattling loudly, and then a voice that sounded familiar. John's blood chilled as he realized what the man was shouting.

"Casey! Casey! I know you're in there, Casey!"

John left his office and crept into the hallway slowly, feeling a horror-movie sensation: fingers on the back of the neck; a fear of every corner and shadow. But there was no jump scare until he got to the main floor and saw the face through the glass. The man waved again, and John, absurdly, waved back.

It was like looking in a mirror, John thought. Or maybe a portal to another dimension, an alternate reality where he hadn't walked away from that crash on the highway years ago, hadn't disappeared into the woods and a new life, but had stayed to face the consequences of what he'd done. A reality in which he had been the one to go to jail for shooting the cashier.

It was Randy. His brother. After all this time, he'd found him. "Let me in."

Now Randy was stalking around the office, putting his hands on everything. Touching Tamara's reception desk, her computer screen and keyboard. Testing the furniture in the waiting area, running his fingers on the upholstery. Inside John's office, he tapped his fingers on the top of the upturned glasses and the stopper of the crystal decanter, then crossed the room and knocked on the desktop with his knuckles. It was as though he was testing everything to see if it was real and not hollow. As though, having spent years in jail, he now needed to explore the outside world with his hands and make sure it was all still solid.

"When did you get out?"

"Few months ago," Randy said. "Parole. They're lighter on second-degree murder. My lawyer decided to go with a defense of I didn't mean to kill the guy, the gun just went off."

It wasn't too far from what had really happened, John reflected. He could have gotten the same light sentence. But jail time was jail time, and he was still glad he'd run. He wouldn't say this, though. He wasn't stupid.

"Since the long-lost-brother defense wouldn't fly," Randy said, "negotiating a lesser charge was the only thing we could do."

"I'm sorry about that," John said. "I really am. I want you to know that. I never intended for this to happen to you."

"But you're not too sorry, are you? Not so sorry that you decided to help me. No, it was good for you that I went to jail for the guy you shot. Me going down for it meant that nobody looked too hard for you."

Maybe John should've tried to deny that, but he didn't. It was true, besides which, a denial would've only made Randy angrier. John wondered where this was going, what his brother wanted now that he was out. Revenge? He started looking around the office for heavy objects he could grab if he had to. The decanter. The tray it was sitting on. His nameplate on the desk, a colored glass paperweight.

"I was afraid," John said, and it was true. Just as he was afraid now.

"I bet you were," Randy said. "You always were a fucking pussy, weren't you? They would've sensed that it in there. Prison would've eaten you alive. Me, I didn't do so bad with it. Kept my head down mostly, acted tough when I had to. It ended up being boring more than anything. Every day the same as the last. Your mind kind of hollows out after a little while."

It sounded horrible—but not that different from his own life, John thought. It had been years since he'd read a book, since he'd been surprised or delighted by an exciting thought. The boy who spent whole afternoons in the community library seemed long dead to him. His life had become a kind of prison of his own making. The accommodations were better, but the despair might be the same.

Randy went around the desk and plopped into John's chair. He didn't object.

"Goddamn, Casey, you did well for yourself. How much do you make here in a month?"

"Enough to get by," John said. "And it's John now, by the way."

"John," Randy said, then laughed. "John Smith?"

"Peters. John Peters."

"I know, I was just kidding," Randy said. "I found your name on your website. You ever think about the fact that, even when you get to pick who you are. you go with the lamest Joe Blow kind of name? Like you're choosing to be a shitty nobody."

"What do you want, Randy?" John asked.

Randy shrugged. "I don't know. Maybe just to see the brother who sent me to jail for fifteen fucking years. I didn't really have a plan after that."

John crossed the room and poured himself another drink. He kept his hand on the bottle even after he'd poured. His back was to Randy, but he was listening for any movement, any rustling as Randy came up out of the chair.

"Maybe I wanted to hurt you."

"That right?" John asked.

"Yeah, that's right. I thought about it plenty of times on the inside. Thought about what I'd do to you once I caught up with you."

"And now that you're here?"

"Now that I'm here, I want something else."

John's body eased. His hand came off the decanter. He turned around.

"What?"

"I'm thinking money," Randy said. "You made a nice life for yourself while I was in prison. The way I look at it, you were able to do all this because I took your rap for you. So you owe me. Call it a dividend."

John nodded. "That's fair," he said. "How much are you thinking?"

"Oh, I don't know," Randy said. "How does a million sound?"

John's teeth clenched to hear the number, but he didn't argue. "It'll take me some time to pull that much together." His mind was already going, thinking about which accounts he'd have to unlock, assets he'd have to unload, money he'd have to move around. How to do it without raising any attention from Scovel, or the feds—or his wife? The savings and money market accounts didn't have enough money, and John couldn't touch those without Regan noticing; the retirement accounts had more, but drawing from those would bring large tax bills and questions from the IRS; and he couldn't touch the business's money without Scovel finding out.

"I'll give you a month to figure it out," Randy said. "One month. Then I start talking about everything I know."

CHAPTER 32

The next morning, John was considering the problem of where to get Randy's money when Tamara knocked on his door and came walking in.

"What is it?" he asked.

"We have to talk," Tamara said. "It's…it's something bad."

John waved her in with a kind of resignation. Everything was bad; more bad barely registered.

Tamara sat. "Before I tell you what I'm going to tell you," she said, "you have to promise not to tell Scovel. He'll kill me. I'm serious about this, John. I'm telling you because you have a right to know. To make plans for yourself. But I really shouldn't tell you. I shouldn't even be talking to you."

"What is it?" John asked, his panic rising. "Tell me."

"I got picked up last weekend."

"Picked up."

"Yeah," Tamara said. "By the police. On a drug thing."

John's stomach dropped. "Tamara. No."

"I was selling. Just some pills at a club I was at. It was entrapment—this lady asked me if I had anything extra she could buy off me. But she must have been undercover, because before I knew it I had cuffs on my wrists and I was in a cop car headed to the station."

"And?"

"And I'm cutting a deal, John," she said. "The Ponzi scheme, the money-laundering, all of it. I can't do this anymore. I have to stay out of jail. I have to get clean."

John's head was in his hands. He stared at a spot on the desktop, a knot in the oak. The world felt as though it was shrinking down to nothing around him, his whole future seeming to narrow to a point no bigger than that wood knot. Reality was closing in, fast.

"You're ruining me," John said. "My life is over."

"I'm telling you to warn you," Tamara said. "So you can make a plan for yourself. Maybe you can cooperate too. Scovel's the one they want; he's bigger than you are. If you can give them anything on him, they might give you immunity."

John blinked, kept staring at that knot. He shook his head to himself. Immunity might be an option for Tamara—not for him. He was in too deep, with too many other crimes that could come to light in the course of an investigation. The fake identities. The cashier he shot dead—a crime he'd let his brother go to jail for. No matter what he did, how much he cooperated with the authorities, he'd never walk free.

"Or you could run," Tamara said.

Running. Yes, that was better. He'd done it before, and he could do it again. Go somewhere, lay low, regroup. Start over. He'd have to leave Regan and the kids behind, but maybe he could find a way to send them money from wherever he ended up. Or take them with him somehow. He just needed time. Time to figure it all out.

"How long do I have?"

"I don't know," Tamara said. "Maybe a month. Maybe less.

I've only just started working with them. I've got to bring them things—financial records, evidence. Recordings. I don't know what yet. They told me to just go in today, pretend everything is fine. Await instructions."

"Stall them," John said.

"How?"

"I don't know. Tell them you can't get at the records. Tell them I'm watching too closely, that I've destroyed things, moved files, whatever. I just need time. I need that month. Please."

"Okay," Tamara said. "But I have to give them something eventually or I'll go to jail. And I can't stall them forever. The paper trail is there; it's discoverable. They'll find what they're looking for eventually. And then they'll arrest you."

"Just a month," John said. "That's all I need."

The month that followed was one of frantic, panicked activity for John. The first thing he did was switch all their personal accounts to be in Regan's name alone, to make it harder for the feds to seize the money. There was a quarter million in a series of savings and money market accounts, then a few million in retirement accounts, each one now in Regan's name after he'd had her sign some papers. A nice cushion to keep her and the kids afloat after he got arrested or went on the run.

His next thought was about gifts, assets he could leave with Regan that she could sell or pawn for some extra cash. He thought about jewelry, about art, about cars, but then decided that the better bet would be something big, a single purchase that could support her for years if she chose to sell it. That left real estate.

He did all the things a rich man buying a house for his wife would do. Got a real estate agent, started looking at properties.

When he found the house on Lake Minnetonka, he knew he'd found the one—Regan would love it, and the price was right, more than a million. He offered on the spot, five percent above asking, then closed out a retirement account to pay in cash; the tax penalty was terrible, but the feds would have a tougher time getting at a whole house than they would an IRA, and the withdrawal would look legit if it was tied to the home purchase.

———

"It's happening tomorrow," Tamara said. "At the office."

It was Regan's birthday; he took the call as she was getting ready to go out, poring through her closets for an outfit she liked.

"Thank you," John said, and then hung up. It was happening earlier than he'd have liked, but he thought he could make it work. He had a plan, and he needed to stick to it.

"Who was that?" Regan said from the top of the stairs, coming down. She wore dark jeans and a ribbed cream sweater that came down to her thighs, and John thought she looked gorgeous, as pretty as the day they'd met. He realized with a pang that soon he wouldn't get to look at her anymore, wouldn't be able to admire the beauty of the woman he'd married, and he cursed himself, then, for spending so much time at the office. For dedicating himself to a job that didn't even give him any joy, only misery. He should've spent far more time with Regan, drinking her in, storing her up inside him for the day he'd have to leave her.

"It's nobody," John said, thumbing the phone dark.

"It's my birthday," she said. "You're not going to spend all your time on your phone, are you?"

"Nope," John said, rising, crossing to the bottom of the stairs, and curling his arms around Regan's waist. He pulled her close until her hips touched his. "I'm all yours."

She loved the house, was totally stunned by the surprise, and John enjoyed the feeling of walking through the rooms with her. For a moment, he could almost believe that they'd get to enjoy the house together, that he'd be around long enough for that. But after closing, when they went back to the empty house and made love on the living room floor, it felt like a goodbye.

That afternoon he brought Regan back home and then left without saying goodbye. He couldn't bear it, feared he'd cry if he tried to give her a peck on the cheek, and then Regan would know something was up. So he simply slipped out the front door instead, spared a single glance back at Regan and the kids. He'd miss them. But they'd be better off without him.

He kept his distance from the office that afternoon—that was where Tamara had told him it would happen, where he'd be arrested—but he didn't run yet. Instead, he hit more than a dozen banks before closing time, places where he and Tamara and Scovel had money ferreted away as part of the laundering scheme, and closed out all the accounts. Asked for the balance in cash, then walked out the door with stacks of hundred dollar bills in plastic bags.

Then he went to the lake house and called Randy.

"You have my money?"

"I have it," John said. He gave Randy the address. "But wait until dark, would you? I don't want anyone to see you."

Randy showed up around dusk, driving up in a rusted-out pickup truck that made more noise than John would've liked. John left the front door open a crack and then went to wait inside, where he'd put all the money in a leather bag on the kitchen counter. He'd found the bag a few days earlier in the back of

Regan's closet, a designer thing he vaguely remembered buying for her at an outlet mall a year back, gift tags still on.

Randy came inside, looking around at the empty rooms. "Some house," he said. "It's yours?"

"Where are you living?" John asked, ignoring his brother's question.

"Grandpa's old shack," Randy said. "You remember."

"I do," John said. "Does Mom ever come out to visit you there?"

"Nah," Randy said. "She keeps her distance."

"I see," John said.

Randy's eyes fell on the leather bag. "That's it? Looks like a ladies' bag. This where you keep your tampons?" He bellowed a laugh.

John's jaw bulged. Randy hadn't changed a bit. "Why don't you look inside?" he suggested, and Randy stepped toward the island, pulled on the zipper.

"So that's what a million dollars looks like, huh?"

"I guess so," John said.

"It's all there? Should I count it?"

John shrugged. "If you really want to. A hundred stacks of a hundred hundreds. Pretty easy math."

"I'll take your word for it." Randy pulled the zipper closed, lifted the bag by both straps, heaved it off the island. "That's it?"

"That's it." John said.

"Well," Randy said. "Good doing business with you, then. See you never."

He turned and walked back toward the front door—and that's when John began to move. He reached with smooth, unshaking hands toward a drawer, slid it open, then grabbed at the object he'd hidden inside: a crumbling red brick he'd found outside the front door. He gripped it in one hand, the chipped edges cutting against his fingers, the flat of it pressed against his palm, and walked calmly to the entrance behind Randy. He'd taken off his shoes so his footfalls would be quiet on the tile, so his brother wouldn't turn and see him coming up behind. Randy was just at the door, putting his hand on the knob, when John caught up with him and swung the brick round, feeling the pleasing momentum of its arc pulling on his arm. He landed a blow on the back of Randy's head, felt the skull cave beneath the force. Randy fell to the floor. Blood pooled on the tile, ran through the grooves of it like water filling a dry riverbed.

What surprised John was how calm he felt, how little what he'd done upset him. He was reminded of how it had felt to shoot the cashier, the out-of-bodyness of the whole thing. Standing there, he could almost convince himself that it had not been him who'd done what he'd done, but someone else, and he'd just happened to walk in on the aftermath.

He took off Randy's clothes, moving his dead limbs and rolling him over to work him out of his shirt, his pants. Then he took off his clothes and put on Randy's, put his on his brother's corpse, along with his wallet with his driver's license and credit cards. It was dark by the time he pulled the body to the water's edge, the heels dragging along the grass and dirt as he pulled it by the armpits. His legs and arms were exhausted by the time he heaved Randy into the boat, but he still had to row to the middle of the bay. Randy was propped up in the bow, and the waves jostled his body so that he looked like he might still be alive and watching John through the darkness. Chilled by the black hulk of his brother in the dark, John moved quickly once he got to deep water, heaving the cinder block into the water. The rope attached to the cinder block unreeled from the bottom of the boat, then tugged Randy's body to the edge—John had tied the rope around the chest. The boat rocked, almost capsized, when the corpse caught on the edge, but with a panicked heave John was able to push it free. There was a splash, then the water swallowed Randy, and then, finally, he was gone.

John rowed back to the shore, left the boat at the dock, ran up the grass to the driveway. He left the money in the trunk of his car in the garage—Regan would find it first, he hoped. Then he got in Randy's truck, started it, and roared away.

He drove north, back to the cabin, the place where this story had begun. He arrived late, after midnight, and slept in a chair: the same tattered La-Z-Boy that had been there when he was a kid. In the morning he thought about going farther, driving up to Canada, then disappearing, but he stayed where he was, paced the floor, and wondered why he wasn't running. What it was that was keeping him in that place.

Soon enough he realized: he was waiting.

Waiting for Regan. Waiting for his wife to come and find him.

PART 3

CHAPTER 33

"You're a fucking asshole," Regan said.

"Huh?"

"I said you're an asshole."

John blinked at her. He'd been talking for a while—forever, it seemed. Not that Regan had let him tell his story without interruption; in fact, it had turned out less like a *story* and more like a long, epic marital *argument*: curving, winding, spinning off into tangents and eddies as Regan disputed parts of his memory of things, insisted that it had happened differently. (For instance, she argued for almost a half hour that *John* had been the one who was turned on by the cons, not her—and on the night of his quasi-confession, she insisted that *she'd* been the one to have just finished feeding Philip, not him.)

Still, his story *had* gotten told, for the most part. Now he felt as though he was climbing out of a dream, still half-embedded in the accounting he was giving of himself, and he experienced her pronouncement as a kind of rupture, something so out of context as to be almost incomprehensible. *Asshole. Fucking asshole.* For a few seconds he sputtered, unable to summon a response, and into his silence Regan poured more words.

"You think that story is going to make me feel sorry for you?"

John opened his mouth for a rejoinder but then stopped when he realized that had been exactly his purpose.

Regan stood from her chair and began to pace back and forth on the cracked concrete pad that was the shack's floor and foundation. John's story seemed to have stirred up something inside her, made it so she had to move. She didn't even meet John's eyes as she spoke—just as he hadn't met hers, mostly, while talking about his past. Sometimes even when you were talking to someone, what you were saying had nothing to do with them.

"You killed someone. You let someone else go to jail for a crime you committed. You made up identities. You walked out on a pregnant woman. You stole from people. Lied to me. Cheated on me. Laundered money for a fucking gangster. And somehow you want me to think that *you're* the victim here?"

Listening to her litany, there were points where John wanted to interrupt and defend himself. But he realized how ridiculous, how paltry, these protestations would sound, and kept his silence.

"Then you walked out on me," Regan said. "You walked out on *us*, on our family—our marriage, our kids. When it fell apart, you ran. Like a coward. You ran instead of staying to face what you'd done. You left me to pick up the pieces. You know how terrifying the last few days have been? Scovel, your gangster friend: he found us, John. He texted me a picture of you fucking your little drug addict girlfriend. You have any idea how that feels, to get a picture on your phone of your spouse having sex with another person?"

"I don't," John said, his voice gone small. "It must have been horrible."

Regan didn't seem to hear him. "I thought he was going to kill us. He actually *did* kill Tamara, you know that? And *I* was the one who had to walk in on her. I was the one who found the dead body of the woman who fucked my husband."

She let out a kind of desperate laugh at the absurdity of it all. She was breathing too fast, practically hyperventilating, and under different circumstances John might have jumped up and grabbed her hands, tried to calm her down, but he didn't think she'd take very kindly to being touched by him right now. She stopped pacing, drew both hands up to her forehead in a kind of panicked, jerky movement, then let them slide over the top and down the back of her head, smoothing down her hair. Then the hands coming down moved again, one to cover her mouth, one to grip the opposite elbow, and suddenly she was crying. Silent, but her shoulders quaking, tears positively squirting out of her shut eyes.

John felt like shit. Worse than shit. There was a special place in hell for men who made their wives cry, and he was in it.

"You're just…" Regan began, "you're a bad person. A bad husband, a bad father. I can't believe I didn't see it before. I can't believe I married…" She trailed off, let her arms fall, gestured toward him, "*This.*"

John was still sitting, planted in the same tattered, mouse-chewed recliner that had been there since the day two decades ago that he went looking for Randy. He felt as though he was being held in place there by a giant weight, pinned down by an invisible hand on his breastbone, a criminal in the dock, forced to hear his sentence.

"I didn't want it to be this way," John said. His voice came out thick, and he was surprised to find that he, too, was crying—tears stinging at the edges of his eyes, his wife going blurry in front of him. "I tried to…to be good. All I wanted was to be what the world wanted me to be. What *you* wanted me to be. I wanted to be—to be *someone*, I guess. Someone worthwhile. Someone you'd be proud to be with."

The tears were coming too thick for John to see Regan's

expression, but her blurry form merely stood on the floor in front of him, not moving, not saying anything.

"I know that probably sounds stupid to you, the way it all ended up," John said, looking off to the side, "but it's true. All I ever wanted was to be someone who someone like you could love. And I figured you wouldn't want anything to do with me if you knew about—this." He lifted an arm and twirled a finger in the air, indicating everything about the squalid shack: the uncovered pipes, the rat droppings in the corner, the unraveling braided rug, the bucket catching a leak in the roof when it rained, the mouse-gnawed boxes of food, the rusty back door hanging off its hinges. This was the core truth of his life, the shameful truth: poverty, squalor, desperation. He was not John but Casey, a scared boy with no future. A criminal. A coward. A human dead end.

He felt something touch his knee, and looked up to find that Regan had come to him, sunk to her knees in front of the recliner, and was now pulling at his arms with some mixture of franticness and anger.

"But you could have told me, you idiot," she said. "You didn't have to pretend, didn't have to hide. You could've told me the business wasn't going well. I could've helped. We could've figured it out together."

John blinked, tilted his body toward her. "What about the rest of it?" he asked. "You really think you'd have loved me if you knew everything? If you knew what I'd come from? I made you love me as John. Could you have loved Casey?"

"I don't know," Regan said. "Maybe. I wish you'd at least given me the chance."

Somehow her hand had found its way into his. Their fingers fumbled together, then clasped, and Regan gave his hand a squeeze. The pressure of it was something he felt all the way up his arm and into his chest; deeper than that even, all the way to the core of him. It felt to him like a possibility: the possibility that he might still be worthy of being loved by Regan, that there was still something inside him—a small something, perhaps, but something—that was worthy and valuable and good.

"God," John said. "I've really fucked everything up, haven't I?"

Regan leaned toward him, and he leaned in too, and soon their foreheads were touching. John closed his eyes and just stayed like that for a while, breathing slowly through his nose, listening to his wife's breath rise and fall with his.

And then—another sound. Outside, distant. The crunch of gravel under tires, the low groan of a car engine.

John sat up, pulled his hand from Regan's, broke the contact between their bodies as he stood. He ran to the front window and peered through the clouded glass.

Past the front steps were a couple of rusting lawn chairs, an old moldy couch, and a long stretch of bare ground for cars to park. Beyond that was a winding gravel lane that snaked its way up through the trees to the blacktop road beyond. John peered up into the trees and saw a flash of shiny black: an SUV wending its way through the switchbacks toward the shack.

John's stomach plunged.

"Fuck," he breathed.

"What is it?" Regan asked.

He whirled around to face her.

"They're here."

CHAPTER 34

John was hers now. He belonged to Regan, body and soul. She had every last bit of him—every piece of his story, every secret shame and embarrassment, every hope, every dream. Every lie, every sin. She knew it all, finally. It was what she'd always wanted, she supposed, what she always thought a marriage should be: to be so connected with a person that there were no borders between you and them, the distinctions blurring until it was almost as though you were a single body, a single mind, a single soul. Two become one.

And yes, she was furious with him. She'd never been angrier. His story was sad, she had to admit—and it was also self-serving bullshit. A typical self-pitying male fantasy. In his own telling, John was not responsible for any of the things that had happened to him, the things he'd done. Someone else was always to blame, usually a woman: his mother to begin with, then Tricia, the girl from the resort. Leah, Tamara. And Regan most of all—Regan and her wanting a nice life, a stable life, wanting kids, wanting to be a mother. Somehow these things, in John's mind, were what had driven him to lie to his clients, to steal money, to break the law. As if he hadn't made his own choices, his own mistakes, every step of the way.

But she loved him too. She realized this as she watched him rush around the room, locking the door, pulling the blinds, running to a wooden chest at the side of the room, kneeling at it. She was stunned at the realization. She still loved John—loved him more, perhaps, than she ever had before. What was *love*, anyway, but the feeling of being tied up with someone, so deeply connected that it was impossible to root them out of your life without pulling out whole pieces of yourself? It didn't have to be a good thing, a pleasant thing. Love could be terrible too.

John unlatched the chest, lifted up the lid.

"What are you doing?"

John reached into the chest and took something out with both hands, set it on the ground in front of him. Regan gasped when she saw it, felt her heart shift into another gear. It was an object she only knew, from movies, as a machine gun, the kind gangsters or terrorists used, pulling the trigger to let off a spray of shots. It was sleek and black, seeming almost to swallow the slanting evening light that fell from the windows across the room.

"Is that real?"

"It's an automatic rifle," John said. "Randy was a bit of a gun nut."

He took out another gun, a handgun, and slipped it into the waistband of his jeans at the small of his back, then stood with the automatic and held it out to her.

"I'm not touching that," she said.

"Take it," John said. "Scovel is here, and he thinks we've stolen a million dollars of his money."

"We have," Regan said.

"Well, all the more reason to defend ourselves, then."

"Can't we just talk it out?"

"Talk it out? He'll kill us, Regan. But not before he tortures us to get us to tell him where the money is. This isn't just some unscrupulous businessman we're dealing with. He'll actually chop off our fingers if he has to."

"Then let's just give him the money," Regan said. "I stashed it at my parents' house. Up in the rafters of the garage."

"No," John said. "No fucking way. I took that money for *you*, so you and the kids could get through this mess and have something for yourself. You got a plan to keep it?"

Regan winced. To say she had a plan was generous. "Playing both sides, I guess. Offering to launder it for Scovel to buy time. While cutting a deal with the FBI to turn him in. Maybe somewhere in all that they'll just forget about the money, or figure it's lost, or something."

"That's good," John said. "That's a good con. You just have to stay alive long enough to be able to pull it off."

He shoved the automatic rifle toward her again. She took it gingerly, feeling its weight pull at her arms.

"Like this," John said, then showed her how to hold it. "You put it against your shoulder when you're ready to shoot, right here." He touched a place right under her collarbone.

"I don't want to shoot anyone," Regan said.

"You're not going to," he said. "Here's what's going to happen. I'm going to go out there and talk to them. But when I give you a signal, I want you to let off as many rounds as you can through that window over there." He pointed to a half-open window on the far side of the cabin. "But don't shoot *at* anyone. I want you to put them into the ground."

"What's the point of that?"

"Scare them. Let them know I've got some firepower in here. They don't need to know it's you. Maybe I've got a friend in here, a backwoods gun-nut crack shot. You'll shoot a few rounds, and they'll go running for cover. Maybe they'll even leave."

"Okay," Regan said, even though she didn't feel okay. She felt as though she was holding a snake; the gun in her arms made her skin crawl. "Will it hurt?"

"There'll be some kick," John admitted. "You might bruise a little. But you'll be okay. It's better than being beaten up and murdered."

"I suppose," Regan said.

Outside, there was the sound of wheels on gravel again, closer now. Doors opening, footsteps fanning out.

"John!" a voice yelled. Regan recognized it as Scovel's. "Come out. We know you're in there!"

"Okay," John said. "You ready?"

Regan moved toward the window and gave John a reluctant nod. She felt sick with dread, felt as though she might either vomit or faint at any moment, but she was resolving to keep it together. She'd given birth to two children, raised them practically on her own. Men never recognized those things as difficult, but they were—perhaps the most difficult things in the world. If she could do that, she could do this.

John opened the door and walked outside, his hands up. Regan pressed herself against the wall and peered through the window as he came down the steps. Scovel stood in front of the cabin, rough-looking guys to either side of him. They had nondescript faces, but Regan thought she recognized them as the men who'd been keeping an eye on her at Minnehaha Park, the ones Scovel had threateningly pointed out to her.

"Scovel," John said. "Good to see you. It's been a while."

Scovel snorted. "Cut the small talk, John. I want to know where my fucking money is."

"It's here somewhere. Buried in the woods. Only I know where it is."

"Bullshit," Scovel said. "Your wife told me she had it. We followed her here. The way we figure it, she brought the money to you, and you're getting ready to run together. So I'm going to ask you again. Where's the money?"

"I'm telling the truth, man," John said. "Regan was lying to you when she said she had the money—she was scared. I had it the whole time. I'm telling you, it's buried somewhere on this property."

"Okay," Scovel said after a beat of silence. "Then you're going to show us where it is."

John shook his head. "I don't think so."

Regan looked back to Scovel. He was quiet for a few seconds, anger passing through his body, rearranging his jaw, his shoulders, his limbs. He adjusted his stance on the gravel, lifted his head again, then said, "Maybe if I pull out a few of your toenails you'll change your mind."

"Doesn't need to come to that," John said. "Just listen to me for a second, would you? The feds are on to us. They've got a warrant for my arrest. I'm wanted for fraud. You're probably a target too. You know that, right?"

"Of course," Scovel said. "What's your point?"

"My point is that you've got bigger problems than a million dollars. If the feds get me, they get the business, they get everything I know—and they get you. But if I get away, they've got nothing on you. Think of the money as severance, okay? You pay me to go away. The feds will never find me."

Scovel put his head down. He seemed to be thinking it over. For a moment Regan thought that might be the end of it; he'd accept John's terms and leave. But then he raised his eyes again, and there was a new hardness there.

"No," Scovel said. "Fuck no. We're doing this my way. You stole money from me, and you gotta pay for that. Only choice you make is whether I let you die fast or take it slow."

"I was afraid you'd look at it that way," John said. He raised an arm toward the window where Regan stood.

Here it came, Regan thought. The signal. She raised the automatic to her shoulder, aimed at the ground, prepared to shoot.

"Stop."

The voice came from behind her, a whispered hiss in her ear. Hands clamped on top of her own on the automatic.

She bucked at first, threw her elbows back at the ribs of the person grabbing on to her, thinking it was one of Scovel's guys—but she stopped after she turned back and saw that it was Armstrong. He wrenched the gun from her hands.

"Fucking hell, Regan," he said. "Are you trying to kill someone?"

"Agent Armstrong," she said, suddenly out of breath. She'd been holding it, she realized. "How did you get here?"

"I had your keys. I changed the tire, drove slow to get here."

"But how did you find us?"

"The car you stole was government," Armstrong said. "It's got a tracker. I coordinated with headquarters to find you. Parked a ways up the road and snuck in through the woods when I saw what was going on. There's a chopper on the way. Backup."

"Will it arrive in time?"

Armstrong hunched down, peered out the window. Regan looked with him. Outside, John was waving his hand, over and over, the signal for Regan to put a hail of bullets into the ground.

"Regan," he called back with increasing panic in his voice. "Regan?"

"You have to help him," Regan said.

"It's four on one," Armstrong said. "I need that backup. Especially if they're armed."

"You're armed," Regan pointed out, nodding toward the automatic rifle that was now in Armstrong's arms.

Outside, there was suddenly shouting.

"He's got a gun!" someone yelled.

Regan looked back through the window. John was going for the handgun wedged in the waistband of his pants at the small of his back. On either side of Scovel, the two men were going for their guns too.

Regan's hands rose to the sides of her head. She covered her ears and screamed.

CHAPTER 35

John wasn't fast enough to get a shot off. He fumbled the gun as it came out of his waistband, couldn't get his finger on the trigger—and then the shots hit him. One in the chest, another in the stomach. He felt the force of the shots before he felt the pain of them; felt his shoulder snap back as though tugged by a marionette wire; felt something rupture in his gut. Then came the searing agony, blooming white hot to swallow him entire as he fell to the ground. When the heat of the pain passed and he could see again, he found he was looking at the sky, the clouds blood red with the setting sun.

"Fuck's sake, you idiots," Scovel growled somewhere out of sight. "I didn't want you to kill him. We need him to tell us where the money is."

"But he was going to shoot you, boss," one of the goons said.

Scovel let out the sigh of a man who was beset by incompetence, an employer whose underlings were constantly letting him down. "Well, let's go talk to him," he said, "before he bleeds out."

John lay on the ground, blinking up at the sky. The taste of salt and iron rose up at the back of his throat, and he felt something wet on his lips and chin. The pain was still incredible, but it had started to subside a little bit. To fade.

He blinked again, and suddenly the three men were standing over him. Scovel and his two goons.

"Where's the money, John?" Scovel asked.

"I'm not going to tell you," John said. There was an unmistakable gurgle in his voice. He felt as though he was speaking through some kind of liquid. Drowning in it.

Scovel lifted his foot from the gravel and pressed it against John's shoulder. The pain came back, lit up the nerve endings throughout John's torso. He groaned, closed his eyes. Some part of him welcomed the pain—it meant he was still alive, still breathing and feeling things—and he summoned a smile as his eyes came back open.

"Fuck"—he began, pulling his head up, concentrating hard to put some breath behind the word, to spit blood on Scovel's shoes before finishing the sentence—"you." Then he let his head drop back to the dirt.

Scovel sighed, took his foot away, and looked up to the cabin. "Someone get in there," he said. "Maybe the wife knows something."

"Got it," said one of the goons, the younger one, and he walked to the cabin.

"No!" John said, rolling to his side, reaching after the guy's pant leg—but it was too late, he was already up the steps and putting his hand on the doorknob. "Don't you fucking touch her!"

The door opened, and a man appeared on the other side. He wore a thin coat with "FBI" emblazoned in yellow on the breast, holding a gun—the automatic John had left in Regan's hands. The man hit Scovel's goon in the face with the butt of the gun as soon as he stepped over the lintel. He slumped to the floor, dropped like a sack of dry cement. Then the FBI agent flipped the gun around, came out of the cabin spraying bullets in the air.

"FBI!" he yelled. "Everybody drop your weapons!"

There was a flurry of footfalls as Scovel's other guy ran off into the woods, but Scovel only sighed, put his hands in his pockets, and leaned back against the SUV.

"Arnold Scovel, I presume," the FBI agent said.

"Yes, sir," Scovel said. "You gonna go after him?"

"He won't get far," the agent said. "We'll find him soon enough. It's you I'm most interested in."

"Yeah?" Scovel said. "Why's that?"

"I'm placing you under arrest," the agent said. "For...well, shooting *him*, for one."

John couldn't see the agent, but he knew he was talking about him.

"I didn't shoot anyone," Scovel said. "I was just along for the ride. I had no idea what my associates were planning to do. If I had, I would have tried to stop them."

"Right," the agent said. "We'll see about that. You stay where you are."

"Oh, you don't have to worry about me," Scovel said. "I'm not much of a runner. My knees."

There were footsteps, and then the FBI agent's face appeared above John's head.

"There's an ambulance on the way," he said. "And just in case there was any doubt, you're under arrest too."

It wouldn't matter, John knew. They were too far out for help to get there in time.

"I hid the money," John said, struggling to speak through the blood filling his mouth, gagging him. "You'll never find it."

"What money?" the agent asked.

"*His* fucking money," John said, pointing a finger toward

ANDREW DEYOUNG

where he thought Scovel was—though he'd become disoriented, no longer knew for certain which direction was which. He'd begun to feel a drunken kind of sensation, the world spinning around his head. "My wife had nothing to do with it. With any of it. You remember that."

"Okay," the agent said. "Whatever. Just don't talk anymore, okay?"

John saw Regan's face next, saw it floating in his line of vision, and at first he thought he was hallucinating, until he remembered—she was there. She was with him. It was really her.

"My wife," he said, absurdly.

He felt a stab of pain in his shoulder once more, dimmer now.

"Hold it tight," the FBI agent said, "and don't let up until the paramedics get here."

He looked down and saw Regan's hand against his chest, holding a cloth there, trying to slow the bleeding. He smiled, trying to meet her eyes, but she was focused on the wound, her face pale, as though she was the one losing blood. Regan was always so good to him. Even now, after everything that had happened. So good.

"Regan," he said. "The kids. You have to tell them…" He coughed, gagged, then swallowed down the blood pooling in his mouth and forced himself to go on. "You have to tell them I love them. They have to know."

Regan nodded. "They'll know. I'll make sure of it."

"And you—" he began, but Regan cut him off.

"No," she said. "Just don't. It can wait."

"It can't," John insisted. "I need to say this."

"Fine. What?"

"With you…" John said. "The person I was with you—that was the best version of me."

John realized as he said it how pathetic it sounded, what a

336

terrible self-judgment it was—the man he'd been with Regan had still been pretty bad—but it was also true. He loved Regan, and he also loved who he'd been with Regan, the man he'd sometimes become, at his best, for her.

"Okay," Regan said, brushing her free hand lightly across his forehead, cupping his cheek. "Quiet now. Help is on the way. Just lie back."

There came a sound from above—a *thwump, thwump, thwump* that John recognized as the rotor blades of a helicopter slashing at the sky. The rhythmic pulse of it grew louder, even as John's heartbeat grew softer, more faint. As he himself began to fade.

"Just a little bit longer now," Regan whispered to him. "You're going to be okay."

"Yes," John said. "Of course I will." It was a lie, he knew. The last lie he'd ever tell her. He was feeling thinned out, woozy and light, and he knew it wouldn't be too much longer now. It was okay, though; if this really was the end, the last thing he saw might as well be his wife. His beautiful wife, the woman who'd made him believe, briefly, that he could be good.

EPILOGUE

It was a simple storefront, red brick with tall square windows and a sign designed in sleek modern lettering hanging above the door. The name Regan had given her business was *abide*, all lowercase, and underneath the name were three more words vaguely detailing what the establishment offered: *design, furnishings, provisions*. Parked across the street, Armstrong squinted to see past the glare on the glass. It didn't look to him like there were any customers inside—it was still early, not even ten—but he could see Regan, sitting at a computer, the light of a huge Mac screen shining on her glasses.

He'd never seen her wearing glasses before. She looked nice in them. Pretty.

"What are we doing here?" Torres asked. She sat in the passenger's seat. Technically they weren't supposed to be here—they were on their way to a new investigation, a nonprofit embezzlement case with some interstate implications—but Armstrong had argued for the detour.

"I don't know," Armstrong said. "I guess I just wanted to see it."

The case was long over by now. It had been more than a year since that day outside the clapboard cabin up north—a year since

John Peters had died of multiple gunshot wounds and Arnold Scovel had been arrested on a host of charges ranging from fraud to racketeering to murder. Armstrong no longer had any reason to speak to Regan, no official reason at least. And yet something had stuck with him about the case. About Regan, if he was honest with himself. He'd read every newspaper article that mentioned her name, watched every TV story where she appeared on camera. Online, he'd tracked the progress of her business from "Coming Soon" social media pages and websites to full operation on a corner of Minneapolis's East Lake Street. But he'd never stepped inside the shop. Never seen it with his own eyes.

"Why do you care so much?" Torres asked now.

"I don't know," he said. "Doesn't it bug you a little?"

Torres was silent, and when he looked at her there was a little smile on her face. He smiled back. Working together for as long as they had, they now knew each other almost as well as married couples did. Torres knew when he wasn't really asking her a question, not even looking for her opinion—only looking for an excuse to tell her what he thought.

"It bugs *you*," Torres said. "So out with it already."

"I don't know," Armstrong said. "I just think sometimes about how it went down. With the money."

Regan had never gone ahead with the deal she'd cut with the federal prosecutor—she'd never worn a wire, never got Scovel on record admitting to money-laundering or all the other crimes he was suspected of. But the prosecutor honored the deal anyway, let Regan keep half of the assets John had left to her in exchange for the cooperation she was still able to give. She testified in court to everything she knew: Scovel's threats, his attempts at blackmail, his admitting to her—albeit not on tape—that he'd killed Tamara. And then, of course, the scene in the woods, Scovel dispatching his men to shoot her husband dead.

It couldn't have worked out any better for her, Armstrong thought. In the press, her cooperation with authorities to bring down a gangster made her a hero. Even John's victims, the clients from whom he'd stolen money, had changed their minds about Regan. It helped, no doubt, that many of them had been repaid in full for the money they'd lost—the initial investment, not the false gains—out of funds the feds seized from Scovel's criminal empire. Money from stolen goods, from drugs, from illegal loans and online identity fraud. All of it went to make right what John had done wrong. And none of it would have been possible if Regan, the con man's widow, hadn't bravely told the truth, testifying against a dangerous crime boss in open court.

Or so the media narrative went. A redemption story.

Armstrong, meanwhile, couldn't shake the sense that he'd been played. That there'd been a deeper con going on all along—and that Regan was the one who'd pulled it off.

"She lied to us," Torres said. "She lied to us plenty. But she cooperated, too, in the end. I don't know. You never tie up all the loose ends from a case. There's always something left, something that'll bother you if you think about it too much. The key is not to."

"I know," Armstrong said. "I can't help it."

"That's because you like her," Torres said.

"No," Armstrong said. Then he let his gaze drift back across the street, back to Regan sitting at her computer, studying something there, a look of deep concentration on her face, and he reconsidered. "Maybe."

"So what do you want to do about it?"

"I think I want to go in. Talk to her. One more time."

Torres sucked air through her teeth. "You sure that's a good idea?"

"No," Armstrong said. "But I'm going to anyway."

Torres shrugged. "Okay."

Armstrong stepped out of the car, glanced up and down the street, and jogged across to the curb. A bell rang over his head as he pushed through the glass door, and Regan looked up from her computer screen. She showed no surprise to see him standing there.

"Agent Armstrong," she said, taking off her tortoiseshell glasses and folding them flat in her lap. She wore a white blouse, a knee-length pencil skirt, black flats. Under her swivel chair, her legs were crossed at the ankle, her smooth calves folded demurely together. "How nice to see you."

"Is it?" Armstrong asked, his voice coming out angrier than he'd intended.

Regan blinked at him. "It is. I always enjoyed seeing you, even when you were investigating John. It was a bad time. But you made it easier for me, as much as you were able to."

Armstrong felt a flush of shame, but he couldn't locate its source. Was he embarrassed to have come in with so much hostility toward Regan, or to remember his foolish deference toward her during the investigation? Either way, he felt lightly chastened, and he didn't know what to say next.

"What are you doing here?" Regan asked, standing.

Armstrong swallowed down a lump in his throat. What *was* he doing here? It seemed so clear to him in the car, but now that he was inside, the sight of Regan had wiped all the thoughts from his head. He glanced around the room as though looking there for some refuge. What he saw looked more like an IKEA showroom than a design studio: couches and side tables, vases and lamps and framed art. On the far wall, opposite Regan's desk at the entrance, there was even a coffee counter with a shiny espresso machine, wrapped sandwiches, desserts under glass.

"Just wanted to see how you were getting along," Armstrong said, then brought his gaze back to her.

She cocked her head to the side and smiled through squinting eyes. "That's sweet of you. I'm fine. Trying to juggle the kids and getting a business off the ground. As you can see."

Regan gestured toward a tucked-away corner behind her desk, and Armstrong rose up on the balls of his feet, craned his neck, and saw her two children, the boy and the girl—what were their names again?—on the floor amid a scattering of toys. They were paused in their play, looking up at him with something like fear in their eyes.

"Oh," Armstrong said, surprised. "Your kids are here."

"They're in day care most days," Regan said. "But it's closed today for some reason. Something about staff training. I bring them in sometimes when I can't find anyone to sit with them."

"I get it," Armstrong said. "You don't have to apologize."

"I wasn't," Regan said, her voice brittle.

Armstrong cleared his throat. "It's the business I was most curious about, actually. It's an interior design business, isn't it? The same thing you wanted to do for the federal prosecutor."

"That's right," Regan said.

"But why all the furniture? The fancy coffee?"

"Well, my interior design consultancy is the core of the business. It's where most of the money comes from. But I wanted there to be more to the business too. Keeping the shop gives me a chance to show off my design sensibility to potential customers, to show them the kinds of furnishings I might put in their homes if they go with me. And the coffee—oh, I don't know. I just wanted people to feel comfortable being here."

Armstrong made a show of looking around. "Not many people here now, though."

"You should have seen it earlier," Regan said, her eyes bulging.

"There's always a morning rush for coffee and pastries. Then things tend to quiet down until lunch. The weekends are when we get most of our initial consulting appointments and walk-ins looking at the home furnishings. The rest of the time I work on client projects. That's what I was doing when you walked in, actually. A nice couple down in Tangletown. They're getting an addition, a sunroom."

"You mentioned consulting appointments," Armstrong said. "How much does that cost?"

"A hundred dollars for an hour," Regan said. "It's a prelude to fully signing on with me for a complete interior design project."

"So all this extra stuff—the furniture, the coffee, the consulting—it gives you a lot of places to put money, doesn't it?"

Regan gave him a placid smile. "I don't know what you mean."

"I'm sure you don't."

Regan pressed her lips together, then gestured toward the coffee counter, regaining her composure. "You want something? I sent my barista on a break, but I help her sometimes during the busy mornings. I'm getting pretty good at a cappuccino. My treat."

Armstrong shrugged. "Sure," he said. "Two, actually. To go."

"Two?" Regan asked as she moved behind the counter.

"Torres is in the car."

"Oh, Agent Torres!" Regan said, her voice bright, as though Armstrong had just mentioned a long-lost mutual friend. "I hope you'll say hi to her for me."

"I will," Armstrong said, then put his hands in his pockets and watched Regan bustling around behind the counter, pouring the espresso shots, steaming the milk, setting out two white cardboard cups. "There's another thing I'm curious about," he said as she began to pour the espresso and the hot milk into the cups.

"Okay?"

"Out by that cabin. Before your husband died. Remember?"

Regan's face went cold. "I don't like to think about it. Or to talk about it in front of…" Her eyes darted past him, and he glanced back to see the kids, still staring, not playing with their toys.

Armstrong lowered his voice. "I'm sorry to bring it up. But I have to. Before John died, he said something about some money. Some money he stole from Scovel."

Regan shook her head. "I really don't know anything about it."

"Scovel said it was a million dollars in cash."

"Yes, that's what I heard." Regan put tops on the drinks, pushed them across the counter, but Armstrong didn't pick them up.

"You have any idea where that money might have gone off to?"

"John said he buried it in the woods," Regan said.

"So you do know something about it."

Regan put her head down and gave him a thin smile that said he was being tricky and they both knew it. "I know what John said before he died."

"And you think it's true?"

She shrugged. "Someone must think it's true. I hear there are people searching those woods looking for it. Treasure hunters coming from all over. There was a story about it in the *Star Tribune*, wasn't there?"

"So you have no idea where that money could be."

"None," she said.

Armstrong studied her face for a long moment, looking for some hint of…what? Guilt? Deceit? Armstrong didn't know.

He reached down and took the coffees, then turned and walked back to the front door.

"I'd love to see you back sometime," Regan said, following after him. "Maybe you could come in for a consulting appointment. Bring your girlfriend. Men don't always think about how to make spaces beautiful, but women do. It's important for a relationship. It makes a house a home."

Armstrong turned back. "I don't have a girlfriend," he said.

"I didn't know that," Regan said, cocking her head. "I'm surprised. A man like you should have a girlfriend."

"A man like me?" Armstrong said, then let it drop, gave a shrug. "It doesn't matter. I'm too busy with my job. It doesn't leave much time for relationships."

"What a shame," Regan said. "You'd make a good catch. For someone. That's what I meant."

A silence descended—a long, electric silence, full of possibility. There seemed to be an invitation in it. The moment called for a decision, and Armstrong made one.

"Goodbye, Regan," he said, then turned and walked through the door before she had the chance to say anything back.

At the car, Torres took her coffee from Armstrong's hand. "Thanks," she said. "You get what you need?"

"No," he said.

"Anything there we should be thinking about?"

"No," he said again. "There's nothing."

Torres considered that for a moment, then nodded. "All right."

Armstrong gave one last glance at the shop. Regan stood at the window, looking out. Above her head was that sign—and looking at it, Armstrong felt annoyed all over again.

"*Abide*," he read. "What the fuck does that even mean?"

A smile came to Torres's face. "I think it's sort of a play on words. *Abide* like live, in a place. A home. But also *abide* like *be*, maybe. *Exist. Persist.* In a sort of…I don't know…a Zen sense. It's clever, if you think about it."

"I guess."

"Just let her have it, Armstrong," Torres said. "It's not so easy, you know."

"What's that?"

"Being a woman in this world."

He still felt like arguing, but there wasn't anything he could say to that. Maybe she was right. Maybe he should just leave Regan alone.

"All right," he said, "you win."

"We're going, then?"

Armstrong nodded. "We're going."

He started the car and drove away.

———————

Regan stood at the front windows, arms crossed over her chest as she watched Armstrong walk to the car. He spoke for a few moments to someone in the passenger's seat—that must have been Torres—then pulled away from the curb and slid down Lake Street.

Maybe she should have been worried. Maybe they were investigating her again. But she didn't think so. The way Armstrong had said goodbye had a finality to it. She'd never see him again. She felt almost sad to think about that. There was a time when she thought something could've happened between them, that if she'd ever choose to be with a man again, it could be a man like Armstrong. A silly thought, she realized. That was over now; whatever there'd been between them—whatever kindness, whatever affection—it was gone.

Regan felt a presence next to her, something brushing up against her leg, and she looked down to see Etta standing there, blinking up at her.

"What is it?" Regan asked. "Do you need something?"

"Was that the man who wanted to put Daddy in jail?"

Regan let out a breath through her nose. She'd hoped the children would've forgotten Armstrong by now, but children's minds were like sponges—they absorbed everything, and didn't let go.

"Yes, Etta," she said. "It was."

"Are bad things going to start happening again?"

Regan sank down to her haunches and looked Etta in the eyes. "No, sweetheart. Nothing bad is going to happen. Not anymore. We're done with bad things for a while."

Etta seemed to think about that. Then she nodded, accepting it. "Okay."

Philip walked up beside Etta—cheeks round with smiling, eyes squinting into the sun at the windows. "Mama happy?" he asked.

"Yeah, bud," Regan said, her heart swelling. "I am happy. *So happy.*"

"Because of us?" Etta asked.

"That's right," Regan said, her voice full with sudden emotion. "Because of you. Come here, both of you. Mama needs a hug."

Etta and Philip fell toward her and she caught them in her arms. She gave each a kiss on the top of the head, breathed in the smell of their hair, and for a moment she was so overcome that she feared she'd burst out crying. This was what it had all been for—this family, these beautiful children she'd brought into the world. Everything she'd done, every decision she'd made, every lie she'd told, had all been for this. For *them.*

The moment passed, Regan regained her composure, and she let Etta and Philip go.

"Come on," she said. "Why don't you go back to playing. Mama's got a bit of work to do."

She rose, and together they walked back to the desk. Philip and Etta went back to their play—Etta to a coloring book, humming and talking to herself as she colored in a cartoon cat, while Philip picked up a toy truck, making motor sounds as he pushed it along the floor. Each retreating to imagination, to dreaming, to the private and fragile world of childhood.

Regan sat at her computer and nudged her mouse to awaken the screen. She pulled up a spreadsheet, the business ledger, and keyed in a new line: *Armstrong consultation.* She added the date, and then the amount: $100. It didn't even register in her mind as a lie—she and Armstrong *had* discussed interior design, after all. They'd even talked about the cost of the consultation.

And then, with movements so smooth and rapid it was almost as though she wasn't even thinking about them at all, she pulled open the desk drawer, thumbed a one hundred dollar bill out of a thick envelope, and put the money in the till.

Her thoughts as she closed the money drawer drifted again to Agent Armstrong. Perhaps it was for the best that she'd never see him again. After what had happened with John, she should probably be done with men for a while, maybe even forever. She was providing for her children, making ends meet, pursuing her dreams—those were the important things, the things that mattered most. What she'd done to get there didn't have anything to do with anybody else. That was her business: her money, her children, her possessions, her choices to live with.

All of it belonged to her now. There was no one left to share the responsibility.

And that was just fine by her.

ACKNOWLEDGMENTS

This book is set in the Twin Cities and parts of Greater Minnesota, the state I call home. Many of the settings are real, but I've also changed the details of real places or invented locations to serve the story—while still hopefully capturing the true spirit of each place. In this, I'm grateful for the kindness and indulgence of my fellow Minnesotans. I suppose I'd be following my compulsion to tell stories anywhere, but I feel especially lucky to live in this state, which supports its writers so well and whose landscapes, cultures, and people inspire my imagination.

Many thanks to my editor, Deb Werksman, for her vision for this book, for getting me out of my own way when that was what needed to happen, and for shepherding me so expertly and patiently through the publishing process. I'd like to extend that gratitude to the whole Sourcebooks and Poisoned Pen Press team: Jocelyn Travis, Susie Benton, MJ Johnston, Heather VenHuizen, Mandy Chahal, Emily Engwall, the visionary Dominique Raccah—and a host of others whose names I don't even know but who touched this book in some way.

Kate Garrick's unflagging support and advocacy as my agent was invaluable throughout, as was her eye for story and character.

Kate was the first one to tell me, at a crucial point in the development of this book, that Regan wasn't as innocent as she pretended to be, that she knew more and was a lot craftier than she let on. About this and so many other things, Kate was—is!—right.

I'm grateful for Margaret LeFleur's reading of a portion of this novel and for the support of her and my broader Midwest writer community: Bryan Bliss, Sara Biren, Heather Bouwman, William Kent Krueger, and too many others to name, friends old and new.

Lastly, I'm especially grateful for the support and love of my family, particularly my wife, Sarah, who read this novel in its nascent stages, and my children, Maren and Rory, who were too young to read it when I wrote it but who inspire me and give my work meaning in ways I can't even put into words. Sarah, kids: I love you so much more than I'm able to express, and whatever is true and good and beautiful in these pages springs directly from the love, from the *home*, that we nurture together every single day.

ABOUT THE AUTHOR

Andrew DeYoung is the author of *The Temps*, a speculative novel about the end of the world. He works as an editor at a children's book publishing company, and he lives with his wife and two children in the Twin Cities area in Minnesota. *The Day He Never Came Home* is his first domestic thriller.